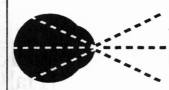

This Large Print Book carries the Seal of Approval of N.A.V.H.

Runabout

Pamela Morsi

G.K. Hall & Co.
Thorndike, Maine

Published in 1994 by arrangement with
The Berkley Publishing Group, Inc.

G.K. Hall Large Print Paperback Collection.

The text of this Large Print edition is unabridged.
Other aspects of the book may vary from the original edition.

Set in 16 pt. News Plantin by Rick Gundberg.

Printed in the United States on acid-free paper.

Library of Congress Cataloging in Publication Data

Morsi, Pamela.
    Runabout / Pamela Morsi.
       p.   cm.
    ISBN 0-7838-1126-8 (alk. paper : lg. print)
    1. Large type books. I. Title.
[PS3563.O88135R86 1994]
                                         94-32215

---

*For Sherry
the other half of the Sylvester Sisters
(two offices throughout the world)*

*She's smart, she's funny, and she
knows as much as anybody*

Chapter One

The April 23 Sunday edition of the *Prattville Populist* headlined the Russians' move toward Verdun. It carried an ink-drawn picture of industrialist Henry Ford, winner of the Nebraska primary for the Republican nomination for President with the quote, "I will run if the people call me." Half of the front page was devoted to speculation on President Wilson's anticipated ruling on the Mexico policy and the unsurprising report that Pancho Villa was still at large. But the real news in Prattville, Oklahoma, that Easter Sunday morning did not make the paper. The real news was that Tulsa May Bruder would be attending Sunday church services for the first time since being jilted by Odysseus P. Foote.

"Luther! Luther!" The loud call was punctuated by pounding on the bedroom door. "Luther, wake up!"

Luther Harlan Briggs moaned beneath a tangle of bedcovers before pulling the sheet off his face and glared at the closed door.

"Damn it, Arthel. You'd better have one hell of a reason for waking me up at dawn on a Sunday morning."

An unsympathetic chuckle could be heard through the door. "It's nearly noon, Romeo. Tulsa May's downstairs. She's got trouble with the Runabout."

Luther moaned again and covered his head for almost a full minute before throwing back the bedclothes and sitting up. "I'm coming," he hollered at the door. "Just let me get my pants on."

He had just managed to get one foot on the floor when a long slim arm slipped out from underneath the covers to wrap around his waist.

"Don't leave yet," a sleepy, feminine voice murmured from somewhere within the tangle of sheets and blankets. Luther gently pushed away the small restraining hand at his waist.

"Emma, you'd best get your sweet fanny out of my bed, it's nearly noon."

The young lady made an inarticulate sound.

"You know I can't understand you when you talk into the pillow." Luther stood in the center of the room, looking for his overalls. When he found them under the bed, he shook them out sharply.

Emma pulled the covers off her head and watched him. Luther grinned back. Emma Dix was a fine figure of a woman with a tiny waist, narrow hips, and perky little bosoms though none of that was currently within his vision. What Luther saw was a tousle of dark auburn hair, so vivid it had clearly come from a bottle, and the remnants of last night's face paint smeared unattractively in the morning sunlight.

8

"Now, Luther honey," she purred hopefully. "Don't you think your customers can wait?" She patted the empty place beside her on the bed.

With a chuckle, Luther shook his head.

"My customers expect prompt service, seven days a week," he told her.

"Well, what about me?" She pouted as she raised herself up on one elbow and allowed the sheet to slip down to a daringly dangerous level.

Luther's answer was low and sexy. "I've been servicing you promptly all night, Emma. And I'd certainly be willing to try seven days a week if you're up to it."

She giggled as he pulled the brown duck overalls up, allowing them to hang loosely at his slim hips as he splashed water into the washbasin and began his morning ablutions. Emma watched him with pleasure.

At twenty-six, Luther Briggs was a tall, strongly built, handsome man who on the coldest day of winter still carried the warmth of summer bronze on his flesh. His thick black hair had just the tiniest bit of wave in the front. He had a fine-featured face that was just short of downright pretty, a long masculine jawline that was saved from sternness by one impudent dimple, and the straightest, whitest teeth that ever smiled at a pretty girl. But his most remarkable feature was his eyes, vivid blue eyes.

Clean and damp, Luther ran a comb through his hair with one hand as he assessed the whiskers on his jaw with another. He hated shaving. For-

9

tunately, he'd inherited enough of his mother's Indian heritage that his beard was sparse. With a shrug he decided to wear his stubble this Sunday.

"Do you want me to wait or go on home?" Behind him Emma pouted. She was a little bit spoiled and a little bit demanding. And very accustomed to men letting her have her way.

Luther hooked one shoulder strap and left the other to dangle as he turned to grin down at her. "Emma sweet, don't you always do exactly what you please?"

She sat up, carefully holding the sheet with more enticement than modesty. "Of course I do. I just want to know what *you* want me to do."

Luther stuck a sockless foot into his right boot and gave her a wicked wink. "I'd like you warm and waiting and I'll be back in twenty minutes."

Luther left the bedroom without a backward glance. His stomach growled loudly, but he didn't stop in the kitchen to see if there was anything to eat. Plunking his wide-brimmed straw hat on his head, he stepped out the door of their second-floor apartment. A wide slat-wood porch overlooked the yard and the Guthrie and River Road beyond. A huge blackjack oak nearly three feet across dominated the entire area. The full, heavy buds on the gnarly branches were near ready to burst with the new green of summer shade.

Parked beneath the tree, a small, snappy, but definitely old-fashioned car popped ominously. Luther's eighteen-year-old brother, Arthel, who still looked too long-legged and too skinny for his frame, stood shaking his head as he talked with a plainly clothed, demure young woman with hair the color of the first carrots of spring. Luther leaned on the second-floor porch railing and grinned down at the two people he loved most in the world.

"Tulsy Bruder!" His words rang out. "Have you been out racing that Runabout against Barney Oldfield before I've even had my breakfast?"

The young woman grinned up at him, hands on her hips. "Any man who has not had breakfast by noon on Sunday morning deserves to go hungry. Now come down here and fix this cantankerous car of yours."

Luther wagged a threatening finger at her. She responded by sticking out her tongue. With a shake of his head he took the stairs at the side of the porch two at a time.

The second-floor porch jutted out over the lawn, providing a wide overhang. Luther used this area to work on bikes or cars, protected against bad weather. The cross pole on the far end of the building held a large wooden sign with white painted letters that read "Luther's Bicycle Shop and Auto-Mobile Garage." Today it creaked slightly in the spring breeze. Though the sign was rustic, the entire downstairs was a modern shop with all the latest equipment for the building and repairing of self-propelled transportation vehicles. Luther stepped to the door, which was never locked, and grabbed a screwdriver, an adjustable wrench, and a rag. If the Runabout couldn't be fixed with those tools, then it probably couldn't be fixed at all.

As Luther took a step toward the Runabout it backfired loudly, making him curse under his breath. "Cut the spark, Arthel," he ordered. "I don't want to have to fix the whole firing mechanism."

As his brother adjusted the knob on the wall panel, the Runabout gave a giant sigh that was almost pain and then shuddered into complete silence.

The hush was deafening. Tulsa May gave an exasperated and infuriated sigh. "Why does this car always quit on me when I really need it?"

"This piece of junk doesn't 'always quit on you when you really need it,' " Arthel said. "It just *always* quits on you."

"Arthel!" Luther scolded. "How can you speak so ill of this wonderful machine? It may be a piece of junk, but officially it's still *my* piece of junk."

"But I'm going to buy it from you," Tulsa May assured him hastily. "Just as soon as I get the money together."

Luther shook his head with a smile. "I hope, Tulsy, that when you get your money together, you'll buy a better car than this one."

"I like the Runabout," Tulsa May declared. "It's pretty."

Luther stepped back as if surveying the vehicle for the first time. It had a narrow wheelbase and a high seat, there was no windshield, it still required a crank start, and the steering was on the right side. But aesthetically, Luther had to agree, the Buick Model G Runabout was a pretty car. The wine-colored body finish, red wheels and running gear, and the five brass lamps and shiny bulb horn were flashy enough to attract the nonmechanical, like Tulsa May, or the youthful, as he himself had been when he'd chosen the Runabout over bigger, better, finer autos.

Luther shared a speculative glance with his brother. "You're absolutely right, Tulsy. And if all you want to do is look at it, I think the Runabout is nearly perfect." He hesitated momentarily and then his mouth curved into a devastatingly appealing grin. "But if you are thinking to go anywhere . . ."

Tulsa May shrugged fatalistically and all three chuckled. Luther reached into the seat and removed the cushion. Beneath the fading red upholstery sat the worn and aging two-cylinder engine.

"The carburetor is probably just full of dirt again. I don't think the Runabout is ready for the undertaker yet."

Arthel shook his head. "I think you should shoot it and put it out of its misery."

His joke was left unanswered as the creak and clomp of an approaching buggy drew their attention.

Tulsa May's eyes widened in distress. "Here,

Arthel, stand in front of me, maybe he won't see me."

Luther looked down the lane. "Tulsy, it does no good to hide. Everybody in town knows this Runabout."

"Why don't you let me hold him, Tulsa, and Luther can rearrange his face and vital organs," Arthel said.

Luther gave his younger brother a warning look. "If he's determined to come here, I'll talk to him."

And it seemed as if the man were determined. The buggy pulled up to the side, and the driver, dressed in a fancy new tweed coat, doffed his hat politely. "Morning, boys, missed you in church. It is Easter, you know."

"Good morning, Doc Odie," Luther answered evenly. He adjusted his stance slightly as he looked up at the other man. His legs were spread slightly as if for balance and his arms were folded across his chest in a slightly aggressive manner. "If I don't go all year, I suspect God wouldn't be especially thrilled to see me showing up on one of his holidays."

The man nodded dismissively. "Good morning, Tulsa May," he said, addressing his former fiancée for the first time.

She nodded politely, but didn't reply.

Odie Foote was a congenial but rather unattractive bachelor in his mid-thirties. His head seemed overly large for his body and rheumatic fever as a child had made him physically weak, with

14

narrow shoulders and an almost concave chest. "Your Easter ensemble is perfectly charming, ma'am," he remarked, smiling at her straight-cut gown of copper-colored Gloria cloth and the wide-brimmed straw hat that was trimmed with a band and bow of the same material. "You do remember, however, that brown is not my favorite color."

Tulsa May opened her mouth to answer, but Luther interrupted. "I believe that your preferences are no longer Miss Tulsy's concern." His words were low and tinged with threat.

Odie hesitated only a moment. "Of course," he said. "I was just speaking as a friend. I do hope that you still think of me as your friend, Tulsa May."

Luther's jaw dropped open in disbelief. "Why in heaven would she think that!"

The doctor looked evenly at Luther. "Why, I suppose because this is a small town and she and I will have to continue to see each other for years to come. Besides," he said with a grim smile, "I know Tulsa May to be of a forgiving nature. And the reverend and I have already worked out our differences."

The brothers' expressions showed that they were not so generous.

"The reverend's heart was obviously not engaged," Luther said snidely.

Doc Odie gave the younger man a sharp look. "Marriage is a serious step, not one taken lightly. The reverend understands that."

Luther's blood was boiling. It was on the tip

of his tongue to reply that a public jilting was also not to be taken lightly. But a hasty glance at Tulsa May's pale face stilled his tongue.

Doc Odie smiled tightly and gave a proprietary glance to Tulsa May as his gloved hand patted the buggy seat beside him. "Since that disreputable automobile is obviously not working again, won't you allow me to drive you to your destination, dear? It will show the whole town that we've let bygones be bygones."

Luther had no idea what Tulsa May's answer might have been. Quickly he answered for her, his tone sharp enough to cut nails. "The Runabout works fine," he said "And Tulsy's at her destination. She came to see her best friends, Arthel and me."

Foote raised an eyebrow in question, but his expression softened. "Boys," he said more quietly, with patronizing intent. "I know you've been like brothers to Tulsa May. But the lady really has no need for such protection. It's well-known that she speaks for herself." He turned to Tulsa May. "Come riding with me, my dear."

She raised her chin with such determination that the brim of her hat knocked against her back, and she gave a huff of disdain. Unfortunately the huff whistled through the gap in her front teeth, making her sound more startled than self-righteous. "No, thank you, Dr. Foote. I've come visiting Luther and Arthel."

The doctor gave her a long look before doffing his hat in a polite nod and snapping the reins

16

against the broad back of his bay mare.

As the black buggy drove out of sight, Arthel sighed heavily. "Just one little bone, Luther. Just let me break one little bone in that gnat's-arse's face."

"Arthel, your language." But Luther chuckled as he protectively wrapped his arm across Tulsa May's shoulders. "Are you all right?"

She nodded. "Thank you." She sighed heavily. "I know he's probably right, but I just can't bear to talk to him. Not yet."

"I don't blame you one bit," Arthel insisted.

"I don't care if you never give Moldy Odie the time of day," Luther agreed.

Tulsa May smiled bravely as she gave each "brother" a grateful hug. "It's not really him, anyway," she said firmly. "If he changed his mind, then he changed his mind. I just wish he'd decided before the concert."

The "concert," otherwise known as the engagement party, held three weeks previously, had been the biggest social event Prattville, Oklahoma, had ever seen. Constance Bruder had wanted the announcement of her daughter's engagement to be remembered forever. A hired band from Guthrie had arrived that afternoon. Briggs's Park was decorated with dozens of pink Japanese lanterns and Mrs. Bruder had purchased one thousand pink hothouse roses to adorn the town green's gazebo.

Tulsa May had been nervous and slightly ill at ease as she stood amid the preparations dressed in a vivid pink gown that matched the roses, but clashed drastically with her hair.

The whole town had turned out for the announcement even though every soul in the community had already heard the news: Tulsa May was to marry the doctor. Unfortunately, just after sunset — and before the announcement — the doctor developed an acute case of cold feet. He had fled.

There had been shocked whispers of disbelief, some titters of laughter among the less empathetic, and a good deal of unapologetic anger. Tulsa May, though not the prettiest girl in town, was a favorite. Everyone agreed she did not deserve such shabby treatment . . .

"It's really not him," she insisted now to Arthel and Luther. "I wouldn't want to be married to a man who didn't want to marry me. But . . ." Tulsa May's cheeks were flushed with embarrassment as she swallowed bravely and spoke the unvarnished truth. "I just hate having the whole town feeling sorry for me."

"Sorry for you?"

She shrugged and nodded. "I guess I should be used to it by now. Half the people in Prattville have been shaking their heads and feeling sorry for me for years. I just never let it bother me before."

She stared out at the horizon. "I guess I've never let *myself* feel sorry for me before."

Arthel started to protest. Luther, his expression stormy, stepped away from Tulsa May and turned his attention back to the Runabout's dust-filled engine. His face was expressionless as he opened the breather over the carburetor. It was simpler to think about mechanics; the workings of internal combustion engines was something that he understood, something that he could control. The actions of most people had no rhyme or reason as far as he could see.

As he tightened the cylinder housing, he attempted to block out the anger and sorrow swelling in his heart. He hated injustice. He hated the careless pain one human could inflict upon another based on circumstances of birth, the color of skin, or physical appearance. He knew knives didn't have to be drawn or shots fired to hurt. He had wounds of his own.

"Mama says I should just pretend that it never happened," Tulsa May said.

"That is the stupidest thing Miz Constance has ever said," Arthel said hotly. "And I can personally vouch that she has said a lot of very stupid things."

"But you have to admit there is truth to it," Tulsa May answered evenly.

"That's 'cause this town is full of men with oatmeal where their brains ought to be!" Arthel's voice was filled with youthful rage. "We should have taken that scoundrel out to the woods for some old-fashioned tar and feathers."

"Oh, Arthel." Her voice held the warmth of a smile. "You are sounding like a chivalrous gentleman these days. You'd better watch out or or you will ruin your reputation as a clodhopper."

Arthel opened his mouth to protest, but Tulsa May gently squeezed his arm. "It really doesn't matter, you know. I'll get over this eventually. My heart's not really broken. I'm just disappointed. I wanted to be a wife. I thought I might be really good at it."

"Of course you would be," Arthel insisted. "You're good at everything."

Tulsa May laughed aloud at that. "I'm *fairly* good at most things; I excel at very few. I read Latin and Greek, but neither very well. I can sew a stitch, but rarely in a straight line, and I may know how to cook but I almost always manage to burn the beans while I'm imagining myself in deep discussions with Descartes or Darwin." Tulsa May sighed with resignation. "I've never been *really* good at anything."

"That's not true! Why . . . why . . ." Arthel sputtered. "Why . . . not everyone can write for a newspaper. You can sure do that."

Tulsa May shook her head. "I'm not even very good at that. My disposition is too sunny."

"Too sunny? What does that mean?"

"Well, when any other reporter turns in a headline, it reads HOUSE AND BUSINESS DESTROYED BY FIRE. When I turn in the same story, it's titled NONE INJURED IN OVERNIGHT BLAZE."

Luther slammed the Runabout's breather back down into place and turned to her. "There is nothing wrong with looking on the bright side of life, Tulsa May. Wanting to see the good in things."

"You are absolutely right," she agreed. "I just wish I could see the good in having the whole town walking on eggshells around me and pitying me behind my back."

Luther set the spark on the front panel and slipped the crank handle into the starter. After one turn the Runabout popped and sputtered momentarily, but as Luther adjusted the engine, it began to purr with the precision of a Singer sewing machine. He covered the engine and set the red upholstered cushion back on the seat before turning back to Tulsa May.

"My dear Miss Tulsy," he said with a very formal and proper bow. "Would you care to take a Sunday drive with me?"

Tulsa May giggled and gave him a thorough once-over. "Wouldn't you like to go and put on a shirt?" she asked.

Luther glanced momentarily up at his residence on the second floor.

"I believe I'll just escort you as I am if you're not offended."

Tulsa May took his warm tanned hand in her own and climbed into the Runabout. She scooted over to the left so that he could drive.

"We'll be back in an hour or so," Luther told his brother as he released the brass brake lever.

"If anyone comes looking for me," he said pointedly, "just say that I had to give the engine a test drive."

21

His younger brother gave Luther a jaunty salute as Tulsa May handed Luther the extra pair of driving goggles and he adjusted them over his eyes. A cloud of dust was left in their wake as they headed south down the sandy pike known as Guthrie and River Road.

As Arthel watched them drive away, one eyebrow was raised in speculation. Luther was up to something. Something important enough for him to leave a hot zam-betty warming his sheets.

"Where is he off to?"

Arthel looked up to see Emma Dix leaning over the second-floor porch. Her chemise and petticoat were partially covered with a bright red fringed shawl.

"Luther's taking Tulsa May for a Sunday drive," he answered.

"He told me he'd be back in twenty minutes." Emma's words were shrill.

Arthel shrugged. "I guess he forgot you, Miss Dix."

Emma's huff of indignation was almost comical, and Arthel pretended to rub his chin as he covered the grin he couldn't quite suppress.

"I'm not the mechanic my brother is," he said matter-of-factly. "But I'd be happy to check out your parts, ma'am."

With a screech of rage, Emma Dix hurried back inside, slamming the door so hard the building's painted wooden sign swung creakily in the breeze.

Chapter Two

The Guthrie and River Road was rutted in all the places where it wasn't sandy, but since Tulsa May was not driving she ignored the rough road and gazed out over the awakening spring meadows of false boneset and prairie coneflower.

"You deserved better than him, you know," Luther said simply, interrupting her thoughts.

Tulsa May swallowed and lowered her eyes. "Maybe he had cause."

"Cause!" Luther exclaimed with disbelief. "What possible cause could a man have for breaking off an engagement in the middle of the engagement party?"

Her familiar penny-brown eyes glanced at him, seemingly darker with sorrow. "His cause was that he just doesn't love me."

"Oh, for mercy's sake."

Tulsa May smiled humorlessly. "I know that you men don't like to talk about love and romance. But you do know that it exists and you know when you don't feel it."

"Tulsy, he asked you to marry him. He must have thought he loved you at the time."

She shook her head. "He never claimed to love me. He thought it was time that he should marry and he thought that I would be a respectable and biddable wife."

"Respectable and biddable?"

Nodding, Tulsa May managed a wry grin. "I can't imagine where he got such an idea, but he had it."

Luther looked at his friend affectionately. Tulsa May was a good and obedient daughter, for the most part. But she prized her independence.

She looked down at her hands, unnecessarily adjusting the seams on her gloves. "Doc Odie thought he could marry without love. But when the time came, his heart wouldn't let him."

Luther blew a furious huff through his teeth. "His heart wouldn't let him? I'd like to rip his heart out and feed it to him for breakfast!"

Tulsa May reached over to pat the strong brown hand that tightly gripped the steering wheel. "My brave protector," she teased. "We are no longer playing children's games, Luther. You don't have to always take my side."

He looked down at her again. Seeing the golden freckled face, the intelligent brown eyes, and the wide smiling mouth with its endearing gap-toothed grin, he smiled.

"I don't *have* to take your side, Tulsy," he said. "But I always will."

The moment was sweet and fresh and lightened Tulsa May's heart as Latin poems and sweet summer music never could.

A jackrabbit scampered across the road in front

of them, startling them and breaking into the moment.

"So did you love him?" Luther asked a moment later.

"What?"

"Odie Foote, remember? Moldy Doc Odie . . . did you love him?"

Tulsa May ignored the silly nickname.

"I . . . well, yes, of course I did, but —"

"Not 'yes, of course,' " Luther corrected sharply. "There are plenty of things not to love about Odie Foote."

Tulsa May nodded and with a sigh made a painful admission. "I guess I didn't love him as I should have. I wanted to be married, I suppose. I feel more disappointed than anything else."

Tulsa May looked down at her gloves again. She hoped her confession didn't make Luther pity her too.

"Good!" Luther said decisively. "He is no great catch, Tulsy. He is the most boring man I've ever tried to converse with, he's as old-fashioned as Old Man Bowman, and he smells of antiseptic."

"He's a doctor! He can't help that he smells like one."

Luther gave her a nod of approval. "You defend him bravely, but I do think things have turned out for the best."

She hesitated before nodding agreement. "Honestly, you are right. He would have been quite disappointed with me and I would have been miserable with him."

"Then all's well that ends well."

"Undoubtedly so," Tulsa May agreed. "I just wish the whole town of Prattville didn't look at me as if they were fearful that I'm likely to drown myself in the river."

Luther reached out to raise her chin. When her bright penny-brown eyes met his vivid blue ones, he smiled.

"Oh, I think I've got an idea of how we can stop the talk around town."

"You can never *stop* talk," she told him, shaking her head. "It's like a river. It's going to run its course and we just have to be patient and let it pass by."

Luther nodded. "There's some truth to that. But the world is not the simple creation of nature anymore. Civilization has learned a thing or two about rivers. We can dig them deeper, dam them up, or divert their course."

Tulsa May looked confused. "What are you talking about?"

"I have a plan."

"A plan? What kind of plan?" She sounded suspicious.

"Now, Tulsy, when you wanted to read Mr. Lawrence's scandalous book, I went to Guthrie and bought it for you, didn't I?"

"Yes."

"When you decided that you wanted to do something worthwhile for the community, who introduced you to Erwin Willers and helped you convince him that a woman could be as good a newspaper reporter as a man?"

"You did."

"And when you wanted the freedom to come and go as you pleased, but Rev wouldn't let you have your own rig, I gave you this Runabout."

"And I do appreciate it."

"If you really want Moldy Odie Foote, Tulsy, I'd see that you'd get the smelly old coot."

Tulsa May gave him a bright, winning smile. "What do you plan to do? Beat the poor man to a pulp and drag him down the aisle?"

Luther grinned. "It would have been a pleasure."

She giggled.

"But you don't really want him. We've established that, I believe. And we can't dam up that river of town gossip," he said easily. "But we can divert it in another direction entirely."

"How are you going to do that?"

"The age-old cure for blighted romances. There is no stronger stimulant for a change in gossip. You, Tulsy, are getting a brand-new beau."

She shook her head in disbelief. "A new beau? I don't think that is very likely. Odie Foote is the only gentleman caller I ever had."

"Well, you just found yourself a new one."

"Who?"

"Why, myself, dearest Tulsy," he answered with a comically high-toned affectation. "If I might be so bold."

Tulsa May laughed out loud. "Oh, Luther, you are teasing."

"I am completely serious."

"It will never work, you know," she said with complete conviction. "There is no chance that we can make anyone believe that you are my new gentleman caller."

Luther grinned confidently. "Of course we can. Where is your legendary optimism? A few Sunday drives like this, a willing escort to church, and an occasional stroll through the park. The matrons in Prattville will be stumbling over each other to spread the news."

Tulsa May's expression was still skeptical. "No one in this town would ever believe that you could be calling on me. We've been friends too long."

"When it comes to matters of the heart, friendship can turn to romance in the blink of an eye."

"But still, Luther, I don't think anyone would think that of you, of us. I mean, well . . ." She hesitated awkwardly. "Couples, well, couples seem to go together. They match, so to speak. Do you understand what I'm saying? They are both very godly or they're both avid hunters or they enjoy flower gardens. They seem as if they belong together. And we . . . I mean you and I . . . well, we just don't look right together. People would find it strange. I'm so plain and blunt spoken and you, well . . ." She took a deep, determined breath. "If you must know, every female in Prattville, whether she's dressed in pinafores or widow's weeds, is pining away in love for you."

Luther stared at her for a long moment and then threw his head back and roared with laughter.

"It's true," Tulsa May insisted. "All the young ladies at church think *you* are the fish to catch."

Luther looked down at her. "Fish to catch?" He chuckled lightly, as if at some private joke. "I think the young ladies of the church are trying to lure me with the wrong bait."

Tulsa May looked at him curiously.

"Anyway," he continued, "what the young ladies think is unimportant. It's the thinking of their mothers and fathers that we must concern ourselves with." He hesitated as if unsure whether to speak his mind. "Tulsy, I have . . . well, I have a reputation of sorts with . . . ah . . . women that are of tarnished regard."

Tulsa May's eyes widened in shock.

Luther cleared his throat self-consciously. "I'm sure that many of the men in town will be aware of that, even if the more innocent young members of the congregation are not."

"A reputation?" Tulsa May looked at her closest friend as if she had never seen him before.

"It's not a particularly good reputation," he said quietly. "And, well, I guess everyone knows that when a fellow with a bit of a past thinks to settle down, he'll pick a gal that's sweet and pure. Something different from the females he's been around."

Tulsa May nodded, still slightly befuddled.

"Everybody in this town, Tulsy, thinks you

are the brightest shine since sunrise. And you are just the kind of gal a man marries."

Tulsa May frowned uneasily.

With a natural grace, Luther laid his arm along the back of the seat and gently squeezed her shoulder.

"You would make a wonderful wife for a man mending his bachelor ways, Tulsy. And I think everyone in Prattville can see that."

The feel of his hand on her shoulder warmed her and touched her in some deep part of her soul that she never allowed herself to examine. Luther Briggs to court her? Even if it was only a sham, the idea of it gave her heart a fluttery thrill that could not be excused away by any rational argument. She looked up at him and swallowed nervously.

"I don't know, Luther," she said. "It seems like a mighty big lie to get into."

Luther smiled down at her. "If you were to listen to every lie told in this town, you'd go deaf in a week from overwork."

Tulsa May still seemed unsure, but Luther was not. The plan had come to him in a flash, but he knew that it would work. He would make it work. Gently, he squeezed her shoulder again. He would do anything to make his Tulsy happy.

They had known each other since Luther and Arthel had come to Prattville ten years before. After their father had died, they had expected to be taken in by their grandmother, Maimie

Briggs. But Miss Maimie, as she was called by everyone, had never approved of her son's marriage to a Cherokee woman so she had rejected her grandsons. Luther had been devastated.

Tulsa May had made them feel welcome that first day, as the two of them had sat sadly in the kitchen of the old Briggs mansion, waiting in vain for their grandmother to ask for them.

"You can stay with us!" Tulsa May had insisted immediately.

What Reverend Bruder had thought of that solution, Luther never really knew. But he and his brother were graciously welcomed into the parsonage and lived there for almost a year before Luther found work that was steady enough to support himself and Arthel. Luther had always been grateful to Reverend Bruder and his wife, Constance, but he'd loved Tulsa May, his Tulsy, as the younger sister he never had.

"It'll be like taking candy from a baby," he assured her. "I'll parade you around town a bit, take you on a picnic, sit with you on the porch in the moonlight, and folks in this town will forget Doc Odie ever even called on you."

"But then how will we get out of it?"

"Don't worry," he assured her. "Once I've shown an interest in you, the other young bucks will be taking a second look. When you see one you like, you break it off with me and no one will be the wiser."

She rubbed one of the buttons on her gloves, worried. She wasn't sure it would be that easy.

Ruggy's Lowtown Saloon was dark and dank and smelled of sweaty bodies and stale beer. For a bar, the atmosphere was perfect. Luther squinted, his eyes adjusting to the dim interior. He made his way to the bar and grinned at the barkeep, an old black man who was polishing barrel-bottom beer goblets with a faded red checked towel. Garbed in a fancy dress shirt, a black corded neck scarf, and a bar apron, Conrad Ruggy dressed as formally in his role as a saloonkeeper as he had as Miss Maimie's butler.

"Evening, Mr. Ruggy," Luther said as he seated himself at the bar in front of the older man. "Did we have a good day or a stinker?"

The old man's face crinkled into a broad grin. "Some of it's been good," he answered. "And some of it has been stinkin'."

Luther laughed. "I suppose you plan to tell me which is which."

Conrad Ruggy and his wife, Mattie, had worked for Miss Maimie Briggs for as long as anybody could remember. Since it was traditional to leave faithful servants a legacy, the folks in Prattville were highly surprised that Miss Maimie's will did not mention her servants at all.

"I want to settle some money on you," Luther had told the old man after the will was read. "I don't claim to have ever understood Miss Maimie, but I know that you should have some money to keep you in your golden years."

Ruggy had chuckled and shook his head. "I don't plan to have no golden years, boy," he said. "I've been black all my life and I see no evidence that I'll be changing any time soon."

"But I want —" Luther had begun, only to be interrupted by the older man.

"What I want, boy, is a job. A good job that I can go to every day and keep my mind busy and make a living for my wife and me. I don't need much pay, just a mite. Just enough so that I don't ever have to live off my little Maud and her man."

Luther nodded, understanding, but scratched his chin as he thought. "Do you know anything about machines, Mr. Ruggy?"

Conrad had laughed. "You mean like that silly horseless of Miss Maimie's? Lord no, I don't know a thing and don't intend to neither." Ruggy folded his hands across his chest and eyed Luther. "I heard you bought that rundown beer parlor down in the Lowtown."

Luther shrugged. "Just bought it for the building. I thought I might fix it up for a warehouse."

"Now, why would you want to do that, boy? Don't you know that the beer business is the most steady in the world, good times and bad?"

"I don't know a thing about beer parlors," Luther admitted.

"Well, boy," Conrad said quietly. "I suspect that this is your lucky day. 'Cause I was raised behind a bar. And I'll set that one up and run it for you."

"And how much do you want to be paid for that?"

The old man grinned. "I just want my share of the business, boy. Fifty-fifty, right down the middle."

As Luther gazed across the smooth, highly polished bar, he knew it was one of the best investments he'd ever made.

"Well," the old man began leisurely. "The good news is that we sold a fair amount of beer this morning and that Blue Turley and the Mitchum fellow are getting up a game tonight in the back room."

Luther looked around hastily to ensure that they weren't being overheard. Gambling of any sort was a serious crime in the state.

"I said I'd keep an eye out for them," Ruggy continued. "For a simple five percent of the take."

"Five percent."

The old man's eyes widened innocently. "Seems fair to me."

Luther laughed. He left all the decisions about the place to Ruggy.

"I'm putting that money aside for the new building," Ruggy said with a broad smile.

Luther's brow creased. "I told you, I haven't decided about the new place."

"But you are going to," he said, unconcerned, "and what better use could you have for that old Henniger building than a bar and billiards parlor?"

"Mr. Ruggy," Luther explained quietly. "It's

on Main Street. Reverend Bruder would be damning my soul from his pulpit for a month of Sundays if I were to open a saloon right in the middle of town."

Conrad chuckled. "Lordy, it's all true what they tell ya," he said. "You can take the boy out of the church, but you can't take the church out of the boy."

"It's not that," Luther answered quickly. "I just respect the preacher, and he stands up for me in this town. I don't want to make trouble for him or myself."

With a nod, the old man let it go. "As you say, boy."

Ruggy went back to polishing the beer goblets and Luther looked around the bar, slightly uncomfortable.

"So that's the good news?" Luther said, trying to change the topic. "What's the stinkin'?"

Ruggy sighed heavily as he set the polished goblet forcefully on the shelf behind him. With a frown the man leaned over the bar nearly nose to nose with Luther.

"That *female* you've been scurrying around with has been here all afternoon."

"Emma?"

Conrad nodded. "I don't approve of no gals of no sort that hang out in places like this."

Luther knew that Conrad only allowed his wife, Mattie, inside to scrub and clean the place, and he would never open the door for customers until his lawfully wedded was safe at home.

"What's she doing here?" Luther asked.

The old man shook his head. "That's what I was fixing to ask you. She come in here about mid-afternoon mad as a wet hen. I told her you hadn't been here, and I didn't know when to expect you. It's Easter Sunday, for Lord's sake. Folks ought to be in church."

Luther couldn't argue with that. "What's she been doing all this time?"

Ruggy made a face as if he'd just had a taste of sour apple. "She's been playing pocket billiards."

Muttering, Luther walked to an open doorway at the far end of the saloon. The pool room was separated from the main room so that the billiards and snooker players would not be distracted by rowdy drinkers. The room itself was bare and simple. A green cloth-covered table dominated the space in front of three large glass windows. Although there were gas lamps for evening play, true snooker players only attempted serious games in the full light of afternoon.

A serious game was presently in progress, but it was not billiards. Emma Dix, giggling seductively, bent suggestively over the table, pool cue in her hand. Blue Turley, a rangy young cowboy, leaned over her back ostensibly giving her advice about her angle on the ball. Ferd Mitchum was sitting on a stool in the corner watching with such glee, Luther assumed that his vantage point offered a good view of the woman's bodice.

When Emma finally took her shot, it was wide,

a truly dismal attempt.

"Oh, poot! I missed again," she complained with a pretty pout.

"You just need practice," Blue Turley assured her with a chuckle. "And I'm here for you to practice on anytime."

The young woman found his suggestive remark amusing. Luther did not.

"Emma!"

All three turned to face him. Emma's eyes lit with appreciation.

"My, my, look what the cat dragged in this evening."

Luther glared at the two men, before turning his attention toward the woman.

"May I speak with you a moment, Emma?"

Handing her cue to Turley, Emma gave him a flirty grin. "See you boys later," she assured them. Her chin high and giving plenty of wiggle to her walk, Emma made her way to Luther's side.

"What are you doing here?" he asked through clenched teeth.

"Why, I'm playing pool." She looked around innocently.

"Emma, this is no place for ladies."

Her grin was positively wicked. "Honey, not being a lady is one of the things you like most about me."

Luther led her out of the pool room to a table at the far back corner of the saloon where he politely offered her a chair.

"I'll have a beer, Conrad," she called out. "Or whiskey, if you got some stashed behind the bar."

"Coffee," Luther said. "Two, black."

"Two coffees coming right up," the old man answered.

Emma was clearly not pleased and frowned unhappily at him until Ruggy brought the tray.

The blue tin mugs, one slightly dented on one side, were seldom used and almost new. Luther touched the handle on his, but it was too hot to pick up. He glared right back at Emma.

"I don't want you coming here anymore," he said, his voice strong with conviction. "No ladies, women, or females of any breed hang out in this saloon."

Emma's eyes narrowed. "I needed to see you," she told him. "What am I supposed to do, wait at your house and watch over your little brother? He's really too young for you to leave alone."

She was baiting him and Luther knew it. If Luther had a weak spot it was his brother. He'd taken responsibility for him from childhood and was almost obsessed with seeing that the younger Briggs had it easier than he had himself. Frequently Emma'd made little jabs about Luther's overprotection. More than once he'd risen to the bait, but not today. Deliberately he let her snide remark pass right over him.

"Perhaps you should spend more time at your own home," he said with an unpleasant smile. "The gossips seem to think you are shirking your duty there."

It was a cut guaranteed to wound and it hit the mark cleanly. Furiously, Emma raised her hand and slapped Luther's face.

Emma's eyes widened as she stared at the brightening red mark against his cheek and a stab of fear coursed through her.

Luther cleared his throat and took a deep breath to calm himself. Glancing around he saw every eye in the place upon him. With deliberately casual unconcern he reached up to rub lightly the injured area.

"Well, at least she didn't break my jaw," he announced to the ogling crowd. His words drew hoots of laughter from the men in the saloon. Assured that no further fireworks were about to occur, the men turned back to their conversations and their beer. Luther looked across the table at Emma.

"I apologize," he said quietly. "I was angry. I can fault you for a lot of things, but caring for that old man is not one of them."

Emma merely stared at the mug of coffee before her. It was cool enough to drink before either spoke again.

"Where did you go?" she asked.

"I had to see a friend."

Raising her eyes, she gazed at him speculatively. "I have friends, also," she said, nodding toward the billiard room where the sounds of shiny duronoid balls cracking against each other could still be heard.

"Blue Turley?" Luther shook his head in disgust. "That no-account wouldn't know an honest day's work if it came to the door with a calling card."

Emma lowered her eyes coyly. "But he's got mighty big shoulders for a woman to lean on."

"Yes, ma'am." Luther snorted. "And you should see some of the dirty-looking hags that have been leaning on them."

She raised her chin as if she intended to make some further comment, but Luther raised his hand to hush her.

"I think that we should stop seeing each other for a while."

The statement was so unexpected that Emma gasped. "What?"

"I'm going to be busy for a few weeks and I think that perhaps we shouldn't see each other for a while."

Emma shook her head. "You can't be serious," she said. She looked around her as if searching for the answer to some strange puzzle. "I won't come down here anymore," she assured him. "I never dreamed you'd be this upset."

"It's not that. Certainly you don't belong here, but you're free to come and go as you please."

"Did that little slap hurt you?" she said, disbelieving.

"Of course not, you —"

"Blue Turley? That little flirtation with Blue? Why, that's nothing, honey, you know that. The closest that rounder's ever come to loving on me is pinching my backside."

"I'm not likely to be jealous of Blue Turley," Luther agreed. "It has nothing to do with you. I have something important in the works and I just don't think we should see each other for a while."

"But —"

"I'm not saying *never*," he added quickly and reached across the table to touch her hand. "I just have some plans and I think it would be best for both of us if we weren't seen together for the next few weeks or so, until I get things worked out and completed."

Emma's jaw tightened. Even in the dim light of the saloon she looked every day of her twenty-eight years plus a dozen more. "No, Luther. You aren't dropping me like some used-up rag on the garbage heap," she said quietly.

"Dropping you?" Luther leaned back in his chair and looked at her curiously. "Emma, we've got no claims on each other. We both know we've just been in this for the fun. No promises have been made."

Her voice was harsh, dangerous, threatening. "Oh no," she agreed. "No promises were made. Not one little promise at all. But I'll make you a promise now, Luther Briggs. You try to drop me, for even so much as a week, and you will live to regret it."

"Emma —"

"I am no faithful hound that comes when you whistle and stays when you say sit." Pushing her chair back angrily, she rose to her feet. "I wish I hadn't already slapped you. 'Cause I would dearly love to do it again."

Chapter Three

His best white shirt shone brightly in the last pink light of evening as Luther Briggs stepped onto the porch at the Bruder parsonage. Before he knocked, he donned the gray tricot jacket he carried beneath his arm, and casually pulled a small celluloid comb from his back pocket and ran it through his thick black hair, which was still slightly damp from his bath. Then he pulled his stiffly starched white collar to make certain it was standing straight up and he tightened his necktie.

Finally, he rapped smartly on the heavily scrolled frame of the Bruders' front door.

No answer came right away. He knocked again, louder and more forcefully.

"Yes! Yes! I'm on my way." Luther heard the complaining voice through the door. A minute later it was flung open by a sweaty and flustered Philemon Bruder.

"Luther?" Reverend Bruder's voice sounded both surprised and pleased. "I certainly never expected to see you here on a Sunday evening."

Luther smiled at the man. Though the preacher's hair had started to gray badly, his handlebar moustache was still a bright carrot-red, and his body tended toward long and lean. These days he sported the muscles more suited to a professional pugilist than a parson, readily visible since he was wearing a sweat-stained quarter-sleeve cotton shirt and baggy trousers.

"Evening, Rev," Luther answered, using the familiar nickname. "What have you been doing, chopping cotton?"

The preacher chuckled. "I'm working out in my gym."

"Your gym?" The whole town knew the minister had an almost devout interest in exercise and bodybuilding, but Luther had not heard anything of a gym.

"You've got to see it, son. I've finally set up a place of my own in the basement. It's small, but it has almost everything: rubber wands, a rowing device, chest pulleys, even a punching bag with gloves. And I just got the new Whiteley Exerciser from the catalog last week. It's much superior to dead weights. Just try it; the manufacturer says you can double the strength of your chest muscles in just eight weeks."

"My chest muscles are fine," Luther assured him.

The he shook his head. "The body and mind must be in top condition for the soul to prosper."

Luther smiled with amused affection at the minister. Physical culture proponents such as Tuke, Jahn, and Sandborne figured almost as largely in the preacher's day-to-day philosophy as did the teachings of the apostles. Ever since the afternoon, nearly ten years ago, when Cora Sparrow gave the preacher her copy of Daisy Millenbutter's *A Ladies' Guide to Good Health, Fine Posture, and Spiritual Completeness*, Reverend Bruder had been as busy converting the lazy to exertion as he was the sinning to righteousness.

Luther was saved from a further discussion by Mrs. Bruder's entrance into the foyer from the rear parlor.

"Luther, dear boy!" she exclaimed in pleasant surprise. "What a delight that you've come to visit." Casting a disapproving glance at her husband, Mrs. Bruder made a face. "Philemon, really! Go wash up and change. We have company."

Constance Bruder was a kind and loving wife and a working matron in the church and community. Luther wondered, however, if Mrs. Bruder had ever had a maternal bone in her body. The year that he had lived with her, she had treated both Arthel and himself like welcome strangers. Not for one moment had she offered even the slightest crumb of motherly care. But it was nothing personal. Miz Constance didn't seem to comfort or understand her own daughter. So how could anyone expect her to really warm up to two half-grown boys?

"Please make yourself presentable," Constance directed her husband. "Familiarity is no excuse for informality."

"Oh no, please." Luther stayed the preacher hastily. "Not on my account. I've just come to sit on the porch with Tulsy."

45

Both of Tulsa May's parents turned to stare at the young man as if he'd suddenly grown another head.

"Sit on the porch with Tulsa May?" Mrs. Bruder's voice sounded puzzled.

"What in the world would you want to do that for?" the preacher asked baldly.

Luther sucked his cheeks in slightly as he controlled the spark of annoyance that he felt. "I've come to call on Tulsy." He spoke each word slowly and clearly.

"To call?"

"On Tulsa May?"

The totally incredulous expressions of the couple worried Luther. Was Tulsa May right? Was this little drama he intended to enact going to be more difficult than he'd imagined?

Tulsa May stared at the large oval mirror that stood in the corner of her bedroom next to her dresser. She turned her face, first right profile, then left, then looked at herself straight on. There was no help for it. She still had a long skinny face, a gap between her front teeth, and carrot-colored hair.

She wondered, not for the first time, what God had been thinking about when he'd created her. Each and every physical trait she had came from her father's side of the family. And while these traits looked fine on her daddy, on Tulsa May they fell far short of the accepted standard of beauty.

She deliberately forced away any self-pity. "Just be grateful you don't have his moustache!" she told her mirror image with a sternness that was spoiled by a giggle.

With a shake of her head at her own foolishness, she glanced up at the rack of hats that hung on her wall. Tulsa May was not overly fond of clothing or accessories, but she loved her millinery. Her mother once accused her of having two dozen hats. Tulsa May was grateful that Mrs. Bruder had never checked the boxes beneath the bed or she would have seen twice that many. Hats were Tulsa May's one true weakness and strongest temptation. But she never scolded herself for it.

If God hadn't wanted her to buy hats, she told herself, he wouldn't have given her orange hair.

Tonight she chose a tiny Venice bonnet that sat squarely on the top of her head. Its dark green velvet facing and bow was accented by a darker silk lace and a jetted aigrette that poked jauntily from the back. It was a charming hat, but its most important feature was that it easily drew the eye away from her unfortunately colored hair.

She attached the Venice bonnet securely with two long jet pins and fiddled momentarily with the arrangement of velvet and lace. Looking back into the mirror, she smiled with pleasure. That image quickly faded as she purposely closed her lips to cover her less than perfect smile. Tulsa May checked her reflection again. Yes, that was better, she assured herself. If she could just remember to keep her lips closed to cover the gap in her teeth, her chin down to shorten her face, her hair would be decently covered and she would be passable.

Not that she really cared much for herself, she was quick to remember. She had fought that demon in childhood and had come through being pleased at what heaven *had* given her, rather than longing for those things that passed her by. But, poor Luther, she thought. He was undoubtedly accustomed to being with more attractive women and she knew that mattered to a man. At least it had mattered to Odie Foote.

"A woman is a symbol of a man's success," her mother had warned her. "It's all well and good to be sweet and kind and smart, but a man wants something pretty on his arm."

Tulsa May had managed to ignore her mother's philosophy and advice for a long time. But it began to seem as if Dr. Foote agreed with her.

"I understand," he had told her one night in the quiet privacy of the front parlor, "that it is proper for a woman to appear suitably drab when she is working for wages." He cleared his throat before he continued. "But you must allow yourself to shine youthfully when I call upon you."

Dr. Foote's idea of youthful shine included bows and furbelows and pale pastel colors. Her mother had dressed her in that fashion for more than a dozen years, but the pretty dresses and fancy ribbons that looked so appealing on other young women made Tulsa May look and feel ridiculous. Neither her mother nor Odie could ever quite understand that.

Well, she thought, they had had their way. With the doctor and her mother in collusion, Tulsa May had been forced into a betrothal gown of rose pink ruffles. She gave herself a disgusted expression in the mirror. Perhaps it was the sight of her in that dress that had made Odie run from the engagement party as if his coattails were on fire.

Downstairs she could hear the sounds of conversation and guessed rightly that Luther had arrived at last. He was such a dear, such a friend. This silly plan of his was sure not to work, but the fact that he devised it was a sweet and generous favor.

"You are just full of ambition," she'd told him on one long-ago summer day as he polished the Runabout in the drive in front of the carriage house at the Briggs Mansion. "With all the plans and ideas you have, you're sure to do important things in your life."

He smiled at her. "Do you know what my biggest ambition is?" he asked.

She shook her head.

"To see that my Tulsy is the happiest girl in Prattville."

She had giggled. "Aiming low, are you?" she asked. "You know there is not a happier soul in town than sunny, smiling Tulsa May."

His eyes had been warm as he nodded in agreement. "And it's my job as your 'almost brother' to see that you stay that way."

And he had done his best, she conceded. Even now that they were both all grown-up, he was still as dear to her as ever.

A smile came to Tulsa May's lips as she imagined the consternation of the young ladies at church. She almost giggled. When they found out that Luther Briggs was courting her, green would be the most common complexion color in the congregation.

A strange, anxious thrill swept through her, causing Tulsa May's heart to beat more quickly. Luther Briggs would be courting her. Immediately she tamped down the delight that skittered in her veins. None of this was real. It was pretend and it was a favor.

Besides, she was absolutely certain that friendship with Luther Briggs was far superior to a grand passion for him. He was sure to be a heartbreaker. And her heart was far too fragile already.

With a last shake of her narrow brown skirt and a careful straightening of the dark green piping on her shirtwaist, Tulsa May hurried down to meet her new and hopefully very temporary gentleman caller.

"Chin down, lips closed, hat in place," she reminded herself aloud.

As Tulsa May reached the landing a few minutes later, she heard her father's voice.

"Well, of course you have my permission, son,"

he said, his tone incredulous. "It's not a question of that. It's —"

Tulsa May was left to wonder about the rest of that sentence. For at that moment Luther glanced up and smiled broadly, interrupting Reverend Bruder. "Tulsy," he called out delightedly. "What a prompt pigeon you are. Most of the girls I call on make me wait half an hour."

Tulsa May rolled her eyes dramatically. Completely forgetting her own admonitions, she raised her chin high and smiled broadly. "Well, I wouldn't want to appear too eager," she said. "Do you think I should go back upstairs and make you wait thirty minutes?"

There was a small huff of disapproval from Constance Bruder, but both young people ignored it.

"My dear Miss Bruder," Luther said, making a courtly bow. "I would much rather spend that time sitting with you."

The reverend seemed ill at ease and puzzled, but his wife gazed at her daughter and young Mr. Briggs hopefully.

"Well, I don't know about this. I —" Reverend Bruder began.

"Leave the young people alone, Philemon," Constance scolded him in a sugar-sweet tone that was as hard as maple candy, then she turned and smiled a much too friendly smile. "Young Luther has always been almost family. The reverend will sit in the front parlor. Luther, you may take our little Tulsa May out to the swing for a bit of privacy, but no leaving the porch. I'll bring some refreshments."

Little Tulsa May was horrified. Her mother was acting every inch the prospective mother-in-law, and Tulsa was tempted to set her straight immediately. As if sensing the impending confession, Luther reached for her hand and gave her a playful wink.

"We will sit on the swing, ma'am," he assured her. "Right in front of the parlor window. And we will certainly call for a chaperon if we decide to take a turn in the garden."

Miz Constance smiled with sickening sweetness.

With his arm offered in grand fashion, Luther hurried Tulsa May out onto the porch.

"That was the most ridiculous thing that I've ever heard," she whispered to him disgustedly. "Has my mother lost her mind? For heaven's sake, we've been out alone together in the Runabout probably a hundred times!"

Chuckling, Luther hugged her familiarly around her shoulders. They walked to the grill-back milk-blue porch swing, whose seat was covered with a folded quilt for padding. "That was before we were *courting*," he told her. The width of the swing dictated a certain closeness of the couple. Luther laid one arm along the back so that they were not so closely crushed together.

"But we're not —"

"Shhh." Luther brought one long finger to Tulsa May's lips. With a familiar, boyish smile he leaned down next to her ear and whispered gently. "Our true plan must be so secret, even we forget about it."

His breath was warm and husky in her ear, raising gooseflesh on the side of her neck and sending a strange, startling sizzle through Tulsa May's veins. She giggled nervously.

"Not one word," he whispered. "Start thinking of me as your brand-new beau."

He leaned back and looked over at her. His vivid blue eyes seemed even darker in the pale evening light. His voice seemed softer than Tulsa May remembered.

"When you can begin to believe it, everyone else in town will too."

If the beating of Tulsa May's heart was any measure, she was halfway to believing it already.

If someone wanted to announce something to the entire community of Prattville, he had two options. He could speak with Erwin Willers about taking an advertisement in the *Prattville Populist*, or he could tell Fanny Penny.

Mrs. Penny, wife of local businessman Titus Penny, was the current gossip champion of the county. In fact, the woman could probably hold her own in a national competition.

Because his "courtship" was not something that could be easily explained in a newspaper ad, Luther headed down to the Penny Emporium on Main Street near mid-morning on Monday to leave a "discreet whisper" with the matronly town crier.

53

The Pennys' businesses had prospered through the years. The Emporium, a grand building, was adjacent to the smaller store, which had once been known as Penny's Dry Goods. The original building was now simply Penny's Grocery and Market. The Emporium, filled with the exciting and up-to-date wares of a fashionable department store, was the fanciest edifice on Main Street: two stories of bright red brick with cheery yellow trim. It perfectly matched the red-brick sidewalk that ran throughout the town. The year 1907 was recessed in brick near the top of the building's impressive facade. A year quite important for the history of the town: it was the year that Oklahoma achieved statehood, the year that the town was named as a county seat, and most important to Fanny Penny, the year the city fathers voted unanimously to change the town's name from Lead Dog to Prattville. An alteration that society matron Amelia Pratt Puser was quoted as saying was a "giant step toward civilization and modern life."

The entrance to the Penny Emporium was as grand as a church, with a wide double doorway with plate-glass windows on either side for display of an enticing array of practical as well as frivolous articles designed to lure even the most resolute passerby into the store.

Like everyone else, Luther took a long look into the glass case that morning before stepping across the threshold. A small brass bell tinkled at the top of the doorway, announcing him.

The store smelled of fancy soaps and new leather from the shoe department in the back. There was one long counter down the right side of the store. Behind it was a hive of pine drawers that extended from the polished wood floor to the high plastered ceiling. A tall ladder attached to a rail at the top could be moved from one end of the room to another to reach anything, anywhere.

Luther stepped up to the counter and leaned against it casually. He didn't shop for fine goods often, since he put most of what he made back into his business or into local real estate. And his biggest project was to save enough at the Prattville State Bank to send Arthel to the A & M College to study engineering.

From behind a curtain at the back of the store emerged a young blond woman who was so exquisitely beautiful her face would have put any of the Gibson girls to shame. Maybelle Penny was the belle of Prattville, the reputed beauty of the county and probably one of the loveliest young women in the state. Perfectly groomed and highly fashionable, at sixteen she already had the ability to set male hearts fluttering whether they were her own age or four times more.

"Well, good morning, Mr. Briggs." She moved toward him in a walk that was carefully calculated to show her at her best. Her hands were clasped primly together at her small waistline, she held her chin high, revealing the perfection of her features, and her skirts swayed gently.

"Miss Maybelle." Luther tipped his hat and then, as if thinking better of it, removed it completely. "Don't you look pretty this morning, ma'am. As, of course, you always do."

Maybelle coyly tilted her head to the side and answered with softly feigned shyness, "Oh, Mr. Briggs, you will turn a girl's head."

Luther was amused at the young girl's pretensions. He'd known her since she was a holy terror in pigtails. It was a bit difficult for him to now see her as a demure young lady.

"We haven't seen you around the shop lately. You must be working rather long hours at the store these days."

Maybelle lowered her eyes with feigned modesty. "I'm not sure that it's proper at all for me to just pop over for a visit as I have in the past. I mean, your home is a residence of gentlemen, with no chaperon."

Luther raised an eyebrow in surprise. "Well, I know that Arthel misses you. He doesn't get into nearly as much trouble these days as he used to with you around."

Her head snapped up, and this time there was an expression of consternation on her face. "Arthel was my *childhood* friend," she said coldly. "I am no longer a *child* to play games and run about town."

Nodding gravely, Luther agreed. "You do still ride your bicycle."

"Well, of course I do."

Luther's serious expression slowly widened into

a grin. "I'm glad to hear that. I was becoming worried that you had simply turned into another boring grown-up."

Maybelle's brow furrowed. She was not nearly as bright as she was pretty and she wasn't quite sure whether a joke had been made of her or not.

"Could I show you something this morning?" she asked, clearly unwilling to prolong a conversation that she wasn't certain showed her in a good light.

"I was needing some help, I'd hoped to speak to your mother." Luther glanced back toward the pale lavender curtain at the back of the store.

"Mama had to help at the grocery this morning," she told him. "The first vegetables of the year will be coming in soon, and she and Daddy needed to do some spring cleaning."

Luther nodded thoughtfully. Clearly, Maybelle did not have the ear of the community, nor was she as nosy as her mother, but he hoped that perhaps he could intrigue her enough to tell her mother. Setting off a chain reaction could be as effective as a direct hit.

"I need to purchase some gloves." He leaned closer to whisper as if relaying a private confidence. "Ladies' gloves."

A bright pink stain colored Maybelle's cheeks and she drew a shocked intake of breath. The purchase of ladies' gloves by a single man could only mean one thing, serious courting. A casual call or just walking out would mean candy or flowers. Gloves had a permanency that was considered quite close to The Question.

Maybelle hadn't heard a word about Luther Briggs and any girl. Most of her friends assumed that the devastatingly handsome Mr. Briggs was still sowing his wild oats. Obviously things had changed.

Woodenly, Maybelle stepped behind the counter to the ladder, which banged and rustled as she pulled it about midway along the wall. She climbed only two steps to reach high enough to grasp the drawer that contained the latest in feminine handwear. Pulling it out of the wall, she carefully laid the box on the counter in front of Luther.

"Do you have a color preference, Mr. Briggs?" she asked in her most professional salesperson voice. "White is always a safe choice. It goes with anything, and it is proper for this time of year."

"Hmmm." Luther was noncommittal as Maybelle laid out an assortment before him.

"Black silk is very practical, of course," she said. "It doesn't show dirt and can be used for years to come." She laid three pairs of black gloves on the other side of the drawer.

Luther still didn't seem impressed.

"What I really had in mind," he said finally, glancing up to smile at her in a manner that could be interpreted as conspiratorial, "was something unique. Something that could be very special for my very special lady. Do you know what I mean?"

Maybelle's rather dumb bug-eyed look indicated that she clearly didn't.

"Something in her style or her colors."

Maybelle's expression now softened until she was positively calf-eyed in admiration. "That is a wonderful thought, Mr. Briggs," she whispered. "How very . . . very . . . romantic."

"Yes, I think so," he said, pressing his lips together tightly to control a grin.

"What . . . what *is* the lady's style and what *are* her colors?" Maybelle asked.

Luther didn't answer immediately. Instead he began looking through the box of gloves, examining and discarding one pair after another. With each assessment, Maybelle offered an eager sales pitch.

"Those have a patented fingertip guaranteed not to wear out before the gloves," she said of one pair.

"The high cut wrist is very flattering to women with pleasingly plump arms," she said of another.

"These," Luther said finally as he picked up a small pair of peach-colored silk taffeta. The gloves appeared almost plain at first glance. As he turned them over in his hands, he admired the tiny round brown buttons and the exquisitely delicate brown embroidery on the back and around the thumb. "These are perfect." He looked up at Maybelle and smiled broadly. "Her style and her colors."

Maybelle gazed at the gloves in his hand, dumbstruck. Luther could almost see the wheels in her brain turning as she frantically searched for the identity of the woman for whom peach and brown were colors and delicate and plain were style. Her puzzled expression indicated that she hadn't a clue.

"I'll pay cash," he told her with a self-satisfied sigh. "Could you wrap them up for me?"

"Of course," Maybelle answered, her voice vague.

It took only a couple of minutes before the peach taffeta gloves were wrapped neatly in white tissue. Luther placed the packet into his inside pocket and with a warm smile he bade Miss Maybelle a good day.

The little bell rang once more as he left the building. Casually, without looking back, Luther crossed the street, hesitating only to wave at Ebner Wyse as he drove his wagon down toward the bank.

In the anonymity of a saddle display in front of Osgold Panek's Leather Goods and Harness, Luther turned to glance back across the street.

The bell at the Emporium tinkled once more as Maybelle stepped through it, pausing only to turn the Open sign to read Closed. He watched her hurry toward the doorway of the grocery and her gossipy mother. He smiled.

FASHION IS AGELESS

Spring Looks for Every Woman

As was evidenced in local churches this Easter Sunday past, modern ladies' fashion is no longer the preserve of the wealthy or the young. Since her capital wedding this year to President Wilson, our First Lady, the former Mrs. Edith Gant, has demonstrated that even women of modest means and matronly years can dress smartly and fashionably. In a recent interview with *The Ladies' Home Journal*, the First Lady offered this advice. "Select your jewelry with respect to your toilette. It should emphasize the predominating note in your costume and accentuate the color of your hair or eyes." For most women this means only minor changes in

Chapter Four

Prattville's annual Spring Blossom Festival had begun as the company picnic of Cimarron Ornamental Flowers, but over the years, the picnic had evolved into a full-fledged town fair.

This heavily attended and entertaining Saturday afternoon event was where Luther and Tulsa May decided to make their first public appearance as a courting couple.

Tulsa May sported a new wide-brimmed straw hat, trimmed in tiny taffeta roses and tied beneath the chin with pale peach gauze, when she picked Luther up in the Runabout.

"Do you mind if I don't wear a coat?" Luther asked her as he straightened his tie and smoothed down his shirtfront. "I know it would look more respectful, but I swear, Tulsy, I feel nearly strangled in that hot gray jacket."

Tulsa May did not object. She thought he looked wonderful. Luther's blue striped overshirt was corded in the placard with darker blue twill and tied loosely at the collar with a matching string tie. His long shirt cuffs were held away from his wrists by fancy ribboned garters of the same color, worn just above his elbow. All that blue intensified his eye color to incredible brightness. Sweet-smelling rose oil adorned his hair and held it perfectly in place. It was covered by a slate-colored fur railroad hat set on his head at a jaunty angle.

"Do you want to drive?" she asked.

Luther shook his head. "No, ma'am, I've driven this vehicle a good deal more in my life than I ever wanted to." He sauntered to its left side and eased into the seat aside her.

Tulsa May glanced back toward the garage. "What about Arthel? Does he need a ride?"

Laying his arm casually along the back of the seat, Luther answered negatively. "Arthel's a big boy, Tulsy. He can get out and about on his own power these days. Besides" — his grin was wide and teasing — "a gentleman doesn't go courting with his kid brother in tow."

She gave him a sarcastic smirk and adjusted the foot pedals into gear. With only a slight jolt, the Runabout chugged forward.

The day looked to be a promising one. The weather was still cool, but a warm breeze was blowing in from the west. Overhead the sky was wide and clear, and an overnight shower had wet the ground just enough to keep down the dust on the road.

"Did you hear about the Spring Blossom Queen?" Tulsa May asked eagerly.

"I heard a while back that they were thinking of having one."

"Daddy was furious," Tulsa May confided. "He said that even the appearance of having someone *rule* over the festival was breaking the First Commandment."

Luther chuckled. "The Rev sure can get his taters in the crib about the strangest things."

She smiled. Luther did know the reverend's foibles. For one long, wonderful year in their childhood, Luther Briggs had lived with them. And in that one well-remembered year, the two "almost brothers" had drawn her out of her shell, and lonely, dreamy Tulsa May had blossomed into the charming prairie flower that she was always meant to be.

Time had passed and much had changed, but that childhood bond remained. There was no one else to whom she would have spoken so plainly.

"I think his indignation is a way of recompense," she said. "Daddy spends so much time with his books and his gym that I think when something he didn't orchestrate occurs in the community, he believes that he's been shirking his duty."

Luther nodded thoughtfully. "You are probably right. Truth to tell, I thought old Rev would give up the pulpit long before now. He just doesn't seem to enjoy it anymore."

"I think he *would* retire," Tulsa May agreed, "if he felt that he could still be useful in some way to the community."

"Well, of course he'd still be useful to the community!" Luther replied.

Tulsa shrugged. "What is so obvious to the

rest of the world is often a mystery to the person in question."

As they approached the high bluff south of town known locally as Cora's Knoll, they were forced to slow with the press of other vehicles. Friends and acquaintances hollered greetings from the slickest rigs, noisiest touring cars, and the plainest old mules.

Old Haywood Puser, his thick mane of heavy white hair and his long beard causing him to look much like Santa Claus, had parked one of his rubber-tire buggies near the entrance to the knoll area and was directing the traffic.

"Afternoon, Mr. Puser," Tulsa May called to him.

The old man bent from the waist in an old-fashioned formal bow. "My dear Miss Bruder," he said with feigned dignity. "I do hope you've come with the intent to write a splendid article about this small entertainment hosted by my step-son."

She opened her mouth to assure him that she would, but Luther spoke up first. Bringing his arm more possessively around her shoulder, he gave the old man a wink. "My Tulsy is not here for business, but pleasure."

Seeing the young man's proprietary manner, Haywood raised an eyebrow in surprise. Then he gave Luther a nod of approval. "Well, it's about time, if I'm allowed to say so. Why don't you park that old autobuggy under the maple tree over there," he said, indicating a spot some distance from the rest of the vehicles. "A young couple may need to find themselves a quiet, shady place if the afternoon gets too hot." He gave Luther a knowing wink.

Tulsa May's face was flaming as she drove into the shade. "How embarrassing!"

Luther looked at her, puzzled. "What on earth was embarrassing about it? Old Haywood is just showing us the consideration as a courting couple he approved of."

She sighed loudly as she pulled down the throttle and allowed the engine to die. "Surely he knows we are not *really* a courting couple."

Luther reached over and gently squeezed her prettily gloved hand. "Courage, Tulsy," he said as his thumb traced the brown embroidery. "If Haywood believes, the whole town will. I don't think they are going to be nearly as hard to convince as you believe."

Tulsa May shook her head, flustered. "It just seems so unlikely."

Jumping down, he sauntered to her side of the Runabout. Grasping her familiarly at the waist, he lifted her to the ground. "It just seems unlikely to you," he insisted. "I know you think of me as a brother, but nobody else in this town has any idea what you or I might be thinking. It's all what it looks like. If it looks like we are courting, then we are."

"I'm sure it just looks incredibly foolish," she insisted as she glanced around nervously.

"Courting is a rather foolish business." His

66

smile was wide and warm. "To my thinking, *nothing* could be more foolish than a burst of sunlight like you wanting to settle down with Moldy Doc Odie Foote. But everyone in town believed it, including you."

Tulsa May tried to think of a snappy retort, but when she looked up into his flashing grin, she could only smile back.

Respectfully he offered his arm and she laid her hand formally atop it. With chins high, they walked together toward the festivities.

The loud piping of a calliope cheerfully tooting "Turkey in the Straw" caught their attention, making them walk faster to the picnic grounds.

The knoll, which overlooked the flower farm and the family home of the owners, Mr. and Mrs. Jedwin Sparrow, was dotted with gaily colored tents, a platform for speeches and music, and booths displaying every type of ware and food imaginable.

As they walked through the lane of booths, a small boy darted between them, a huge piece of chocolate cake stuffed in his mouth.

"Woody Sparrow!" Grace Panek called after him in a scold. "Don't you be snitching one more piece of this cake or I'll blister your backside."

Young Woody didn't even bother to look back as he rushed on, pausing only for a quick stop at Lily Auslander's table to make a sticky, chocolate-fingered grab for a wiener and roll loaded with Lily's special sauerkraut.

The fair had never been more elaborate. Booth

after booth featured displays of flowers, both fresh and dried, food, drinks of sweet milk, buttermilk, spring water, and lemonade. Games of chance were absent but a shooting gallery was set up with targets, and a horseshoe tent was already under way.

The crowning touch stood at the very top of the small hill, overlooking the Cimarron River. There sat a brightly painted and gaily mirrored merry-go-round. The steam-powered selection of gaudily festooned wooden horses traveled up and down and all around, as the excess steam was pumped into the calliope.

"I can't believe it!" Tulsa May's eyes were as round as saucers. "How could everybody in town be talking about the crowning of a Spring Blossom Queen while they managed to keep this a secret?"

"Maybe that's how they did it," Luther answered as he watched the spinning mirrors and colors atop the hill. "Jedwin Sparrow is a shrewd businessman. I'm sure he used the queen idea to create a diversion."

Tulsa May demurely adjusted the angle of her hat and attempted to act her age. "I've never ridden a merry-go-round," she whispered quietly to Luther as if making a lurid confession. Her legs were suddenly full of jitters. Glancing around, she was grateful that no one was staring at her unseemly behavior.

Luther's grin was broad and his laugh was as comforting as a warm sheepskin. "Tulsy," he said. "You can be as adult as you like. But I can't wait another minute to ride on that thing."

A crowd had already formed on the near side of the whirling stage and youngsters darted in and out trying to sneak through the press of adults to be first in the line.

"This is the best idea Jedwin Sparrow ever had," a young matron with two bright-eyed children in tow proclaimed.

"It wasn't Mr. Sparrow's idea," Maybelle Penny piped in. "Mrs. Sparrow and I thought of it. Her husband just handled the details."

Dressed in a pale blue gown with white eyelet at the wrists and throat, Maybelle looked especially lovely. And from the way she held her head and casually patted her hair, she was well aware of the fact.

"Well, it's just wonderful." Tulsa May reached across to the younger girl and grasped her hand with excitement.

Maybelle was smiling back at her warmly, when suddenly her expression changed. Shocked, the young girl stared at the elegant peach taffeta gloves that graced the hand that held hers.

"Your gloves?" Maybelle's question was an incredulous whisper.

"Oh, thank you," Tulsa May answered, assuming she was receiving a compliment.

The operator of the merry-go-round chose that exact moment to stop the whirling carousel. Everyone rushed forward. Luther jumped up on the round platform, then turned and easily pulled his partner up beside him. Then he headed toward the wildest-looking horse. "Might this be a pleasing mount for you, Miss Tulsy?" he asked, gesturing to a gaily decorated black wooden pony with a carved windswept mane and a tail made of genuine horsehair.

As she nodded, Luther grasped her around the waist, his hands warm and sure, and lifted her up to sit sidesaddle.

"Now, don't fall off," he admonished.

In mock terror, Tulsa May grasped the long pole that ran through the horse's neck and chest. "Oh, stay here and protect me from this dangerous animal."

Luther tweaked her nose playfully. "Sorry, ma'am," he answered in a deep Texas drawl. "This cowboy has his own horse to wrangle." He threw one long leg over the blue and white pony next to hers.

"You're a little far from the ranch, aren't you, cowpuncher?" Tulsa May asked.

Dramatically, Luther raised an eyebrow. "Just call me Kid, ma'am," he said with low-toned gruffness. "Carousel Kid."

Tulsa May was hooting with laughter when she caught sight of the bench directly behind them where Maybelle Penny sat primly between Rossie Crenshaw and Fasel Auslander. The young woman's unspoken censure was so vivid that Tulsa May covered her mouth in embarrassment and turned her attention demurely to the horse in front of her. Chin down, lips closed, she told herself. The loud, breathy music of the calliope began again and slowly, as if uneager for another trip, the horse beneath Tulsa May lowered toward the floor and then began to rise again.

Smiling once more, Tulsa May looked ahead as the merry-go-round picked up speed. A lock of curly carrot-colored hair worked free of her rather severe coiffure and sneaked out from beneath her hat brim to fly in the breeze.

As the merry-go-round turned, situated as it was along the far side of the knoll, she could see nothing beneath them but the Cimarron River far below. Tulsa felt as if she were flying in thin air. Breathless with delight, she turned to Luther. His vivid blue eyes were bright as starlight. Silently the two shared the magic of the moment.

"Tulsy! The ring!" he suddenly called out to her.

Glancing back she saw the shiny, brilliant brass ring dangling along the side of the merry-go-round. She knew capturing it would mean a prize.

Clinging precariously to the pole, she leaned as far as she could. Beyond the loud music of the calliope and the excited giggles and shouts of children, Tulsa May could hear Luther Briggs cheering her on.

It was closer now, daring her, luring her. It glimmered in the sunshine, bright and shiny, perfectly round, like a halo or a wedding ring.

Tulsa May grabbed. Nearly unseating herself in the effort, her hands clamped only around emptiness. She'd missed. Her eyes turned to Luther in disappointment only to find him cheering. She felt a tug on her arm and looked down in disbelief. The brass ring dangled loosely upon her wrist.

The high-backed wooden wheelchair got stuck momentarily in the buggy ruts and Emma Dix had to put her back into it to get the contraption moving again.

"Willie! What a delight!"

Emma cringed slightly when she saw the man walking toward them. Keeping her eyes down, she nonetheless continued forward.

"Good day, Preacher." The wasted old man in the wheelchair spoke in greeting as he waved weakly in acknowledgment of his old friend.

Reverend Bruder clasped the pale, age-spotted hand in his own and smiled down in genuine affection.

"I'm so glad you were able to join us, Willie," he said. "There's to be singing this afternoon and it just wouldn't be the same without you."

The old man chuckled in modest gratitude before gesturing to Emma. "My little gal wouldn't have it no other way but for me to come," he said with more than a hint of pride. "Little Emma is the best daughter a man ever had, Preacher. And I thank the good Lord every day for returning her to me."

Reverend Bruder cleared his throat nervously and gave the barest nod of acknowledgment in Emma's direction.

For her part, Emma seemed as ill at ease as the preacher. When Dr. Foote joined the three it seemed nearly a godsend.

"Mr. Dix." Doc Odie hailed the frail man in the chair first. "It's good to see you outside for a change."

"The weather's perfect." The reverend looked up at the blue sky.

Doc Odie nodded in tacit agreement. "There's some thunderheads building up north," he said, gesturing to some dark clouds on the distant horizon. "But the wind's blowing them to the east, so they may miss us. As long as the sun shines, it'll be right good for your health to get a breath of fresh air."

The old man nodded. "My Emma, she brought me," he told the doctor in a quavering voice.

Doc Odie smiled easily at Emma before turning his attention once more to her father. "You are a lucky man indeed, Willie Dix," he said. "Not only do you have a devoted and bright daughter, but a competent nurse." He raised his eyebrows in a warm, friendly smile. "And a pretty one to boot," he whispered.

Willie laughed out loud. It was a pleasant, joyful sound that had been missing from community gatherings for the past few years.

"My Emma is the image of her dear mother," Dix told the doctor proudly. "But truth be told, I'm not too modest to say the girl got her good sense from me."

The gentlemen made the suitable replies. Emma, however, still stood somewhat to the side.

Finally, Odie Foote changed the subject.

"Preacher, I've just come from your house," he said. "I was thinking to escort Miss Tulsa May, as a friend of course, to show that there are no hard feelings. But I guess you and Mrs. Bruder already brought her."

Reverend Bruder puffed up slightly with what could only be the sin of pride. "No, I didn't bring her at all. Tulsa May seems to have cast her interest in another direction these days."

"Another direction?" Doc Odie was clearly puzzled.

"She has a new gentleman caller," the preacher stated baldly.

Doc Odie stared at Reverend Bruder as if the older man had lost his mind.

The reverend's smile could have been considered triumphant. "Why don't I push Willie around the grounds?" he said to Emma. "I know everyone will be wanting to see and talk to him."

"That's a wonderful idea, Philemon." Willie turned to his daughter and gave her a warm smile and a small wave. "You don't need to be spending such a pretty day with me, Emma. Just go have some fun with the other young people, and don't give your worn-out old daddy another thought."

Without another word, Reverend Bruder grasped the push handles on the chair and began to move away from Emma and the doctor.

As Emma stared after them, her stance gradually changed from anxious to defiant.

"That preacher's sure got it in for me," she said to Doc Odie. "I swear if he were any more

74

disapproving I'd be wearing a scarlet *A* on my chest."

The doctor, who'd been staring after the two of them, was nearly startled back into the conversation.

"What? Oh, pay him no mind, Emma. He doesn't really know you. And after that awful engagement concert fiasco, he's not overly fond of me either."

Smiling at the doctor, Emma was secretly grateful for the opportunity to find a partner in crime.

"Who in the world could be Tulsa May's new gentleman caller?" Doc Odie asked, clearly caught up in his own concerns.

Emma shrugged. "It could be anyone."

Doc Odie looked doubtful. "Not anyone in this town."

Shaking her finger at him, Emma scolded. "Now Doc Odie, Tulsa May is sort of pretty in her own way. And she's very sweet."

The doctor nodded. "You are kind, Emma," he said. "Tulsa May is the type of woman a fellow can relax with, settle down with. But 'pretty' is a far cry from that woman's looks."

"Well, maybe 'comely' is a better word for her. She draws people to her."

"It's that all-fired optimism of hers," Doc Odie replied. "I tell her all the time that she talks sunnier than a socialist and just as foolish."

Hearing Emma's deep throaty laugh, Dr. Foote smiled broadly and then offered his arm. "Your father wants you to relax and spend some time

75

with the young people," he reminded her. "I'm not all that young, but I can be a passable escort."

With a polite nod of acceptance, Emma laid her hand on his tweed-covered sleeve and walked beside him into the crowded booth area. If people were surprised to see Emma on the doc's arm, nobody commented.

Emma held her head high and smiled. In her heart she imagined that she was young again, not so much in years as in experience. She imagined that she was once more the prettiest girl in Prattville. She imagined that she was still innocent and giggly. That she'd never met Fremont Bateman. Never fallen in love with him. Never run off to marry him. She imagined that she was once again young enough not to know how a married man could lure a foolish girl into a lifetime of sin.

Maybelle Penny passed in front of the couple, flanked by two spiffed-up young men and leading half a dozen others. She did not deign to glance toward either. Still, Emma couldn't help but smile at the pretty young girl in the new spring dress. She had once been much like her.

Maybelle stopped in front of a crowded, noisy corner booth. Her entire entourage gathered around her, obstructing all other movement in the booth area.

"Well, if it isn't Sitting Bull himself." Maybelle's voice rang out. "What are you doing? Praying for the return of the buffalo?"

Arthel Briggs looked up from the crank on the

76

ice-cream bucket he was turning. His eyes were as brown as chestnuts, and his cheekbones were high and sharp. His thick, almost blue-black hair was parted directly down the middle and grew a little long on the sides, the style enhancing the remnants of his Indian heritage. He was quiet, calm, controlled. Leisurely, he allowed his eyes to wander from white kid toetips to blond top-knot. "Oh hello, Maybelle," he said finally.

"Put you to work, did they?" young Rossie Crenshaw asked.

Arthel's expression broadened into a smile. "They were just looking for the fellow with the strongest muscles."

There was a rumble of conversation and brags among Maybelle's male contingent, before Rossie stepped over the low-hanging rope that separated the area. Rolling up his sleeves, he eagerly went to take Arthel's place. "Let a real man put his back into it."

"Wonderful, where can we find one?" Eustace Maitland asked sarcastically.

Arthel walked over to the rope near the far side and wiped his damp palms on a ragged cotton towel. He glanced up and saw Dr. Foote and Emma, to whom he nodded in acknowledgment.

Emma stiffened as if she had expected Arthel to wink suggestively at her or make an off-color comment. He did neither.

"What kind of ice cream are you making?" Doc Odie asked.

"Mostly apricot," he said. "Mrs. Wyse gave

us some of last year's preserves to mix in. They were pretty brown, but I suspect it will be tasting all right."

"How long have you been cranking?"

Arthel shrugged. "Quarter of an hour, not longer. We'll have something to serve pretty soon."

"Well, Cochise," Maybelle interrupted as she moved to his side. "I think you and me should have a powwow. I just saw the funniest thing in my life and I have to find out the whole truth right this minute."

Arthel looked down at the pretty, petite blonde at his side. Part of him saw the childhood pest that used to follow him around like a shadow. But another part, a part he was not yet willing to acknowledge, saw a beautiful young woman in the perfect blossom of youth. Maybelle Penny gave him a sweet smile and dimpled prettily. Arthel was expressionless.

She gave a half-glance at Emma and a flirty little wave to the doctor before launching into her wide-eyed, gigglingly told tale.

All three listened with rapt attention.

"— so he said that the gloves were for a special woman he was calling on," Maybelle explained midway through her story. "And I swear on a stack of Bibles I saw Tulsa May Bruder wearing those very same gloves this afternoon."

There was a long silent pause.

"Yes, so?" Arthel said.

"So?" Maybelle practically squealed. "So, who

was the special girl he was calling on? And why didn't she accept the gloves?"

Arthel's stone-faced visage broke momentarily as he stared at Maybelle.

"What makes you think that the special girl didn't accept them?"

"If she had, then Tulsa May wouldn't have them."

With a loud pop, Arthel slapped the towel with more force than necessary. Shaking his head, he spoke to Maybelle as if she didn't quite have good sense. "Tulsa May *is* the special girl."

"What!" The exclamation was a chorus. Maybelle, Emma, and Doc Odie stared at Arthel in disbelief.

Chapter Five

Just before noon the political speeches began. Luther joked to Tulsa May that he did not believe this to be a very clever organization of the agenda since listening to Oklahoma politicians had caused more than one stalwart citizen to lose his lunch.

He and Tulsa May stood at some distance from the speaker's platform, but had no trouble hearing. They had spent most of the morning eating and had no appetite for lunch, but Luther did manage to get a heavily laden tin of apricot ice cream. With a couple of makeshift wooden paddles for spoons, the two shared the treat.

Tulsa May's prize for catching the brass ring was a bright red feather that now stuck jauntily out of her straw hat, though it clashed vividly with her bright orange hair.

As the speeches progressed, the crowd pressed in and the two found themselves in close company with half a dozen people, including Carlisle Bowman and John Auslander.

Bowman looked at Luther strangely. "I hear all over the place that you brought Tulsa May here."

Without glancing over at her, Luther knew the

young woman's cheeks were flushed with embarrassment.

"Yes sir, Mr. Bowman, I did," Luther replied
easily. "And we're having a mighty nice time."

Bowman snorted with disdain. "In my day a
fellow didn't stand around at political speeches
when his gal was near and her daddy weren't."

Luther almost pointed out that the reverend
was only a few hundred yards away, but Tulsa
May interrupted.

"I enjoy political speeches, Mr. Bowman," she
said.

Luther wasn't sure if she'd understood the older
man's implication or was just too much of a lady
to notice.

"As a reporter for the *Populist*," she continued,
"it's important that I take an interest in everything
that makes news."

Bowman appeared ready to give his opinion
of young ladies who work for newspapers when,
fortunately, young Fasel called out.

"Looky, here comes our 'Voice in Washington.'
So drunk, as usual, that he can hardly stand."

Congressman Elias Curley had the long, lanky
body of an Abraham Lincoln. Unfortunately, he
also had the vices of Ulysses S. Grant. By the
time his turn came at the podium, the congressman was somewhat unsteady on his feet and his
nose could have been used as a beacon on a foggy
night. Although there was some laughter and
shaking of heads, the community forgave him because he said the things they wanted to hear.

Curley cleared his throat loudly and raised his hands high over his head to capture the audience's attention. "We," he hollered out to the crowd, "in this great forty-sixth state of the United States, are a peace-loving people."

There was a momentary pause as he cast his gaze across the crowd. Nodding heads were seen throughout the crowd and murmurs of approval could be heard everywhere.

"There are those who would cry out for the blood of this country!" Again he hesitated, letting his words soak in. "Those who endeavor to steal our boys from their seats in the schoolroom and their places behind the plow." He paced unsteadily from one side of the podium to the other. "There are those who would send our boys to far-off places. Places we've never heard of," he yelled. "Places we can't even pronounce," he added more quietly.

"The continent of Europe, my friends, is half a world away," Congressman Curley continued. "And the folks living there are a people of many languages and of many minds. If they have divided up in two camps and propose to destroy each other, what business is it of ours?"

"Amen." Reverend Bruder's voice was heard plainly near the front of the crowd.

"Whether the future of the Old World is ruled by the Kaiser and the Central Powers, or by England, France, and the Allies, will not amount to a hill of beans come harvesttime in Oklahoma!"

The roar of the crowd was partly for his words and partly for the wild gesturing of his arms that nearly knocked him off balance.

"I follow the lead of President Wilson," Curley declared. "I want an America of peace, an America of neutrality." The congressman paused to sigh with great drama. "That's what I want for America and that's what I want for Oklahoma. And now, my friends, if what you want is what I want, then I know come November you'll be marking your X in the box for me."

The crowd roared its approval and Congressman Curley hurried to the side of the speaking platform where he sat down, apparently not a minute too soon.

"I don't care how bad a drunk that man is," Carlisle Bowman declared. "He is just plain right and I'm voting for him again."

"I sure ain't interested in fighting no war in Europe," Roscoe Nunley agreed.

"But the war is coming," Tulsa May said. "We can't stay out of it much longer, it's coming right to our door."

"That's nonsense, girl," Bowman assured them.

"It's the truth," Tulsa May insisted. "I don't work on a paper without knowing what is going on. That sneaky submarine-boat strategy is killing as many Americans as it is Europeans."

"Wilson said not to sail on European boats," Bowman protested.

Tulsa May shook her head. "The submarine

commanders can't even tell whose ship they're blowing up. They're hitting everything in the water."

Luther nodded gravely. "What she's saying is true. When they fire off those torpedoes, they don't know if they're aiming at friend or foe, navy or civilian."

"Those submarines *are* really a sneaky, underhanded way of fighting," Roscoe offered.

Bowman nodded shortly then turned to John Auslander. "What about the Kaiser fellow of yours?" he asked. "Why is he doing such a thing as hiding and shooting?"

Auslander's eyes widened in surprise. "I know nothing of the Kaiser. I came to America when I was twelve years old."

Young Fasel interrupted his father. "In a way I wish we would go to war," he announced to the crowd. "I'd be the first to sign up to get a shot at the Kaiser and all his army!"

The young man's words of bravado brought boisterous excitement to the crowd. Tulsa May felt a tug on her arm and allowed Luther to lead her away from the argument heating up.

They moved to the relative privacy of the area behind the speaker's stand. The sky was clouding over and a brisk, cool breeze ruffled Tulsa May's skirts. She held her hat in her lap.

"Did you see John Auslander's face?" she asked quietly.

Luther looked at her a long moment. "I was hoping that you hadn't."

Tulsa May shrugged. "I don't know what makes the old man sadder, the Kaiser's aggression or his son's defection."

Luther slipped a comforting arm around her waist. "Maybe those Europeans will patch up their differences and settle down to making a living."

She smiled broadly at him. "Now you're talking like me, all hope and no reason."

"We might *not* get involved in a war," he said.

Tulsa May gestured to the dark bank of rain in the distance, and the flashes of lightning. "We might not get rained on tonight either," she said. "But the clouds are sure looming."

The political speeches completed, the first of the entertainment began. Tulsa May waved at Jedwin Sparrow, whose daughter Ellie slept against his shoulder, while he welcomed the crowd from the podium.

In the ten years since he'd begun his business, the flower farm had achieved national recognition for its dried and wax-preserved floral products. Now, with new ice-cooled and refrigerated railway cars, Cimarron could sell fresh flowers in both Guthrie and Oklahoma City. And once a year the whole community benefited from the success of the Cimarron Ornamental Flower Farms.

"I see nothing but growth and good times for this industry," Sparrow announced to the crowd. "And as we succced, the entire city of Prattville succeeds with us."

85

That brought enthusiastic cheers from the assembly.

Haywood Puser, local mortician and Sparrow's stepfather, edged up to the side of the podium and wordlessly took the pretty young child from Jedwin Sparrow. The day had already been a long one for the children, but the festivities had only begun.

"In all the years we've been having this little to-do," Sparrow said, "we've tried to make each one better than the last. We've finally figured out that our celebration had something missing." Hesitating dramatically, he grinned at the crowd. "I suggested to my wife that it might be corn liquor." This statement brought a roar of laughter. "But, you know, women understand these things better than us men. And the women of this community have convinced me that what the Prattville 1916 Spring Blossom Festival needed was a queen."

"I'd rather have the corn liquor!" a heckler yelled from the back.

Jedwin chuckled. "As the owner and manager of the Cimarron Ornamental Flower Farms, I am delighted tonight to present our very first Spring Blossom Queen."

There was a moment of restlessness in the crowd as everyone looked around curiously to see what woman would step up to the podium to be crowned.

"Now, I know that most of you think that I'd probably choose my wife for festival queen,"

Jedwin said. "But she told me she was *already* taking care of a three-hundred-acre flower farm, a brand-new house, four unruly children, and a husband who had practically no hair left at all."

The crowd laughed loudly as Jedwin patted his receding hairline with mock dismay.

"So, folks, my second choice just had to be the prettiest little spring blossom in Prattville. My friends, my employees, good people of this city, I now present your Spring Blossom Queen, Miss Maybelle Penny."

Shouts broke out from the entourage that followed the pretty Miss Penny like a shadow, while the four strongest employees of the Cimarron Ornamental Flower Farms carried in a cane-back chair on skids. The chair was lavishly decorated with colorful flowers and twined with vines. Seated thereupon was the lovely Spring Blossom Queen dressed in an elaborate high-waisted gown of soft silk messaline and white net. In her lap, the queen carried a fancy ribboned wicker basket. As she slowly made her way through the crowd, she nodded regally from her throne and threw handfuls of pretty, fragrant flower petals upon the assemblage.

Tulsa May cheered. "Isn't she beautiful!" she said to Luther breathlessly.

He nodded. "Maybelle is a very pretty little girl, but she thinks a little too well of herself."

Tulsa May giggled. "What else would you expect of a queen?"

When Maybelle reached the speaker's stand,

she was helped to the stage by Sparrow. As her
throne was secured into slats at the side of the
platform, Queen Maybelle waved and smiled and
addressed the crowd. A delicately woven coronet
of pink blossoms was placed on her head and
she was then escorted to her throne.

Jedwin Sparrow handed her a scepter of flowers
and greenery trailing long silk ribbons. Maybelle
held it high in the air. "Let the music begin!"

Old Mort Humley hurried up to the platform
with his fiddle. He gave a jerky bow to the queen
before setting the scarred and much abused violin
against his collarbone and scratching up a tune
as he jigged around the stage. Mort played with
more enthusiasm than talent, but it was enough
for the good people of Prattville.

While square dances were more typical in the
community, Mort could not fiddle and call a set
simultaneously. So he stuck to the round dances.
That suited the younger people perfectly since
it allowed the young gentlemen to hold their ladies
more closely.

"Shall we dance?" Luther asked, taking Tulsa
May's hand hopefully.

She hesitated. "Papa doesn't approve of dancing."

"I am quite aware of the Rev's views on the
'musical excuses for the encouragement of un-
lawful congress.' " His words were spoken with
such a dead-on imitation of her father that Tulsa
May laughed. "Come on, Tulsy. The Rev didn't
want you working for wages or driving your own

car either. That hasn't stopped you much in the past."

Looking up into his vivid blue eyes, Tulsa May found it impossible to refuse. "You'll have to teach me," she said shyly.

"It will be my pleasure."

Luther led her out to the dancing area directly in front of the podium, carelessly tossing his hat to the corner of the platform as they passed.

He walked Tulsa May right square onto the middle of the floor and placed her left hand on his shoulder, holding her right in his own. As his palm rested lightly against her waist, Tulsa May could feel its warmth through her shirtwaist. They were a full arm's length apart, but the closeness was still heady — very, very new for Tulsa May. Swallowing bravely, she watched and listened raptly as Luther began to demonstrate a very conservative one-step.

Tulsa May looked down at her brightly polished brown high-button shoes as if they might run away on her, and followed as best she could. After a few turns it felt surprisingly easy.

"You're a natural!" Luther told her. "No one would believe that you've never danced before."

"I sure hope Papa believes it."

Luther raised his head to glance around the crowd. "The Rev's over to the right, next to Clyde Avery. He looks a little like he got a mouthful of bad poultry, but I think he's apt to survive."

Tulsa May laughed out loud. It was such a warm, hearty sound that Luther spun her gaily around, nearly taking her breath away.

"You've got the one-step down, Tulsy," he said. "Do you think you are ready to spiel?"

Her eyes widened. "It would be scandalous."

"Yes, ma'am," Luther agreed.

Tulsa May's conscience pricked her only for a moment. "Let's give it a try."

"Just hang on, honey," he said. "We're about to set Prattville, Oklahoma, on its ear."

Slouching up to her, Luther bent his back to put his chin on her shoulder. His arm came around her tightly and pulled her up against the soft cotton stripes of his shirt, closer than a horseshoe on a hoof. The spiel was patterned after the movements of a waltz, only done in double time. They pivoted and spun, whirling swiftly in the middle of the dance floor.

Tulsa May giggled in surprise at the strange, new sensation as Luther turned her again and again in faster and faster circles.

"Oh, my!" was the only intelligible statement that she could come up with.

Luther laughed at her breathless exclamations. Her step was quick and she followed with dexterity, but Luther had spun with more accomplished dancers. He was an experienced "tough dancer" and had spieled in dance halls near and far, but somehow, it had never been quite so much fun before.

The dancers around them began to fall back to watch as the young couple tore up the floor in the latest ragtime rage. Roses bloomed in

Tulsa May's cheeks as she became aware of eyes upon her all around.

But another, more disconcerting sensation was also plaguing her. As her gentleman escort bounced her fashionably around the stage, her bosom, restricted only by her crepe de chine corset cover and the pleated voile bodice of her gown, jiggled against him. Embarrassed, Tulsa May moved back slightly. To her consternation the jiggling only increased. Quickly, she pressed herself once more against Luther. It seemed that the only way to control the unseemly spectacle was to meld the softness of her bosom to the hardness of his chest.

Luther appeared quite oblivious to Tulsa May's predicament and completely delighted at her decision to snuggle up close. She felt him smiling against the side of her neck. His warm whispers of encouragement sent shivers of electrified goose-flesh down her bodice to the points that she pressed so firmly against him.

"I think the Rev is about to have a conniption," he said. "That is, if Miz Constance doesn't have one first."

A flash fire of mortification sprang to Tulsa May's cheeks and she pulled back sharply from Luther's embrace. Once again unbound breasts began to wobble like apples in a washtub. Hurriedly, she pushed herself protectively once more against the warm masculine chest.

She was choosing the lesser of two evils, she told herself.

It was infinitely more ladylike to snuggle-spiel than to jiggle.

"Merciful heavens!" Emma overheard the whispered exclamation from Fanny Penny, who stood not four feet away from Willie Dix's wheelchair. "It was pitiful enough that she got herself publicly jilted. Must she make a complete fool of herself in front of the whole town?"

"Whatever do you mean?" came the reply. Emma surreptitiously glanced in that direction to identify the speaker. It was Cora Sparrow, Jedwin's wife.

"You know exactly what I mean," Fanny continued loudly. "An old maid kicking up her heels with a young bachelor. It's downright embarrassing!" Mrs. Penny made a tutting sound of disapproval.

"You are being silly, Fanny," Cora soothed. "Luther and Tulsa May are of a similar age. And they are just friends, and they always have been."

Fanny's tone was huffy with disapproval. "If that is how *friends* dance, I would think her parents shouldn't allow her to have any."

Although Emma genuinely disliked Mrs. Penny and would gladly disagree with her on whether the sky was blue or green, depending on which side the woman chose, Emma didn't like the looks of Luther's new spieling partner either.

Emma's day had been a long one. Except for the temporary respite when Doc Odie escorted her among the booths, she'd been entirely alone with her father, struggling with his wheelchair over the grassy terrain. Oh, folks came over to talk — with her father. Willie Dix had been song leader at the community church for years. He was known and loved by all and they didn't hesitate to greet him. The friendliness of Prattville residents toward an ailing old man, however, did not extend to his daughter. She had been ignored, looked through, and occasionally openly snubbed by the ladies of the town. The gentlemen's words were usually more polite but they slid their gaze familiarly across Emma's body, their eyes speaking volumes more disrespect than the tongues of their wives.

Emma Dix was a fallen woman. No amount of explanations or excuses would ever change that fact. And Emma did not have the will to even try. Were it not for her father, she never would have returned to Prattville. She had worked as a barmaid in Wetumka and Muskogee and discovered that the darker side of city life offered its own brand of friendship and acceptance. She could have stayed there, maybe married a down-on-his-luck gambler or liquored-up cowboy. No one there would ever have heard of Fremont Bateman, and he'd be as gone from her memory as he was from her life.

But she had come back to Prattville to take care of her father because he loved her and she loved him. So she put up with the sly looks and the disapproving stares and did her duty as a daughter to the man who had given her life.

"Isn't that your man up there ragging with the preacher's carrot-top?"

Emma started since the words were whispered intimately in her ear. She turned to find Blue Turley, shined and spiffed and standing at her right shoulder.

She raised an eyebrow haughtily. "What are you doing here, Turley? Did the pool room burn down?"

His chuckle was low and humorless and held a trace of lewdness. "Just thought I'd see how the other half is living. What about you? Pretending to be something you ain't?"

Emma smelled the scent of moonshine liquor on his breath, and chose not to answer.

Turley motioned once more to the dance floor. "I heard down at Ruggy's place that he done dropped you fair and square. Everybody's talking about who that mighta been for. Now me, I woulda never expected it to be little Tulsa May."

"They are friends," Emma said primly.

Turley hesitated, watching the couple pivot and swirl before them. "Yep, I'd say they look right friendly like."

Emma held herself stiffly beside him, not deigning to answer. Turley casually stepped close in behind her and slipped a hand around her waist.

"Now that little preacher's daughter has a fine reputation," he continued. "But she sure ain't got what you got."

As if to illustrate his words, Turley let his hand

wander the curve of Emma's backside and surreptitiously squeezed her fanny through the material of her dress.

Startled, Emma jumped and hastily moved forward against her father's wheelchair and away from the man's unwelcome touch. Setting her jaw tightly, she replied, between clenched teeth, "I'm here for an outing with my father."

Turley raised an eyebrow. He stepped to the side of the wheelchair and gave her father a patronizing smile. Then irreverently, he patted the shoulder of the old man and asked much too loudly, "How you doing today, Willie?"

Dix raised a rheumy eye to the young man standing beside his daughter and his cheerful smile narrowed into one long thin line. "You're that fellow they call Turley, ain't you?"

"Yes, sir," the younger man answered loudly, as if the man were deaf.

Willie Dix gave Blue Turley an assessing look which was long and steady enough to make the younger man uncomfortable. Finally, Emma's father nodded with hesitance. " 'Spect you best be moving on now, Turley."

Willie glanced up at his daughter's pale face and gave her a tender smile. "Emma dear, could we scoot up a bit closer to the stage? I'm enjoying watching all this dancing."

"Good Lord almighty!" Clyde Avery exclaimed. He glanced apologetically at the reverend, who was standing beside him. "Excuse me, Preacher," he said hastily. "That's . . . well, that's some dancing."

Reverend Philemon Bruder stood stone-still watching his only daughter act in a manner that could be described in the best of terms as imprudent. He glanced at his wife who was herself bug-eyed.

Never had he allowed a member of his family to engage in any sort of dancing activity. And on numerous occasions he had sermoned on public dancing at community celebrations.

"What on earth is she thinking of?" he heard his stunned wife whisper.

The preacher was more than a little confused himself. There was a part of him that wanted to walk onto the stage, stop the music, and grab his errant offspring by the wrist and drag her home. She should be sent to her room for a week of prayer and chastisement!

He sighed. There was another part of the reverend that watched his little girl, whom he loved so much, dancing and laughing and looking happier than he'd seen her since she'd been made a public embarrassment at her own engagement party.

"Philemon —" Constance began to protest.

"Reverend!"

An indignant voice beside him halted whatever Constance was about to say.

Titus Penny, proprietor of the Emporium, and his obviously angry wife Fanny stood staring with disapproval at the young couple on the dance floor.

"Titus, Fanny," he said calmly. "It certainly is a lovely evening."

"Reverend, I am shocked," Mrs. Penny said firmly. "I know that young Briggs is a friend of Tulsa May's. But this unseemly behavior —" She gestured to the spieling spectacle on the dance floor.

The preacher's jaw hardened dangerously. He felt his wife stiffen beside him.

"If we might have your permission, Reverend," she continued. "I would like to nip this outrageous display in the bud, before any of our other young people are corrupted."

The reverend regarded Fanny unhappily and then glanced over at her husband, who clearly looked ill at ease and seemed to wish that the ground might open up and swallow him.

"Make your point, Titus."

Fanny pushed him aside. "We simply wish to state our disapproval."

Bruder glanced back at the dancers. Laughing, Luther Briggs held his little Tulsa May closer than plaster to a wall, his cheek pressed against hers. Righteous indignation sprang through the reverend's veins. There was no way he would countenance this behavior.

"Titus would like to discreetly come to your aid," Mrs. Penny whispered. "He could quietly cut in and return your daughter to you to be escorted home."

It was the tone of voice more than the words that snapped a tiny spring of resentment that festered within the preacher. The tall Reverend Bruder turned to Mrs. Penny, and literally glared down at her.

"My dear Fanny," Constance Bruder answered her with a dismissing wave of her hand. "That certainly will not be necessary. Our Tulsa May is of legal age and neither married nor betrothed. The only disapproval that she must concern herself with is our own."

"But certainly, Constance, you don't —"

Mrs. Bruder continued. "The actions of my daughter are not taken without my knowledge and are none of your concern."

"You knew she'd be *dancing?*" Titus asked, genuinely puzzled.

Reverend Bruder glanced at him and then at his wife and finally once more at the dancing couple. He cleared his throat lengthily.

"As you know," he stated finally, "I have long been a proponent of physical exercise for the health of the body and the strengthening of the soul. Dancing . . ." He hesitated, clearing his throat another time. "Dancing is merely a social form of physical exercise. Good people have engaged in it since biblical times. Although I myself am not a practitioner of this particular form of exertion, I see no justification for forbidding my daughter a healthy social form of calisthenics."

Open-mouthed with shock, the two stared at the reverend. Constance remained beside her husband, her head high and clearly proud.

Titus Penny ignored Fanny's huff of disapproval and took a moment to watch the dancers. He swallowed hard. "Well, Reverend, I guess it does look pretty healthy at that."

Chapter Six

The rain held off until nearly dusk, but when it began to come down it was fierce. Within seconds after the first drops fell, a deluge poured out of the sky and the residents of the Prattville community ran for cover.

Luther and Tulsa May, who were still lingering near the dance floor when the rain began, immediately hurried through the downpour to the parking area. Everyone else had the same idea and the ensuing rush resembled a panic. Horses whinnied in fright and little children began to cry, unsure of what was happening. A sudden streak of lightning startled a jittery bay mare. She reared, frightened, and slipped in the mud, falling on her side. Still in her harness, the mare struggled and nearly toppled the buggy that was attached to her.

"Go on to the car!" Luther yelled to Tulsa May. He was already soaking wet, with water dripping from the brim of his hat. His hair looked blacker than tar plastered to the sides of his face, and his vivid blue eyes were brilliant in the storm, as if the lightning itself was captured in them. "Go on, hurry, you'll be soaked."

Tulsa May followed his order, but realized that

Luther had forgotten one of the less cheerful facts concerning the Model G Runabout. It had no top.

Reaching the autobuggy, Tulsa May opened the turtleback spare-tire cover behind the seat to retrieve a large black muslin wagon umbrella. While holding the umbrella, Tulsa May climbed clumsily into the driver's side of the Runabout. The umbrella came open with a gentle whoosh and Tulsa May quickly checked the eight metal ribs to ensure that none were bent backward and vulnerable to the wind. That done, she slid the umbrella's thirty-six-inch pole into the running board and tightened the seat fixture that held the umbrella secure.

Through the gray mist of rain she saw that Luther, with the help of Kirby Maitland, had helped the fallen mare back on her feet. Though she was still fussy and nervous, Luther had a hand on her halter, and seemed to be calming her. Kirby, the farrier, ran his hands along her flanks and sides, checking for injuries.

Tulsa May watched from her semidry perch as the two men waited for the horse's owner. She was cold and dripping wet, but she was smiling. It had been a wonderful day. A day almost out of a dream. Even now as the rain dripped off her bedraggled red feather, she couldn't help but sigh with pleasure.

Finally, Osgold Panek and his wife, Grace, made their way to the buggy.

Luther watched the mare take off safely before

101

he began making his way across the road. He didn't even bother to hurry. He was soaked through to his union suit, far beyond any concern for the downpour. The fancy blue shirt was plastered to his rangy muscles like a second skin, his soggy black trousers clung to his legs, and his patent-leather gaiter tops oozed water from the soles and would never be the same.

Nevertheless, when Luther looked up to see Tulsa May in her umbrella perch, he grinned. That grin was so broad it was clearly visible through the combined dimness of the approaching evening and the pouring rain. She couldn't help but smile back.

"You seem awfully happy for a wet fellow."

Luther removed his hat from his head, causing a small waterfall. He bowed deeply. "Many women have claimed, ma'am, that I am made of pure sugar," he told her with formal politeness. "You, however, can see for yourself that I do not melt, even in the sloppiest of spring rains."

She chuckled lightly at his genteel foolishness. Tulsa May knew that he loved to get himself up in fancy clothes, so she was pleasantly surprised to see he could still enjoy the dubious pleasures of getting a good soaking in a summer rain.

"Get up under this umbrella before you catch your death of cold!" She pretended to scold him and a few moments later the Runabout sputtered to attention. Tulsa May adjusted the throttle as Luther rounded the car, taking time to light all five of the lamps before jumping in the far side to take his seat.

Buggies and autocars were still making their way from the nearby fields to the now wet and slippery Guthrie and River Road. Patiently waiting her turn, Tulsa May glanced over at Luther. The umbrella was a makeshift solution that didn't work as well as it might. The cover of black muslin only reached halfway across the passenger's seat and a small but steady stream of rainwater was pouring directly on Luther's head.

"Move over closer, out of the rain," Tulsa May said.

Luther shook his head. "I'm wet already. A little more won't matter a bit."

She might have argued the matter had a familiar voice not called to her from the road.

"Miss Tulsa May," Doc Odie hollered from the relative dryness of his buggy. "Come join me here at once!" He glanced patronizingly over at Luther. "I'll see the young lady home, Briggs, and without the threat of pneumonia."

Luther, only a moment ago so unconcerned about the weather, suddenly scooted close beside Tulsa May and brought his arm around her, pulling her close. Tulsa May's heart skittered at the unexpected warm contact.

"There's plenty of room for two under here," he called back to Doc Odie. He grinned at Tulsa May in a comically wicked way. "And don't worry about that pneumonia, Doc Odie. I think I can

103

manage to keep one little gal pretty warm all by myself."

Tulsa May's breath caught in her chest and she couldn't have spoken a word if she'd wanted to.

Doc Odie looked incredulous, but he flicked the reins against the horse's back and took off at a clip.

"I think the old coot may be jealous," Luther announced, pleased.

Tulsa May's hands fluttered nervously to her throat as she managed to compose herself. "Now that is something to be optimistic about," Tulsa May said. "It would certainly be all right with me if he turned out to be one of the folks who believed the gossip about us."

Luther hugged her tightly against him and smiled. "We'll make him believe it, Tulsy."

She felt his warm breath against her cheek.

"We'll make them all believe it," he said. "It just takes time."

Tulsa May's heart was pounding so loud she could hardly hear what he was saying. Then he drew his hand back from where he'd been holding her waist.

"I'm wet, Tulsy. I'll make you cold."

She glanced across at the rain-slick cotton shirt that clung so faithfully to the hills and hollows of his broad, muscled chest. Somehow she didn't feel *cold* at all.

Finally, a lull in the retreating line of buggies and autocars allowed Tulsa May to enter the roadway. Visibility was poor and the five fancy brass lamps that appeared so sporty in daylight offered only a moderate amount of actual light on the path before them. And because the Runabout was designed before the invention of the windshield, rain blew right into their faces. Being forced to concentrate on her driving had cleared the fuzzy warmth that had temporarily dulled her brain.

"Can you see where you're going?" Luther asked with some concern.

"Not well," Tulsa May answered honestly. "But I've driven this road a million times in worse shape. I can get us to the parsonage wearing a blindfold and one hand tied behind my back!"

Luther laughed and reached over to grasp her right wrist. "Am I going to be the one to blindfold you and tie you up?" he asked.

An odd little thrill of excitement sizzled through Tulsa May. She didn't understand her reaction to such a silly statement and looked at him, puzzled. Luther cleared his throat a little nervously and began concentrating solely on the road ahead of them. Tulsa May was left with a curious sense of wonder as she expertly drove the Runabout through the dark muddy ruts toward town. His body, still pressed closely to her own, felt warm and strong. A shiver ran across her skin, like lightning darting across the sky. Strange. She still didn't feel cold at all.

Maybelle Penny had not given up her throne easily. When the first drops of rain began to fall, people hurried this way and that. Stubbornly, Maybelle kept her seat, sure that the sky would not dare to rain on her. For that reason, it was pouring like buckets, and not a soul was in sight, when Maybelle Penny, 1916 Spring Blossom Queen, rose to take shelter. Her dress, however, seemed reluctant to go with her. When she took one step down from her throne, she was jerked rudely from behind.

"Waaaa!" she yelled like a madwoman then her feet slid out from under her and she landed face-down in the muddy ground in front of the stage. Dazed, for a minute she couldn't figure out what had happened. Her feet were still on the platform, her knees were on the ground, and her face was in the mud. As she rose up on her elbows, she heard a loud ripping sound. In horror she gazed at the fluffy ruffled hem of her new white messaline silk dress. While she had been seated at her queenly throne, somebody had nailed it to the floor.

"Titus!"

Screaming her younger brother's name in fury was not enough. Angrily, she pounded the muddy ground beneath her, and a wet glob of dirt splashed back in her face.

"Oh!" She shook her fist at the darkness of the sky that poured down on her.

Clumsily, she tried to get up. More than one nail still held her hem to the stage, and ripping her skirt off to free herself was not a suitable option.

Desperately she tried to turn around to reach

the nailed hem of her skirt, but her movements only served to increase her frustration, digging her deeper into the mud.

"You need some help, my queen?" a low amused voice asked.

Maybelle turned as best she could to find herself face-to-face with a pair of muddy brown leather work boots. Slowly, she crooked her neck until she could see up . . . up to the grinning face of Arthel.

"Don't just stand there, Geronimo! Help me up!"

The young man's chuckle was almost lost on the howl of the thunder. "Are you speaking to me, Queenie?"

"Who else is there, Crazy Horse?" she snapped. It was the worst of all possible luck to be in the silliest, most embarrassing position of her entire life and to have it witnessed by pigheaded, know-it-all Arthel Briggs!

"What are you waiting for, Cochise!" Maybelle screeched at the young man standing above her in the mud. "Do you have a war party coming over the hill?"

Squatting down beside her, Arthel smiled and looked self-satisfied. "Cochise? Geronimo?" He shook his head with feigned resignation. "Well, Queenie, I sure hope one of those fellows comes by soon to rescue you." He gestured to the soiled front of her dress. " 'Cause you're going to get pretty damned cold and wet waiting here in the mud."

At her puzzled expression, Arthel saluted her smartly.

"Have a nice evening, Miss Maybelle," he said as he rose to his feet and began walking off into the darkness.

For a moment she just stared after him.

"Wait!" Maybelle called out finally. He kept walking. "Come back here!" she screamed.

He didn't even pause.

Trying to rise to her knees, Maybelle only managed to slip in the mud one more time. There was a loud ripping sound.

"Oh, no," she moaned. The back of the skirt had separated from the bodice.

Her lips were pursed still in a pretty pout, but out of necessity, she swallowed her pride. "Arthel!" she yelled. "Arthel! Please! Please come back and help me."

He stopped in his tracks, and a moment later he was back beside her, grinning as widely as the winner of a pie-eating contest.

"Always eager to help out the queen."

Grasping Maybelle around the waist, he lifted her back onto her throne.

"Just look at this mess," she complained. The rain was still coming down furiously and she looked like a wilted orchid the day after the ball.

Arthel was working to pull the remaining nails free of the gown. "This was some neat trick," he noted calmly.

Maybelle clenched her fists and growled like

108

a mad dog. "When I get my hands on Titus —" she threatened.

"It wasn't just Titus," Arthel said matter-of-factly. "I saw Clark Wyse and Jimmy Trey Sparrow with him."

Maybelle's eyes widened with fury. "You *saw* them nailing my dress to the floor!"

Her expression was pure fire. Realizing immediately that he'd said the wrong thing, Arthel tried to soothe her.

"I didn't know it was going to rain" was his defense.

"You!" Maybelle was so filled with rage she almost tripped again.

"Arthel Briggs!" she screamed.

The ripping sound this time was louder than the thunder.

"Well, at least you are free," he told her as he handed her the entire back part of her dress.

The parsonage was still dark when Tulsa May pulled up under the elm tree at the far side of the porch.

"Come on inside," she told Luther. "Let me make you some warm tea before you have to head back out in this weather."

He gratefully accepted her offer and they made a dash to the porch. Luther shook the water out of the black muslin umbrella cover as Tulsa May opened the door.

"We'd best take our tea in the kitchen," she told him. "As wet as we are, Mama'd have a fit if we sat in her parlor."

"The kitchen is fine with me. The first time I ever talked to you was in a kitchen."

"That's right," she said as she led him toward the back of the house. "With all that happened, I'm surprised you even remember that."

When they reached the kitchen, she turned away from him to hang her soaked hat on a peg to dry. The fancy red feather she'd won on the merry-go-round was clearly ruined, but she left it tucked in the hatband just the same.

Luther watched with pleasure as she took down the tea things from the cupboards. It was a comforting sight. "Of course I remember. It was the only good thing that happened to me that day."

She turned her head sharply in surprise. Their eyes met for only a moment before he turned his attention to the stove, opening the grate to stoke the wood. "When Mrs. Puser came down to say Miss Maimie didn't want us, our own grandmother didn't want us" — Luther shook his head as he stared at the red coals in the fire — "it was the unhappiest moment of my life. Worse than Mammy dying, worse than Papa dying. After all . . ." He grabbed a stick of wood from the box and shoved it onto the sparking blaze. "They hadn't chosen to die. They couldn't help leaving us. Miss Maimie *chose* to send us away."

There was a quiet silence between them as Tulsa May, her brow furrowed, pumped water for the kettle. "She regretted it, Luther," she told him.

"I think right away she regretted it. That's why she always kept her eye on you, always wanted to know what you were doing. That's why she hired you to work for her."

Luther made his way to the far end of the kitchen. Hands in his pockets, he gazed unseeing out the windowpane where streaks of spring rain ran in rivulets down the glass. "She kept her eye on me," he agreed. "But not Arthel." He turned and walked to the table, sitting down in a ladderback chair. "She never cared about Arthel, because Arthel looked like Mammy. Arthel was Indian."

There was no humor in his grin. "But not me, I was a little gift from God: I'm a ringer for Luther Briggs. Yep, lucky me, I take after my daddy, blue-eyed, good-looking, squaw-man Luther Briggs. And Miss Maimie." He shook his head. "That old woman loved her errant son. She wanted him back. She wanted *her* Luther Briggs. She never gave a damn about me, Luther."

Tulsa May turned to him. "Is that why you gave all the money away?"

He gazed silently at his muddy shoe. When Miss Maimie died, the whole community was surprised at the reading of her will. Luther was her hired chauffeur, and never by any word or action had she ever acknowledged the boy as anything but her employee. But in her will, she claimed him as her only blood relation and left all of her money and property, every bit of it, to Luther.

"Yes, that's why, Tulsy," he admitted quietly

to her. " 'Cause she left it to *me* instead of Arthel and me."

He took a long deep breath as if releasing his anger.

"We didn't need her help!"

Luther's head jerked up as if he had every intention of saying more. But his expression suddenly changed. His eyes wide, his mouth open, he stared.

"What is it?"

Luther made a little choking sound and attempted to clear his throat. But he did not look away.

Tulsa May followed the direction of his gaze and stared too. Her crepe de chine bodice and the white muslin camisole beneath were both dripping wet, plastered against her body as if she were completely naked. The shape of her breasts were not disguised in any way and her dark nipples stood in stark relief to the paleness of the surrounding skin.

"Oh!" Tulsa May immediately folded her arms across her bosom. Blushing furiously, she looked up in horror and shame at Luther, still sitting stunned at the table.

With some difficulty, he dropped his glance finally to the floor and loudly cleared his throat. "Is that tea about ready, Tulsa May? It's getting late and I should be getting home." He shifted awkwardly in his chair as if he were sitting in a clump of bull nettles. "I wonder where your parents are?"

His bland comments gave Tulsa May a moment to recover her wits. She grabbed her mother's bib apron from the hook near the door and hastily slipped it on. "I'll have that tea for you in one minute," she told him with deliberate cheerfulness. Her hands were fumbling as she tried to tie her sash.

The silence in the kitchen was almost tangible. Tulsa May was beyond mere shame, she was furious at herself. Other women always seemed to have the good sense to glance in the mirror, so that they knew to staighten their ruffles or fluff their skirts. Tulsa May always avoided mirrors and this humiliation was the price that she paid. She wouldn't make that mistake again.

She cast a quick glance toward Luther. Oh, how she must have embarrassed him. To have to see a woman sticking out like that, especially a woman who was his best friend. How awkward for him! How mortifying for her!

She shook her head, still horrified. First she'd spent the whole evening bouncing her bosom against him on the dance floor and then she'd practically shown him her naked breasts. It was too distressing to even think about.

Fortunately, the water began to boil and she could concentrate on making tea. She kept her eyes determinedly on her task and didn't glance in his direction until the tea was steeping.

"Here we are," she said, smiling brightly at him, hoping to dispel the tense atmosphere.

"Thank you," he answered cordially.

She seated herself across from him at the table and smiled with determined nonchalance as she struggled to think of a fit subject for conversation.

"Didn't little Maybelle look pretty tonight?"

Luther raised his gaze from the walnut wood grain of the kitchen table. "She is a pretty girl, all right," he answered. Then with a grin he added, "Pretty spoiled."

They chuckled lightly for a moment since they both recalled Maybelle's childhood reputation for tantrums and tirades.

"She's sweet though, inside, and she will grow out of that pettiness."

He shrugged in tacit agreement.

She could think of nothing further to say about the Spring Blossom Queen.

"The merry-go-round was such fun." Tulsa May tried again. "I could have gone round and round forever. And then to catch the ring!" Her enthusiasm brightened her face attractively.

"The rain didn't do that feather much good," Luther pointed out.

Tulsa May glanced toward the dripping hat. "It does seem a bit worse for the weather," she admitted as she gazed at its sodden disrepair. "But I'm sure it will dry perfectly fine."

"You are being optimistic again," he said, teasing her.

"Guilty," she confessed, but she still did not quite feel as comfortable with him as she had before.

"Try to think of something not so cheerful,"

he challenged. "I dare you to come up with three discouraging thoughts."

"Hmm —" Tulsa May looked deliberately thoughtful. "Well, I suspect nearly every new spring dress in Prattville will have to be laundered tomorrow."

"That's probably true," he agreed.

"And I suspect Woody Sparrow will have a tremendous bellyache tonight."

"If he doesn't he should have."

"And I think that I will, in the near future, hear several sermons about the evils of dancing."

Luther laughed out loud. "It was fun, wasn't it?"

"Yes," she answered quietly.

"I'll have to take you again sometime."

Tulsa May was very conscious that Luther looked straight into her eyes as they talked and did not allow his gaze to stray for even one minute downward to where the apron now covered her. His determination to look only into her eyes was almost as disconcerting as having him looking at her bosom.

"I understand that you've bought the Henniger building on Main Steeet," she said, abruptly changing the subject.

He nodded. "It was a good price; I thought I might as well have it."

Checking the tea, Tulsa May surmised that it was dark enough and began to pour into her mother's semiporcelain Evangeline teacups.

"Are you planning to open up a store?" she asked.

"I was considering using it as a warehouse when I bought it," he admitted. "But since then, I've been thinking that the location is much too good to waste with storage."

Tulsa May nodded. "Two scoops and a dollop of milk?" she asked as she looked down at his teacup.

"You remember what I like very well."

She looked mischievous. "I remember a lot of things . . . I remember when you hid my paperdolls too!"

"You were too old for paperdolls."

"Still, they were mine."

"I gave them back."

"Well, yes you did. But you made me search three days for them. And then you never did tell me where you'd put them."

"You would never have found them on your own," he said smugly. "I put them in that book Miz Constance gave you for your birthday."

"What book?"

Luther grinned. "Don't you remember? It was called *A Modern Guide to Deportment in the Best Society*. I knew you'd never look inside."

Tulsa May laughed and covered her face. "You're right, I never did."

Finally, the tension seemed to be easing.

"So now you are planning to be a Main Street businessman."

"If I can think of a good business to put there.

Something that I would enjoy owning. I don't think I'm ready to sell belt buckles or tombstones."

Tulsa May smiled at him. "I'm sure that whatever you do with it will be the perfect thing."

A noise at the front door ended their conversation. The Reverend and Mrs. Bruder had arrived home at last.

Tulsa May didn't wait for her parents to discover them. "We're in the kitchen," she called out.

Mrs. Bruder yelled hello before hurrying up the stairs. The reverend, however, came back to stand in the kitchen doorway. He was wet and tired and did not look the least bit happy. He gave Luther only the slightest nod of acknowledgment.

"Tulsa May, it is not really proper to entertain a gentleman when your parents are not at home."

Luther drank down the remaining tea in one gulp and immediately rose to leave.

"It was raining, Papa," Tulsa May said in defense. "I invited him in for some tea to warm him up."

Reverend Bruder pursed his lips thoughtfully. "I understand, but it is still not proper. However" — he glanced disapprovingly at Luther before returning his gaze to his daughter — "after your carryings-on tonight on the dance floor, dear, I'm not surprised that you forgot about propriety."

"It's my fault, Rev —" Luther said.

"— *I* wanted to dance, Papa. I'd never done

117

it and I wanted to try it."

"Well, I hope you've gotten over that nonsense."

"Actually," Tulsa May answered bravely, "I rather enjoyed it. I think I would like to do it again."

Luther cleared his throat nervously.

"I won't have you hanging out at wild dance halls." The reverend, his eyes narrowed, made this admonishment as much to Luther as to Tulsa May.

"No danger of that, Rev." Luther was visibly uncomfortable with the discussion. He cleared his throat. "I was hoping, sir, that I might be allowed to escort Miss Tulsy to church in the morning."

The preacher raised his eyebrows and folded his arms before him, surveying the young man with surprise. "You intend to darken God's door once again, Luther?" He shook his head and then glanced at his daughter. "My, the Lord does work in mysterious ways."

SPRING BLOSSOM FESTIVAL HUGE SUCCESS

Evening Rain Doesn't Dampen Enjoyment

Cimarron Ornamental Flower Farms held its annual Spring Blossom Festival on Saturday at Cora's Knoll near Prattville. It was estimated that nearly two hundred people were in attendance for the festivities, which included a steam calliope merry-go-round and speeches from local politicians.

Miss Maybelle Penny, daughter of Mr. and Mrs. Titus Penny of Main Street was crowned Spring Blossom Queen in a ceremony that included the presentation of a

Chapter Seven

He was a boy again. The wind swept his long black hair into his face and he brushed it away. He heard her call his name. Or did he hear it? Perhaps he felt it? She was behind him. His mother. His mother as he remembered her, not his mother from the photograph that sat on the delicate parlor table in the front room. That mother was a pretty, young, dark princess with her hair dressed in an elaborate style. That mother was wearing a fancy dress and had her face lightened with rice powder. This was his mother with the long black braids that hung nearly to her waist and the once bright calico dress, much faded and worn at the elbows.

"Greasy!" she called once again to him, in that way of hers that made it sound like "Greezie."

He turned to run back to her, but he felt weak and she was a long distance away. His father was there too. Looking very tall. Looking very alive. He struggled to reach them, briefly frightened that he would not make it. But then he was beside them. They were smiling down at him. His father ruffled his hair. "Son, come take your brother," he said in the deep, strong voice that Luther remembered, although he couldn't see his father's lips moving. "He's younger than you and he's your responsibility. You must keep him safe and keep him with you."

Luther looked down into the blankets. Arthel was a baby once more. Tied into his papoose cradle, he had the same black hair on his forehead and the same shriveled-up face that Luther remembered. The little baby eyes crinkled up and he opened his mouth as if to howl, but no sound came.

"Be careful with him now," his mother admonished as she strapped the leather binding on Luther's back. "You must watch what you do. You must keep your little brother safe."

"I will, Mammy," he said, in a soft sing-song voice that sounded nothing like his own.

Both his parents smiled at him proudly. His father gestured for him to go ahead, and as he hurried before them on the road, he could feel the warm weight of his brother on his back. He felt the comfort of his family's nearness. He was happy. Walking. Walking. Walking up the steps of the Briggs mansion.

The door was open and he went inside. He stood at the bottom of the stairs. Was he supposed to climb up? He turned to ask his mother. She was gone. His father was gone too. The path they had trodden together had vanished with his family. He tried to call out to them, but he couldn't make a sound.

They were gone. Forever.

Tears came to his eyes, but he wiped them

away with the back of his hand. He turned once more to face the stairs. Yes, he was supposed to climb them. His parents had sent him here expecting him to continue on. He would do as they had hoped.

He tried to raise his foot, but he couldn't move. Staring at his leg as if it were not his own, he tried again. He still carried the baby Arthel on his back. The weight had grown too heavy. He tried again, forcing his feet to move. But he could not.

He looked up the long length of stairway before him and searched for a solution. But none seemed right. Should he remove the papoose cradle? He could leave Arthel at the bottom and return for him when he was stronger. No, he couldn't leave a baby alone here. He'd promised his mother to keep him safe. His father was counting on him. But he couldn't stay forever at the foot of the stairs.

He tried once more to climb. Desperately, he clutched the rail and tried to pull himself forward. He couldn't pull himself up, he couldn't crawl there on his hands and knees. Sweat broke out all over him. He couldn't make it up the stairs, not now, not ever.

Panic came over him like a blackness that robbed the air from his lungs.

There was no place to go back to.

There was no way to go forward.

He tried to cry out, but the words wouldn't come.

Luther sat up in bed. He was covered with sweat. He looked around at the familiar room and his familiar place as his breathing returned to normal. With a shake of his head, he put his feet on the floor and climbed out of bed. Staggering to the washstand, he doused himself with cool water from the pitcher and stood silently in the darkness. Nightmares had never been a problem for him. He had always faced his fears in broad daylight and that was hard enough. As a stunned sixteen year old he'd found himself suddenly orphaned. He'd been grieving and afraid but he subdued his own feelings. If he were frightened and lonely, how much more so was Arthel? At eight, Arthel had been a much beloved and sheltered child. It was his birth that had finally brought his parents together. He was accustomed to attention and spoiling and unconditional love. He needed family. It was the one thing that Luther had been unable to give him.

Cursing beneath his breath, Luther pushed away any thought that he might have fallen short. He'd given Arthel the most that he could. And he tried his damnedest to give him even more.

Returning to the bed, Luther determinedly covered himself with the worn cotton bedsheet, flung one arm across his forehead and admonished himself decisively to go back to sleep.

He lay perfectly still for several minutes before he admitted to himself that falling back to sleep might not be easy. He supposed that he should go ahead and get up. It was nearly dawn and

Arthel would be making coffee pretty soon.

As he relaxed, his mind drifted back to the events of the night before. He remembered with pleasure dancing with Tulsy. She was really quite good at it, he decided. Given an opportunity, they could really scrape some sawdust together. Of course the reverend wouldn't like that much. He wondered briefly what the reverend would have thought if he'd known that Luther had seen Tulsy with her shirtwaist soaking wet.

A low sexy smile parted Luther's lips and he sighed.

The Bruders' kitchen had all the sweet smells of home. Tulsa May stood there, innocently, yet somehow suggestively. Her carrot-colored hair was mussed. She was his Tulsy, his plain and ordinary Tulsy. But, beneath that sweet, sopping silk dress she was naked. Her perfectly round, plump breasts shimmered like orbs of brass in the yellow-orange glow of the coal oil lamp. And they were crowned with dark nipples. Huge nipples. Luther had never seen such nipples. The sight of them had made him weak.

He moaned slightly now as he relived the memory. He had stared. He knew that he had stared. That had embarrassed her, and he was sorry about that. But, at least he had only stared, he thought as he drifted back into sleep.

In his dream he walked toward her until he was standing only inches away. Gently he traced his finger along the soft familiar curve of her lip. She was his Tulsy, his friend. Then his finger left the corner of her mouth and began moving down . . . down . . . down toward the soaking wet bodice that drew him. Lured him. She looked up at him and then down to his hand on her bosom. There was no fear in her face.

Luther grasped her shoulders to pull her closer, closer until her breast touched his mouth. Gently he tasted the sweet rainwater that dripped from the drenched fabric that clung there. His tongue came out to catch another drop, but that was not enough. Pulling her closer still, he took her nipple between his teeth, caressing it with his tongue. So sweet. It was heaven. It was everything. It was not enough. He had to have the rest of her. All of her.

He opened his mouth further and sucked at her breast, pulling the areola within his mouth. She tasted of violet water, and the lingering scent of talcum was fresh and sweet and soft. He pulled his mouth from her bosom. He gazed up into her penny-brown eyes.

"Tulsy," he whispered hoarsely to her.

He opened his eyes to see the full light of dawn just pouring in through the window. His erection was rigid and throbbing. With a sound that was half-sigh and half-curse, he turned on his stomach, pressing his aching flesh into the soft warmth of his feather tick.

"Tulsy," he groaned into his pillow. His eyes closed for one long moment and then popped open in shock. "Tulsy?" He said the word aloud, as if he couldn't quite believe it.

Immediately, he turned and rolled out of bed. He stared back at the cotton bedsheet, the familiar scrap-tie quilt and the white painted iron bedstead as if they were traitors. He took a deep breath and released it slowly. Still unsteady on his feet, he hurried once more to the water basin and liberally splashed himself, head and shoulders, with cold water from the pitcher. He shook all over like a dog coming out of the river, splashing droplets against the furniture and across the mirror.

Grabbing up a towel, he dried his face and then gazed in the mirror as if he didn't know himself. His expression seemed to stare back blankly. It was the strangest moment of his life. Imagine, him having thoughts like that about Tulsa May Bruder?

The kitchen was empty, but the coffee smelled wonderful. Carefully, Luther wrapped a towel around the hot handle of the coffee pot and lifted it to pour himself a mugful. Arthel was the only person in Prattville who could make good coffee without using eggs. Luther had tried on several occasions to get the hang of it himself. But his own coffee was a poor substitute. Arthel had a way with a cookstove just as Luther had a way with engines.

"Morning," he said as he stepped out onto the second-floor porch.

Arthel was seated in one of the rockers that looked over the road and the bluff beyond. "Damnation!" he said with a shake of his head. "Must

126

be Judgment Day for you to be up before sunrise."

Luther shrugged and seated himself in the rocker next to his brother.

"Don't kid yourself, little brother," he said, only half joking. "Some of us get judged every day."

Leaning back in the rocker, Luther put one long bare foot on the porch railing, holding himself in a perpetual half-recline. "Couldn't sleep," he said simply. "And I promised Tulsy that I'd take her to church this morning."

Arthel laughed out loud. "Now that's the most amazing thing I've heard you say this week. And it's been an amazing week."

"Well," Luther admitted as he took a tentative sip of scalding hot coffee. "The Rev was a little wound up about the dancing last night."

"He wasn't the only one," Arthel said. "What in the world got into you to be holding Tulsa May like that? And in public too."

"What do you mean? We were dancing." Luther's mouth thinned. Though with his dream still fresh in his mind, he did feel guilty.

"Oh, I know. I've seen you dancing plenty of times," Arthel agreed with a wry grin. "But Tulsa May is no betty. You've got no business snuggle-spieling with her."

Luther's voice was dangerously quiet. "Little brother, I am twenty-six years old. When it comes to the ladies in my life, I can do whatever it is I decide to do. And I do so without your permission."

Arthel raised an eyebrow in challenge, but said nothing. He turned his attention back to the eastern sky and Luther followed his gaze. Quietly they watched the grays, blues, pinks, and yellows of the Oklahoma dawn.

"Did you get a ride home last night?" Luther asked finally.

"Yep," Arthel answered. "Mr. and Mrs. Penny gave me a ride in that fancy Chevy Touring Car."

"Oh?"

When Arthel made no response, Luther continued. "Was Maybelle with them?"

"Well, sure."

"I thought maybe she'd gone home with one of those dozens of fellows following her around."

Arthel squirmed a little uneasily in his chair. "I don't know who she came with, but she left with me."

"Now, that's real interesting," Luther said.

Arthel refused to take the bait. "Actually, it was even more interesting than you think."

"Oh?"

"Titus nailed her dress to the platform floor."

"What!"

"You heard me. That rascally brother of hers, along with Jimmy Trey and that Wyse boy, must have snuck half a dozen nails in her hem."

Luther hooted with laughter. "Lord, what happened when she tried to get up?"

"The Spring Blossom Queen fell flat on her face."

Luther shook his head in disbelief. "How could

they do that without her noticing?"

Arthel was laughing now too. "It was the music. All that dancing and old Mort stomping around on the stage. She just didn't pay that hammering a bit of mind."

"You saw it?"

Nodding, Arthel took a long swig of coffee. "I didn't have the heart to stop the little devils. It reminded me of the scrapes we used to get into when we lived with the preacher." He shook his head. "Lord, I wished I'd thought of it myself. You should have seen her in that fancy dress, wallowing in the mud like a wounded hog."

Luther choked on his coffee at the image that formed in his mind and Arthel had to whallop him on the back a couple of times so that he could catch his breath. "For shame, Arthel. A gentleman never laughs at the expense of a young lady."

"I think this particular young lady owes me some laughing," Arthel said firmly.

Luther nodded with understanding but without approval. "I take it you rescued this damsel in distress," he said.

"I tried to," Arthel said, with mock humility. "But you know that hotheaded little gal. She jumped right up again and ripped the whole back of her skirt clean from the bodice."

"No!"

"Would I lie to you?"

"How'd you keep a straight face?"

"I didn't."

The two brothers laughed uproariously together for several minutes, until tears had formed in Luther's eyes and Arthel was holding his chest.

"Sure to the world, Arthel, I leave you for a minute and you get yourself into a peck of trouble."

"It's the kind of trouble a fellow could get used to. Would you have believed that under that sweet little white dress Maybelle was wearing a bright pink petticoat and pink ribbons on the ruffles of her bloomers?"

"Bloomers! Now, Arthel, that's getting much too dangerous," Luther said with as much caution as laughter. "It's not your time of life to be thinking about ladies' underwear."

Arthel shoook his head. "When a fellow starts thinking about them, I suspect it's time to start thinking about them."

"I suppose it's all right for you to be thinking," Luther said slowly, "but remember you've got college and all that. Wouldn't want some gal to trap you. So thinking about it is all that you ought to do."

Arthel's grin was broad. "Big brother, I am eighteen years old. When it comes to the ladies in my life, I can do whatever it is I decide to do. And I do it without need of your permission."

The Briggs brothers were not the only ones to see the dawn that morning. Tulsa May Bruder watched from her window seat, her knees hugged to her chest, her eyes thoughtful. Her serviceable muslin gown was gray from many washings, patched at the elbows, and the embroidery at the yoke was picked with broken stitches, but it was as comfortable as an old friend and she refused to send the dress to the rag bag. Her hair was unbound and hung past her waist like a thick, wavy orange shawl. The early morning sun made its length shine like strands of gold.

She took turns in her observation. She would stare out the window a while and then rest her chin upon her knees to contemplate her bare feet. Neither sight really captured her attention.

She had not slept well. She'd stayed up late to write her story on the festival, hoping the effort would tire her out, but it hadn't worked. Even after Doc Odie's humiliating public jilting, Tulsa May had been able to lose herself in sleep. She'd simply closed her eyes and told herself that things would look better in the morning. Taking the worst and making something good of it, was the one thing with which she had great experience. But last night there was no bad news or sad thoughts to keep her awake. It was simply some strange unsettlement within her as if there were a room in her heart that had been closed up so tightly and for so long that she'd plainly forgotten that it existed. Last night, she'd taken an unexpected peek through its doorway. She was scared.

A creak of a door and the groan of floorboards warned Tulsa May that her father was making his way down the stairs. His office was directly

131

below her room, and as she sat in total silence, she frowned, waiting for the sounds of him entering the study to work on his sermon.

But the study beneath her remained quiet and Tulsa May could faintly hear the sounds of her father's steps on the basement stairway. She smiled and released a long-held breath. He was going to work out in his gym. If she hurried, she could be dressed and gone before he ever knew she was awake. The last thing she wanted this morning was to have a "little talk about her carryings-on last night."

With the wild rush of a younger girl, she jerked a clean dress out of the wardrobe and threw it across the bed. Hastily — and certainly unladylike — Tulsa May washed her face and hands, brushed her teeth, and slipped into clean underwear. Dressed, with her shoes in her hand, she sneaked out of her room and tiptoed down the stairs. She was out the back door and halfway down the well-worn path at the back of the house before she tied the sash at her waist. She put her shoes on while sitting in the privy. It was only then that she realized she hadn't bothered to put up her wildly tangled hair. She searched the pockets of the dark blue day dress for hairpins, but didn't find even one.

With a shrug, she rose to her feet, adjusted her clothing, and headed out. Pulling her hair together and combing it with her fingers, she made one loose braid and stuffed its red masses into her straw hat as she walked the back alley toward Briggs Park. It was a path she knew well.

Since the diphtheria epidemic of 1906, when she, only little more than a girl, had begun taking care of Miss Maimie Briggs until her death, Tulsa May had dutifully taken this path at least once a week to visit Miss Maimie. Faithfully but not cheerfully. Tulsa May visited Miss Maimie as if she were swallowing a home-cooked tonic, very unpleasant to taste, but undoubtedly good for her.

Tulsa May did it to keep herself humble. While her father praised her quick mind to the skies, and most of the ladies in town shook their heads and assured Tulsa May that she had "sweet ways," Miss Maimie had been a good deal more blunt.

"I hope you aren't hoping for a splendid match," Miss Maimie had said one unpleasant Saturday afternoon. "If you manage to make any match at all, it will surprise most people in this town."

Tulsa May had neither felt very hurt, nor taken offense at this sentiment. She knew that her mother and most of the ladies in the town felt the same way. Tulsa May actually *admired* Miss Maimie's acerbic tongue and the way she used it to manipulate people. Not that she, herself, would ever aspire to so cold-bloodedly control others, but as a curiosity, Tulsa May found Miss Maimie's approach to personal relationships quite entertaining.

Unfortunately, there were times when Miss Maimie's perception was too acute.

"You don't come to see me, miss," the old

133

woman said. "You spend half your time over here visiting my chauffeur."

Tulsa May had answered with a smile on her face. "I'm not your employee, Miss Maimie. I visit of my own free will and can therefore spend that visit in any manner I choose. Besides," she continued quickly, "Luther is more than your chauffeur. He's your grandson."

The old woman's eyes had narrowed. Nobody ever dared remind Miss Maimie of her kinship with the handsome blue-eyed half-breed who bore her son's name.

For a moment Miss Maimie hesitated. Then a thoroughly unkind gleam came into her eyes and she smiled too sweetly at Tulsa May.

"I understand that young Luther is your *friend*," she said.

Tulsa May had felt her throat go dry. "Yes, he is."

Miss Maimie nodded. "I guess a girl like you has to take what she can get. Of course, your heart shows in your eyes every time you look at him." The old lady sighed loudly. "Unrequited love is *so* romantic."

Even now, years later, Tulsa May could almost hear the acid in the old woman's words. Yet each word rang with truth. Tulsa May stopped at a stone and pine bench beneath a cottonwood tree on the edge of the park. Through the budding trees of springtime, she could still make out the rooflines of the fine big house. Miss Maimie was long gone, the Briggs Mansion was now the

Millenbutter Hospital, and no living being knew Tulsa May's heart. Except Tulsa May herself.

Leaning forward, she propped her elbows on her knees and rested her face in her hands.

Your heart shows in your eyes every time you look at him.

A girl like you has to take what she can get.

She watched a tiny trail of ants making their way through the grass in front of her feet. How they knew where to go or how to get back was one of God's mysteries. Why a woman would fall in love with a man she could never have, was another.

Tulsa May couldn't say when she first knew she loved Luther. There had been no bolt from the blue, no decisive moment of change in her feelings.

Oh, she'd had a crush on him right from the start. What girl in Prattville didn't? Every dreamy-eyed maiden in town sighed when he walked past. That thick dark hair, the vivid blue eyes and broad dimpled smile were not something that the young female heart could ignore. She remembered once passing Indian clubs with Sissy Maitland during a Prayers and Posture Meeting for Young Ladies.

"He is the most beautiful man that God ever created," Sissy said wistfully.

"He's not a man at all," Tulsa May quickly corrected her. "He's only sixteen, barely older than us."

Sissy had shaken her head. "He's plenty enough

135

of a man for me," she declared. "Besides, those Indian boys grow up faster. They are out killing buffalo or whatever when white boys their age are still in the schoolroom."

Tulsa May gave a sharper twist to her throw of the club, and almost managed to hit Sissy in the head.

"Luther is not an Indian boy and he's certainly never hunted a buffalo!" Tulsa May declared hotly.

Sissy agreed, but for all the wrong reasons. "He is so good-looking that you can almost forget he's got mixed blood. But when you see that little brother of his . . ." She shook her head. "Well, you know . . ."

Tulsa May's jaw tightened now as she continued to stare at the trail of ants at her feet. Sissy had married Cleo Guttmand and moved to the oil fields in Shamrock. Luther had never given the small-minded girl so much as a second look, and Tulsa May was glad. But she knew her own feelings at the time were almost as shallow.

All her life she'd known that there was more to people than their outward appearance. She prided herself on being someone who looked beyond the exterior, where all folks had their good points as well as their failings. So she was determined that she would really get to know Luther Briggs. Once she knew his faults, that would cure her of any idealized girlhood fancy.

It had not been easy. That broad dimpled smile was given as often in discomfort as genuine warmth. Though affable to all, Luther Briggs was not the kind of young man to allow anyone to see inside him. Walls of reserve had been built by rejection and responsibility. But Tulsa May had been relentless. And when he came to trust her, she had finally been allowed to view his heart. What she had discovered, she had fallen in love with.

She sighed heavily and used the pointed toe of her shoe to dig a giant crater in the ant trail at her feet. The line of ants hesitated momentarily, bunched together as if discussing the sudden change in the geography and plotting a new strategy. It was less than a minute before one intrepid insect began to skirt the edge of the crater and rediscover the rest of the familiar trail.

Tulsa May loved Luther Briggs, but she knew today as she had so many years ago that her love would never prosper. And to reveal it would end a treasured friendship.

The clomp and clatter of a buggy coming up the road drew her attention, causing her to peer wide-eyed through the stand of trees. She couldn't see the road or who approached, but on Sunday morning at daybreak the most likely person traveling to the hospital would be Doc Odie.

Tulsa May pulled her hat down farther over her long half-braided tail of carrot-colored hair in horror and jumped to her feet. Doc Odie had often complained of her untidiness. It would be so humiliating to be caught in a public park with her hair undone. Anxiously, she hurried down the deserted alleyway back toward the parsonage.

Once she had been very serious about marrying Odie Foote, and she had carefully tried to gain his approval. She was not proud of that fact. She had always insisted that she didn't need a man to make her life worthwhile. All the feminists of the day were certain that marriage, for women, was a form of legal slavery. But she wanted children, a little family of her own. And if the ladies of the movement could manage that without marriage, they were much braver than she.

Still, she wondered how she could have ever considered marriage to Doc Odie. She would have been expected to give up writing for the newspaper.

"It is unfeminine."

And she would not be allowed to own a car or drive.

"Far too dangerous."

Her interest and opinions on politics and current events would have to be kept to herself.

"A woman's brain is simply not structurally large enough to grasp the complexities."

Odie Foote was difficult, stubborn, and opinionated. He and her mother got along perfectly: both seemed to find more faults in Tulsa May than graces.

But he had asked her to be his wife. Why, she honestly couldn't imagine. She had stared at him with disbelief.

"I'm not sure," Tulsa May had admitted later to her mother.

Her mother had wrung her hands at the words. "Honey," she'd said worriedly. "Odie Foote might well be the only chance you ever have."

Tulsa May had paled at the thought and her resolve had weakened. Her "only chance" for a family. So she'd swallowed her misgivings and had said yes, for all the good it had done her. Apparently, Doc Odie had been unable to swallow his own misgivings.

As she hurried along the alleyway, Tulsa May glanced back a couple of times to assure that she had not been seen.

For years Tulsa May had read the work of Stanton and Anthony and others in the feminist movement. She believed that women should have the right to vote and she prayed that they would get it. She didn't think that a spinster was a "waste of nature" or that the success of a woman was measured in terms of how well she married. She knew these thoughts were as radical as those of the most fervent bluestocking.

But there was that other part of her. That little tender growing place in her that wanted to feel her belly swollen with child. That wanted to hold that child in her arms and teach the child Euripides as well as how to play cat's cradle.

Tulsa May blew out a sigh of near self-disgust. It was glandular, undoubtedly. The same traitorish glands that gave her fat, pouty nipples also gave her the desire for a child to suckle them.

That thought gave her a strange jolt of pleasure she couldn't quite understand. She shook it off.

Having children was apparently a treasure not to be realized. Without marriage they were impossible. But what about the rest of it? The tenderness of being held by a man? The taste of his lips on her own. Would she be forced to forgo that also? Momentarily and unwillingly, the smiling image of Luther Briggs crossed her mind, but she pushed it away. Best friends never marry. Any hope to the contrary could risk ruining a wonderful friendship. Losing Luther Briggs as best friend would hurt a thousand times more than any public jilting Doc Odie could ever manage. No, best friends could never marry. But could they share some of the tenderness of a man and a woman? Was being held very far from dancing together? And was being kissed much beyond that?

Chapter Eight

Fortunately for both Luther and Tulsa May, the Reverend Bruder's sermon was not about the evils of dancing. But the community did not escape the Spring Blossom Festival uncensured.

"Gossip, while not expressly mentioned in the Ten Commandments, was inherently a sin of bearing false witness," the preacher contended. As no one ever repeated things and got them exactly right.

Luther had seated himself beside Tulsa May in the shiny, slickly polished oak pew reserved for the pastor's family in the front of the church. Ostensibly, this was to give moral support to the preacher. More likely, Luther thought, it was done so that the people of the church could scrutinize them during the sermon. That, at least, was certainly true today.

Luther gave the reverend his complete attention. Since he hadn't been in church in several years, and every soul in Prattville knew that, every eye in the congregation was focused upon him. The preacher's words notwithstanding, Luther Briggs's attendance at Sunday service was certain to be the main theme of local gossip for the coming days.

During the years following the deaths of his parents, Luther had been, peripherally at least, a part of the preacher's family. He and Arthel had suffered, or profited from, some of the same inspection that had always been a part of Tulsa May's life. It was different, of course. They were orphans and half-breeds and children to be pitied. They were also the grandsons, unclaimed though they were, of town matron Maimie Briggs.

Those were sometimes sad, sometimes lonely days for Luther. He missed his parents terribly and felt a deep burden of responsibility for his younger brother. The Bruders were very kind to offer them a home. And although he was grateful and cared very much for Rev and Miz Constance, he did not love them. He wanted the love of Miss Maimie. She was a part of him, a part of his family. And he wanted his family back. More than that, he needed a family for his brother.

Tulsa May had understood.

"I go over there nearly every day, Greasy," she had told him. "You just show up with me. What is Miss Maimie going to do? Throw you out the door?"

Luther was afraid of just that. Tulsa May always looked for the best in people and she'd even managed to find something likable about Miss Maimie. But he knew that there was something very, very bad in the old woman.

He'd gone over on his own one afternoon, dressed in his Sunday suit, his hair slicked back with the reverend's best pomade. Conrad Ruggy opened the door.

"Good afternoon," Luther greeted the old man formally. "Is Mrs. Maimie Briggs at home?"

The fact that Miss Maimie was *always* home notwithstanding, Luther wanted to observe the polite formalities.

The old black man's eyes were sharp as he surveyed him. "Why don't you step into the library, sir," he'd said as he opened the door wider. "I'll see if Miss Maimie can have visitors."

It had been an interminable wait alone in the big library that was stuffed full of paintings and bric-a-brac and held very few books.

"Miss Maimie will see you now," Conrad had announced.

Luther had felt a wave of nausea sweep over him. But he raised his chin and followed the aging butler to the very formal front parlor.

He stepped across the threshold and nearly lost his nerve. He'd seen Miss Maimie before. She'd attended the Sparrow wedding and later he'd caught glimpses of her on her occasional visits to town. Somehow she seemed even more formidable close up.

They stared at each other for a long, assessing moment. She was his grandmother. The woman who had given birth to his father. A woman who had loved his father maybe as much as he had. She was looking deeply into his eyes as if seeing something unexpected. For a moment her face was relaxed and open and there was something . . . something there that Luther could not quite make out. Then as quickly as it had come, it was gone. Her expression was a cold, haughty mask of displeasure.

"Well, boy," she said in a stiff, unyielding voice. "You wanted to see me. I assume you have some business."

Luther opened his mouth, but then he had no words. Maimie Briggs did not want him for a grandson. She did not want to make a home for him and his brother. She did not want to love them or to have them love her in return.

"Well," she snapped impatiently. "Do you have business or not?"

"I'm looking for a job," he blurted out.

The words surprised both of them. He already did plenty of daily chores at the parsonage and he was still attending school. He knew the reverend still considered him a child and would never expect him to pay his own way.

"A job?" Miss Maimie managed to sound both skeptical and derisive. "What on earth could you do?"

"I'm very good at working on machines," he told her. "I can fix about any kind of motor or engine that you might have."

Miss Maimie scoffed. "Young man, I do not have any machines," she said. "No motors, no engines."

He knew that she was trying to disconcert him. But she did not. The same stubborn haughtiness that was her trademark also flowed through his own veins.

"Well, if you don't, you should," he told her high-handedly. "This is the twentieth century, after all. Just because you were born in the past doesn't mean you have to live there."

Sitting in church now, years later, Luther still smiled at the memory of Miss Maimie's face. Unconsciously, he reached for Tulsa May's hand and squeezed her fingers. She'd always shared in his small victories over Miss Maimie. She glanced over and smiled at him curiously before they both turned their attention back to the preacher.

It seemed Reverend Bruder had barely gotten wound up on his chosen subject when the sermon was over. The congregation stood to sing as Mary Beth Muldrow began playing the invitational hymn. They shared a hymnbook, with Tulsa May paging through to find the right song.

Luther chanced a quick glance at Tulsa May and then wished that he hadn't. When he looked at her familiar smile, he saw something else, something new, something that immediately reminded him of his wicked dream. He jerked his gaze back to the preacher, but couldn't control the heat that climbed up his neck. He tugged impatiently at his stiffly starched collar. Clearing his throat, Luther sang a deep bass harmony to Tulsa May's high, breathy soprano.

"Not a burden we bear,
Not a sorrow we share

145

But our toil He doth richly repay;
Not a grief nor a loss,
Not a frown nor a cross,
But is blest if we trust and obey."

This is Tulsy, Luther reminded himself silently as he stood only inches from her, the clean, familiar scent of her favorite talcum drifting to his nostrils. *Tulsy. Not some Saturday-night sweetie whose name you can quickly forget.*

Finally the invitational ended and he could take a step back, grateful for the distance. He was angry at himself for merging fantasy with reality. Tulsa May was the kindest, most gracious friend he had ever had. He shouldn't repay that generosity with crude thoughts.

When the service was over, he escorted both Tulsa May and her mother to the back of the church with extreme formality. The noise and bustle of the departing congregation gave him some perspective.

Woody and Jimmy Trey Sparrow headed to the church door with such exuberant enthusiasm, they nearly knocked their grandfather down. Haywood Puser only managed to right himself with the help of old Osgold Panek. The two men shared a light laugh and shook their heads.

Maybelle Penny was attempting to open her lacy pink parasol.

"Don't open that inside the building!" Beulah Bowman admonished her.

Maybelle shrugged with unconcern. "I don't

believe in silly old superstitions."

Mrs. Bowman huffed up with disapproval as she moved away, muttering about bad luck.

Maybelle raised her nose as she allowed young Fasel Auslander to convey her to the door, her umbrella hanging unfolded over her arm.

Miz Constance quickly drifted away into the crowd, clearly having news to spread. Luther, however, didn't rush, though Tulsa May was clearly anxious to leave. But Luther knew that it was important to take their time. Slowly, deliberately, he led her toward the exit, careful to speak to each and every member of the congregation. They needed to be seen and he intended to make sure they were.

"Morning, Luther, good to have you in church again," Opal Crenshaw greeted them politely. "Tulsa May, what a delightful hat!"

"Thank you," she barely had time to mutter before Erwin Willers, publisher of the *Populist*, slid up beside them with a friendly wink.

"You making your own news these days, Tulsa May?" he teased.

She flushed brightly.

"Luther Briggs!"

Turning, they were confronted with Amelia Puser, the leading society matron of Prattville.

"Mrs. Puser." He gave the mortician's wife a polite nod. "What a pleasure to see you looking so lovely this morning."

Amelia flushed proudly with the strength of vanity that even more than fifty years of living couldn't quite conquer. Her delicately featured face remained surprisingly youthful and her wavy blond hair was miraculously lacking in gray. The result of Madame Olivia's Cosmetology Products, which she received in plain brown wrapping from a mail order catalog. Her black silk taffeta gown was trimmed with georgette crepe in the very latest style with a throw-tie belt that emphasized her still fashionably narrow waist.

"And what a surprise to see you." Pointedly, she glanced over at Tulsa May, whose hand still lay gently on Luther's arm. "So, is it true what I'm hearing?" She fluttered her black lace fan prettily before slapping it playfully against the young man's lapel.

Luther smiled at her and then glanced down at the young woman beside him. He saw that her pale, slightly freckled face was more rosy than usual. Possessively he patted her hand.

"Now, Mrs. Puser," he answered with a charming grin. "How could we ever know what you've been hearing?"

As the smartly dressed older woman raised an eyebrow, Luther gave her a polite but dismissing nod and moved onward.

"Good to see you, Luther." Clyde Avery offered a friendly greeting.

"It's sure a sight to see you in church," Ross Crenshaw admitted.

Luther smiled in answer.

"Titus, Mrs. Penny." He acknowledged Maybelle's mother, who held her ten-year-old son's hand securely in her own.

Slowly Luther moved through the crowd with Tulsa May on his arm. There were nods and welcomes and greetings. But behind their backs there was plenty of whispering and speculation. Could it be true? What an unlikely couple! They've always been together so much. How long had it been going on? Did Doc Odie know about this? Was that what *really* happened to the engagement? Luther felt Tulsa May tremble nervously beside him. Glancing down, he saw that her cheeks were fiery red.

"Steady, Tulsy," he whispered. "We're off to a flying start. Don't balk on me now. We're just going to walk right out of here and over to your front door."

"They're all looking at us," she said in a hushed tone.

"And that's just exactly what we want," he said. "Smile when you look up at me, Tulsy. You don't want them to think that you're unhappy."

She did smile at him, bravely, and his answering grin warmed her somewhat.

The crowd was behind them, lingering in the churchyard, watching, whispering, the preacher's admonition against gossiping completely forgotten. Tulsa May's hand lay gracefully upon Luther's arm as he led her to the parsonage and up the two wide steps to the porch.

He turned to her and they both sighed heavily.

"Don't you dare to look," he said. "Every eye

in the congregation is watching this front porch."

"I hate being the center of attention," Tulsa May said with a sigh.

Luther nodded and placed his thumb beneath her chin, raising her gaze to his. "That's why we started this, remember? We can't stop the river from flowing, but we can dam it up and divert it in another direction."

Tulsa May chuckled humorlessly. "Right now, I feel like we are in for a flood."

"It's only temporary," he assured her. "I'd bet they've already stopped feeling sorry for you. We just have to keep it up long enough for them to stop talking about you."

She agreed. "I just didn't think it would have to be so public."

Luther grinned. "In a small town, Tulsy, everything is public."

"I suppose you are right."

"I *know* I'm right. People think they've got a personal interest in knowing everything about everybody."

"But we're going to put one over on them," Tulsa May replied.

"We sure are." He was too close to her again, he warned himself. He could smell the welcoming warmth of her and he was drawn to it. He should step away, he told himself. She was standing with her back against the porch pillar. Civility demanded that he give her more space. Somehow, he moved closer. "Let's give them something to think about."

Before she had time to question him, he leaned forward, lightly touching her shoulders, and brought his mouth down to her own. He had meant it to be a sweetheart's kiss, swift and sugary. But he had not expected her lips to be so soft. He had not expected his body to immediately respond. He had not expected that they both would tremble.

"Luther!" Tulsa May's exclamation was breathy against his mouth. As her lips parted, Luther took advantage. She surprised him. Somehow he'd thought, *if* he had thought, that the taste of her would be sweet and wholesome, like fresh sliced peaches or warm molasses. The spicy, exotic enticement of her lips was totally unanticipated. She was totally new and unknown. Not his familiar Tulsy at all. He moved his mouth eagerly across her own. Wanting more, wanting —

Abruptly he pulled back and stared down at the woman in his arms. This was Tulsa May Bruder, his childhood playmate, his best friend, his Tulsy. How could she — ? How could he — ?

She stared up at him wide-eyed. Shocked.

Luther laid his head on top of hers and drew her warm body against his. He had to hold her close again, but he could not look into those familiar trusting eyes. What was happening to him? His heart was beating so loudly it nearly deafened him. Or was it her heart? They were so close, it was difficult to tell.

"Greasy?" The sound of his familiar childhood name brought him to his senses.

151

He took a deep cleansing breath and stepped back from her. "That should give them something to talk about this week."

Tulsa May stared in surprise. Clearly, she had forgotten that the kiss was meant for an audience.

Doc Odie pulled his team of bays up in front of the faded shotgun-style house on Second Street. The crepe myrtle in the front yard nearly obscured the tiny porch. But Emma Dix was already standing at the door by the time Doc Odie's feet touched the ground.

"He's real bad, Doc," she told him quietly. "Getting caught out in the rain like that yesterday." The young woman shook her head. "I don't know what I was thinking about."

Doc Odie stepped up on the porch, medical bag in hand, and patted her shoulder comfortingly. "You were thinking about having a good time and allowing your father to enjoy himself also. He seemed very happy to be out among friends yesterday."

Emma nodded, but from her expression it was clear she had no plans to forgive herself.

Doc Odie followed her into the house. The long, narrow front parlor was as neat as a pin. The handsomely upholstered furniture, although nearly a decade out of style, was impeccably clean and so carefully mended that not even the slightest fray in the material was visible. Ornate hanging lamps, augmented by delicate crystal prisms, provided the light for the parlor and were in perfect condition. Their glass chimneys sparkled, the wicks were trimmed, and the wells were full. The cream-colored silk draperies at the windows were perfectly pleated and sun-bleached for lightness. The room was filled to bursting with tiny bric-a-brac and fancy furbelows, each one the late Mrs. Dix's most prized possession. They were all carefully dusted and placed just so on the numerous tables, cupboard and knickknack shelves throughout the parlor.

The pristine perfection of the room was somewhat spoiled, however, by the sick bed near the potbellied stove. Willie Dix lay small and pale against the worn, graying bedsheets. His thin steel-colored hair was damp from the cool cloth that lay across his brow. His wheeled chair sat empty at the foot of the bed like an admonition.

"Morning, Doc Odie." The old man's greeting was rasping and hoarse. "What brings you here on a bright Sunday morning?"

Doc Odie knelt beside the old man's bed. He pulled a large sheepskin bag out of his case and removed his stethoscope. First the doctor adjusted the earpieces upon his head, then he laid the horn-shaped scope against Willie's chest. Doc Odie listened quietly to the raspy breaths, his expression not betraying whatever thoughts might be in his head.

After a moment, he removed the horn and helped Willie to raise himself to a sitting position. "What do you think I'm doing here on a Sunday morning?" the doctor asked him with a smile.

"I've come to get a closer look at that pretty daughter of yours."

Willie smiled feebly. "My Emma is a precious girl, Doc. I don't blame you for trying to impress her, but if you're here counting on making a miracle cure of my old-age affliction, I think you'd have better luck just buying one of them fancy gas buggies."

Doc Odie smiled affectionately as he moved the scope horn along the old man's back listening to the sounds of his heart and lungs. "I'm not sure I agree with that," he told Willie. "I'm more likely to understand how to get you going than one of those noisy automobiles."

Gently, Doc Odie laid Willie back down in the bed. The old man's breath came quickly, as if the exertion of sitting up was overwhelming.

"Your chest is pretty heavy this morning," the doctor said.

Willie waved away the concern. "Ain't nothing that one of my Emma's mustard plasters can't fix."

Doc Odie nodded gravely. Turning to Emma, he gave her a hopeful smile. "Why don't you fix your father one of those plasters he sets such store by."

With a timid smile, Emma hurried to the kitchen.

Doc Odie returned his attention to his patient, his expression serious. "There's not much left of those old lungs, Willie."

The old man nodded. "I'm ready to meet my

maker, Doc," he said. "I ain't gonna be begging for more time here below."

The two men stared silently at each other for a long minute.

"It's going to be rough on your daughter," Doc Odie said quietly.

Willie shook his head. "It'll be the best thing in the world for her. She shoulda never come back here. Folks is not good at forgiving in this town. Always blame the woman, they do. Even when she's little more than a kid, like Emma was."

"It was a long time ago," Odie soothed.

"People got long memories," Willie replied.

The doctor only nodded.

"I never hated a soul in my life, till my Emma took up with that Bateman." Willie glanced toward the kitchen sadly. "You know, Doc, they's just some men in the world that can't be happy without making some fine, decent woman miserable."

"Emma has turned out fine, despite her past," the doctor said.

"Not despite it," Willie corrected. "Because of it. She's a fine woman, and I'm proud of her. She's seen the worst life can dish out, and she's come through it with her soul as her own. Some lucky man, somewhere, someday, is going to be right fortunate to capture her attention."

Doc Odie smiled down at the old man. "I'm sure you're right."

"I know I'm right," Willie said. "But I don't

155

think just being right is going to be enough this time. I think I'm a-going to have to make some plans."

Doc Odie raised one graying eyebrow in question. "What kind of plans are you talking about?"

"I got some money saved up," Willie told him. "I want Emma to have it to start a new life. Doc Odie, you see that she uses it for that."

"Emma's your heir, Willie," Doc Odie answered. "Of course everything you have will go to her."

The old man shook his head. "But she's like to spend it on a fancy funeral and a ticket out of town."

"Perhaps leaving town would be the best."

"Nope, Doc," he said. "It ain't the best. Once you start running from life, well, you just can never run far enough. Emma's got to stay here. She won't never get away from the gossip following her if she don't turn on it and face it down."

The doctor considered the old man's words and nodded slowly in agreement.

"I love that girl, Doc," Willie continued. "I know what she's got to do. But once I'm gone, I don't want her having to do it alone. You've got to help, Doc. I'm counting on you."

"Me?" Doc Odie was incredulous.

"You got to tell her what to do."

"Miss Emma does not generally ask for my counsel."

"She'll accept it just the same when you tell

her it's come from me," he said. "I won't have her wasting her life running from town to town. Or being wasted on some useless ne'er-do-well who can never appreciate her for what she is. She deserves a good marriage, Doc. And a man who'll value her."

"Yes, Willie, I think she does."

The old man smiled. "I want you to see that she gets that man."

"What?"

"You don't fool me, Doc. I know you can get just about anybody to do just about anything when you set your mind to it. I'm counting on you to set your mind to finding my Emma a husband."

Doc Odie cleared his throat nervously. "Anybody you specifically have in mind?" he asked.

Giving the doctor a long look, Willie grinned broadly, showing the missing space of two teeth on the left side. "Well, that Briggs boy that's got the autobuggy shop seems a likely choice."

"Luther Briggs?"

Willie nodded. "He's right sweet on her, I understand."

Doc Odie was surprised at the news. He also found that it didn't sit well with him. "Luther's rather young," the doctor protested.

"He's old enough," Willie said. "Old as my Emma, at least. I think he'd make a decent husband when he takes it to himself to settle."

"Well, perhaps so, but —"

"I think she's more than a bit fond of him too. Else I wouldn't be going that way."

"If they are already interested in each other, I don't see that there is anything that I need to do."

"Interested is one thing, wed is another," Willie stated emphatically. "I want you to see that they get hitched up good and proper. And I'd really like to see you do it before I'm six feet under."

Doc Odie opened his mouth to answer, but the words froze on his lips as Emma reentered the room.

"Here we are, Papa," she said, as she walked in from the kitchen. "This will break up the tightness in your chest in no time."

The hot aromatic poultice was wrapped in thin cotton toweling. The doctor pulled back the bedclothes as Emma carefully laid the plaster on her father's bare chest.

The old man made one painful gasp and tensed up rigidly as the heat blanched his skin. A moment later, Willie lay back with a sigh to allow the home remedy to work its magic.

"Oh, Emma," the old man said gratefully. "You are a good daughter to take such fine care of me."

The young woman didn't answer but only smiled warmly at her father.

"You'll be feeling better in no time," Doc Odie said, for Emma's benefit.

She looked at him quickly, as if testing the honesty in his words. Doc Odie nodded assurance, and she sighed as deeply as if she'd been holding her breath for hours.

"Thank you for coming by, Doc Odie," she said. "Can I fix you a cup of coffee or tea?"

The doctor politely shook his head. "Don't trouble yourself, Miss Emma," he said formally. "I'll be back to check on your father first thing in the morning."

MILLION HOGS IN SINGLE YEAR

Growth Is Steady, Future Bright

Experts at the stockyard report that they will soon reach the point of one million slaughtered per year. Growth in hog production within the country has been steady, and the outlook for the future has been most encouraging indeed. Stockyard and slaughterhouse jobs comprise the largest single industry within the limits of the city, and according to the stockyard's fore-

Chapter Nine

Monday morning, bright and early, Luther Briggs was using the acetylene torch to build a head gasket for Erwin Willers's Packard. Welding was one of those things that Arthel did better and he usually left it up to him. It was noisy and smoky and required strong concentration. But this morning it seemed like a perfect occupation.

His brother had been determined to talk about yesterday's trip to church and dinner with Tulsa May. Normally he would have been glad to share his visit with Arthel. About yesterday, however, Luther didn't have a word to say.

As far as he was concerned, it was one of the longest days he'd ever spent. From the time he'd come to pick her up, he had felt clumsy and tongue-tied and not himself at all. He had been afraid to even look at Tulsa May. Every time he did, the memory of that dream returned. He was ashamed, but he couldn't seem to dispel his imaginings. And after that unbelievable kiss on the porch, he was definitely on shaky ground. So he'd tried to keep his eyes on Rev and Miz Constance. Anybody but the woman he wanted to look at. The woman whose breasts he'd seen through her underclothes.

Just thinking about that made his hands tremble and upset his concentration. So much so that when Luther felt a tap on his shoulder, he jumped as if a shot had been fired.

"Crenshaw wants to see you," Arthel yelled to him over the sound of the welding torch.

Luther nodded and began turning off the spigot that supplied the acetylene to the welding wand. Within seconds, the flame fizzled and died. Luther carefully laid the hot wand across a cool metal surface and removed his goggles. He looked up and tipped his head in greeting at Ross Crenshaw who was standing on the threshold of the front door.

"Morning, Mr. Crenshaw," Luther said. He moved to a small table at the far side of the shop. Throwing his heavy leather gloves on the rickety worktable, he grabbed a worn cotton rag and wiped his hands before stepping forward to accept the older man's handshake.

"Luther." Crenshaw glanced curiously around the shop. "Looks like you've got plenty of work to keep you busy these days."

Luther was very proud of his business. People came all the way from Guthrie to be treated right by a mechanic whom they trusted, but he would never say that to Crenshaw. "We're making a living," he admitted modestly. "Times are clearly getting better, I think."

"It's a miracle if they are," Crenshaw replied in a bit of a huff. Being head of the county's Republican Party, the older man had a disenchantment to maintain.

Luther wiped the sweat from his brow with the rag he held and used the opportunity to smile to himself.

"If we get Wilson for another term, we'll be sure to throw off the last of this little panic."

It was like waving a red flag in front of a bull. Crenshaw immediately took the bait, lambasting the President's domestic policy. "It's war that's on the voters' minds now," he said firmly. "If Wilson gets in again, we are sure to stay neutral and never get a chance at the Kaiser."

"Most folks don't want a chance at the Kaiser," Luther answered quietly. "That's Europe and clearly none of our business."

The older man shook his head. "If we ever hope to be an equal in the world of nations," he said, "we're going to have to make the whole world our business."

Luther refrained from comment. He hated the idea of war, but he hated the Kaiser too. Why couldn't the Europeans take care of their own problems? He didn't have the answer. Crenshaw didn't have it either, he was sure. Maybe there wasn't any answer.

"Politics and business are clearly two subjects that do not mix," Luther said finally. "And I'm enough of a businessman to be more concerned with the latter than the former."

Crenshaw nodded, accepting the truce. "You've always been quite a go-getter," he said.

Luther felt no need to comment on that. "Saw

you in church yesterday," Luther said instead. "Your family's looking well."

"Yes, sir, we're fine. I saw you in church too. I suspect I'm there about every Sunday. We don't get to see much of you, though."

"Maybe that'll change."

Crenshaw nodded. "Rumor is that you're calling on the preacher's daughter."

He raised one dark eyebrow. "Is that the rumor?"

"She's a real kind girl," Crenshaw replied. "Kind and decent, that's what matters in a woman over the long run."

Luther was not ready to discuss the long run with Ross Crenshaw. "So what brings you to the shop today? Are you having trouble with that new Ford of yours?"

He shook his head. "No, no, runs like a sewing machine. The Ford's the best car ever made," he stated baldly. "I know you've always seemed partial to those Billy Durant cars, but I swear that Henry Ford is a national treasure to this country."

"He makes a good car," Luther agreed half-heartedly, not even tempted to get back onto the subject of politics and national treasures.

When the younger man didn't take the bait, Crenshaw reluctantly moved on to the business at hand. "No, what I came to talk to you about, boy, is that Henniger property you've bought on Main Street."

"Oh?"

"Nearly everybody in town is wondering what you're planning to do with it. I thought I'd just ask outright."

Luther smiled. "Well, asking outright is exactly the thing to do, Mr. Crenshaw," he said. "But, truth to tell, I haven't decided what to do with it."

"Oh, come now," Crenshaw said, disbelieving. "You can level with me, boy, I ain't the preacher come calling."

"It's the truth, I'm telling you. And I'd tell the preacher the same. I bought the building because the price was right and I was looking for a warehouse."

"A warehouse?"

Luther shrugged. "I guess I wasn't thinking too clear. It wasn't until after I'd signed the papers that I decided that a warehouse on Main Street just wasn't the thing."

Crenshaw's expression was closed and disapproving. "That story won't wash, boy. Some say you are about the sharpest knife in the drawer. You don't go putting down good money by accident."

Actually, that was exactly what had happened. As soon as Luther heard about the building being for sale, he felt almost compelled to purchase it. He even surprised himself at how adamant he'd been. Once it was his, he wasn't sure why he'd even wanted it.

"The rumor is," Crenshaw continued, "that you're going to open up another beer and billiards joint like the one you own in Lowtown."

Luther wiped his hands on the rag again thoughtfully.

Crenshaw's visage was stern. "I just wanted you to know that the good people of this town will not approve of that."

"Oh?" Luther felt the ire rising inside him. "Which good people are those?"

"I was talking to Fanny Penny just this morning and she is downright worried about what might happen to the businesses downtown if some kind of immoral *joint* were to move in."

Luther's smile was decidedly cool. "Mrs. Penny should spend more time working at the Emporium and less time in idle talk. That probably would have a more positive effect on her business."

Crenshaw shook his head. "I'm not about to be telling Fanny how to run her business."

"But you'd like to tell me how to run mine." Luther's jaw was set tightly and his eyes were narrowed.

The older man opened his hands in a gesture of surrender. "I'm not telling you nothing, Luther. Just giving a bit of fatherly advice."

"And what is that 'fatherly advice'?"

"I know your place down in Lowtown is well run and clean. I've been by there myself a time or two. Not a lot of bad elements hanging around there."

"It's Ruggy's place," Luther pointed out. "I only own an interest in it."

He nodded agreement. "True, but folks here

tolerate it more 'cause it's yours than because it's his."

Luther couldn't argue that. Oklahoma was no more equal in its treatment of the races than anyplace else in the country.

"We all think *that* place is fine. You just leave it there. Don't be thinking to bringing such a place up to Main Street."

His arms folded across his chest, Luther looked distinctly displeased. "We?" he asked. "Who is asking here?"

Crenshaw shrugged. "I guess I am."

"Do you want to buy my building?" Luther deliberately held his temper in check.

"No," Crenshaw replied easily. "I ain't got more than a couple of nickels to rub together with prices being what they are."

"Then if you don't want the building for yourself, what I do with it is strictly my own concern."

"I'm just telling you what I think," Crenshaw said. "I'm telling you what the whole town thinks."

"Well, I thank you for that, but please tell the whole town that I'll be doing what *I* think," Luther answered.

Crenshaw shook his head. "That's what I was afraid of. I was afraid you'd be thick-headed. All the Briggs folks are. You know, boy, thwarting the propriety of the community is what got your father into trouble. And look how you and your brother have paid."

The blood drained from Luther's face and then

came back pounding with bright red fury. But when he spoke his voice was as soft as a whisper and deadly. "Anything that me, my brother, or my father might have owed to this community has been paid in full," he stated flatly. "I think, sir, that you can see yourself out."

Tulsa May was between a rock and a hard place. She had no desire to face the good people of Prattville. But she could not bear to go one more day without visiting the foundations department of the Emporium. And she needed to turn in her latest news story.

With that firmly in mind, she'd donned a cute little brimless straw hat circled by a broad satin rose ribbon that met in the front at a satin button and sprouted two wide curled quills that hung high before her. She headed for town early, hoping that no one else would be stirring. The last thing she wanted was to talk to anyone about anything. Especially when that anything concerned Luther Briggs. Her feelings were so confused and close to the surface, she wished it were fashionable to veil her face. As it was, the whole town could probably see right through her.

The heels of her shiny "peggy" pumps snapped smartly against the brick sidewalks and echoed rather loudly in the light haze of the early spring morning. The spindly new dogwood trees that sat in square little plots along Main Street were heavily budded and close to blooming. The trees had been Cora Sparrow's idea and had been donated by Cimarron Flower Farms. Their fragile beauty was the only thing in Prattville that managed to capture Tulsa May's attention.

She hurried into the office of the *Populist*, hoping to turn in her work and pick up her new assignments without much fuss. Erwin Willers, however, had other plans.

"Well, here she is," he exclaimed loudly as if making an announcement, though the building held only his desk and the huge printing press. "The biggest news story to hit Prattville in weeks! Too bad I can't print it. I swear, Fanny Penny is going to run me out of business."

His light banter was friendly, but disconcerting. Tulsa May found herself blushing furiously and wishing that she hadn't had to come into the office.

"Here's that article on the National Automobile Association's project to create a national map of roads," she said.

Willers nodded and took the copy from her hand. Tulsa May watched him read it. He stood several inches shorter than she, giving her a perfect view of the top of his head where only a small strip of graying brown hair broke the monotony of bright pink bald skin. "Nothing will ever come of the mapping business. There are just too many roads and they change all the time. Besides, why would someone in Oklahoma need to know the roads in Mississippi?"

"Maybe to go for a visit?" Tulsa May suggested.

"Humph," was the man's only reply. "What

about the Romanian prince fighting with the Allies on French soil?"

Tulsa May screwed up her mouth with distaste. "It's not really newsworthy, Mr. Willers. There are plenty of Romanians and Latvians and every other kind of person fighting in that war."

"Not all of them are princes," Willer corrected her. "And not all of them are married to American girls. Human interest, Tulsa May, got to give folks that human interest."

"You'd think that folks would be more interested in the issues involved than the personalities of the combatants."

Willers simply laughed off her comment, but Tulsa May wasn't surprised. In the three years that she'd been writing for the *Populist*, she'd learned that although her work was appreciated and treated fairly, her opinions were almost totally dismissed. Willers hadn't wanted to hire her in the first place.

"A newspaper office is no place for a woman," he had declared adamantly.

Her father had agreed completely.

"Papa, I can't just sit here in this house and let my mind go to waste," she'd argued. "You wanted me to be well read and knowledgeable. Now that I am, should I try to forget it?"

"I never meant for you to go out and work for wages," the reverend had insisted.

Tulsa May hadn't known what to say. But behind her she'd heard Luther Briggs chuckle. "I'm surprised at you, Rev. Never thought you were one to have a person hide her light under a bushel."

It had been Luther who had convinced her father, and it had been Luther who stood at her side when she'd convinced Erwin Willers. But it was her own work, her own words that kept her at the job all this time. Maybe she could never win Mr. Willers over to her way of thinking, but her writing went straight in the paper just as she wrote it.

"I want that Romanian prince by tomorrow," Willers told her firmly. "Come on, I know you can do it. Just pretend he's the boy next door and your heart will pour out all over the page."

Tulsa May sniffed, but nodded. "All right, but if I do that, I want a whole column on the Secretary of Interior's ceremony to award the Sioux tribesmen full citizenship."

"Done," Willers agreed. "And if you have time write me a filler on the Anti–Horse Thief Association Picnic at Carrier last weekend."

"But I didn't attend," Tulsa May protested.

Willers shrugged. "I'm sure it was a great success, food, games, music. Just give me something. Nobody from Carrier reads this paper anyway."

Assignments in hand, Tulsa May left the *Populist* office for her other errand. Like a prisoner walking the scaffold, she made her way to the Emporium. Her mind free of picnics and Romanian princes, she could think only of the one true basic necessity of feminine existence, a foundation garment.

She had agonized over the problem of her bodice. She never wanted to be seen "jiggling" again, and when she'd finally decided on a solution, it had seemed so simple. Having never been particularly fashionable, she would now deliberately go out of fashion and into modesty by wearing an old-fashioned corset. If only no one were to suspect either her errand or its cause.

The nearly deserted streets raised her hopes, but they were to be dashed. Glancing through the glass at the Emporium, she saw that the place was already full of people. Momentarily, cowardice reigned, and she thought about turning for home. But she admonished herself for her foolishness. She expected the town to gossip about her. Her plan with Luther actually depended upon it. She did not, however, relish an audience.

Quietly, she let herself in through the front door, sighing under her breath at the unseemly loud clang of the shop's bell overhead. Every customer in the store looked up. And every one of them stared at her.

Fanny Penny stood with Amelia Puser. Priscilla Maitland was listening to Opal Crenshaw and Beulah Bowman. Grace Panek was being filled in by Bessie Willers. And Lily Auslander was whispering to Myra Avery. The silence in the room was very nearly deafening.

"Good morning," Tulsa May greeted the women with exaggerated politeness. She couldn't quite keep the nervous tremor out of her voice or the blush out of her cheeks. With deliberate

171

bravado and determined efficiency, she began removing her gloves as if absolutely nothing about the morning was even the slightest bit unusual.

A guilty murmur of welcomes and smiles were given. It was clear that Tulsa May Bruder had been the subject of speculation and conjecture, and her sudden appearance had embarrassed them all. Of course, most of all, it had embarrassed her.

Maybelle Penny, by nature less guilt-burdened than any other lady in town, quickly moved to Tulsa May's side.

"I'm so glad you've come in this morning," she said with giggling sincerity. "I've been just dying to talk with you."

"Oh, really," Tulsa May said in a bland tone as she neatly deposited her gloves in her handbag. "Whatever about?'

"Luther Briggs, of course."

Maybelle's smile was guileless and her laugh was positively trilling. "So, is it really true that you are keeping company with Pratt County's most handsome heartthrob?" The pretty young woman's question burst out as if she couldn't hold her curiosity in check for another moment.

Tulsa May looked up at the women around her. Instantly, the store's customers all turned to other concerns. They began busily surveying whatever goods were put before them, attempting to appear unconcerned about young Maybelle's question. Tulsa May, however, was not fooled. The room was totally quiet as each woman strained to hear what answer she might give.

"We're only . . . I mean we're just . . ."

"Courting?" Maybelle finished for her. Tulsa May wanted vehemently to deny it. But what was the purpose of Luther's efforts to send the gossips off on the wrong trail if she were to come to town and nullify everything he'd done? She could not, however, manage to actually say aloud that Luther Briggs was courting Tulsa May Bruder. She stood silently wishing she'd never allowed Luther to talk her into such a foolish adventure.

When Tulsa May said nothing to contradict her, Maybelle squealed delightedly in a girlish fashion that Tulsa May found somewhat irksome. "That's what Arthel told me, but I couldn't believe it. You and Luther Briggs! It is just completely amazing."

Tulsa May's blush darkened, and young Maybelle became aware of the meaning of her words. She clamped a hand over her mouth in horror and then began stuttering and stammering through an apology.

"I found it a little difficult to believe myself," she said, giving Maybelle a warm, sisterly hug and a forgiving smile. "My mother also says that there is no making sense of folks and I suppose in this instance she's right."

Reaching out to take Maybelle's arm, Tulsa May casually began to lead her to the back of the store, away from prying eyes and listening ears. "It *is* a little surprising when a long-term friendship takes a sudden unexpected turn."

Maybelle looked relieved to have her careless words overlooked. Gratefully, she dropped the subject of romance at least for the moment.

"Yes, I know exactly what you mean," she told Tulsa May.

"You and Arthel?"

Tulsa May's question obviously hit home as Maybelle's cheeks flushed bright red and her chin came up defiantly.

"Me and Chief Buffalo Brain?" She managed a very high-handed and superior scoff. "There is certainly nothing between us."

"That's what I meant," Tulsa May said easily. "You were such good friends and inseparable as children, now you seem barely able to tolerate the other's presence."

"Yes, well . . ." Maybelle seemed ill at ease now and eager to change the subject. "Are you looking for a new hat? I swear you wear the sweetest hats in town."

Remembering the purpose of her errand, Tulsa May was, once more, discomfitted. She hated to talk with Maybelle, but discussing her problem with Mrs. Penny would be infinitely more humiliating.

"Actually, no," she said quietly, looking back to assure herself that she was no longer within hearing distance of the other women. "I need to purchase a new foundation garment."

"Oh, certainly," Maybelle answered in her shop-girl voice. "If you would step over to this counter."

She led Tulsa May to the far side of the room where discreet cupboards and drawers contained the latest in ladies' undermuslins and lingerie. "Would you like something prettily trimmed?" she asked sweetly. "Or maybe a bright color? Copenhagen-blue is all the rage."

Maybelle lined her wares attractively along the counter so that each could be seen and compared with the others. Tulsa May looked down in dismay at the collection of Grecian Girdles and Coutil corsets. She glanced guiltily behind her. "I was hoping for a different style."

"A different style?" Maybelle looked at her curiously. The young girl gazed down at the wide variety she had set out for display. "We have front lacers," she said, indicating the garments in question. "And back lacers with front hooks." She pointed those out too. "We've got these with elastic webbing. They are perfect for sports. Or you can purchase these with steel boning for formal occasions." Maybelle smiled pleasantly at her customer. "We've nearly every type of ribbing or girdle you could possibly want."

Barely nodding, Tulsa May swallowed nervously. Her voice was only slightly above a whisper. "I would prefer something a little more . . . ah . . . well . . . something old-fashioned."

"Old-fashioned?" Maybelle raised her eyebrows curiously. "Old-fashioned in what way?"

Tulsa May's expression would have made a casual onlooker think that she had just robbed a bank. "Do you have something that comes up high?"

"High?" Maybelle's brow furrowed as she gazed at Tulsa May's midriff. "How high?"

Her face brightly flushed now, Tulsa May glanced around nervously again before placing her hand at the level of her collarbone. "About this high," she said.

Maybelle's eyes widened momentarily. Her mouth formed a little O, then she too guiltily looked around.

The other women were busily dissecting yesterday's much-mentioned and speculated-about kiss on the preacher's own porch step. Her arrival at the Emporium didn't slow down the gossip in the least, only brought the volume down to a whisper.

Highly involved in their own controversies, none suspected that two near criminals were planning untold social misdeeds at the ladies' under-garment counter. Assured that no one was looking in their direction, Maybelle put a warning finger to her lips and then indicated that her cohort in crime should follow.

Nervously, and feeling very much like a felon, Tulsa May trailed Maybelle to the back of the store. Surreptitiously, they slipped behind the thick violet drapery that separated the public part of the store from the "employees only" section. Tulsa May had to hurry to keep up with Maybelle, who wove in and out through the narrow shelves in the dimly lit storage area. It was clean and orderly, but there was a faint odor of mustiness about the place. Tulsa May had never been back there before, and she had no desire to do so again.

She was about to tell Maybelle she'd changed her mind when the girl finally stopped. Maybelle bent down to the very bottom shelf to retrieve a box that seemed to have been hidden behind another.

"Mother would have a conniption if she knew these were here," she confessed to Tulsa May. "She expressly forbade me to order any."

Tulsa May's eyes widened in surprise. "You bought something for the store without your mother's permission?"

The deed was apparently so common, Maybelle didn't even bother to respond.

"Mama just doesn't understand. Things were different in her day, not at all like now. In her day women wanted big bust lines and tried to improve upon nature, I can't imagine why. Now she thinks that altering the bosom in any way is somehow indecent," Maybelle continued. "But I swear these are the height of decency to me."

"Maybelle, what are you talking about?" Tulsa May asked, clearly confused.

The younger woman looked down at the box she held hesitantly and then looked up at Tulsa May. "Are you looking for an old-fashioned garment that . . . well . . . that keeps you from feeling quite so exposed?"

Tulsa May blushed vividly, but nodded.

Maybelle sighed with relief. "I've tried to explain to Mama," she said. "But she just will not understand. She constantly tells me how *lucky* we modern women are not to be bound up in those awful corsets of her day." Maybelle's tone of voice was a waspish and exaggerated imitation of her mother. "We are so fortunate, Mama thinks, that the new fashions only corset the lower body. It is so *healthy* to have one's natural bosom unconfined." Maybelle shook her head, clearly not in agreement. "I don't consider having my bump-lumps bobbing as I walk down the street any advantage at all."

Tulsa May's mouth dropped open in wonder. "You too?" Her relief was obvious. "I thought I was the only one."

"Well, you're not."

"It's just so . . ." Tulsa May began tentatively. "Well, it's just so embarrassing."

"Mama says it's my own fault," Maybelle confided. "She says if I'd just move more slowly and with more dignity, I wouldn't jiggle."

"I try that myself," Tulsa May said. "I am always walking at half the pace I want, and I try to avoid any abrupt moves or steps."

Maybelle was nodding.

"But sometimes," Tulsa May finished, "sometimes, you just have to hurry."

"That's right," Maybelle said. "I feel exactly the same way. And it's not just us, apparently," Maybelle told her proudly as she removed the lid from the secret undergarment box. "There are enough women like us that they've come up

178

with a whole new idea in corsets."

Tulsa May stared in awe as Maybelle brought out a very stiff-looking type of camisole. Taking the material in her hands, Tulsa May examined it. The garment was made of heavy white cambric and eyelet embroidery and boned with elastic stays. A series of tiny metal hooks were used for the closure.

"It works like a corset for the bosom," Maybelle explained. "Only better. See how roomy it is," she said, showing Tulsa May the contoured front bodice. "It gives you the security of a full corset, with the comfort and health of your natural un-restricted bosom."

Tulsa May's eyes were as big as saucers. "Oh, Maybelle, it looks wonderful."

"It *is* wonderful," the younger girl admitted. "I've been secretly wearing one myself since last summer. It is absolutely the latest thing, and I don't care what Mama says, when women find out about these things, they are all going to wear them."

"I certainly am," Tulsa May stated flatly. "What are they called?"

Maybelle shrugged. "Some of the order catalogs call them bust corsettes. But the modistes have given them a much more elegant French-sounding name."

"What is that?"

"They call them brassieres."

"Brassieres," Tulsa May repeated in a reverent whisper.

CITY MAY LAND
CARNEGIE LIBRARY

City Council Promises Monies

The securing of a Carnegie Library is in sight for the city of Prattville after several years of effort on the part of local workers, including Mr. and Mrs. J. E. Sparrow and the Reverend Philemon Bruder. At the last meeting of the city council, members promised to set aside the sum of $1,500 for the maintenance of the library during the first year of operation, as stipulated by the Andrew Carnegie Foundation of

Chapter Ten

Luther Briggs found himself trying to avoid Tulsa May. He knew this was foolish since the sooner the two made enough gossip to no longer be interesting, the sooner they could begin planning a parting of the ways. The whole plan had made perfect sense when he'd thought of it. Once the fellows in town began to see Tulsa May in a new light, why she'd be able to pick and choose. A woman like his Tulsy should never have to settle for someone like Doc Odie.

But somehow the situation seemed to have spun out of control. Even thinking about her distracted him. Her nearness disturbed him. And, damnit, he cursed himself, his growing desire for her was downright disconcerting. His imposed celibacy, he assured himself, was the real reason behind his dear friend's startling new appeal. But, the idea of slipping into old ways with Emma or some other sweet young thing was somehow not very tempting.

Luther decided that he needed a new approach, a way to make gossip without being alone with her. It should have been easy, he thought. Young unmarried couples were under constant scrutiny. However, Luther found that was not enough.

Even though Reverend and Mrs. Bruder might be sitting in the parlor, just inches from the porch window, Luther and Tulsa May were outside on the porch. And Luther was very knowledgeable about the ways a young couple could spark and spoon undetected right under the parents' noses.

This was the problem on his mind as Luther pulled his shiny black Model A-2 Commercial to a stop in front of Penny's Grocery and Market. He and Arthel were building a refrigerated cold box for the grocer. Arthel had arrived before dawn to start the building, while Luther had stayed behind to load up the truck and drive over with the piping.

The grocery building, looking slightly out of place against the bright brick sidewalks, was Penny's original store. Now, even though the bulk of his business was next door where his wife and daughter ran the Emporium, the Grocery and Market was still Mr. Penny's most beloved concern.

"Morning," Luther called as he stepped through the door, careful to shut the screen behind him. The floor was strewn with baskets and crates displaying produce for sale. He helped himself to an apple from the bin, briefly rubbing it against the leg of his trousers before taking a bite. The taste was a bit mealy, but it was late in the season. The spring fruits and vegetables were just beginning to come in, so there was plenty of room to walk around. During the summer, the store was so full, it was hard to walk inside. Every

182

farmer's wife in a ten-mile radius sold the excess of her garden at Penny's. He was considered the fairest grocer around and especially kindly toward the ladies.

"Good morning, Luther," the older man called out over the sound of hammering. Titus Penny was nearing forty and gray at his temples, with a fine streak of silver in his waxy moustache. "That brother of yours has been working up a storm since daybreak," he told Luther proudly. "I swear that young man is going to make something of himself in this world."

Luther nodded in agreement. "Arthel's not shy about hard work. And he's got a good head on his shoulders."

"I guess your family just comes by it naturally. And if this cold box he's building works as well as you think it will, well, it just might mean a whole new line of work for you."

Luther laughed. "No, sir," he said. "The last thing I need is *another* line of work."

His laughter was contagious and the grocer jovially joined in.

"Let's at least have a look at our new marvel of modern technology," Luther suggested.

The two men walked to the far back of the building into the area formerly used for storage. The "box" that Arthel was building covered a quarter of the storeroom. Right now it looked like two boxes, one about a foot smaller in every respect than the other. Arthel was so engrossed in getting the perfect fit on the corner he was working on, he didn't even hear the two men enter.

"Your brother's here," Penny called out to him.

Arthel looked up from his position on the floor. "About time," he said with a broad smile and feigned irritation. "I was just beginning to think I was going to have to figure out how to put this contraption together by myself."

"Did you actually expect help with the carpentry from me?" Luther shrugged in a grand gesture of helplessness. "You know how often I hit my thumb with the hammer."

"Pipe delivery is your specialty, I suppose?" he said.

Luther gestured toward the back door. "I'll bring the truck down the alley and unload them right back here."

"Good idea," Arthel agreed.

The design of the cold box was not Luther's idea. For years, double-walled boxes with ice had kept perishables cold. And for the past few years refrigerant pumped through panels by a small motor had been widely tested. Luther, however, had decided to use a combination of both methods. The cold box at Penny's Grocery would easily be able to store fresh meat, and milk could keep inside for over a week, while eggs would be edible for at least a month.

"So, the wood fitting's done," Arthel told Luther as he brought the last of the thin copper tubing in from the truck. "What do you need me to do now?"

"Nothing much," Luther answered with a deceptive grin. "I just need you to bend some pipe."

"Sounds easy enough," Arthel said.

Of course, it wasn't all that easy. Luther's plan involved filling the empty insulating space between the inner and outer walls of the cold box with coils of thin copper piping. A naturally supercooled liquid would be pumped through the pipes, creating a very cold space that would cool the interior box. For the best results, Luther wanted the copper pipes coiled tightly and close together. But if the coils were too tight or had any kinks, the flow of the refrigerant might be cut off completely, or at the least the motor on the pump would be overworked.

Arthel set up the welding torch outside the back door to solder the tubing together. Occasionally, Luther spelled him in twisting the coils.

By noon the coils were in place and hooked up to the pump. The two young men were shirtless and sweaty as they set the inner box within the mesh of tubing. Arthel hammered on the end pieces as Luther stood back and watched.

"I sure hope the dang thing works," Luther said.

"It will," Arthel said confidently.

"The refrigerant should be arriving in a day or two. Then all we have to do is fill up the pipes and start it pumping through."

Titus Penny came back into the storage area. "It looks wonderful! It's so large."

"It ought to hold just about everything you can need," Luther told him with only the slightest hint of boast in his voice. "As soon as those chemical tanks arrive from Oklahoma City, I'll come back to get it started."

Penny slapped Luther companionably on the back. "This is really something. I swear, Luther, you ought to open up a refrigeration shop in that building you've bought across the street. It would be a great new business for the town."

Luther's smile dimmed, but only slightly. "I haven't decided what I'm doing with that building yet. As soon as I know, I'm sure everyone in town will too."

In another quarter of an hour, the two young men had loaded up their scraps and tools and retrieved their shirts. Arthel had jumped into the driver's seat.

"You know what I'd like to do?" Luther said. "I'd like to take the afternoon off and just lie down by the water at Frogeye Creek."

"Sounds good to me," Arthel agreed. As he reached the end of the alleyway, he turned out into the street and then honked his horn loudly.

Luther sat up in the passenger's seat. Tulsa May, dressed primly in a dark green walking skirt, had just emerged from the newspaper office.

"What's the latest news?" Arthel called out to her. He'd stopped the truck in the middle of the street and Tulsa May was obliged to walk over to talk to them.

"Oh, the world just carries on as usual," she answered as she stepped up to the door on Arthel's side. She glanced into the interior, and smiled at Luther. "The picture show at Guthrie is Mary Pickford in *The Foundling*. The state house voted twenty-eight thousand dollars for bridge contracts, and Victrola Company's new musical record for May is 'O Sole Mio,' by Enrico Caruso."

"Guess I don't need to buy a paper then," Arthel said. "I got the best of it straight from the horse's mouth."

Tulsa May put her hands on her hips in feigned fury. "I do not, sir, consider myself a horse."

"Youngsters!" Luther complained with a long-suffering sigh. "Arthel, you should have said that you got it from the *prettiest* mouth on the paper."

Tulsa May actually blushed at his compliment, and Luther felt stupid for having embarrassed her.

"We're heading out to Frogeye Creek," Arthel said to her. "Why don't you run home and pack us up a good home-cooked picnic and come along?"

Tulsa May's eyes widened and her cheeks paled. She looked past Arthel to see that Luther appeared very uncomfortable. "I . . . ah, no . . . I don't think —"

"It sounds good to me," Luther said quickly. "We were planning to go out there and I'm sure Miz Constance has a little something in her kitchen to stave off our hunger."

"Well —"

"Oh, come on, Tulsa May," Arthel said. "Luther may get to see you all the time, but I sure don't."

Recovering herself, Tulsa May smiled deviously. "I can't really go out to the creek with two young men. I'll only come on one condition."

"What?"

Frogeye Creek was a lazy-flowing sweet-water tributary that twisted in and around three sides of the town of Prattville before joining with the Cimarron River. North of town, down a dusty red dirt road and back in a pretty wooded glade, the creek made a small falls, not more than four feet high. The creek then pooled into its widest, laziest point. This area, a familiar spot to all locals, was a summer swimming hole as well as the usual site of church baptisms.

On this particular afternoon, two automobiles, one shiny commercial vehicle loaded up in the back and one old but well-loved wine-colored one, were parked in the shade of the trees. Closer to the water a heavily laden picnic cloth was spread across the grass.

Maybelle Penny, dressed as daintily as the first flower of spring, held a pretty pink parasol above her head to protect her from the few rays of sun that shone through the heavily leafed branches.

The other young lady was also protected, but she had worn the wide-brimmed straw hat more to hide her hair than to shield her complexion.

The gentlemen lounged casually nearby. Luther Briggs was amused. His brother was sullen.

"I swear, Tulsa May." Maybelle giggled. "Your

mother does make the sweetest cinnamon bread I've ever tasted. Do you want another piece, Luther?"

Arthel looked up from his plate, displeased, his tone as cold as winter. "If he wanted another piece, Maybelle," Arthel said, "he would take one."

Maybelle glared haughtily at the younger man. "Oh, excuse me, Sitting Bull. I forgot that good manners are a white man's custom."

Arthel's cheeks swelled up like a toad ready to spit.

Tulsa May glanced over at Luther, who loudly cleared his throat. She suspected he was trying to hold back a laugh.

Originally, Arthel had flatly refused to accompany Maybelle on the picnic.

"Do you want to ruin my day?" he'd asked Tulsa May when she'd suggested the idea.

"Maybelle would be perfect," Tulsa May insisted. "I can chaperone her and she can chaperone me. I'm not going without her."

Maybelle had not been much easier to convince.

"I don't want anybody to see me with *him*," she'd said fussily.

"There won't be a soul there besides us," Tulsa May assured her. "Besides, I need you there. My parents would never let me go alone on a picnic with Luther Briggs."

Putting one over on the adults was what had finally convinced Maybelle, and the young lady was determined to enjoy herself.

189

She was not the only one with qualms about the outing. Luther found that if he kept his gaze squarely on Tulsa May's familiar freckled face and gap-toothed grin, she was his same Tulsy as always. Unfortunately, his eyes seemed to be defying good sense, and repeatedly through the afternoon, his glance slid down to the discreetly covered bosom he had imagined so vividly in his dreams.

Tulsa May suffered her own demons. She feared that her true feelings must be shining in her eyes. For her part, she tried not to meet Luther's gaze at all. This ran directly at cross-purposes to Luther's own plans.

The only real distraction for the two was Arthel and Maybelle's bickering.

"Let's put up the swing," Luther suggested finally. It was something sure to keep them gainfully occupied for a good half hour with little chance of private conversation.

Arthel agreed without enthusiasm, but set out to fetch the rope from the truck while Luther walked with one lady on each arm along the bank of the stream to search for the perfect tree. Tulsa May spotted a huge red oak, nearly as wide around as a kitchen table, which stood strong and sturdy near the top of the falls.

"We could hang it from that long branch there," she said, indicating a thick, bark-covered limb high above them.

Luther looked skeptical. "It won't be easy to climb up there."

"We don't want the *easiest* swing," Maybelle assured him. "We want the best."

He studied the branches above him. "Oaks are the hardest trees to climb," he mused aloud. "And the lowest place for a foothold is nearly eight feet up."

Tulsa May was about to resume the search when Maybelle piped up.

"Oh, but you gentlemen can do that." Maybelle gave him a wide-eyed, winsome smile that she used frequently to get her way. "And this one is perfect. We'll be able to swing right out over the falls."

"It might be a little dangerous," Luther said.

"I love dangerous!" Maybelle proclaimed. No one contradicted her. Arthel just looked disgusted.

It was hard to believe that Arthel Briggs and Maybelle Penny had once been seen together as commonly as ham and beans. Before Maybelle was old enough for the schoolroom, she had taken to the young boy and had followed him like a shadow for years. For his part, Arthel had enjoyed the worship of the pretty little pest. And ultimately, they had become companions.

Yet two summers previously, their friendship ended abruptly. The two had been hiding out in the big pecan tree that overlooked the pretty little white house known as Briggs Cottage. It was their special place, their secret place.

Arthel was whittling a broken twig as the fourteen-year old Maybelle sat cross-legged on a large branch. Barefooted and scrape-kneed, Maybelle was daydreaming of her future and the empty cottage below them. Built by Arthel's father, the cottage was a replica of the Briggs Mansion downtown. To her young mind, the empty cottage built for a bride was exquisitely lovely. The expression on her face was far away, soft and wistful.

"What in the world are you thinking about?" Arthel had asked her. "You look sort of dispeptic."

"I was thinking about us. Arthel, that little cottage is so romantic, don't you think?"

He glanced down at the weathered small white building and shrugged. "Yeah, I guess so."

Maybelle sighed. "I think that's where we ought to honeymoon."

He stopped his whittling. "Honeymoon?"

Maybelle smiled. "Well, I know it's more fashionable to go down to Turner Falls or the Eureka Springs. But don't you think it would be romantic, just the two of us in that sweet little house?"

At sixteen, Arthel was hardly ready to think about marriage. And gazing across a pecan-tree branch at a scraggly, flat-chested fourteen-year-old with grass stains on her skirt was not something to put him in mind of it.

"What makes you think we're going to get married?" he asked. "I don't recall posing the question."

"Well, of course we're going to get married someday," Maybelle replied, somewhat puzzled. "I can't imagine marrying anyone else."

Arthel snorted. "Well, I must have a better

imagination than you."

It was a childish argument that went on for half an hour. In the end, both were unkind, both were cruel.

"You're not even thinking about marrying me, and I'd already decided that I would go against the wishes of my parents to marry you. Do you think Mama and Daddy would *want* me to marry an Indian?"

Part of knowing someone very well was knowing the soft spots, easy to injure. Arthel's soft spot was his Indian heritage. And Maybelle's careless, bratty words hit right on target. The half-whittled wood he was working on snapped in two beneath his fingers. Her words had broken the branch as surely as they had severed the friendship.

Arthel dropped to the ground and walked away. Since then he had taken up a course of ignoring Maybelle. A course he continued to follow. Maybelle had also taken up a course. A course of annoying him, calling him anything to get a rise out of him and avoiding being alone with him.

That was until now. "Come on, Luther, this is perfect."

Luther took one quick look at Tulsa May, who shook her shoulders, deferring to him. Maybelle's hands were clasped in a hopeful gesture. All he could do was shake his head.

"I suppose it will be fun to swing right over the falls," he admitted.

"Yea!" Maybelle cheered happily, clapping her

hands gleefully like a child.

By the time Arthel arrived with the length of rope slung over his shoulder and carrying the swing seat, all three of them were waiting hopefully. Luther took the seat, a sanded and shellacked pine plank about four feet long, and leaned it against the side of the tree.

"This looks like a likely tree to us," Luther said.

Arthel glanced upward. "Looks pretty high."

"Let me give you a leg up," he said. "And you shimmy up to that first big branch on the creek side."

"Me! Why do I have to climb the tree?" Arthel protested, his arms folded across his chest stubbornly.

Luther shrugged. "There are times when age has its advantages. This is one of those times."

Arthel raised an eyebrow and appeared chagrined. However, after a quick glance at the ladies, he slipped the coil of rope around his neck to free his arms and stepped into his brother's offered hands. "Up I go, old man, but don't forget I did this for you, if I fall and break my head."

"Your head is far too hard to break," Luther assured him as Arthel climbed higher up to stand on his brother's shoulders. Within moments he had scaled the trunk and had the ends of the rope hanging down toward the ground. To test its strength, he slid off the limb and hung by one dangling rope end and then the other. Neither gave or slipped and the branch barely wiggled with his weight. Satisfied, he let himself down the rope, hand over hand, until he was only a couple of yards from the ground. Then he dropped easily, landing without problem.

"Perfect," Tulsa May congratulated.

Luther patted him on the back.

Maybelle only stuck her nose higher in the air.

When the seat was tied in position, they had Maybelle test it before they were satisfied.

"Okay, who's going to try it first?" Luther asked.

"Oh, of course Maybelle will," Arthel answered quickly. "You know she requires special treatment on every occasion."

Maybelle's cheeks flamed with fury and embarrassment. She *had* expected to be first, but now she no longer could.

"Tulsa May should go first." She gave a superior stare at Arthel. "Age before beauty, of course."

Arthel's eyes narrowed angrily, and Maybelle gasped as she suddenly realized what an unkind thing she had said.

"I didn't mean —"

Tulsa May laughed. "The way I see it, Luther and I have the same advantages over you two youngsters."

Mindful of her skirts, Tulsa May accepted the seat tentatively, as if unsure that she might end up flat on the ground. As her confidence increased, she began to swing slowly.

"Now, Tulsy," Luther complained. "You'll

have these children thinking you *are* positively ancient."

"Just let me try it out a little," she protested. "How do I know this thing won't drop me like a stone in the creek?"

"Did you hear that, Arthel? The woman is questioning our engineering abilities!"

Arthel chuckled. "Believe me, Tulsa May, you are much safer in this swing than you ever could be in that pile-of-junk Buick that you drive."

"Shhh! You mustn't talk that way in front of her."

"Her?" the three others questioned.

"Well, of course she's a 'her'," Tulsa May insisted. "Like a ship or a boat, an automobile is obviously female."

Luther grabbed the ropes and began to swing her higher. "Guess you are right, Tulsy," he said. "Cars are like women. They're so pretty you're willing to spend all your money on them. Then they leave you stranded on some deserted road in the middle of nowhere."

Arthel laughed a bit too heartily.

Maybelle shot him a dirty look.

Tulsa May shook her head. "No woman has ever left *you* stranded on a deserted road."

Luther only gave the swing a strong shove, propelling her out over the falls for the first time.

Tulsa May's squeal dissolved into laughter. She was clearly enjoying the ride and began pumping the swing to new heights.

"Hang on," Luther warned. "If you fly off we'll

have to be fishing you out of the creek."

"Worried about me?"

Luther shook his head. "Don't want to get my new overalls wet."

"Well, then you'd best come and protect me," Tulsa May answered.

With that, Luther took a running grab, and pulling himself up by the ropes, he placed his booted feet on either side of her.

Tulsa May squealed with laughter. It had been years since they had shared a swing, but the motions and rhythm were familiar.

The wind whispered around her face, tugging the loose carrot-colored strands that had escaped from the tight web of pins beneath her straw hat. But for once she didn't worry about her hair.

"This is wonderful!" Tulsa May exclaimed as the two of them floated high above the white rippling water. The clean sweetness of bursting summer buds floated up on the cool breeze.

As they swung back toward land, her body leaned into his. He'd grown much taller since their last tandem swing. Once she could lean back and rest her head against his stomach. She realized that now her head reached only to his thighs. She hastily jerked her head forward, trying to sit up straight, and save her modesty. But the closeness of his body, the top of his muscled legs against her shoulders, could not be ignored. She wet her lips nervously. The gleeful giddiness of a few moments earlier vanished. The warmth of him, the scent of him, seemed to surround her.

Her heart felt as if it were expanding. Her body was quivering.

"My turn, my turn," Maybelle declared petulantly, unable to wait a moment longer.

Tulsa May dropped one of her feet to the dirt to slow herself, grateful for the interruption. Luther dropped off the back of the swing and easily stilled it.

"Fun?" he asked. His vivid blue eyes looked straight into hers.

Tulsa May felt herself blushing. Could he see it? Was it there in her eyes? Actually, she hoped that she just appear flushed from the exertion. "Oh, yes, very much fun. Just like when we were kids."

"Yes," Luther agreed. "Just like when we were kids."

He offered his hand and she jumped out of the swing.

Maybelle almost instantly took over the seat.

"I'm going to swing so high, I'll be able to touch that branch on the far side of the falls," she declared.

Luther and Tulsa May looked skeptical.

"Well, if you're going to get that far," Arthel said. "You are certainly going to need some help."

Grabbing the ropes, Arthel too jumped on to ride tandem.

"Idiot!" Maybelle screeched from her precarious perch. "Get down from there. I don't want you to ride with me."

"Too late," he replied as he pushed them off.

But their position was awkward. The movement of his knees pushed her hands away from her hold on the ropes. She cried out half in fear, half in fury. At last, she managed a more secure position by wrapping her arms around both his legs and the ropes. This pressed her body rather too close to his.

Luther watched the two of them, displeased. "Arthel should have let her swing alone. If she gets in a snit it will be the devil to pay for all of us."

Tulsa May giggled. "Oh, I imagine Arthel can handle her. They are best friends."

"Not anymore."

"They still are," Tulsa May assured him. "You don't stop being best friends just because you start feeling more."

Luther glanced at her quickly and then turned away.

Tulsa May closed her eyes, horrified. She wanted to kick herself, or bite her tongue. She prayed he wasn't reading anything into her comment.

Luther looked back at the young couple. The spoiled Miss Penny was squealing and laughing loudly now, kicking her feet wildly as if she were afraid she might plunge to a watery death. She was clearly, however, not the least bit afraid. And her enthusiastic kicking only succeeded in giving Arthel, her rider, a generous view of her exceptionally lacy pink undermuslins. Arthel's animosity seemed to have disappeared and he was now smiling broadly.

Luther's brow wrinkled in concern. He wondered if he should do something. Arthel and Maybelle were both very young and probably very foolish. When it came to men and women, those two could be a dangerous combination.

"Don't they look just darling together?" Tulsa May said beside him.

"What?"

"Arthel and Maybelle," she answered. "They are the most perfect couple, I think."

"They can't stand each other," he declared emphatically.

"Oh, don't be silly," Tulsa May told him. "They are a match for sure."

A match? Luther wasn't certain. He saw only a couple of rowdy, lawless children flirting with a headlong race away from the straight and narrow.

However, that was not quite the thing to tell a decent young woman like Tulsy, so he simply smiled agreeably and said nothing.

Secretly, he just hoped his brother kept his head, and that young Maybelle's virtue would prove to be more formidable than it currently appeared.

Chapter Eleven

After lunch the ladies had agreed to nap leisurely on the quilt for an hour as the gentlemen headed for the swimming hole.

But once they were alone, it had not been easy to persuade Maybelle to take that nap. "Do you think they are down there stark naked?" she'd asked Tulsa May as she slipped off her boots.

"Don't even think of such a thing," Tulsa May said sharply. Then she firmly closed her eyes, hoping Maybelle would not pursue her improper conversation.

When Luther and Arthel returned, they were damp headed, but their clothes were perfectly dry. Tulsa May tried to forget Maybelle's question.

"You shoulda come and joined us," Arthel said with a grin. "The water was just right."

"I suppose you think it'd be 'just right' for two unmarried females to swim with two unmarried males?" Maybelle answered with a tone of indignant reprimand.

Tulsa May looked at her curiously. "Arthel was only joking."

"Moral turpitude is not something that should be joked about." Maybelle sniffed.

"Especially when one is speaking with a person totally lacking in humor," Arthel replied politely. "But of course, I wasn't talking to you, Maybelle. I try to avoid that at all costs. It's so lowering."

The pretty young woman's cheeks puffed out in fury. "Why . . . why . . ." She fumbled for a stinging reply.

"Now, you two. Don't start another fight." Luther was looking toward the sinking sun, concerned. "It's getting very late. Tulsy, why don't you drive Maybelle home in the Runabout while Arthel and I follow you to make sure that you don't have any trouble."

"What?" Both Arthel and Maybelle sounded put out.

"Don't be silly, Luther," his brother said. "It's really not that late."

"You and Tulsa May have hardly had a minute alone," Maybelle protested. "You must at least ride home together."

Luther stared at the two, amazed. For two people at each other's throats, they were awfully anxious to spend time together. But he wasn't sure it was a good idea. And not just for Maybelle and Arthel.

"If it gets dark, we can't be alone on the road with the ladies," Luther said. "What would their fathers think?"

"Oh phooey, Luther," Maybelle complained. "You talk like an old-maid Sunday school teacher. This is the twentieth century, you know."

The young woman's sudden lack of interest in

propriety did not go unnoticed, but Luther didn't comment.

He glanced at Tulsa May for help, but she kept her thoughts strictly to herself. He considered arguing the case another minute, then gave in. If there was anyone more stubborn than his brother Arthel, it was probably Maybelle Penny.

"Okay," he finally agreed. "But you two are going first. And Tulsy and I will be right behind you."

Although the young couple had been at each other's throats all day, Luther suspected his younger brother would try to linger on some darkened road stealing kisses from the grocer's daughter. And he hoped to prevent that.

"The Runabout is much more likely to break down than the Commercial," Arthel said "We should follow you."

"If the Runabout has trouble, then I'll fix it. Now you two get going before Maybelle's father begins to worry."

He didn't have to ask twice. Luther barely had the Runabout cranked and in gear before the Commercial completely disappeared from view.

"Does Arthel always drive so fast?" Tulsa May asked.

"Not always," Luther answered with a disgusted sigh. Adjusting his goggles, he gently let up on the throttle and the Runabout chugged forward at its very moderate pace.

Beside him, Tulsa May was quiet. Luther wondered what she was thinking. Her profile was fine and rather delicate for a woman who was so strong. Strong? The thought had come to him suddenly but he knew that it was true. That determined chin and tidy little hat couldn't hide the strength that had always drawn him to her. But there were secrets in her eyes. And whatever was on her mind, he knew she would not share. And Luther knew he was to blame.

He was attracted to Tulsa May, he could no longer deny the obvious. But he didn't have to act upon his impulses either, he reminded himself. She was a sweet, loving friend, almost a sister. He hoped that someday she would make some lucky man a wonderful wife. But Luther Briggs was not in the market for marriage, he reminded himself. He had a business to run and a brother to raise and educate. He would wait to marry until the time was right. And now was not the time. Now, women were for fun and foolishness. To Luther marriage was a serious step. He knew firsthand the pain that came from taking marriage vows lightly.

His father had married his mother Cherokee fashion, without real consideration or foresight. His grandmother, Miss Maimie, had been livid, and since there had been no legal ceremony, she'd threatened to withdraw her financial support, coercing Luther Sr. into abandoning his Cherokee marriage and firstborn son and taking to wife Cora, a nice, respectable white woman. Ultimately this house of cards collapsed, Miss Maimie withdrew her support anyway, and two fine women were hurt. Luther, Sr., returned to his Indian wife and Arthel was born. They had eight good years together before they died, but the years they had wasted, the years Luther had lived alone with his mother, were irrevocably lost.

Luther vowed to himself that he would never be so foolish. He'd marry only once, for love alone. But his first responsibility was to Arthel. When he was finished with his schooling and started off in the world, then it would be time for Luther to settle down. But that was a long time off, a very long time. Too long for a woman like Tulsa May to wait. She would have half a dozen children before he'd be ready to head to the altar. No, he couldn't seriously consider marriage to Tulsa May. Not that he thought she'd consider marrying him.

And she was far too fine a woman to trifle with. Momentarily he wondered if anyone ever had. Doc Odie? That was certainly logical, though somehow the thought of Tulsa May cuddling with Doc Odie made him feel slightly ill.

It never happened, he assured himself. And Tulsa May was probably the prude of prudes. Of course, she'd always seemed cheerful and adventuresome, but that was in life. Could she be that way in a man's bed? He shook his head. Impossible. Then the image of her breasts beneath the damp shirtwaist entered his mind.

He glanced over at her and swallowed. The late afternoon was darkening quickly. Was she frightened to be alone with him on a deserted road at night? That was foolish. Tulsa May wasn't afraid of very many things. And she certainly would never be afraid of him.

He wondered what her mother might have told her about dark, deserted roads, unchaperoned rides, and men. He wondered what Miz Constance had to say about men. He had heard the Rev's spiel.

"What a husband and wife do in the privacy of their own bedroom is not to be speculated upon," Reverend Bruder had told him, red faced and plainly embarrassed as they sat alone and uncomfortable in the pastor's study. "When you have need to be fruitful and multiply, God will direct you in the appropriate way."

Luther had nodded solemnly and managed to keep a straight face. Fortunately, his own father had enlightened him several years earlier.

"It looks like the bitch and the hound or the bull and the cow," his father had told him. "But there's more to it than how it looks. People are thinking beasts, Greasy. And thinking beasts can love. Thinking beasts can also be hurt. Treat *every* woman with the respect and tenderness that you would treat *any* woman. And son" — he'd smiled sadly and tousled Luther's hair — "try not to make promises that you won't be able to keep."

That was exactly what he had done. Luther glanced over again at his Tulsy in the seat beside him. This time she smiled back shyly and then turned her eyes to the road before them. He had promised to pretend to court her just long enough to turn the gossip. He meant to keep that promise.

As they passed a small, almost hidden glade at the side of the road, a flash of shiny black metal caught his eye. He began to slow down.

"What is it?"

Luther pulled off to the side of the road about a hundred yards ahead. "It's Arthel and May-belle," he said simply.

"What?"

"If my eyes don't deceive me, that's my A-2 Commercial back in the trees we just passed."

Tulsa May turned in the seat and rose up on her knees to look back behind them. "Do you think they've had car trouble?"

"No," he answered quietly. "I believe they stopped here on purpose."

"Why?" For a moment Tulsa May's expression was puzzled. "Do you think they are . . . I mean, could they . . . it's —"

"They are sparking and spooning," Luther replied as casually as he could.

Tulsa May slipped back down in her seat staring straight ahead. "But, well, I thought they'd be a match eventually, but right now they don't even seem to like each other."

Luther shrugged.

Tulsa May glanced back over her shoulder nervously. "Should we . . . should we . . . do something?"

Luther wondered the same thing, but shook his head. "Not yet. I'll give them a couple of minutes. Then, if they don't head out on their own, I'll go break it up."

"That sounds like a good idea." Tulsa May nervously cleared her throat and became suddenly very concerned with the slant of her hat. Removing the long steel pin, she reset the angle and pinned it again, before adjusting the ribbon and straightening the ties.

The two sat stiffly and silently in the car for several minutes. Luther looked down at his tamed fingers, ostensibly checking for grease under his nails. There was none.

Tulsa May, her hat now readjusted, tucked in her hair, straightened the brooch at her throat, and picked imaginary lint from her brown poplin skirt.

In the distance the setting sun was turning the clouds bright pink, coloring the evening sky. It was beautiful, inspiring, romantic.

"Do young couples regularly do this sort of thing?" she asked finally.

Luther gave her only the most cursory of glances. "Yes, I guess most do. Arthel and Maybelle are a little young."

Tulsa May nodded. It was quiet again.

"Didn't you and Doc Odie — ?" Luther wanted to kick himself as soon as the question was out of his mouth. It was none of his business, and he certainly didn't want to know.

He heard her clear her throat. "He kissed me many times," she answered. "But he would certainly never try anything out alone and unchaperoned like this."

Luther nodded.

"Doc Odie is a gentleman," she said quietly.

"Doc Odie is an idiot," he replied under his breath.

"What?"

"Nothing."

"You said something."

"I said Doc Odie was an idiot."

"Why do you say that?"

"If I had a chance to get you alone out in the country, I'd sure try to kiss you."

Tulsa May stared at him for a moment in disbelief, her face fiery red. Then she shrugged off his words as mere flattery. "Well, you *are* alone out in the country with me!" she said.

He turned toward her, his vivid blue eyes dark with an emotion that she didn't immediately recognize. When she did, she covered her face with her hands in shame and turned away.

"I didn't mean that as it sounded," she assured him quickly. "I was merely making a joke."

Luther no longer cared what she meant. Leaning forward, he laid an arm along the back of the seat behind her and gently pulled her hands from her face.

"This is silly, I —"

"Shhh," Luther whispered as he drew her closer. "It's just a little kiss, Tulsy. Aren't we good enough friends to share just a little kiss?"

Tulsa May's heart was beating like the bass drum at the Fourth of July Parade. He was close. Very close. Too close.

"Luther, I —"

He didn't let her finish. With a tenderness that surprised even himself, Luther brought his mouth to hers. It was the gentlest of kisses. A mere touching of one pair of lips to another. A kiss that might have been considered brotherly. But no brother's heart ever pounded like his.

He could have smiled and pulled away and let it go at that. But he did not. Tulsa May brought her hands to his shoulders. He felt her heart beating against his chest, the softness of her bosom against him, and he opened his mouth over hers.

She was sweet and tender and warm. He allowed his tongue to wander the soft pink territory of her lips. The taste of her was heaven. It was home.

Luther's blood was pumping faster through his veins now, and he tightened his grip around her. She felt so good.

"Oh!"

Her little breathless exclamation as she pulled herself away from him brought Luther to his senses. He looked into her familiar face, surprised. She was *his Tulsy,* orange-haired, freckled, and gap-toothed, still. Yet the word that rushed to his lips as he gazed at her was "beautiful." He left it unuttered.

Glancing away, he laid his right wrist across the top of the steering wheel. She also stared straight ahead. The moment was uncomfortable. Tulsa May needlessly straightened her clothes. He was embarrassed. He had lost a small portion of control. And with Tulsy. He was nearly tempted to whistle. Instead, he stared across the horizon.

"Tulsy, I'm sorry," Luther said, finally. "Honestly, I hope you don't think that I stopped here because I thought . . ." He hesitated. "You know that I have the highest respect for you and —"

"I know." Tulsa May's reply sounded small and distant.

Luther turned toward her again. Her expression was one of abject misery.

"Oh, Tulsy, please don't cry," he said soothingly. "I was wrong to take advantage. But I couldn't stand it if I thought I'd cut you to the quick."

Tulsa May's eyes looked suspiciously watery, but he saw her visibly mustering her courage and blinking hard against the tears. "I'm sorry, Tulsy. I didn't mean to offend."

"Please don't apologize anymore." She was staring down at her hands, which were covered with the beautiful peach taffeta silk gloves that he had given her.

With his eyes focused on the rutted dirt road, he reached a hand across to her and laid it circumspectly upon her own. The touch was tender, reassuring, but also familiar.

"I swear that I will never let that happen again."

"I know." Her answer was a whisper. A long moment passed. Then slowly, tentatively, she took his hand that lay so gently upon her own and brought it up to the side of her face. Gently, she pressed the strong masculine palm against her cheek. She sighed before giving a self-depreciating little laugh. "I know it will never happen again," she said, forcing ironic humor into her tone. "Why on earth do you think I'm about to cry? I'm twenty-four years old, and no one has ever kissed me like that. Not Odie, not anyone. I don't expect that it *will* ever happen again. These tears aren't virtue. They're an old maid's disappointment."

Luther listened to her words as he felt the warmth of her cheek against his hand. She was so soft. Had there ever been a woman so soft? Was all her skin as smooth and silken as the curve of her jaw?

"Tulsy?" It was a quiet question.

Pressing his hand one last time against her face, she pulled away from him. He once again gripped the shiny brass steering wheel; he sat up straighter.

"Tulsy?" It was the same question, though his voice was an octave lower.

"It's getting late. We should go."

His expression didn't change.

"Don't you think you'd better check on Arthel and Maybelle?"

He shrugged. "My little brother is on his own."

She was looking straight ahead. He clasped her chin between his fingers and turned her head to look at her. Her eyes were as bright and shiny as new copper pennies. But he couldn't hold her gaze. She lowered her lashes, unwilling to let him see her heart.

Pulling away, she gave a tense little laugh.

"Don't pay any attention to me. I guess a deserted country road at sunset can turn the head of even your addle-brained best friend."

"Tulsy, do you want to kiss me?"

"I suppose I'm as guilty as half the girls in this town." She tried to make it a joke, but her nervous giggle and the somewhat flustered wave of her hand didn't seem quite steady.

Again, he reached for her. This time, his arm that had stretched so benignly along the seat back slipped down. He grasped her shoulder and pulled her closer. He felt her trembling against him.

"Now, Greasy," she said with a forced cheerfulness that was only a shadow of the real Tulsa May. "You're being as silly as I am."

He scanned her face. Her penny-brown eyes so bright . . . her lightly freckled cheeks, pretty with the pink blush of embarrassment . . . her lips, so soft and warm and sweet . . . and so very close.

"Tulsy," he whispered. "If I want to kiss you and you want to kiss me, the only thing silly would be for us not to do it."

With that he brought his lips down to hers. He heard as well as felt the nervous intake of her breath. "Let's not be silly."

Gently, he opened his mouth over her own for taste. He almost moaned aloud.

"Luther, I —"

"Open your mouth a little, Tulsy."

Carefully, as if he feared she might bolt, he brought his lips against hers once more. With only the slightest pressure he sealed her to him.

She started. "What's that?"

"It's just kissing, Tulsy."

She swallowed nervously. "It's a strange kind of kissing, with our mouths all open like that."

He was only inches away fom her. He could feel the warm sweetness of her breath against his cheek.

"It's the *best* kind of kissing. Not the little-sister kind or the maiden-aunt kind. If we're best friends and going to be kissing, we ought to be doing the best kind."

"I don't know if we really ought —"

She had no opportunity to finish her statement. He hushed her mouth with his own, inhaling whatever protest she might have made into the sweet sensation of the best kind of kissing.

She was skittish and fluttery against him for only a moment. Then Luther felt her relax against him, her arms snaked around his neck to hold him closer. He almost smiled at her unguarded enthusiasm. Reluctantly, they parted.

"I think it *must* be the best kind of kissing," Tulsa May whispered breathlessly against his cheek.

Luther chuckled lightly and pulled her tightly to his chest. He felt the shape of her against him. A tiny thread of memory wove through his concentration. He remembered vividly their dancing embrace. Her body had been pressed against him then, but now somehow her body felt different. But the sensation of her lips trembling

214

against him was too tantalizing to hold his thought a moment longer. He brought his mouth to hers eagerly once more.

Luther meant only to please her. But when he both heard and felt the tiny, luscious moan at the back of her throat, he himself was enticed. Without deliberation, he twisted in the seat to bring her closer. Their kissing became more wild.

Her tidy little straw hat had been knocked askew, its pin missing and its ribbons partially undone. Finally, Luther jerked it from her head and cast it aside. A moment later, his hands were in her thick carrot-colored hair, scattering pins and combs. He suddenly wanted to caress those bright orange-colored curls that he knew embarrassed her and that she kept hidden from the world.

"Luther?" Her voice was breathy. "What are you doing?"

"Tulsy, I love your hair," Luther whispered as he buried his face in it. It smelled fresh and clean with a light scent of gardenia. "It's beautiful," he said as he loosened her braid, allowing huge handfuls of the bright orange silkiness to drift through his fingers and spread across her shoulders. Even in the dim light of dusk her hair seemed to shine from its own inner glow. Luther twisted the long curls in his hands, placing gentle kisses upon them before pulling her almost prone upon him and allowing those shiny curls to cascade down over him.

Her breath was hot in his mouth and his hands

215

were eager. Luther felt his control slipping perilously close to the danger zone. That sweet-smelling hair, that soft, soft skin, that warm, beloved, and ardent body pressed against his own. It was so good. It was so right.

"Oh, Tulsy," he whispered only a moment before he gave her the best type of kiss again.

She sighed deeply. Their embrace was as much emotional as physical. There was something that —

The loud honk of a Buick A-2 Commercial had them jumping from each other as if a bomb had exploded.

As the truck pulled up beside the Runabout, Arthel and Maybelle stared, both wide-eyed in disbelief.

Luther glared at his brother, a look of fury on his face. "We were waiting on you," he snarled.

Tulsa May was frantically attempting to straighten her hair and find her hat.

"Well, we're on our way back to town, so there's no need to *wait* much longer." With a short nod, Arthel slipped the A-2 Commercial in gear and headed down the road.

GORE WOULD RELY
ON MORAL FORCE

The "Blind Orator" Speaks in Philadelphia

Oklahoma Senator Thomas P. Gore spoke last night before the American Academy of

Political and Social Science in Philadelphia. Gore, known as the "blind orator," declared to those present that the United States should rely upon moral, rather than military, force and should dedicate itself to the principles of humanity and the ideals of peace, arbitration, and international justice.

Chapter Twelve

Willie Dix, pale and quiet, lay on the small cot in the front parlor. Doc Odie had stopped in to listen to the harsh rasps in his chest and leave a bottle of paregoric. The doctor removed the profusion of wool blankets that covered him and unbuttoned the shirt of the gray flannel union suit that the old man wore. Placing the cold metal horn of his stethoscope against Willie's chest, he listened expressionlessly to the draw and flow of his breath. Silently Willie let the doctor examine him. But when he saw his daughter leave the room, he spoke.

"Are you working on that scheme I come up with?" He whispered the question.

The doctor looked down at him only momentarily puzzled. "What scheme is that?" he asked, already knowing the answer.

The old man's expression was frank. He knew the doctor had not forgotten. "My Emma is going to need a man to take care of her when I'm gone."

"Hopefully, that won't be too soon," Doc Odie replied in an even professional voice.

"It's going to be soon enough that I best set my house in order. Emma is all I've got and I can't leave her nothing 'cept a memory of me."

The doctor nodded thoughtfully, but didn't reply.

"She's a good, loving woman," he said. "Kind in ways her mother never could be. It'll be a lucky man who's got the sense to look past her mistakes and take her for the woman that she is."

Doc Odie glanced toward the kitchen, where the young lady was making dinner.

"You needn't convince me, Willie," he said quietly. "I've seen how she takes care of you." Gently, he probed the old man's chest with his fingers. "But I don't think your idea about Luther Briggs will work."

"Why not?"

"Luther Briggs is keeping company with Tulsa May Bruder these days." Doc Odie held open Willie's eyelids and examined the white for hints of yellow.

"Humph," Willie replied. "I thought that little carrot-top was your gal."

"Not anymore."

"Yep," Willie said, eyeing the doctor critically. "Seems like I heard you left her a-waiting at the altar."

Doc Odie stopped. The old man's words touched a nerve. "I did not leave her waiting at the altar. I just broke the engagement."

"Splitting hairs," the old man replied, waving away his explanation. A cough from deep inside his chest halted the conversation.

Willie's face became red with the exertion. Doc Odie raised him up to a sitting position and patted his back forcefully. Willie finally recovered his breath.

Doc Odie laid him back down on the bed and the old man rested again on the soft goosedown pillow, his face now almost stark white. His eyes were huge and dark and his hands trembled. He was exhausted, but he would not let the discussion rest.

"So you jilted little carrot-top," he said with some difficulty. "You marrying-shy?"

"No. I'm just good at keeping myself from making a mistake. I thought the Bruder girl would do for a wife."

"But she won't."

The doctor shook his head. "For someone she would, I suppose. But if a man's got to spend his whole life looking at one woman, don't you think it ought to be some woman he likes to look at?"

Willie pondered his words for a moment before nodding sagely. "They say a man sees with his heart as well as his eyes."

Doc Odie rebuttoned the old man's shirt and recovered him with his wool blankets. "I guess one part of my eyesight is better than the other." He stood and began loading the equipment into his bag. "Well, Willie. I suspect you'll be with us a while longer." He glanced up as Emma came through the doorway. Obviously, she'd heard; she looked relieved.

"I thought he was looking better this morning." She looked over toward her father and her affection was evident.

"He does look better," Doc Odie agreed.

Willie managed a hoarse chuckle. "I look better 'cause that gal of mine has got me shaved up slicker than a sinful banker on Saturday night."

"Oh, if I let you have your way," Emma argued good-naturedly, "you'd be wearing a long gray beard like Santa Claus."

Doc Odie picked up his bag and straightened his coat, clearly making ready to leave.

"Would you care for tea, Doctor?" Emma asked graciously. At the end of every visit, she'd asked the same question. He always politely refused and it was on the tip of his tongue to do so today. From the corner of his eye he saw Willie watching him. He couldn't forget the help that he'd promised.

"I'd be very pleased to take a cup of tea with you, Miss Emma," he answered.

The young woman was visibly startled, but quickly recovered herself. "Certainly, let me just put on the water."

As she moved back into the kitchen, Odie patted Willie on the shoulder reassuringly before following her.

"I'll just have a seat right here," he said, indicating one of the plain wooden chairs at the small table. It was recently whitewashed and scrupulously clean.

"Odie, you needn't take your tea in the

221

kitchen!" Emma told him.

"I like kitchens," he answered simply. "Especially this one." He looked around at the cosy, well-scrubbed, well-lit room painted in gleaming white and yellow and decorated with checked gingham curtains.

There were several awkward moments as they waited for the water to boil. But once the tea was brewing in the pot and Emma was seated across from him, the doctor began to relax.

"I've been talking to your father some," he said.

"I know. And I do appreciate it. He gets so lonely with no one but me to visit with. It's very kind of you to take the time."

Doc Odie was somewhat uncomfortable that she thought it was a strain on him.

"I enjoy your father," he corrected her. "He's a very good and wise man. I wish I'd known him when he still had his health."

Emma nodded. "It was too much for him. Me, running away like I did. And then losing Mama. I think he just couldn't manage anymore."

Doc Odie placed an elbow carefully on the table and looked across at Emma. The doctor's tawny brown hair was thinning on top and graying at the sides, but his pale blue eyes were clear and youthful as he spoke calmly and with conviction. "Your father's condition has nothing to do with either you or the loss of his wife. If you had stayed home and married one of the local yokels and your mother had lived to ripe old age, your

222

father would still be dying today."

Emma looked up at him, startled. "You can't know that."

"Know what?" Doc Odie asked her. "That he's dying or that it's not your fault?" He didn't give her time to answer. "We *both* know that he's dying. And I hope you will come to believe that it is not your fault."

Emma looked away, and Doc Odie let the subject drop.

"Willie's been talking about you a good bit." This brought her gaze to his once more. "He's worried about what's to become of you once he's gone."

The young woman shrugged. It was a beautiful gesture, full of pride and courage and determination. "I'll be fine," she said with complete confidence. "I can take care of myself."

Philosophically speaking, Doc Odie would have disagreed that *any* young woman could take care of herself. But Emma seemed stronger than most. She had a way about her that could almost change his mind.

"I understand from your father that you've been seeing Luther Briggs."

Emma nearly choked on her tea. The doctor obligingly patted her on the back.

"I surmise that your father is wrong?"

The young woman hesitated. Clearly this was a very personal question. The kind of question whose answer could set the gossips upon her once more. She looked across the table at Doc Odie wondering if she dared to be truthful. Somehow, she felt that the doctor could be trusted. "Not wrong exactly," Emma admitted, looking him straight in the eye. "Luther and I have certainly been to our share of roadhouse dances and moving pictures in Guthrie, but he has never called at the house. And he won't be."

"Oh," the doctor said very quietly. Immediately he understood the nature of the relationship. A fellow who would sashay a lady around the next town, but not call at her own home was clearly up to no good.

"Your father was hoping that perhaps you and Briggs might have a more serious relationship in the future."

Emma shrugged again. "I hardly can say anything about that."

She held her chin high and proud. The doctor felt a surge of admiration. She was clearly an unusual woman.

"Yes," he agreed thoughtfully. "Men seem to have all the choices in this world. You've heard, I suppose, that he's taken up with Tulsa May Bruder."

She gave a disdainful sniff. "I'm sure he's not serious about that," she said. "Even you couldn't settle for that connection."

"No, not *even* me." The pique in his voice and fire in his eyes held the two staring for a long moment before Emma broke into laughter.

"I apologize, Doctor," she said. "I was letting a sip of green jealousy get the best of my tongue.

I meant no offense."

Doc Odie was surprised to find himself smiling back at her. She had an unusual voice, he thought. There was almost a musical quality to it that was strangely compelling. Beautiful and compelling, it was no wonder that a rich, selfish man like Fremont Bateman would have lied to try to possess her.

"Please don't worry about me, Doc Odie," she told him. "When I say that I can take care of myself, I mean it."

The doctor nodded, not taking his eyes off her. She was strong in heart and soul; somehow, he'd always known that. But here in her bright, clean little kitchen she seemed even more so. Like Willie, he began to think a man would be lucky to win her. Maybe even he . . . but quickly he pushed the thought away. Despite her past, she was more woman than he could ever hope to win. She would want someone young and strong and as fine to look upon as herself. Someone like Luther Briggs. And certainly, if she wanted Luther Briggs, she'd only need to snap her fingers. Doc Odie was sure that no man could resist a woman like Emma Dix.

"This thing is just like magic!" Titus Penny exclaimed as he stood in the middle of the cool box.

"Not quite magic," Luther said with some pride. "Just some innovative engineering."

The refrigerant had arrived on the morning

train and Luther now had it circulating through the pipes in the thick wooden walls, with the result that the inside was now quite chilly.

Titus shook his head. "You have a real gift, son. Not every fellow has got an understanding of machines like you do. You shouldn't be wasting it on those smelly automobiles."

Luther glanced up at him, puzzled. Penny had been a patron and supporter of his shop since the first day Luther had opened. "I don't consider my business a waste."

Titus folded his arms across his chest and spoke to the younger man in a slightly superior, fatherly manner. "It hasn't been a waste. But that was yesterday's news. You've the mind and youth to look toward the future."

"I think the automobile is very much a part of our future."

"Surely, we'll all be in autocars in just a few years. That's a certainty. But those car designers are really working overtime up north. Pretty soon now, they will have perfected the automobile and it won't need any fixing up or changes. What will happen to your fix-it business then? Everybody will just buy themselves a Ford or a Hupmobile for keepers and the bottom will completely drop out of the repair market."

Luther looked skeptical. "From what I see as a mechanic, the automobiles don't appear to be anywhere near perfection."

"But it's coming," Titus insisted. "Mark my words, it's just over the horizon. Why, I read just the other day that they've developed a tire that should last for five thousand miles!" Penny shook his head in disbelief. "That's a full lifetime's worth of travel."

Luther shrugged. "Well, I believe I'll wait and see. There's no reason to give up a profitable business over the possibility of future problems."

"Well, you wouldn't have to give it up completely," Titus agreed quickly. "Maybe you could get your brother to run it while you pursue other interests."

Luther shook his head. "My brother is going to college," he said flatly. "What other interests would I be wanting to pursue?"

Titus grinned broadly and began twisting his grayed moustache. "Well, I was thinking about that building you own across the street."

Luther sighed heavily. "As I've told you and nearly everyone else in this town, I haven't made any plans for that building."

"I know, I know," Titus agreed. "But now I've got a plan for you. I mean for us, that is, for the building."

Luther merely waited for Titus to continue.

"How about . . ." the older man said with great drama, "a big sign across the street reading, 'Briggs–Penny General Engineering.' "

Luther raised an eyebrow but kept his silence.

"Can't you see it?" Titus gestured to the walls of the cool box with pride. "If you can finagle a setup like this, son, then there's no telling what kind of machines you can make."

"And you want me to make them across the street?"

Penny nodded. "You just build whatever you've a mind to, and I'll take care of the rest."

Luther nodded. "That's where the 'Briggs-Penny' comes in."

"I'll bankroll your projects," Titus told him. "And I'll sell whatever gadgets you come up with. If one of your inventions turns out to be a real money-maker, we split it right down the middle."

"Right down the middle?" Luther looked at him assessingly. "What if nothing turns out to be a 'real money-maker'?"

"Oh, fiddle, don't worry about that, son. If you don't ever come up with nothing but this cool box, it's enough to give us both a good stake in the future."

Luther grinned then, with eyes twinkling. "Mr. Penny, you already own half the town, what makes you think you *need* a stake in the future?"

Titus flushed slightly. "There's new things coming along every day. I sure don't want to be left behind." As if suddenly remembering something, Titus stepped out of the cool box and gestured for Luther to follow. From beneath a counter on the far side of the store, the older man pulled out a large white box. "Come take a look at this," he said with a conspiratorial grin.

As Luther stood across from him, Penny opened the box on the counter and laid out several strange white garments before him; his laugh could almost have been considered a giggle.

"My Fanny set up a fit about these things," he confided. "She said they was indecent, but I know an innovation when I see one."

"An innovation?"

Penny nodded proudly. "It's the very latest thing in ladies' undermuslins."

Luther picked up one of the pale, lacy garments with one finger and held it before him curiously. "What is it?"

"It's called a brassiere," Titus told him proudly.

"What does it do?"

Penny chuckled. "Now that's the catch." Leaning toward Luther, he spoke just above a whisper. "The women wear it on their bosom."

Luther held it up, examining it more closely. The narrow band of white cambric was lightly boned at the sides and the bottom, and hooked together at the center, forming two distinct cups that a man could easily imagine being filled with soft female flesh.

"It's a corset?"

"Well," Penny related eagerly, "that's what the manufacturer calls it. But my Fanny says no. She was in a huff for days."

"Why?"

"Well, it seems that the brasssiere not only holds the bosom in, it holds it up." Penny raised his eyebrows meaningfully, but Luther didn't immediately catch on.

"Try to imagine all the old brood mares in this town sticking straight out like they was sixteen-year-old fillies."

Luther's eyes widened at the image. And he looked more respectfully at the garment he held.

"Fanny said we weren't having none of it," Titus continued. "She said it was a scandal in the making. I had to order these secretly and hide them out here in the store."

"You don't agree with your wife?"

Penny shook his head. "These are going to sell like hotcakes. There ain't a woman in this town, or any other, that won't rob her own egg money to look younger."

Luther nodded in agreement as he turned the brassiere in his hands, examining it with awe. "Can't you just see Sunday afternoon in the park?" he said. "There won't be any room for the gentlemen. It will be crammed with bosoms."

Titus couldn't quite imagine that. "Surely they won't wear them on Sunday?"

A flutter of noise at the front of the store startled them. Penny jerked the brassiere out of Luther's hands and buried it in the box with the others, hastily stashing it below the counter.

"Morning, Mrs. Puser," the store owner called out.

Luther turned to nod politely at the undertaker's wife, who was dressed smartly, as always, in the most fashionable of mourning clothes. Her afternoon silk was the darkest summer violet and was traced along the front and back panels with fine black threads. She carried a neat little basket, trimmed in a near matching lavender.

"Good morning, Titus, Luther," she said with

the regal dignity of a reigning queen. "I'm here to purchase your best greens, Titus, and I won't be persuaded to take anything less."

"Yes, ma'am," Titus answered as he hurried around the counter. Glancing back, he spoke once more to Luther. "Just think about what I've said," he told him. "I think we might manage a good business together and you couldn't come up with a better use for that building."

"I'll give it some thought." Luther picked up his hat and turned to the door, but Mrs. Puser waylaid him.

"You are talking about that building you purchased across the street?"

"Yes, ma'am," Luther admitted.

"What exactly are your plans for that place?"

"I don't have any plans as yet, Mrs. Puser. I'm still thinking about it."

"Well, I have a wonderful idea," she said, giving him a slightly flirtatious smile that showed her dimples. "I was talking to Mr. Puser about it just the other day —"

Chapter Thirteen

Tulsa May sat at the hand-polished solid oak type-writer desk in her room, her fingers resting on the shiny black metal keys of the machine. She was trying desperately to concentrate on the article she had planned for the paper. The Coleman Safety Egg Case Company was to open a plant just north of town; they planned to hire a dozen men and would require at least a thousand pounds of straw a year for making strawboard boxes. The new industry was to be a great boon to the community. It was an important story, and Tulsa May was glad that Mr. Willers let her cover it.

A *truly* important story, Tulsa May told herself over and over, but somehow she couldn't quite keep her mind on her writing.

Finally, with a self-disgusted sigh, she rose to her feet and turned away from the sheet of paper on the roller. She'd only typed one sentence.

Her faded blue calico housedress had been her mother's; it was a couple of inches too short and sported a bodice worthy of a woman twice her size. It was typical of her working wardrobe. With no one to see or care what she looked like, she went for comfort. But since the day of the picnic,

Tulsa May had discovered that comfort depended as much on the state of the heart and mind as from the constrictions on the body.

She began pacing the room nervously. Again, in her mind, she relived the events in the Runabout. Again, she could see the sunset, smell the faint masculine odor of soap and axle grease, and feel the hairs rising on her arms in an almost electric reaction.

Luther Briggs had kissed her. Oh, he had kissed her before, as a sister. And he'd kissed her thoroughly that day on the porch. But this time, he had *really* kissed her. There was no crowd to amaze, no plan being carried out, no reason except that he had wanted to. Luther had kissed her as if he were a man and she were a woman. She stopped pacing in mid-revelation and shook her head disdainfully. He *was* a man and she *was* a woman. But surely he — She couldn't finish the thought. Could he really have wanted to kiss her? Had she felt *his* heart pounding, or just echoes of her own?

With some trepidation she walked over to her mirror. With hesitant, gentle strokes she touched her lips. They looked the same as always. There was no indication that a man had kissed her with passion. Or that she had kissed him back. Her lips were soft. Had they felt soft to him? Had they trembled then as they did now with just the memory?

"Oh, Luther, Luther," she whispered softly. Being in his arms was like a dream. But oh, such a wonderful dream. God help her, she didn't want to ever wake up.

Luther's hands had touched her. His lips had touched her. He'd held her tightly in his arms. It was a miracle, certainly. But were miracles real?

She looked herself in the face. It was the same face she'd seen in this mirror for years. Not a face she liked or admired, but one she'd grown accustomed to. When Luther Briggs had looked at her, had he seen this face? When she had looked in his eyes, he had stared at her in a whole new way, as if it had been someone else.

But it had been her, Tulsa May Bruder. And Luther Briggs had known it was her and he'd kissed her. Twice. And he'd told her that he'd wanted to kiss her.

A thrill shot through Tulsa May. All these years she'd never even allowed herself to dream and now . . . now . . . Sighing heavily, Tulsa May dropped down onto the vanity bench. Just thinking about those moments made her knees so weak, she could hardly stand. Could it really happen? Could he really *want* to kiss her?

Gazing into the mirror once more, Tulsa May disdainfully eyed the tiny lace cap that covered her hair. It looked like the type of hat someone's grandmother would wear.

Tulsa May's mother had hated the cap, but Tulsa May had insisted that it kept her hair neat. It *did* keep her hair neat, but in fact, she wore it for a much sadder reason. Even in the privacy of her own room, Tulsa May hated having to look at her hair.

She knew that to be foolishness. God had given her that hair with as much forethought as he'd given her her keen intellect and sunny personality. But it was orange. She'd always thought of it as her cross to bear rather than her crowning glory. She had learned to live with her homely face and her gaping teeth. But she hated to look at her hair.

Luther, however, had not only looked at it, he had run his hands through it. He had kissed it softly, almost reverently.

Slowly, she pulled the little cap from her head and cast it onto the vanity. The tightly pulled, perfectly smooth knot at the back of her head was as tidy as it could be. Determinedly, deliberately, she began removing the pins and unwinding the knot. She was the one young lady in Prattville who'd never spent an extra hour before the mirror, experimenting with the latest fashion coiffures. She had never pored through fashion books, looking for a brand-new style, though perhaps she had lingered a time or two over the occasional hair-dye advertisement in the paper.

The tightly secured orange curls, once released from their confines, swirled about her face and shoulders with about as much dignity as pigs on a picnic. Her hair was everywhere. She grabbed big hanks of it to pull out of her face. Long corkscrews of ugly bright orange fell about her shoulders. She picked one lock up, examining it carefully. It was soft and sweet smelling. Again she remembered the feel of Luther's hands as he ran his fingers through its length. She smiled. But then she looked more closely.

"Carrots," she said aloud. Making a face at herself in the mirror, she spoke sarcastically. "How romantic. Her hair was the color of carrots."

She shook her head firmly and the curls flew in all directions.

Luther had said that he loved her hair. Surely he had lied. "Nobody could love this hair," she said aloud.

She reached for her cap, then hesitated, looking at herself once more in the mirror. Her oval walnut-backed hairbrush with the Russia bristles lay next to the cap. With a sense of purpose, she picked up the brush instead and began pulling it through the waves. At full length, wet or braided, the bright orange mass reached past her waist. When it was dry, the tight curls fell only midway down her back.

She began to count. One hundred strokes was the correct number, Mother had always insisted. But this afternoon she only wanted to feel the bristles against her scalp, see herself with her hair down in broad daylight. And remember the touch of Luther Briggs.

The bright light of the afternoon sun poured through the window and shone on her hair. The bright golds and fiery reds glowed with a beauty that she had never seen before.

Tulsa May ran her fingers through the silky tresses, her expression puzzled. "It's really not so bad," she said aloud.

The words were a surprise to her ears. She almost smiled at her own reflection in the mirror.

A smart knock on the door captured Tulsa May's attention. She hastily came to her feet as if having been caught with her hand in the jelly jar.

"Come in," she said.

Constance Bruder bustled into the room. If she was surprised to see her daughter standing guiltily in the middle of the room, she didn't comment. "Good afternoon, Tulsa May. Why are you doing your hair at this time of day?"

Mrs. Bruder, dressed in an attractive new spring morning gown, sat down with businesslike efficiency on Tulsa May's bed. Her thick, straight hair of chestnut brown was just beginning to be streaked with silver. Currently she wore it in an "upswept." Her new floral crepe dress was Copenhagen-blue printed with tiny pink rosebuds that matched the long sleeves of snowflake net. The bright, girlish colors were typical of Mrs. Bruder's taste. But the excited expression on her face was atypical. "I need to have a word with you, Tulsa May."

Mentally cringing at her mother's tone, Tulsa May tried to hold off the inevitable. "You know this is my working time, Mama," she said. "I've got a story due to Mr. Willers this afternoon."

Mrs. Bruder waved away her concern with a light giggle. "I haven't heard that machine rattle in half an hour. And the peace and quiet is welcome, I do assure you."

"But Mr. Willers —"

"Erwin Willers is the least of my concerns. Tulsa May, do you realize that the whole town is talking about you?"

Blushing, Tulsa May nodded and turned to watch her reflection in the mirror. With a grim expression Tulsa May sat once more on the vanity bench and began to tightly braid the bright orange curls she had so recently admired.

"It doesn't matter what your father preaches to this town about gossip," her mother continued. "People will do it anyway, which is normal and natural, of course, and usually perfectly innocent and . . . well, I've been known to engage in that harmless pastime myself, but it just will not do for folks in this town to be talking about *my* daughter."

"I'm sorry, Mama," Tulsa May said as she wrapped the tightly braided rope of hair into a coil and secured it tightly at the crown of her head. "I'm sure by summer it will all be past."

"What will all be past?"

Tulsa May hesitated. "Why, the speculation about Luther and myself. Once it's over and he stops calling, it will be old news."

Mrs. Bruder regarded her daughter. "Perhaps," she acknowledged with a thoughtful nod. "Then perhaps it won't be over at all. Maybe this gossip will just lead to more."

"More?"

"Perhaps," her mother said, nodding. "Maybe a betrothal."

"A betrothal?"

Constance Bruder was smiling now. "I never really thought that young man would be quite your type. But love is strange."

"Mama, Luther Briggs is not in love with me." Her statement was matter-of-fact, but forceful.

"Then why else is he paying call?" her mother asked, her eyes sparkling with pleasure.

Rising to her feet, Tulsa May thrust her hands into the pockets of her dress. Her first impulse was to begin walking back and forth across the room. But she knew that her mother hated that habit. "Ladies stroll, they do not pace," she always said.

Tulsa May knew that she should tell her mother everything, the whole stupid, silly idea. But somehow, she couldn't manage the confession. She shook her head decisively. "I'm not getting my hopes up and neither should you."

"Oh, fiddle!" Constance exclaimed. "You've got a better chance for that man than anyone in town and you know it."

"Mama —"

"It's certainly true. It would be the luckiest day of that young man's life if he could persuade you to be his helpmate."

"Oh, Mama, don't be ridiculous."

"Ridiculous? Tulsa May, I'll never understand

how you can see the bright side of the darkest cloudy day and still not see the sweetness in your own heart."

When she looked down at her mother's hopeful expression, some of Constance Bruder's own words came to Tulsa May's mind.

"Men don't marry women for the goodness of their hearts."

"Where on earth did you ever get an idea like that?"

"You told me."

"What? Never."

But she had. Tulsa May clearly repeated one of her mother's favorite adages. "Women are easily an object of pity, Tulsa May. Better to have the whole world mad enough to spit than one dear soul to feel sorry for you."

Mrs. Bruder had the good grace to blush. "Now, Tulsa May," she said with absolute conviction. "You know I would never have said a thing in the world to hurt your feelings."

She shook her head. "Mama, I know that you've always loved me. But I also know that you've worried. I'm not pretty enough to make a good marriage, and you're worried about my future. It's understandable."

"Why, Tulsa May, where do you come up with this foolishness? You are as sweet and charming a girl as any Mama could want. And any man who can't see that is not man enough to deserve you anyway."

Tulsa May sat down on the bed beside her

mother and hugged her close. "Yes, Mama," she answered with a long-suffering sigh. "You are right as always. Odie Foote didn't deserve me."

"Doc Odie?" Constance sniffed. "I knew from the first that he wasn't the one for you."

The fact that her mother and Odie had been like two peas in a pod seemed to have slipped Constance's mind. "He just wasn't the one for you," she said again.

"And neither is Luther Briggs."

Mrs. Bruder wagged a finger at her daughter in disagreement. "Now, I wouldn't be so sure about that."

Feeling a lecture coming on, Tulsa May took her mother's hand into her own. "I'm a nice person, or at least I try to be. And I'm smart, I know that. I'm just as bright as anybody in this town, including Papa and Doc Odie. But I know that I'm not a pretty girl, Mama. That's all right. I'm used to myself, and I don't mind. But I *am* plain, Mama. And men don't want a woman that's plain."

Constance Bruder shook her head. "You make plainness sound like a fate worse than death."

"It is a kind of death," Tulsa May answered. "It's a social death. I remember once Miss Maimie told me that 'a plain woman rarely rises above the bottom of life's heap.' " Tulsa May gave her mother a humorless grin.

"Why, that old biddy," she said "How dare she talk to you that way? It makes me so mad I can't hardly see straight." Mrs. Bruder was red-faced. Her indignation was a sweet sight for Tulsa May to see.

"What other nonsense did that old woman tell you?"

Tulsa May shook her head for a moment as she thought back. "She said I am the *worst* kind of plain woman."

"The worst kind?" Constance pursed her lips in disapproval. "What on earth did she mean by that?"

"The worst kind are the ones that tend to forget how homely they really are. They just go on with life, forgetting their place. Expecting to have the kind of life other women take for granted. Pretty soon, the worst kind of plain woman is making a fool of herself over some man. Thinking that he cares when what he really feels is pity."

"Pity! That's the silliest thing I ever —" She stopped abruptly. "Is that what you think about Luther? Do you think he's calling on you out of pity?"

"Luther Briggs is my friend," Tulsa May answered, her face flushing. "He has been since we were children."

"Yes, he has been," her mother agreed. "But men don't go calling on women they consider just friends."

"Mama, he's just —"

"Has he kissed you?"

"What?"

"I asked if Luther has kissed you."

"Mama that's not —"

"I know it's not any of my business. And I also know from your reaction that he *has*. He doesn't sound like a friend to me."

"Friends kiss," Tulsa May insisted.

Mrs. Bruder shook her head. "Friends hug when they are glad to see you. They give you a peck on the cheek when the news is good and they lend a shoulder to cry on when the news is bad. But they never kiss."

Tulsa May stood and turned away from her mother. She felt strange and jumpy and all confused inside. She walked over to the mirror in the corner of her room. Standing there, she looked at the obsessive neatness of her hair and remembered how only a short time ago it furled about her face in all directions. She stared at herself for long moments. Again she felt the bitter taste of Miss Maimie's words. She would never be pretty. Plain, homely, ill-favored, it didn't matter what descriptive term was used. As Miss Maimie had said, she could never have any hope with a young man like Luther Briggs.

"He did kiss me," she admitted softly to her reflection.

She heard her mother's sigh of delight behind her.

Did a kiss, even a very sweet and wonderful kiss, guarantee that a man cared for a woman?

Perhaps it *was* pity. For despite what her mother said, Tulsa May knew that Luther was her friend. Her mother was very wrong about that. Suddenly she hoped that her mother wasn't wrong about everything.

The tiny bell over the doorway jingled as Emma Dix stepped inside the Emporium. The morning had been a busy one for Emma. Her father's condition appeared worse. But he was becoming fussy about her hovering over him. Finally the old man had insisted she go to town.

"A pretty girl ought to be out buying pretty things," he'd told her. "Not sitting next to the sickbed of an old man."

She'd been reluctant to leave the house ever since he'd become soaked in the rain. Once outside, though, Emma felt better than she had in days and she was determined to enjoy herself.

Several ladies were already inside the store, talking animatedly as Emma walked in. At the sight of Emma the chatter miraculously ceased. That was typical, but today Emma refused to allow their reactions to bother her. Holding her chin high, she gave the other customers only vague greetings.

Since the scandal when she'd run off with Fremont Bateman, Emma Dix was *almost,* but not quite, beyond the pale. *Almost,* for the simple reason that no one in Prattville knew for sure what had happened. Emma had left and Emma had come back. Much speculation was made about what she had done in between. But no one knew the facts.

Facts for most small towns wouldn't have been

necessary, but there had been that terrible misunderstanding several years ago about Cora Sparrow, and all the ladies who had shunned her because she'd been divorced were later forced to make embarrassing apologies when the true facts about her marriage were revealed. Since then, Prattville had become reluctant to make hasty judgments.

But many in town *had* made up their minds, and quite negatively, about Emma. And Emma, unlike Mrs. Sparrow, had not been maligned unfairly. If the whole truth about her past ever came out, the entire town would be shocked.

For several months, Emma Dix had lived in open adultery with a married man. When she found she could no longer abide that life, she was out on the streets. Opportunities for young single women were hard to come by, so she'd become a barmaid. She'd decided any honest work was preferable to being a rich man's whore.

She had wanted to marry, to reclaim her reputation, but bachelors with honorable intentions didn't often linger in bars. She had been so lonely, so alone. And she'd had more than one ill-fated love affair during those years.

Now she had come home. It had been a clean break from the past and an opportunity to change her ways. But she hadn't changed. Instead she had begun a secret and illicit liaison with Luther Briggs.

Of course, that was different, she told herself. She wanted to marry Luther Briggs. She'd always had her eye on him. Luther was the most handsome man in town. He was smart, had a steady business, and enough money to keep them comfortably.

If she could have coaxed him into courting her openly, she would have. But he hadn't seemed interested in a serious alliance. So she had offered the bait she knew men found difficult to resist. And she hadn't been sorry. Luther Briggs knew just how to please a woman in bed, and his Indian heritage kept him nearly as much on the edge of society as her past kept her. It seemed to her a perfect match.

Unfortunately, the potential bridegroom had proved to be a bit more difficult than she had anticipated. And now he'd broken off with her completely.

Emma refused to worry. Luther Briggs would be back. Doc Odie was right. A woman like her could have pretty much whatever she wanted. What she wanted now was the life she'd so carelessly thrown away years ago.

Her chin still high in the air, Emma made her way down the counter of the Emporium with a politely civil nod to each of the ladies present as she passed. After a few uneasy moments, she was ignored again and the chattering of gossip resumed in mid-sentence.

Emma stood casually near the hosiery counter, ready to wait. It was a game Mrs. Titus Penny played. She was too careful to openly slight Emma or cut her directly. But she ignored the young woman's existence until the last possible moment and then she hurried through any transactions as if her business were contaminating.

Emma was on to the game and had perfected the bored visage of the browser to protect herself from the slight.

However, today only a few moments passed before young Maybelle, Mrs. Penny's daughter, hurried up to her.

"You take care of Mrs. Bowman," the young girl called out. "I'll help Miss Dix, Mother."

Emma got an excellent view of the expression on the elder Penny's face. Clearly the woman was furious. It was all Emma could do to keep a straight face.

"I'm sorry you had to wait," Maybelle said in her most pleasant storekeeper voice. "I'm afraid Mama and the ladies are quite caught up in the latest gossip."

"Gossip?" Emma felt the color drain from her face. She hoped that nothing new had come out about her. She'd confided in Doc Odie about Luther, but she would never believe *him* to be untrustworthy.

Maybelle leaned slightly forward, her bright blue eyes sparkling with excitement. "The whole town is speculating about Luther Briggs and Tulsa May Bruder."

Emma's relief was immediately followed by chagrin.

"It seems to me that those two have been friends for a lot of years," Emma said deliberately. "I

247

can't truly imagine anything more to it."

"I couldn't either," Maybelle admitted. "I mean, Tulsa May is very nice, but she's just so . . . you know, so . . . ordinary. And Luther is *so* handsome. I was just sure it was a tempest in a teapot."

Emma nodded.

"Even after he bought her those gloves," Maybelle said. "Those peach and brown ones were really beautiful and he said they were for someone special."

Emma hadn't heard about the gloves and her mouth tightened.

"Even then," Maybelle continued, "I really thought they were mostly just friends."

"I'm sure that is exactly what they are."

Shaking her head, Maybelle widened her eyes and leaned forward to whisper. "I went on a picnic with them to Frogeye Creek. They headed out first, in a rather big hurry it seemed to me, and Arthel and I followed, unable to keep up with them."

Her slightly uncomfortable hesitation at her own fib heightened the drama.

"We came upon them on the road. They were sparking and kissing and —" Maybelle's voice dropped even lower. "She had her hair all undone."

Emma stood staring at her, frozen in place. "I don't believe it!"

"I saw it with my own eyes," the younger woman insisted.

"He must be toying with her or . . . or . . ."

"Or he must be really in love."

Maybelle's bright, hopeful, dreamy gaze cut Emma to the quick. Her knees suddenly seemed a little shaky, then a fury overtook her. How dare he! She suddenly forgot her past and reputation, and remembered only that she had given herself to Luther and he had carelessly tossed her aside. Her breath seemed strangled in her chest. She wanted to hurt Luther. To make him suffer for treating her badly. She didn't know how she was going to do it, but Emma was going to make Luther as miserable as she was right that moment.

"Now, what was it that you wanted?" Maybelle asked.

Emma wanted to scream "Nothing" and race out the door. But she couldn't give the gossips, or Luther Briggs, the satisfaction.

"Stockings," she answered a little louder than necessary. "I believe I'd like to look at some stockings."

For twenty of the longest minutes of Emma's life, she remarked, criticized, and complained about the quality of the Emporium's silk hosiery. Finally, when she'd rejected every pair that the store had, she made her way out, the little bell jangling behind her.

Once outside, she exhaled deeply, as if she had been holding her breath. She was still furious.

It was the biggest humiliation of her life. Luther Briggs had thrown her over — and for an ugly duckling like Tulsa May Bruder. Thank heaven that no one in town knew. Still, *she* knew and the knowledge seared.

Her heels sounding sharply on the red-brick sidewalk, Emma angrily began to make her way down the street.

It was sheer bad luck that Luther was leaving the grocery and market, finally managing to excuse himself from Mrs. Puser's endless suggestions for good and proper uses of his new building. He looked at Emma, surprised.

"Luther!" Emma's startled exclamation sprang from an uneasy feeling of having conjured up her own thoughts.

Almost as startled as she was, Luther could think of exactly nothing to say. Politely he tipped his hat as he might for the most casual of female acquaintance and without a word began crossing the street.

Emma watched his back as he walked away from her. He had walked away without even saying hello. Her fury turned to rage. And her thoughts became fused on revenge. Revenge. She would make Luther Briggs pay. And she didn't care at what cost.

Chapter Fourteen

Emma was not the only one to watch Luther Briggs cross Main Street that morning. Doc Odie, returning home from an early house call, spotted him also. The doctor had been thinking a lot about Willie Dix and about Emma. Willie was not long for this world, that fact was clear. And Odie had made the old man a promise he was not sure how he was going to keep. Reluctantly, Doc Odie pulled his team to a stop and followed Luther into his building.

Luther stood in the middle of the lower floor of his Main Street building. Slowly, he turned around, giving the place a thorough once-over. It seemed that everybody in town, except him, knew the perfect use for this building. Usually he was decisive, but somehow none of the options he thought of felt exactly right.

"Good morning, Luther."

Turning to the doorway, he saw Doc Odie hesitating on the threshold.

"Morning, Doc," he replied. "Come on in, I suspect I ought to hear your two cents' worth as well as everybody else's."

The doctor did come inside, but his expression was puzzled. "My two cents' worth on what?"

"On this building." Luther looked around again and shook his head. "Everybody in Prattville knows what I should do with it except me."

Doc Odie glanced around at the bare plaster walls, but his expression was more annoyed than puzzled. "I don't care what you do with the building. You can burn it down for all it means to me. I've come to talk to you about something really important."

"Oh?" Luther sensed from Odie's rather aggressive tone that the subject would not be pleasant. "What did you want to talk to me about?"

The doctor paused. He obviously was searching for the right words when he just blurted out his question. "I want to know your intentions toward a young lady."

Luther's serious expression slowly faded into a genuine grin. "Oh, you do?" He couldn't keep the laughter out of his voice. "What's the matter, Odie? Feeling a little jealous these days?"

The doctor sucked in his cheeks angrily and his eyes bulged in fury. "My feelings have nothing to do with it!" he proclaimed sharply. "It's the young woman that concerns me."

Luther shook his head, actually laughing. "Now, Doc Odie, you had your chance and you got cold feet. Don't expect me to step aside now that you're realizing what a mistake you've made."

"Mistake?"

"Besides, Doc, I honestly don't think you've got a chance with her. Tulsy is not the kind of woman to let a fellow treat her lightly and then walk back in whenever he's got a mind to."

"Tulsy?"

"Miss Tulsa May."

"I'm not talking about Tulsa May."

Luther was confused. "Then who in the world are you talking about?"

"Emma Dix."

"Emma?"

"Yes, Emma," the doctor answered. "Old Willie isn't going to last much longer. I'm afraid he'll be going to his reward in a matter of weeks."

"That's too bad," Luther said. "He's a fine old man and I've always liked him."

"He likes you too," the doctor said. "In fact, it was his idea for me to come and talk to you."

"Talk to me about what?"

"About Emma, of course. Very soon she will be alone in the world with no one to take care of her."

Luther shrugged. "Don't worry about Emma, Doc. That woman can take care of herself."

"Perhaps so, but she certainly shouldn't have to." The doctor looked up solemnly at the taller man. "I think it's time that you married the girl, Luther."

"Married!" Luther was genuinely shocked. "Marry Emma?" He shook his head and laughed. "Doc Odie, you've got to be joking."

"I don't find anything about this topic amusing."

"Emma Dix, the sweet little woman, sitting by the fire and mending my overalls? You don't need much imagination, Doc, to see the humor in that."

"The young lady would make a fine wife."

"Not for me she wouldn't."

The doctor took a step closer, his thin arms folded stubbornly across his chest, his expression belligerent. "Where is your sense of honor, young man? Your sense of duty? I realize you haven't had the most fortunate of upbringings, but surely even you understand that when you've been dancing to the tune, the time will come to pay the fiddler."

"Not if the music has been offered for free," Luther said emphatically. "I don't owe Emma Dix a blessed thing on this earth."

"How can you say that when you've been seeing her on the sly and no doubt sullying her reputation?"

"Emma's reputation was pretty well sullied before I ever laid a hand on her."

"You are despicable!" the doctor proclaimed through clenched teeth. "You've been seeing this woman in less than honorable circumstances and you can joke and cast her off in her hour of need as if she were *nothing?*"

"I never said she was nothing," Luther answered with growing irritation at the doctor's high-handed attitude. "I like Emma. She's a good old gal and we've had some good times together. But she knew from the start that I wasn't interested in anything beyond a little fun. And neither was she."

With a hiss of fury, Doc Odie raised his hand as if to strike the younger man. Stepping back out of his range, Luther glared at the doctor.

"You best not be starting something that you won't be able to finish, Doc. How dare you come down here and lecture me. Duty? Honor?" Luther snorted in disgust. "Where was your duty and honor when you left a sweet, innocent, trusting young woman like Tulsa May to face the pity and gossip of every busybody in this town?" His eyes narrowed and he surveyed Doc Odie as if he were a worm. "I never promised Emma anything. Not companionship, not security, not even a permanent place in my bed. But you, you promised Tulsa May lawful, holy wedlock and all she got was a ruined party and a lifetime's worth of embarrassment."

"This is different," Doc Odie mumbled, suddenly a bit unsure of himself.

"You're damn right it's different! Now take your worthless promises and your holier-than-thou attitude and get out of my sight before I lose my temper and start picking on somebody not nearly my own size."

Maybelle pushed her bicycle under the overhang at the Briggses' shop. She ran a hand over her hair to assure herself that all was in place before announcing herself.

"Luther?" she called inside the building, knowing full well that he was still in town.

Only a moment later, Arthel came to the door, wiping his hands on a greasy rag. His glossy black hair had grown a little long and was tucked behind his ears. He was shirtless under his overalls and Maybelle was surprised at the unexpected width of his shoulders and the muscle definition in his arms.

"Well, good afternoon." His smile was broad and welcoming. "Luther's down in town." He gave Maybelle a long, pointed look before he continued. "But I'm always here for you, honey."

Maybelle tossed her bright blond curls in an attractive show of pique and stuck her nose in the air. "I need someone to fix my bicycle tire. I suppose even you could manage that."

" 'Spect I could," Arthel answered. "Pretty girls' bicycles are my specialty."

Maybelle raised a skeptical eyebrow. "Oh, really? Why, Cochise, I thought you were more into buffalo killing and war dancing."

Arthel's eyes narrowed slightly, but he ignored the jibe. Wordlessly, he moved past Maybelle to the bike.

She hadn't intended to antagonize him. In fact, she'd come out to the shop hoping that he'd be alone. But his light tone made her mad. How dare he talk down to her as if she were some silly, ignorant nobody. He acted as though he barely knew her.

Squatting beside her, Arthel checked the tire, easily pulling it completely off the rim. "The inner tube is practically rotted. It will need a new one."

He looked up at her, but her icy gaze quieted whatever question had been on his lips. Without asking her permission, Arthel removed the rim from the frame and carried it, the tire, and the inner tube into the shop.

He neither spoke nor looked back. It was as if Maybelle had ceased to exist. And he'd made no indication that she should follow. Sniffing genteelly, Maybelle was more than a little annoyed at being left standing awkwardly in the doorway.

She remained there all of a minute and a half. Then with a mumbled comment to herself about his lack of manners, she entered the work room uninvited. Arthel didn't even bother to look up.

"This inner tube must be as old as you are," he said finally.

Maybelle shrugged with unconcern as she walked around the room, pretending interest in the tools and metal parts hung on the walls. "I haven't ridden in a long time."

He looked up at her and grinned. But she was staring at a wrench as if she'd never seen anything so fascinating. "So you decided to have it fixed today in case you might want to in the future?"

"It was certainly time that I had it fixed," she said.

"I suppose it is."

Arthel began to whistle. Maybelle found that particularly annoying.

"And here I was thinking," he continued casually, "that you were coming out here just to see me."

Her face flushed a rosy pink, but it was nothing like the bright red that she saw when Maybelle turned to look at the man grinning at her. *He was laughing at her!* She held her discomfiture in check by stoking her anger.

"I most certainly did not come here to see you, Geronimo," she answered sarcastically. "There is an Indian just down the street from me, in front of the cigar store."

Arthel raised his eyes to her and nodded slightly as if conceding the point. "But I understand," he replied, "that he's not nearly as much fun on a dark, lonely road as I am."

Maybelle's cheeks were flushed a very becoming rose, but her teeth were clenched in fury.

"Oh, that," she said, feigning unconcern remarkably well. "I suppose that because I let you kiss me a few times, you think it means something special to me. That *you* mean something special to me."

"And it's not anything special." It was more a statement than a question.

Waving away the subject with a flighty giggle, Maybelle shook her head. "Certainly not. Really, I am not some pale prairie flower to be overwhelmed by the wicked redskin's attention." She laughed lightly and then sighed with studied sophistication. "I've kissed so many men that another one, more or less, doesn't mean a thing to me."

Arthel looked at her questioningly for a moment and then nodded. "So which am I?"

"What?"

"Which am I? More or less?"

"I have no idea what you mean."

Rising to his feet, Arthel came to stand directly in front of her. He was head and shoulders taller than she was and something about him looming over her was disconcerting. Maybelle stepped back. He followed.

"You haven't answered my question."

"What question?"

She retreated once more, but again he stepped forward.

"About my kisses."

"What about them?"

"Do you want more or less?"

Maybelle stepped back one more time and, unfortunately, found her back against the wall. She placed her hands against the rough-hewn logs and felt trapped. And she didn't appreciate it one bit.

"Your kisses were perfectly adequate for a young man of your age," she told him haughtily.

Arthel nodded solemnly. Then slowly, oh so slowly, his expression blossomed into a grin. "I guess I just need practice. I would imagine that a woman like yourself could teach me a thing or two."

Laying a hand on each side of the wall beside her, Arthel effectively cut off any possible escape route. Maybelle glanced nervously toward the door. For all her haughty, brave words, she'd shared little more than schoolgirl kisses with the other boys who had called on her. And before the picnic she'd never been alone with a man. Then it had seemed so wonderful. Now, it only seemed downright scary. The doorway was empty and the road beyond it was quiet and deserted.

"Don't you dare try to force yourself on me!" she said angrily, her hands clenching, ready to bare her nails if necessary.

Arthel leaned forward, closing the distance between them. "That's what you'd expect of a wild Indian like me, I guess." He crooked his head slightly and brought it within inches of her own. "See, you are teaching me already. First rule, never force the lady."

He was so close, Maybelle could feel the heat of his words against her cheek. Her heart was beating like a tom-tom and she trembled. Her own hands suddenly seemed superfluous. She didn't know where to put them. So she used them to grasp the straps on Arthel's overalls.

"I don't like this silly game you're playing," she said. "You are making me very nervous."

Arthel's lips were even closer now. "Is that against the rules or just an observation?"

"Yes! I mean, no! I mean —"

"Ah," Arthel answered. "Games are against the rules, but making you nervous is not."

He took one hand and laid it gently along her cheek, caressing the soft smooth skin. "Is this making you nervous?"

"Please, I —"

"Please what?" he asked so softly, his lips almost touched her own.

She tried to turn away from him, but it seemed as if he were everywhere, on all sides, enveloping her.

"Please —" she begged again.

"Please stop?" he asked.

"No —"

"Please kiss you?"

"Oh, please —"

"Please let you go?"

"Yes, yes, please."

"Say my name."

"What?"

"Say my name, Maybelle. I want to hear it."

"But —"

"That's all, Maybelle. I just want to hear my name on your pretty lips once more."

"I —"

His lips were only a hairsbreadth from her own.

"Say it."

"Oh, Arthel!" she gasped at last, throwing her arms around his neck and melding her mouth to his.

The basement of the Bruder parsonage was dank and rather dark and filled with the mixed odor of drying roots and sweat. The rhythmic sounds of fists thudding against a punching bag were the only noise.

When Luther entered, he followed his ears to Reverend Philemon Bruder. The preacher was clad in an athletic suit of gray cotton worsted with large damp circles beneath the armpits. His fists were raised, as hand over hand he struck the dangling pigskin target. Clearly he'd been exercising for quite a while.

"Afternoon, Rev," Luther called. "Looks like you're about to beat that thing to death."

The preacher gave the bag one last punch before turning to the younger man with a sigh. "It's the best thing in the world, Luther. You really ought to try it."

Luther shook his head. "I work hard enough as it is, Rev. I don't need to make work for myself."

"Now, that's where you're wrong," Reverend Bruder told him as he grabbed up a towel and mopped his brow. "The kind of exercise you get working will never strengthen the body and leaven the mind."

"I'm not sure I'm much in need of either."

"That's where you're wrong, son," the older man insisted as he rubbed the towel over his graying carrot-red hair before wrapping it around his neck. "Physical exercise will make you a better man, not just outside but inside. I've been at it for ten years now, and I know what I'm saying."

Luther just grinned.

"Take that shirt off and I'll start you on some light weights."

"No, I don't think —"

"It'll toughen your body and cleanse your soul."

"I don't need toughening or cleansing," Luther protested.

"Seems to me," the preacher said softly, "that a young man who takes my daughter on a picnic and doesn't get her home until after dark might be in need of a way to work off some steam."

Luther flinched, but he didn't reply. Seeing no option, he removed his shirt without further protest.

Reverend Bruder led him to the corner where he'd set up his Whiteley Exerciser. The contraption of weights and pulleys was attached to a reinforced wall at the far end of the basement.

"Just turn this way," the preacher said, turning him from the equipment. He handed Luther two padded leather hand grips. "All you do is pull and the weights rise up," he said. "You can pull them in tandem, but it's easier when you start to pull with one arm at a time."

Luther nodded, not the least interested in the instructions. He intended to work on the exerciser for a few minutes and then escape the basement gymnasium at the first opportunity. He would have never come if the reverend had not sent for him. Halfheartedly, Luther pulled at the hand grip. His muscles clenched. His eyes bulged. But the weight didn't move.

"It's too heavy."

The preacher tutted. "I'd never have taken you for such a puny sissypants. I lift twice that much."

Luther glared at him. Determinedly, setting his

jaw, Luther slowly pulled at the hand grip. Behind him, the attached weight reluctantly rose and his arm extended to its full length. Light beads of sweat broke out upon his brow.

"Very good," the preacher said. "Now don't just drop it. Let it fall back into place nice and slow."

To his credit, Luther tried. However, the weight dropped back into place much too fast, clanging loudly. The preacher didn't comment.

"Now let's try the other arm," he said.

"Us?" Luther asked.

Reverend Bruder only smiled. Casually, the preacher straightened his bright orange moustache to his satistaction and then folded his arms before him.

Luther's second pull was nearly as difficult as his first. But within a few moments he was managing to lift and lower the weights with some efficiency.

"How long before I've sufficiently cleansed my soul?" he asked.

The older man smiled benignly. "Depends on how blackened your soul might be."

Luther looked at the preacher directly. "I hope you know that as far as your daughter is concerned, there is no need of cleansing."

Reverend Bruder observed him silently for a moment before nodding. "So you two are just friends."

"We've always been friends."

"And there is nothing else?"

Luther almost reassured him, but he did not. When Luther didn't answer, the reverend made a small "ahhh" sound, as if making a discovery.

Luther dropped the hand grip abruptly and it clanged loudly back into place. "Tulsa May is of age and a decent God-fearing woman. I understand your fatherly interest, but I can't see that any of this is your concern."

The preacher raised an eyebrow. "Have we progressed so far in these modern times that a father cannot ask a young man's intentions?"

"My intentions, Rev, are to continue to call upon your daughter as long as *she* welcomes me."

"Good," the preacher said decisively. "I couldn't be happier."

"Well, bully for you," Luther answered, jerking on his shirt. He was slightly light-headed and his arms already ached, but he ignored his physical discomfort.

"I do think that exercise would be good for you, Luther," the reverend continued. "I was young and wild once myself, you know. And there is nothing to take the edge off quite like working up a good sweat."

Luther mumbled something noncommittal.

"That's why I think the YMCA would be such a good thing for the community."

"The YMCA?"

"Young Men's Christian Association. Surely you've heard of it."

"They have one in Guthrie," Luther answered. "If you're a member you can stay all night there instead of in a hotel."

The preacher nodded. "Yes, of course they do that. But that's not really what I'm interested in."

"Oh?"

"The YMCA sponsors gymnasiums for young men, like yourself, to work out some of those frustrations of youth in a boxing ring or lifting weights."

"Sounds like a good idea," Luther admitted.

"It's an excellent idea," the preacher said. "Don't you remember all that I've told you about the philosophy of body and soul harmony?"

The reverend had received a copy of Mrs. Millenbutter's book, *A Ladies' Guide to Good Health, Fine Posture, and Spiritual Completeness,* more than ten years earlier. For a while, her regime of balance, meditation, and exercise was almost a local craze. Most of the town had long ago gone back to general laziness, but Reverend Bruder had retained his interest and had studied even further.

"I certainly remember as much as I want to, Rev," Luther answered.

"So do you think a YMCA would be a worthwhile addition to the community?"

"Sounds all right to me, Rev."

"Good, I knew you'd see it that way."

"What way?" Luther looked puzzled. "Are you asking me for a donation?"

"More than a simple donation," Reverend Bruder said excitedly. "With that new empty building

266

right on Main Street, I want to give you the opportunity of being an integral part of the association."

Luther stared at him for a moment. "Rev, I've told you and everybody else that I haven't decided about the building."

"Of course you haven't. But now that you know we need it for the YMCA, your decision should be a great deal easier."

"Rev —"

"You just admitted to the good that exercise can do."

Luther didn't remember admitting anything of the kind. He started to make a reply, but a mischievous gleam came into his eye.

"Yes, Rev," he said. "I am a great believer in exercise. As is your lovely daughter, Tulsa May."

The preacher's brows lifted.

"But she and I have our own brand of exercise," he continued. "Something more suited to our natures and eminently more pleasurable."

The reverend's expression darkened.

Luther actually smiled. "She's been begging me since the Spring Blossom Festival, and tonight I believe I'll take my Tulsy dancing. There's nothing like spieling to a good ragtime to cleanse the soul."

Chapter Fifteen

Luther knew his plan was a mistake the minute he pulled the Runabout to a stop in front of the roadhouse at Perkin's Corner. Friday night had seemed a safe bet; the local cowboys and roustabouts were only off on Saturday night. And without them there was sure to be less drink and fewer drinkers. However, the dusty ground in front of the roadhouse was jammed with buggies, saddle horses, and vehicles of all types. And the jangle of piano and banjo was loud enough to be heard even from the road.

"Maybe we shouldn't," he suggested to the young woman beside him. It wasn't as much a casual suggestion as a conviction. So far today, nothing had gone exactly to his advantage. After his irritating encounter with the Rev, his muscles had ached all day. His mind had been in such a turmoil that he'd installed a clutch backward and nearly stripped it completely. And then there was his brother.

"You're sure all dressed up," he'd commented when Arthel had stepped out from his room in a fresh white shirt and his hair smelling of pomade.

"Got a big evening planned," he told Luther

with more than a hint of bravado.

Luther grinned. "Going out on the town, are you?"

"Not really on the town," Anthel answered with a laugh. "I'm just going down to that old pecan tree in the yard of Mrs. Sparrow's little cottage."

"Why in the world would you be going there?" Luther asked.

"It's where I'm meeting Maybelle Penny." Arthel's grin broadened. "That pecan tree is where Miss Maybelle broke my heart," he said. "And tonight, it's where that little gal is going to mend it."

Luther's expression was deadly serious. "That's not a good idea, Arthel. You start stealing kisses with that little girl and her daddy will see you end up married to her."

Arthel shrugged. "It wouldn't be the worst punishment I could imagine."

A furious huff escaped Luther's lips. "What about college? Good Lord, Arthel, it's what we've worked for and wanted for years. You're only a few months from A and M; marriage will end that dream forever."

His expression also becoming serious, Arthel grasped his brother's shoulder. "College is *your* dream for me, Luther. It's what *you've* wanted and worked for."

"I promised Mammy and Pa that I'd take care of you!"

"And you have," Arthel answered. "Now, I'm all grown-up, and I can take care of myself."

Luther had wanted to say more, but he was too stunned for words. Even now he could hardly think of what to say, but tomorrow, he promised himself, the two of them would have a long talk. Arthel was just being young and foolish. Luther would convince him to go to college.

"You're still thinking about your brother?" Tulsa May's words startled Luther back into the present.

"Just worried, I guess."

Tulsa May nodded. Luther had told her the whole story on the drive. "Would you like for me to talk to him?"

Luther grinned. "If I can't make him see sense, I'll be very grateful to have you try."

They smiled warmly at each other. He snaked an arm around her waist and hugged her to him lightly. It had been done in the guise of friendship, but Luther was honest enough with himself to admit that he simply wanted to touch her. As always, she felt so good, so warm, so right. He pulled away.

"If we had any sense at all," he told her, "we'd know that we shouldn't step one foot into that roadhouse."

Tulsa May giggled. She was wearing her best brown dress, the gloves Luther had given her, and a brand-new hat, a near brimless pale beige straw, banded by dark brown satin, that fit close to her head like a helmet. "Of course we shouldn't. Isn't that what my father told you a hundred times before we left home? But we're here now and I really would like to try dancing again."

Her grin was mischievous, and Luther found himself giving in against his better judgment. Roadhouses could be stormy places: beer, music, and dancing were often stirred together into a mix of rough talk, wild antics, and dirty fighting.

"All right," he said, grasping her hand in a protective gesture. "But stick close to me. These places can get a little wild. And they certainly aren't used to young ladies of your caliber."

Tulsa May laughed again. Lady newspaper writers were undoubtedly of a caliber all their own.

Luther helped her down and offered his arm like a gentleman at a cotillion and they made their way to the doorway of the boisterous road-house. She was flushed and excited and felt none of the anxiety that bothered Luther. While he saw rough, rowdy men and hard-drinking women, Tulsa May's shining, optimistic eyes saw only laughing, happy folks having a grand time.

"Oh, this is going to be fun!" she told Luther as they stepped inside the open door of the dimly lit room. The establishment, whose official name was Fiddler's Hall, was one long, narrow room. A counter at one end served beer — and any "special requirements" to trusted customers. At the other end was a small stage, raised less than a foot from the main floor, surrounded by lanterns that brightened the faces and instruments of the cigar-smoking piano player, gimp-legged fiddler, and an itinerant banjo picker. They were dutifully jangling out a square as a tall, swarthy-looking fellow with a dashing black moustache called the tune.

Tulsa May looked around with delight.

"This doesn't look like our type of crowd," Luther said, close to her ear.

She stared up at him, puzzled. Once again she let her eyes wander the crowd. Nothing appeared dangerous. Certainly, some of the most clamorous were a bit less than perfect gentlemen, and most of the ladies were dolled up in face paint, but Tulsa May felt no threat. Of course, being at a roadhouse with a man *was* a danger to her reputation. But she was not concerned. After the kisses she'd shared with Luther on the way home from the picnic, she'd begun to think that a good reputation might not be the most desirable thing in the world.

"It looks like such fun," she told him. "Couldn't we stay for just a few moments? Maybe just a dance or two?" Her smile was bright and hopeful. "You did promise to take me dancing."

Luther sighed in defeat. "You win," he said. "You want to try this square?"

Tulsa May nodded excitedly and they moved out onto the floor. Two couples who'd been dancing sixes quickly broke away and another joined them in a square. One man was a big, bearded, ruddy-looking fellow whose girth strained the fabric of his worn overalls. His lady friend was skinny and pale beneath the layer of face paint that had begun to congeal in the wrinkles around her eyes. There was no time for introductions and the caller led them in a quick sequence of movements that

Tulsa May didn't quite understand. She bumped into the big man twice and once into Luther trying to go the wrong way.

Laughing, she was more amused than embarrassed. And fortunately her partners felt the same. Finally, the black-moustached man called for bows to partner and corner and the dance was done. Tulsa May was still laughing.

The big, ruddy man held out his hand to Luther. "You're the mechanic over at Prattville, ain't ye?"

"Luther Briggs," he replied, offering his hand.

"I'm Elm Tripten and this here is Carrilee McDonnal."

Luther offered the lady a polite nod. Tulsa May thought her answering smile overly friendly.

"Who's this little gal that don't know the steps?" Elm's broad smile revealed a missing tooth on the right side.

With only an infinitesimal hesitation, Luther introduced her. "This is Miss Tulsa May Bruder of Prattville."

The big man's brow furrowed in recognition. Tulsa May readied herself for being recognized as the preacher's daughter. It always happened, no matter where she went. She hoped it wouldn't put a damper on the evening.

"You're the little gal that writes for the *Populist*?" Elm asked at last.

Tulsa May was so surprised she stared at him mutely for a moment before finally nodding her head.

"Well, it's about time!" the big man said with delight, clapping his hands together. He gave a big grin to Carrilee before turning his attention back to Tulsa May. "I've been saying for months that it ain't fair that fancy folks that takes their entertainment in salons and moving-picture palaces get writ up in the paper and those of us who're more keen on a sizzling fiddle got to hide out like we was shamed."

As the fiddler began to saw a jig, Elm grabbed her hand. " 'Scuse me, honey," he said to Carrilee. "Don't mind if I give the newspaper gal a spin, do ya, Luther?" he asked, not bothering to wait for an answer.

Luther stared after them uncertainly, but Tulsa May gave him a reassuring grin as she laid her hand on big Elm's shoulder and stepped to the tune.

His hold for the one-step was loose and proper. Tulsa May felt rather overwhelmed by the sheer size of the man, but his actions were those of a gentleman. Clearly, his intent was to talk.

"I know they's some that don't hold with dancin'," he told her. "Some of them, like holier-than-thou preachers, can harangue about it from daylight till dark. But I cain't see no sin in it at all. It's just pure fun and that's what them sour preachers cain't stand." He hesitated, giving her an opportunity to disagree with him. When she didn't, he continued. "Ain't no Jesus teachin' agin it," he told her. "Why, even them folks in the Bible done it. Would they be doing it in the Bible if it was all bad?"

"I don't suppose so." Tulsa May was very grateful that Elm didn't know that her own father was one of those "sour preachers."

"It's like steppin' inside of the music," Elm continued. "You hear that good fiddle and you feel that frailing banjo and then you move your feet and you're not hearing it no more. You're akin. Does that sound foolish?"

Elm's big, hairy, sincere face was winning. Tulsa May found herself smiling at him in delight. He was a rough, hard-working farmer with hands as big as bear paws, but he had the heart of a poet.

"I think I know what you mean," she said. "Moving with the music is like becoming a part of it."

He grinned broadly, again displaying the missing tooth. "Now, I knew you was one smart female the first time I read one of them stories of yours in the newspaper."

Blushing at the compliment, Tulsa May shook her head. "I'm really not a very good reporter. Mr. Willers says I've no head for the facts."

Elm shook his head with displeasure. "That Mr. Willers is a mule's backside. You get the facts just fine. But more, when we read it, well, it's like we see it the way you see it. Not cold and distant, but like we was there." He grinned again as a thought occurred to him. "Reading your newspaper stories is like steppin' into the music."

Tulsa May was honored by the compliment. But she was embarrassed also. A moment later she brought the subject back to the music and allowed Elm to explain to her all that he knew. She listened with as much interest as good manners as he led her around the floor. From the corner of her eye she spotted Luther standing next to the beer stand at the back of the hall. Even in the dim light she knew he was clearly the handsomest man in attendance. Tulsa May scolded herself for this observation. Luther was certainly a fine figure of a man, but the important thing was that he was honest, hardworking, and honorable. And he was her best friend. All the dreams and kisses in the world weren't worth losing that friendship, she reminded herself for the hundredth time that day. And she very much needed to keep sight of the fact.

Most of the men around him were partaking of the local brew and talking and laughing loudly. Luther stood quietly among them. Anyone not looking closely would think that he was with them. But he was not. He was not drinking, not talking, not laughing. He was watching . . . watching her.

Tulsa May felt an inexplicable little thrill sizzle across her skin. Again she felt the touch of his lips on hers and the feel of his hands as they caressed her hair. Once more she was there in the seat of the Runabout, understanding for the first time what the feel and taste and smell of a man could mean. The memory brought a flush to her cheeks. She swallowed and forced her attention back to Elm.

When the music stopped, there was no need to look around for Luther. He was right there to claim her. Possessively, he draped his arm around her waist and she remembered the very public kiss on the parsonage steps. For a moment she felt he might try something similar to demonstrate their relationship, to mark her as his own. She smiled at him reassuringly.

"Thanks for the dance, Elm," she said politely to her partner. "And I appreciate all the information you've given me on dancing. Perhaps I will write up something about it."

The big man grinned broadly. "I'd be much obliged, miss."

Tulsa May placed her hand in Luther's and smiled up at him. Luther had been jealous of Elm? It seemed a ludicrous idea. Quickly, Tulsa May assured herself that she had imagined the entire incident.

The banjo player began raking his fingers rapidly back and forth across the strings in the frailing or clawhammer style. It was a loud, attention-getting maneuver, not something to be danced to, but rather a signal that the man with the black moustache would be calling another square.

Luther and Tulsa May quickly joined another couple in a foursome and again Tulsa May tried to match the spoken words with the movements required. It wasn't easy. Directions such as "circle the wagons" and "pitch the hay" were not self-explanatory. In fact, Tulsa May thought the movements had to be seen to be believed. She did her best, never giving up. And when the dance was finished, she clapped as loudly as anyone. Mostly in gratitude that the dance was over.

"You're not much for square dancing?" Luther asked, unable to hide his grin.

Tulsa May shook her head. "When I said I wanted to go dancing, I think I was thinking of more spieling with you."

Luther's vivid blue eyes became darker. It really wasn't quite proper to bring a woman like Tulsy to a roadhouse at all and certainly not to do any snuggle spieling. Somehow, Luther couldn't manage to summon up the propriety needed to refuse her. "All I want in the world is to give you your heart's desire," he said.

The fiddler began playing a slow sweet tune, undoubtedly meant for a sedate waltz. Luther grinned in mischief, clearly intending to take credit for the change in music. "You ask for a round-set, ma'am, and I see you get one."

Tulsa May giggled.

He led her out on the floor, but to her surprise, instead of taking a waltz position, he snuggled down into a spieling posture. His chin rested upon her shoulder and his body was pressed tightly against her own. She felt the blood rushing to her cheeks and feared that he could feel the erratic beating of her heart. Then she realized that she could feel the beating of *his* heart. It was a scary, wonderful, intimate feeling. She could feel every movement in the muscles of his arms and chest. With his knees bent to reach her height, a thick, masculine thigh occasionally pressed in unseemly familiarity against her own. Her breathing became rather more labored than the slow, sure waltzing movement merited. She felt those embarrassing nipples rising and hardening as her bosom was crushed against his chest. She sent up a little prayer of thanks that God had seen fit to create the brassiere, and that Maybelle had seen fit to sell her one.

The flesh on her arms and neck seemed to flash hot and cold in response to the proximity of Luther's body. Surely, this was what her father was thinking of when he spoke of dancing as sinful. It was far too pleasurable not to be sin.

With wary, hesitant glances, Tulsa May checked to see if the rest of the crowd was staring. No one seemed to notice anything unusual. She sighed with relief and was ready to throw caution to the wind and simply enjoy the warm, wonderful man who held her. Then she spotted a couple at the door.

Guiltily she pulled back from Luther's embrace.

"What is it?" he asked, clearly fearing he had somehow frightened her.

"Look." She pointed toward the doorway. "It's Emma Dix. What a surprise to see someone that we know."

When Emma Dix had ridden up on the back of Blue Turley's dusty bay saddle horse, she'd noticed the Runabout immediately. She was disgruntled and more than a little angry, certain that she was for a confrontation. However, the sight of Luther and Tulsa May on the dimly lit dance floor, snuggled up closer than a mustard plaster on a cold chest caught her unawares. Tulsa May's welcoming smile nearly knocked the foundation out from under her completely.

Tiny hairs bristled on her neck as she felt the warmth of Turley's breath against her ear. "Ain't that your fella out there, Sugartail? Seems he's squeezin' himself against the carrot-top again."

"Shut up, Blue."

"Yes, ma'am," he answered.

Emma didn't have to look at him to know that he was smiling.

"I don't have to say nothing," he continued in his sarcastic Western drawl. "Why, I'm sure you can see it all right before your eyes."

The dance had hardly ended when Tulsa May hurried over to them. Luther followed behind her with visible reluctance.

"Start a fight," Emma whispered.

"What?" Blue looked at her in disbelief.

"Start a fight with Luther. I want to see you beat him black and blue."

Turley surveyed her curiously. She was cold, angry, and deadly serious.

"Why would I want to do that, Sugartail?" he asked with a wheedling whine. "Even Briggs is likely to get in a couple of damn good blows."

Emma swallowed hard and then looked at him.

Her words were quiet. "I know what you've been hanging around me for, Turley," she said. "You beat up Luther Briggs, really beat him up, and you'll get it."

Turley's eyes gleamed. "Well, damn me for a sorry cowboy, Sugartail. I'd beat up the devil himself if it meant rollin' on the bedsheets with you."

"Beat him up, Turley," Emma said quietly as the other young couple hurried toward her. "Just beat him up. I wish I could do it myself."

"Emma, don't you look charming!" As always, Tulsa May's sincerity was too transparent to be questioned. "I love that new hairstyle; curly-bob bangs are so modern."

Emma's lack of answering warmth went unnoticed as Tulsa May rambled on in a rush of excitement. "Isn't this just the most fascinating place you've ever seen? I'm having a wonderful time and it's so good to have friends turn up to share the fun."

As there was no immediate answer, Tulsa May turned to the gentleman at Emma's side. "I know I've seen you around town," she said. "But I don't think we've been properly introduced."

"No, ma'am," Turley replied with only the barest tip of his cowboy hat. "Don't believe we've been introduced at all, or otherwise."

Tulsa May waited for Emma, or at least Luther, to make the introductions. When after a very long moment of embarrassment neither spoke up, Tulsa May just handled it herself.

"I'm Tulsa May Bruder," she said, extending her palm like a man for a handshake.

Turley grasped her fingers and squeezed them intimately and then, to top off this rather unusual reception, he gave her a wicked wink.

Slightly shocked, Tulsa May quickly covered her surprise by laughing. "I've heard you cowboys are Romeos. But you might as well save your flirting for Emma. I'm much too easily impressed to be any challenge at all."

Turley's grin held more than a little bit of spite. "Yep, I've heard Luther boy here ain't much up to challenges."

Her eyes widening in surprise, Tulsa May stared at Turley, puzzled. The strangeness of his comment and the abrasive underlying tone caught her unawares. She turned to Emma.

Miss Dix offered no explanation for her escort's rudeness. Without a word to Tulsa May she turned to Luther.

"Dance with me." It was more an order than a request.

After an uncomfortable glance at Tulsa May, Luther led Emma out onto the floor.

Watching them walk away, Tulsa May had a strange feeling that something bad was about to happen. She hardly had time to examine the thought before the cowboy grabbed her hand.

"Guess that leaves you with me," Turley said beside her. "Come on, Carrot, let's take a turn across the floor."

Tulsa May hadn't a chance to agree before Blue

Turley pulled her out onto the sawdust and into his arms. The piano was jangling a perfect spieling tune, and to Tulsa May's horror, Emma's cowboy snuggled down and grasped her so close she could barely breathe.

"Sir, I must object —" she began in a gentle undertone. Turley, however, began his wild pumping one-step and turn with such enthusiasm, Tulsa May found herself in the unenviable position of "hold on or fall down."

The room spun around them at least half a dozen times before she was able to get her bearings. He smelled somewhat sour and the stench of tobacco clung to his vest. Unlike the pleasant feel of dancing with Luther, Tulsa May felt trapped and sticky and slightly sick.

Turley had allowed the hand at her back to dip indecently low.

Tulsa May gave a startled little protest that Turley disregarded completely. Not about to be ignored, she removed her hand from his shoulder and struggled to push his unwelcome paw back up to the neutral territory of her waist.

"Relax, Carrot," the cowboy told her with a chuckle. "I ain't a-trying to steal your bustle."

"I would appreciate it greatly, sir, if you would not hold me in this manner. It is inappropriate and demeaning."

Turley raised an eyebrow at her words and then shrugged. "Figure I got a right, Carrot," he said. "Your Luther-boy been holdin' Emma pretty close."

Surprised, Tulsa May glanced around the room until she saw the other couple. Emma was obviously very angry and was talking a mile a minute. Luther's eyes, however, were not upon his dancing partner but on Tulsa May and he didn't look the least bit happy.

"Luther's not holding her close," Tulsa May protested. "Why, he's barely touching her at all."

"Barely touching her *now*," Turley countered. "He's touched her plenty, and *close*, in the past." He leaned nearer, speaking the next words against her ear. "They been real, real close. She's been his gal, if you know what I mean."

Tulsa May struggled in his arms. "No, I don't know what you mean. Luther never called on Emma; I would have heard if he was courting her."

The cowboy snorted. "He weren't courtin' her, Carrot. He was . . . well . . . I suspect an innocent young thing like you wouldn't know nothing about that, would ya?"

With a jerk worthy of a traveling wrestler, Tulsa May pulled away from him. "I do not care for what you are implying, sir."

Tulsa May turned her back to walk away, only to feel his hand grab her arm.

"Don't walk away from me, Carrot. When I'm with a woman I'm the one to say when she goes and when she stays. A gal don't dare go walking away from me. I don't like for women to do that one damn bit."

Genuinely angry, Tulsa May turned on him.

"I don't care what you like, sir. It's bad enough that you manhandled me, but I will not allow you to slander two fine, good people that I consider my friends."

"Friends." Turley's chuckle was mean.

Tulsa May meant to ask what he meant when she felt the touch of a hand on her arm. She turned to find Luther beside her, his mouth set angrily as he stared at Turley. With a little flourish, he took her into his arms and danced her out of the vicinity. Pressed close against him, she could feel the suppressed anger and the power of his control over it.

"Was he insulting you?" Luther asked quietly.

"Oh, no, not me," Tulsa May answered, not wanting to rile Luther further. "He was making some suggestive statements about you and Emma."

Luther blanched slightly. "I think that we should go," he said.

Tulsa May nodded. Glancing around, she saw Emma and Turley with their heads together, and became genuinely worried. "All right," she answered. "I think I've had enough of dancing for one night."

With his arm wrapped loosely around her waist, they made their way to the door. Elm waylaid them. "You young folks leaving already?"

"Believe so," Luther answered.

"Well, it was nice to meet you, Miss Newspaper Gal," he said, following them outside to the dimness of the roadway.

Tulsa May smiled at him. "I'll keep in mind what you told me."

"You do that and I'll be looking to dance with you again real soon."

"You seem in a mighty big hurry, Briggs."

The voice was Blue Turley's. He'd come up behind them, his arms folded before his chest belligerently, his tone argumentative and his voice overly loud. "A fella would think you was running scared."

Luther gave Turley a long look, but didn't bother to speak. With a nod to Elm, who'd stepped back slightly — sensing trouble between the two men — Luther continued to escort Tulsa May away from the door.

But Blue followed them. "I ain't heard that you's a coward, but I suspect it could be so."

Luther ignored him.

Emma Dix appeared at Blue's side. Tulsa May was grateful; surely Emma could calm the cowboy down. It was with stunned disbelief a minute later that she realized the woman was urging him on.

"Hey, yellowbelly," Turley called as he followed them out into the yard. "If you're gonna run from me, you'd better run faster or farther than you are now."

The music inside the roadhouse had stopped. The word "fight" had quickly circulated through the floor and the dancers began flocking out through the door, anxious to catch a glimpse.

As the crowd gathered, it became clear that Tulsa May and Luther were not going to be able to make a discreet retreat.

"Get in the Runabout," Luther said calmly.

"What's the matter with him?"

"He's just another cowboy looking for trouble. Now wait for me in the Runabout."

After making sure that Tulsa May was following his direction, Luther turned back to Turley. "I've no interest in getting into a fight."

Blue grinned. "I 'magine not," he said loudly enough for the crowd to hear. "Afraid you'll get that pretty face of yours busted up?"

"I'll not fight you over Emma, Turley," he said quietly. "That's all over and she knows it. There's no need to fight."

"Fight over Emma!" Turley's loud exclamation was followed by a hearty laugh. "There ain't no fight over Emma, pretty boy. I already won her."

"Then there is no cause to fight."

"What about that little Carrot of yours?" he said, pointing to Tulsa May seated nervously in the Runabout.

"Miss Bruder is none of your concern," Luther said.

Turley grinned. "Nope, not yet, she ain't. She 'pears to be your property all right. But I been thinking. There's something about that gal I've been wondering about for some time. I was hoping you'd have the answer."

"What is that?"

Turley leaned forward as if realizing the coarseness of what he was about to say, and spoke just above a whisper. But Luther clearly heard the words. "Is the fuzz underneath her skirts as orange as that on her head?"

Turley grinned. Luther smashed his fist right into that greasy smile. The blow loosened Turley's front teeth and cut Luther's knuckles. Although both men had clearly felt the blow, neither hesitated. Turley rebounded with a punch to the side of Luther's face. Luther brought his swing lower, nearly doubling the cowboy in half as the wind whooshed out of him.

Tulsa May screamed in horror at the very first blow. She was too far away to hear the argument, but she'd never expected Luther to start slugging.

The crowd quickly started cheering for one or the other and betting on the outcome. Tulsa May slipped down from her safe perch on the Runabout and hurried forward. She was determined to put a stop to the whole thing. How infantile and ridiculous, she thought. They are fighting like a couple of schoolboys!

As Tulsa May approached the scuffle, Luther caught sight of her. He turned his head to warn her off, but the words never came out.

Turley, taking advantage, slugged him dead-on. Luther went down like a felled oak.

"Oh!" Tulsa May's initial shock quickly turned to anger. With Luther hurt and bleeding on the ground, all her virtuous thoughts about peaceful compromise were forgotten. Howling like a banshee and her teeth bared, she jumped on Turley's back and began pummeling him on the head.

Caught off guard and already weakened, the

cowboy fell to the dirt. Tulsa May went with him, scratching, biting, and slugging.

Only a minute later she was forcefully pulled from a loudly complaining Turley's back. She struggled against the arms that held her.

"Hold up there, Newspaper Gal," she heard Elm Tripten admonish her. "You gonna embarrass your fella if you don't let him fight on his own."

Glancing toward Luther, she saw that he'd now risen to his feet, and although he was breathing heavily, he was waiting patiently for Turley to stand up also.

The cowboy did, only a minute later, and the two began senselessly pounding each other once more. Blood was running down Luther's face and he swayed unsteadily on his feet. Turley looked better and stronger and was the veteran of more brawls. But Luther was coldly angry. Turley deserved a beating and he wanted to be the one to give it to him.

The fight continued.

Tulsa May was horrified at what she saw, but she couldn't turn her face away. She found herself gritting her teeth and jerking her arms as if she could add force to Luther's blows.

After Luther managed to score several clear hits on Turley, the cowboy realized that he was losing the advantage. With a fierce growl, Turley threw himself at Luther. They fell to the ground. Over and over they rolled across the dusty ground, wrestling now instead of punching, equally matched in age, strength, and determination.

The bets were flying among the onlookers. The odds had now moved to even money. Tulsa May struggled slightly in Elm's grasp.

Dust clung to the blood and sweat on the men's faces. Teeth bared and muscles straining, each tried to overpower the other with strength of will as well as flesh and bone.

In the end, it was nature that determined the fight. It was simply bad luck that in one move when Luther found himself underneath Turley, his head rested on a wide thick oak-tree root. Turley immediately realized his advantage and began pounding Luther's head into the unyielding wood.

On the second or third blow, Luther loosened his grasp and his eyes rolled back in his head. Tulsa May screamed. Elm let her go and raced ahead of her.

"That's it now," the big man said as he pulled Turley from the limp form on the ground.

Turley struggled against Elm's grip.

"That's enough!" Elm shouted angrily. "You've knocked him out already. I'm not about to let you kill him."

Slowly regaining his composure, Turley stood over his victim, breathing heavily and staring.

Tulsa May was on her knees beside Luther. "Bring me some water," she called out to anybody within hearing distance.

Nobody moved as she gingerly began exploring the wound on the back of Luther's head. It was bleeding. That was a good sign.

"Somebody get me some water!" She looked up to see Blue Turley still standing over them looking down at the man he'd laid low.

"There's no water here," he said quietly. "Bring the Carrot some whiskey," he called out behind him. "She needs to tend to her man." Turning his attention to another area of the crowd, the ghost of a smile appeared on his face. "And my gal best be tending to me."

Tulsa May watched as Emma Dix separated herself from the crowd to stand beside Turley. Her expression was strange and vague as she gazed down at Luther. When she caught Tulsa May's eye, that vagueness turned to shame.

"Let's get out of here," she said to Turley. He wrapped an arm about her shoulders and leaned upon her a little more heavily than was necessary as they made their way through the crowd.

Chapter Sixteen

Luther moaned deep in his throat and tried to stir.

"Don't move," Tulsa May admonished as she knelt over him. "You've been hurt."

"Here's a jug of whiskey, ma'am," Elm said as he squatted down beside her. "Outside this stuff will clean his wounds and inside it will revive his spirit."

Luther moaned again. "My spirit doesn't need reviving," he complained as he tried to sit.

"Please lie back down," Tulsa May told him. "I don't want you to faint."

He looked at her curiously through the one eye that wasn't swelling. "Lord help me, Tulsy," he said. "If I faint, just shoot me. I don't think I could live with the embarrassment."

Elm chuckled. "You don't look much worse than the other guy."

Luther glanced at the other man skeptically. "Did he walk out of here?"

"Yep."

"Then at least let me get to my feet."

"You'll do no such thing!" Tulsa May grabbed the brown pottery jug that contained the moonshine whiskey and jerked the cork out of the top. From her skirt pocket she retrieved a dainty white linen handkerchief. She tipped the whiskey jug across her knee and splashed a very liberal amount of the acrid-smelling liquid on the pretty hanky.

"Good Lord, Tulsy!" Luther exclaimed. "You're going to smell like a distillery."

"Let me worry about that. Now lean up if you can and let me look at the damage on the back of your head."

Luther did as he was bid. His only hesitance was in response to the queasy feeling that overtook him. He hoped Tulsa May was wrong and that he wasn't about to faint.

"Ouch!" Luther jumped slightly as the whiskey-dampened hanky made contact with the wound. "Damn it, that hurts!"

"Sorry," Tulsa May answered. "I need to get you home where I can look at this in the light."

"Lord Almighty, Tulsy," Luther answered. "All I need is to take you back to the parsonage with my face all smashed up and you smelling of whiskey."

"Parsonage?" Elm was incredulous.

"My father is Reverend Bruder," Tulsa May admitted.

Elm looked down at Luther wide-eyed. "Boy, I thought you had good sense. If I'da known you to be foolish enough to bring a preacher's daughter to a dance hall, I'da never of bet my money on you."

Luther sat on the ground cringing as Tulsa May

washed his wounds with the stinging corn liquor. "That's why the preachers talk against gambling," he answered Elm. "Because there is no such thing in life except death and judgment."

"Help me get him to the car." Tulsa May spoke with authority to Elm. The big man squatted down and picked up Luther like a baby.

"Damn it, let me down! If Turley can walk out of here, so can I."

Elm allowed Luther to stand, but continued to support him as they made their way to the Runabout.

"Lean against me, boy," Elm said. "Don't you know that pride cometh before a fall?"

"I've already fallen several times," Luther snapped. "I think I'm getting used to it."

Carefully, hesitantly, Luther, with Elm's assistance, climbed up into the passenger seat. But the exertion took a lot of the sass out of him and he sat rather quietly. Elm lit the acetylene headlamps and Tulsa May cranked the engine.

"You take care of this fella now, Newspaper Gal," Elm called out over the sound of the motor. "I might get me one of these autocars one of these days, and I might need to get it fixed."

"Don't worry, I'll take good care of him," Tulsa May said.

"And you," Elm continued, pointing at Luther. "You take care of this little gal here."

"I'll do my best," Luther said, forcing a smile.

"And you find her a more genteellike place

to go dancing. This ain't no place to bring a special gal."

Luther nodded. "Hope you didn't lose too much money on me."

The big man laughed loudly. "Six bits I lost," he said. "But I'd pay it again to see that fight. Nothing like a little bloodletting to let a man know he's had a good time."

Luther's face hurt too much to chuckle, but it wasn't necessary. They could still hear Elm's booming belly laugh as they headed back down the road to Prattville.

His strength draining, and sparkling little stars appearing in his peripheral vision, Luther realized that he was about to faint. "If you're driving, I believe I'll take a rest." He slumped down in the seat and attempted to fake a yawn only seconds before the blackness overtook him.

"That's right," Tulsa May said. "You just sleep a little bit and you'll feel better."

When his head lolled onto her shoulder, she smiled and adjusted her position slightly to make him more comfortable.

She couldn't look at him, he was too close. But she could feel his nearness, his warmth. The scent of him, earthy, masculine, and punctuated with the wickedness of corn liquor, seemed to surround her. She sighed.

Her expression darkened slightly as she thought of the fight. She hadn't heard the words between them, but when two young men had their teeth bared and their eyes were flashing it was bound to be a fight over a woman. And Tulsa May was pretty sure that woman was Emma Dix. She was curvy and fine featured, so it was not hard to imagine how men could come to blows over a woman like Emma.

Even while concerned for Luther, Tulsa May had noticed the look on the other woman's face. What did that look mean? Did she love Luther? And if Luther was truly calling on her, why was it a secret?

Instinctively, Tulsa May let out the throttle on the Runabout and the little car went scurrying with unusual speed down the deserted dirt roadway.

The wind blowing on his face revived Luther enough to realize that he had his head on Tulsa May's shoulder. He sat up a little too quickly and the blackness threatened to overcome him again. This time he managed to ward it off. He took deep gulps of the night air and the fog in his brain began to dissipate. They were almost back in town.

"Tulsy, you can't take me to your father's house," he said. "It's bad enough that my face is smashed up worse than a sailor's at the rodeo. But we both reek of whiskey."

Tulsa May's brow furrowed thoughtfully. She shook her head. "There isn't anywhere else to take you."

"Pull over," he said.

"Here?" Tulsa May asked with surprise.

He nodded. "The river is on the other side

of those trees. At least I can wash up before I take you home." Tulsa May pulled the Runabout just to the side of the road and shut off the engine.

"Just wait here," Luther suggested as he eased himself out of the passenger seat.

"Don't be ridiculous!" Tulsa May said. "What if you were to faint and fall into the river?"

Luther shook his head. "Then I would be saved the ignominy of your having seen me do something so stupid."

Tulsa May didn't argue further; she simply climbed down from the car and followed him into the woods.

The night was clear and only slightly breezy. The moon overhead was just at three-quarters, but it shed enough light for the two to find their way to the river.

The reddish-brown sandbar near the river appeared almost silver in the moonlight. Luther walked upon the bank slightly unsteadily. He knelt at the river's edge and reached down to splash the lazily swirling, reddish Cimarron water on his face. He shook his head slightly at the chill.

"Here," he said to Tulsa May as he undid the buttons on his shirt. "If you're going to stand here, you might as well make yourself useful."

Tulsa May's eyes widened slightly at the sight of his bare chest in the moonlight. When he handed her the shirt, she scrupulously searched for rips or tears. Then she moved to stand behind him. Still, the sight of his naked back was strangely unsettling. She cleared her throat nervously.

Searching for an appropriate way to help, Tulsa May removed her now bloodstained hanky from the back of his head and screwed her mouth up thoughtfully.

"Well, you've stopped bleeding," she said. "I was really becoming concerned."

Luther took the dirty handkerchief from her and began dunking it in the cool water. "Head wounds always bleed a lot," he said. "And it's good if they do. If you get knocked out and you don't bleed outside, you're probably bleeding inside, which is no good at all."

Tulsa May watched as he scrubbed at the dainty piece of linen. "It's ruined already," she said. "You needn't work so hard to get it clean."

Luther held the hanky before him in the moonlight and knew she was right. But he was sorry.

"Tulsy, I suppose it is ruined. Funny, I keep trying to help you and I keep making things worse." His words were quiet and sincere.

"Worse?" Tulsa May seemed surprised. "How in the world have you made things worse?"

The words that came to Luther's mind were not the ones that he spoke. "I've made you the object of gossip and idle speculation. I never intended that."

"Don't be silly," she said. "Creating gossip was exactly what we *planned* to do."

"Well, it was a stupid plan," Luther answered bitterly. "I should have had more sense. Taking you dancing in a place like that was just asking for no-accounts to cast aspersions on your name."

Luther was so angry Tulsa May actually laughed.

"What on earth is so amusing?" Luther asked, his jaw set stubbornly.

Tulsa May shook her head, still smiling. "Who cares what people think? Having aspersions cast on my name is a new experience. I might even enjoy it."

"Tulsy, this is serious," he said, turning toward her. "I can see how this must look. A fine, decent young woman like you chasing around some dance hall, alone with some punch-drunk half-breed and smelling of liquor."

"My goodness, Luther. You make my life sound almost exciting."

Near anger, he grasped her in his arms. "You are the most important woman in the world to me. I would rather die than do anything to distress you."

His declaration was heartfelt and sincere, but Tulsa May paid little attention. She was staring at the wide expanse of damp, muscled flesh before her.

"You don't have much hair on your chest," she said. Realizing the very personal nature of her comment, Tulsa May opened her mouth to apologize. But any words she might have said were swallowed up as Luther dipped his head to join her mouth with his.

His lips were warm and soft, but there was

nothing gentle about his kiss. His mouth teased and lured and mastered her own until they moved as one, in sweet pursuit of pleasure.

Tulsa May felt no shyness, no aversion. She wanted his kiss, his touch, she wanted him. And her body said those things that her words could not. She fitted herself against the contours of his body, so different from her own. His flesh was warm and slightly damp from the cool river water. The sparse swirls of hair on his chest were thin and dark, but somehow she couldn't resist running her fingers through them. The sensation beneath her fingertips was sensuous and startling. It raised gooseflesh on her arms and a shuddering thrill down her spine. She pressed herself more tightly against him.

"Luther," she moaned as a shudder ran through her.

"You're cold?" The question was a whisper against her lips. He pulled her more closely into his arms. She was trembling against him. But he was trembling too.

He took several deep breaths trying to quiet the passion stirring inside him. "It's part of my Indian heritage," he whispered.

She looked up at him curiously. "What?"

"Not having much hair," he explained. He held her at arm's length, looking at her face in the moonlight. This was his Tulsy, he had to remember that. "I bet Doc Odie's got plenty of hair, even if it is gray."

"I wouldn't know," Tulsa May answered. "The

only shirtless man I've seen before now was my father."

It was an intimate admission. It frightened and excited them both.

Tulsa May was blushing, but she cleared her throat noisily and tried to recover her composure. This was Luther, her best friend. She mustn't allow him to know how much he affected her. Attempting to lighten the mood, a joke sprang to her lips. "Daddy looks a bit like an orange bear."

Luther's laughter was a little strained. But the strange spell was broken, he told himself. He would let her go now and they would forget that they had just kissed. He would let her go now . . . now . . . He should let her go now. But he didn't.

"My father was a very hairy fellow too," he said, postponing the moment of parting. "I remember taking baths with him at the creek near our place when I was a boy. He had a big thick pelt of jet-black hair all over his chest."

Tulsa May swallowed. She couldn't imagine the father — all she thought of was a naked Luther bathing. She tried to continue the conversation. "So when people say you are *just* like your father, they don't really know the truth."

Luther's weak smile faded. "No, I'm not just like him." He looked at Tulsa May very seriously. "And I certainly plan not to make any of his mistakes."

Tulsa May had heard her share of rumors about

Luther's father, but she knew Luther was honorable and good. "I don't see any chance of that happening."

Luther shook his head. "It very well could." He released her and stepped away. "My father ruined a decent woman's reputation. If we don't stop this foolish game we've been playing, I might well ruin yours."

Tulsa May didn't immediately know if the game he referred to was the pretension of courting or the kisses they had shared. She felt cold and alone without his arms around her.

"Tulsy, I hope you know I didn't lure you down here to kiss you. Lord knows that's the last thing I should be doing."

"I know you didn't try to lure me," she answered quietly.

With a huge sigh, Luther gestured to the world around him. "It's just moonlight and river that makes me act this way."

"It's all right, Luther."

"No, it's not all right. This must stop." Luther clenched his teeth with determination. "This must stop now."

Tulsa May said nothing. She couldn't hear anything over the sound of the breaking of her own heart.

"We've created enough gossip," Luther said with conviction. "There is no reason why I should call on you anymore."

Her face paling, Tulsa May continued to just stare at him, struggling to keep herself composed.

"I'm sure, the way gossip travels, that by to-morrow night everybody in town will have heard about the fight." He began pacing nervously across the sand. "It stands to reason that you would be appalled and disgusted by such behavior," he said. "And you certainly should be. Fighting and carrying on in a common roadhouse. It's not at all the thing for a fine woman like you."

Still Tulsa May made no comment.

"I'll let it slip that you gave me my walking papers. That should be enough for folks to chew upon until some new scandal comes up."

He turned to look at her then. She seemed small and pale in the moonlight, but she nodded. "Of course you're right, Luther. We've played this game long enough."

He grabbed her chin and lifted it to look into her eyes. They were misted with tears.

"Tulsy?" he whispered "Oh, Tulsy, I never meant to hurt you."

"I'm not hurt," she insisted. "I'm just disappointed."

Luther gazed at her closely. "This has been more than a game, hasn't it?"

Cold fear filled Tulsa May's heart. He was looking into her eyes. Could he see it? Could he see that she loved him, longed for him, ached for the romance he could never give her? Desperately, she sought words that would give lie to the truth in her eyes.

"I'm just thinking of how much I wanted to

go dancing again," she said with a shrug. "I'll miss it."

Luther's eyes softened and he stroked the side of her jaw tenderly. "Dancing?" he whispered. "Tulsy, I'll always be here if you want to go dancing."

Gently, he took her hand in his grasp and laid his palm against her waist. He snuggled up closely against her and began to lead her in a rhythmic, romantic waltz. Luther, his voice low and sweet, sang softly into her ear as they turned and swirled in the moonlight near the slow, seductive sound of the running river.

> "Night and the stars are gleaming
> Tender and true;
> Dearest my heart is dreaming,
> Dreaming of you!"

Blue Turley's room was in the upper floor of the stockyards' office building. The outside stairway was dark and narrow, but Blue and Emma might well have been better able to negotiate it had the cowboy not been carrying his tack and saddle, and had he not celebrated his victory over Luther Briggs by imbibing nearly half a jug of corn liquor on the way back to town.

"Emma, sweet Emma, I've been waiting for this day for many a moon," he told the woman at his side drunkenly.

She made no reply. From the moment she'd seen Luther lying on the ground, she'd known that her bargain had been stupid. She'd felt no elation, no vindication at his defeat. She'd felt only strangely sad for a friend who was hurt. A friend. That's what Luther had always been to her. They had shared some laughter, some happy times, and some pleasure. But there had never been love. Luther had been her friend. Perhaps she hadn't realized that because she had so few.

"The first day I seen you," Turley continued, clearly delighted by his turn of fortune, "I said to Ferd, 'I'm gonna have me a little taste of that one.' That's what I told him, sure as the world."

Emma shuddered with distaste. She had lain with Luther just for the pleasure of it. Could she lie with Blue Turley for services rendered? Somehow, for all her sordid reputation, this seemed worse, much worse, than anything she had ever done.

"This is it, this is it," Turley said as they reached the top of the stairs. He pushed open a weathered and scarred door. The mingled smells of horse sweat, leather, and old boots was unpleasant. "Welcome to my little home-sweet-home."

Emma hesitated at the threshold for only an instant. Turley slung an arm around her waist and pulled her inside. She glanced around nervously as she freed herself from his grasp. The center of the room held nothing but a worn cot covered by a disreputable-looking, moth-eaten blanket. On the left, a couple of crates had been hammered together to form a washstand. And a cracked mirror was nailed to the wall above it. On the far side of the room, Turley carefully laid out his tack. Saddle, bridles, lariats, and horse blankets were stored with some care. Turley's own clothes lay around on the floor in casually thrown heaps. The cowboy walked right across his dirty laundry as if it were rugs.

"It ain't much, but it's mine."

Emma began to feel as dirty as the room looked. "Blue, I've been thinking about this and —"

With a hearty laugh, Turley pulled Emma roughly into his arms. "I've been thinking about it too. Been thinking about it so much, I cain't even sleep good at night."

"I'm not really —"

"You think you've been having fun with Luther Briggs. That metal-heap wrangler don't know half the moves and tickles I can show you. Wait till you see how a real cowboy can scratch what's itching ya."

"Turley, I —"

"Damn." Turley laughed as he ran an eager hand along her backside. "It's gonna be a real pleasure to pleasure you. Ha! I made a joke. But sticking it to you ain't no joke. I bet you like it real good, Emma Dix. Now, don't you worry. When it comes to lovin', I'm real, real good."

Emma began struggling in his arms. His breath was fetid with stale whiskey and he smelled of dirt and sweat and blood.

"Don't!" she protested. "You're hurting me."

Turley loosened his grip only slightly. "I ain't aiming to hurt you, Emma Dix. I'm just aiming to *fuck* you." He whispered the offensive word close to her ear.

"Wait! Stop it now. Blue, wait, I —"

Turley pulled her down on the bed and rolled on top of her. "Emma Dix. Oh, you feel right good to me, Emma Dix. Is your middle name 'Likes'?" He snorted with laughter. "I made me another little joke. Get it? Emma Likes Dix."

The sound of ripping cloth was loud in Emma's ears as Turley grabbed at skirts.

"Stop it!" she cried. "You've torn my dress. Stop it!"

Turley wallowed over her, laughing and joking. "I'll buy you another rag, Sugartail. Something real pretty, all red with sparkly things on it."

"Let me go!" She fought against him. "Let me go right now!"

"Ooooh, damnation, Emma. I like a gal that shows a bit of spirit."

As his grimy hand delved between her legs, Emma began to struggle back in earnest. "Leave me alone!" she screamed.

Turley clawed at her drawers, unconcerned at her protest.

She kicked. She scratched. She screamed. She struggled. But Blue Turley was much too big and much too powerful.

Trying to fling him off her, Emma grabbed for the iron bedstead to get leverage. She was only trying to free herself when her hand encountered the bootjack Turley had left hanging on the bedstead. Grasping it in her hand, she didn't give herself time to think. With a powerful cry of fury, she brought it down with all her strength on his head.

"Yeow!" Turley hollered.

The sound was wild and angry. He grabbed for the bootjack in her hand, but she managed to evade him. There was no stopping her now. With all the strength she possessed, she slammed the makeshift weapon against his temple. This time he did not cry out. Again she brought the bootjack down on his head. And again and again and again.

She was hysterical now, crying, trembling, shaking. He was still. He'd stopped holding her down. With shaky, labored breathing she pushed herself out from under him. She came to her feet at the side of the bed. Nervously she brought a hand to her brow, only to see it covered with blood.

"I've killed him," she whispered as she stared wide-eyed at his still body.

She moved away from the bed. She stared down at the bloodied bootjack in her hand. With a tiny cry of terror she dropped the makeshift weapon to the floor and gazed at it in horrific fascination as if it were a snake.

Emma wrapped her arms about her sides as if suddenly seized with a chill. She turned away from the sight of the bed and found herself staring at her own visage in the mirror. Her hair was wild, her face paint smeared, and her hands were bloody.

"Oh, Papa!" she said aloud. "I've finally done it. I've finally completely ruined my life."

She turned back to stare at Turley for a minute. She couldn't feel sorry that she had stopped him, no matter the consequences. But she felt tremendous sorrow that only now did she realize how carelessly she had been throwing away her own life.

Tears began to fall then, tears of sadness, of self-disgust and anger. She had made a mistake. One terrible mistake. But it had been long ago. She had said that the town would never forgive her, but, in fact, she realized now she had never forgiven herself. Turning over a new leaf and living an upright life had been just too hard to even try. She had thought herself unworthy of anything good or decent or fair. And now, she had killed a man. Now, she would no longer have a chance to try to redeem herself. Now, as a murderess, she never could.

She covered her face with her hands and thought of her father. Willie had loved her through all her mistakes. He would even love her now, when she had killed. But he needed her love and care. He deserved to die in peace, knowing that she had found the life he'd wanted for her. But instead, his last days would be filled with the truth of her shame, her disgrace, her imprisonment.

A low moan came from the bed. Emma screamed.

With shocked disbelief, she looked back at Turley as he began to stir slightly.

"He's not dead," she whispered. "He's not dead."

A wellspring of anxiety and hope surged inside her. If Blue Turley was alive, she still had a chance. She could still change her life. She could still give Willie Dix the peace that a loving father deserved.

"Turley?" She spoke his name in little more than a whisper. She must keep him alive. If she was ever to have a life, a real, ordinary, honorable life, which was suddenly the only thing that she wanted, she must see that Turley lived. She must bind his wounds and make sure that he was all right.

Emma stepped toward him. Fear and loathing filled her throat with nausea. She shuddered. She couldn't touch him. She couldn't touch him again, ever. But neither could she leave him here to die.

When the answer came to her, the fear on her face melted. With a sigh of relief, she turned and raced out of the room, taking the stairs two at a time. The night on First Street was noisy and boisterous, but here, near the stockyards, the only sounds were the bawling cows in nearby pens.

The street was well lit and probably safer, but she skirted it anyway. Hurrying down deserted alleyways littered with garbage and refuse, Emma made her way without caution through the roughest and most dangerous area of Lowtown. She crossed the tracks into Prattville proper. She didn't let up her pace. Running on, she ignored the street that led to her home where her father waited safely.

Emma raced down the red-brick sidewalks of Main Street. The gas lamps glowed brightly to light her way. There were few people out and about, but she noticed none of them anyway. She hurried on. To Luther Avenue, through the city park where picnics were held and the townspeople took their Saturday promenades.

"Please don't let him be out somewhere," she prayed aloud. "I haven't asked a thing in a long time, but I'm asking this."

A light was still on in the study on the first floor of the Millenbutter Memorial Hospital. Emma could have cried with gratitude.

"Doc Odie!" she called as she raced up the stairs. "Doc Odie, come quick!"

Chapter Seventeen

A thoughtful silence had fallen between the young couple riding up Guthrie and River Road in the Model G Runabout.

Luther's suggestion that they should discontinue their charade left Tulsa May feeling sadly bereft. She tried to remind herself that she was very lucky to have had these few weeks and that the sweet, wonderful memories would last her a lifetime. However, this was one occasion when Tulsa May's legendary optimism seemed to fail her.

Luther himself didn't feel much better. Strangely, the idea of returning to his life before he started escorting his Tulsy all over town somehow seemed dismal and boring. But he could think of no other way. She stirred his passion. And he knew himself well enough that he seriously doubted the future of his self-control. Tulsa May was sweet and warm and welcoming in his arms. The safest way to handle that was to get as far away from her as possible. That, or marry her.

Marry her. The fact that the notion even crossed his mind was slightly amazing. But somehow the idea did not in any way dismay or disturb him. He offered a shy glance in her direction. Could the old wives' tales be right? When a fellow got ready to settle down, did he really want a different kind of woman than the kind he'd chased?

Closing his eyes, he tried to imagine next year and the year after that. Arthel would be in college. Luther would be struggling to afford to keep him there. There would be long days of labor and sleeping late only on Sunday. There would be no one to share his dreams, his hopes, or his failures. Briefly he thought of other women he'd known, which led him to Emma. No, he didn't love Emma. He liked her, but he didn't love her. He had never shared anything with her beyond a bed. He'd kept the inside of himself — the joy, the elation, the anxiety — to share only with the people that he loved. He had kept those things to share with Arthel . . . and with his Tulsy.

But marriage? It was a big step. Especially so for Tulsy, he thought. Only weeks ago she had been planning to marry Odie Foote. There was no way a woman like her could make a lifetime choice so easily. And despite the passion in her kisses, he was sure she thought of him as a passing fancy. Someday they'd simply be friends again. Her response was merely innocence, he assured himself. Tulsa May simply didn't know she was supposed to act coy.

Just when he thought the long, silent drive would never end, they arrived back in Prattville. Tulsa May, her hat pinned perfectly in place, was steering the Runabout down Main Street en route to the parsonage. She was quieter than usual.

He had been stupid to kiss her again, he thought. She was probably shocked and embarrassed. Shocked and embarrassed and confused. His excuse of being too full of moonlight and river was an unsatisfactory explanation. Nor was it much of an apology. But he hadn't felt much like apologizing. He tried to wish that he hadn't kissed her. But that regret just wouldn't come.

Main Street was warm and welcoming in the glow of its new gas street lamps. It was after ten o'clock and the bright yellow flame turned the bright brick sidewalks an attractive mauve and reflected into the glass storefronts.

"Look, it's Haywood Puser." Tulsa May's puzzled tone made Luther look up.

The man was hurrying toward them down the street.

"He's calling for us to stop," she commented with surprise.

Luther shrugged. "I wonder what in the world he wants?"

Tulsa May slowed the Runabout until it came to a halt directly in front of the older man.

"Good evening, Mr. Puser," Tulsa May said politely.

"What's wrong, Haywood?" Luther asked.

The old man's face was lined with concern.

"What happened to your face, boy?" he asked.

"I ran into a door."

Puser nodded. "He must have been a big one. Luther, where's that brother of yours tonight?"

"Arthel?"

314

"You got any other?" The old man folded his arms across his chest impatiently.

"Why, he's at home, I suspect," Luther answered carefully.

Tulsa May could hear the lie in his voice, but apparently Puser didn't notice.

"Are you sure about that?"

"Well, no, I can't be certain," Luther admitted.

Haywood put his lips together in a thin line of worry and disapproval. He heaved a sigh. "I certainly hope that is exactly where he is."

"What's happened?" Tulsa May asked. Fear niggled at her and her heart began to palpitate nervously. "Is someone hurt?"

Puser didn't immediately answer, but scratched the back of his head thoughtfully.

"No, no one's exactly hurt," he said evasively.

"Then what has happened?" Luther demanded.

"Well." He cast an uncomfortable look in Tulsa May's direction. "You know Ebner Wyse, that old fellow who lives next to the Sparrows' little honeymoon cottage on the edge of town?"

Luther nodded silently, looking concerned.

Tulsa May felt a hard pit of fear form in her stomach.

Puser rubbed his hands together in a nervous gesture.

"Ebner cain't sleep too well these days. Age does that sometimes. And when he cain't sleep, well, he just sits outside on his porch or walks around his yard."

"So?"

315

"So he couldn't sleep tonight and he was just out in the moonlight minding his own business." Haywood glanced once more at Tulsa May before continuing. "He thought he heard noises over at the cottage. That place has been deserted since Cora moved out to the farm with Jedwin. Ebner thought somebody might be trying to steal something or up to some mischief. Sure enough, he went to check about it and flushed out a young couple." Haywood glanced red-faced at Tulsa May. "My humble excuses, Miss Tulsa May, but Ebner says these younguns was as naked as the day they was born."

"Oh!" Tulsa May's wide-eyed exclamation earned her another apologetic look from the older man. She glanced with growing concern to the man beside her. She could see Luther's jaw tighten.

"Ebner didn't get a look at the gal at all," Haywood said. "But he swears the fellow was an Indian."

Luther was silent for a long minute. When he spoke, his voice was deliberately calm and casual. "My brother and I are certainly not the only Indians in Prattville."

Haywood nodded in agreement. "That's exactly what I said myself," he admitted. "But old Ebner went a-tattling to the preacher and now a gang of menfolk is meeting at the parsonage. They've been looking into who is where they's supposed to be and who is missing. One of them menfolk is Titus Penny and he ain't all that sure where

316

little Maybelle is right now. She apparently snuck out of her room after supper. Penny thinks she went to meet Arthel."

Luther nodded.

"It don't look good," Haywood said solemnly.

Clearing his throat with dignity, Luther smiled down at the undertaker with feigned confidence. "I'm sure I can convince them that they are mistaken. Arthel and Maybelle barely bother to speak to each other these days. And I doubt that either would be involved in anything so foolish."

Haywood shook his head. "I don't know," he said. "Younguns that age are almost always unbelievably foolish."

Luther secretly agreed, but didn't dare to say so. "It's probably some lawless young couple from across the tracks," he assured Puser.

"I sure hope so," Haywood answered. "But you two better get up there and put out the fire just the same."

"That we will," Luther told him.

Haywood doffed his hat at Tulsa May. "You're looking right-out pretty these days, missy. And a good evening to you both."

Tulsa May smiled back politely, but her heart was still racing and her stomach churned with anxiety. She knew Luther so well, and she sensed his distress.

Pulling out the throttle a little more than necessary as she pulled away from the curb, the Runabout sputtered and backfired loudly. They rode in silence once more, but this time it was not uncomfortable; there was a sense of mutual understanding between them.

"Luther —" Tulsa May whispered as they raced down the street to the parsonage. "What will we do?"

"Don't worry, I'll think of something," he quickly assured both her and himself. "I've watched after and taken care of Arthel all my life. I promised Mammy and Pa. I won't fail him now. I can't."

Tulsa May nodded in agreement, but she couldn't swallow the knot of fear that settled in her throat. "And I won't fail you," she whispered.

At least half a dozen angry men, including the mayor, the deacons of the church, and the preacher, stood on or around the preacher's porch as Tulsa May and Luther drew up. Titus Penny was easily recognizable for the bright redness of his face and the anger that puffed out of his cheeks. Every face turned to stare at them as Tulsa May pulled the Runabout up into the little drive beside the house.

"Where is that brother of yours?" Penny called out to Luther before Tulsa May could even get the car stopped.

Luther's face was pale with worry and the aftermath of his fight, but he forced a welcoming smile to his lips. "Why, he's home tonight," Luther answered calmly.

Casually, he stepped down from the Runabout and turned chivalrously to help Tulsa May do the same.

"What happened to your face?" Ross Crenshaw asked as the couple moved closer to the lighted porch.

"A breather fell on me when I was beneath a car," he answered.

"A breather do that much damage?"

"It was a heavy breather," Luther assured him.

"I asked you about your brother." Titus Penny's growl was low and dangerous.

"I told you he's at home, Titus. I worked him so hard today, he said he was going straight to bed."

"He's not there," Fasel Auslander said, looking angry and indignant. "Rossie and I were already over to your place. There's not a soul at home."

"Oh?" Luther tried another tack, but his head was throbbing badly. "Perhaps he's down working on my new building on Main Street. You folks aren't the only ones in town who have ideas for that place."

"Working on the building at night?" Even the reverend appeared skeptical.

"What's this all about?" Tulsa May asked. She knew Luther was still recovering from his fight. He really should be home in bed instead of creating stories. Besides, she simply wanted to hear the worst and face it. And help him face it. "Do you need Arthel for something?" Her expression was sincere and innocent enough that even Luther momentarily believed her confusion.

The men on the porch glanced at each other. This was not a subject to be discussed in front of ladies, certainly not young, unmarried ones. All were far too embarrassed to speak up. Keenly aware that his innocent daughter should not be touched by this latest Briggs scandal, Reverend Bruder was about to order her upstairs to her room, when Erwin Willers spoke up. As the publisher of the *Populist* he was accustomed to speaking frankly with Tulsa May; it didn't occur to him to clean up the story for a young lady's ears. "Got a scandal brewing," he told her with the typical enthusiasm of a newspaperman. "These fellows seem to think that young Briggs is involved."

"My Maybelle's missing!" Titus Penny declared with fury. His anxiety was clearly overwhelming his sense of propriety. "And Ebner Wyse said he saw an Indian boy forcing himself on a woman at the Sparrow cottage."

Luther's mouth dropped open in bona fide shock. *Forcing?* Was Titus Penny going to say Arthel *forced* himself on Maybelle? It wasn't true. Arthel might be foolish and wrongheaded sometimes, but he was neither violent nor cruel. But would they all believe the worst?

"Now, Titus," Mr. Wyse said. "I didn't say exactly *force*." Ebner was somewhat embarrassed. "I mean, the gal were laughing and giggling like she weren't too much agin it."

Penny's face reddened and his jaw hardened with anger.

"Force or no force," Clyde Avery stated determinedly, "we cannot allow our young people to act immorally within the city limits. We are

320

a decent, civilized, moral community."

"Oh, for heaven's sake, Clyde," the preacher chided. "Trust you to worry more about the reputation of the community than the souls of two of our young people."

"The preacher's right," Ross Crenshaw said. "Young Arthel is to be pitied. Why, the boy had practically no upbringing at all. Just a brother who had not much better rearing himself."

Tulsa May gasped at the insult. Luther saw red. "My brother is as moral and upright as any of your rowdy brood of jut-swilling whiners! If Ebner didn't *see* my brother, then it *wasn't* my brother." Luther was struggling for the right words. "All he saw was an Indian. Do I have to point out the percentage of the population of this state that fits that description?"

"But," Ross insisted. "There aren't many Indians that spend their time around this area of town."

Faces were stiff with temper. Voices were raised in anger. Tulsa May feared that things were close to getting out of control. She'd already seen the results of that once tonight, she didn't want to witness it again.

"Where did you say it was?" she asked quietly.

"At the Sparrows' honeymoon cottage," Ebner answered. "Right out in the open under that big pecan tree."

Tulsa May let out a strange little giggle that startled the men into total silence. As they stared at her, she grasped Luther's hand and brought it up to her cheek. He looked at her as if she'd lost her mind.

"I guess we'd better confess, honey," she said, wrapping her arm through his. "That wasn't Arthel and Maybelle out under that pecan tree." Again she giggled. It was an unnatural sound. "It was me and Luther."

"What!"

The chorus of shocked men included Luther himself, but fortunately no one noticed.

"I . . . I . . ." The Reverend Bruder's face turned white as a sheet and then bloomed into fiery red.

The sight of his anger frightened Tulsa May, but she knew she had to protect Arthel. "Papa, please, you look positively apoplectic," she said anxiously.

The preacher's eyes were bulging and he seemed unable to speak. The townsmen were staring at the couple in total horror.

Luther felt the sweat seeping down the back of his collar. He glanced over at Tulsy. She was pale now too, watching her father struggle for breath and self-control. Surely they couldn't believe this of her! Luther was aghast. How could anyone imagine that Tulsa May Bruder would fornicate on the ground with any man, let alone a man who was not her husband. He couldn't let them think of her that way.

"We're married," he blurted out.

"Married?" The chorus of voices once again sounded stunned.

"Ah . . . yes . . . we're married." He grabbed Tulsa May's hand and squeezed it, hoping to both give and get strength. "That's why we're home so late, Rev," he said. "We went to Guthrie and got ourselves hitched."

The reverend continued to stare at them for a moment in disbelief. Then, as if his strength had suddenly failed him, he sat down on the porch step.

"Married?"

"Yes, Papa." Tulsa May hurried up to the steps and squatted down in front of him. "I'm sorry we gave you such a scare. But we're married." She glanced back at Luther with a worried expression. "I love him, Papa," she said. "I want you to be happy for me."

"Happy?" The preacher continued to look at her almost without comprehension. The men around them began to mumble in surprise, but the preacher ignored the sounds. "Why would you run off and get married like that?" he asked.

Tulsa May was momentarily stuck for a reply. She glanced again at Luther. Ebner Wyse was patting him on the back and offering congratulations.

"Well, we . . . I . . ." She stumbled for words. "You know how Mama is," she said finally. "She would have wanted to have another big to-do with paper lanterns and bridal gowns and everything. I couldn't go through that again, Papa. Luther and I just wanted to get married."

The preacher nodded thoughtfully. "Yes, that's

your mother all right." Still he looked puzzled; he lowered his voice to a near whisper to ask the next question. "But daughter, what on earth were you doing at the Sparrows' cottage?"

Tulsa May looked toward Luther for help, but he appeared to be as dumbfounded as she was. She looked back into her father's loving, trusting eyes.

"Honeymoon?" she answered.

By the time Doc Odie and Emma returned to the dirty little room over the stockyards' office, Blue Turley was sitting up at the side of the bed.

"You bitch!" he screamed at her as she walked in behind the doctor.

Emma froze in place; fear was still coursing through her veins. Her bottom lip trembled, but she was far too alarmed at her own actions to cry.

Turley moaned then from the pain in his head. He lay back on the bed. "What did you hit me with?" he asked through clenched teeth.

"Bootjack," she answered quietly.

Doc Odie spied the bloodied weapon on the grimy pine floor and picked it up and handed it to Turley.

The cowboy gave a vivid curse and threw the bootjack toward the washstand. It hit the wall, shattering the dingy mirror that hung there, before dropping into the tepid water in the basin.

"Miss Emma, if you'd wait outside," Doc Odie said with gentlemanly courtesy. He escorted her to the door with a smile of reassurance before turning back to the cowboy on the bed.

"Let's see your head, young man."

Odie didn't like the way the fellow looked at Emma, much less the way he talked to her. But he was a doctor and tending the sick and injured, regardless of his personal feelings, was a part of his vow of service. He didn't, however, vow to be kind and sympathetic to any patients who'd gotten exactly what they deserved.

Emma had given a less than complete accounting of what she'd been doing in this room, and why she'd been forced to strike the man. Out of breath and clearly terrified, she had burst into his study, too winded to do much more than beg him to get his bag. He'd hitched up his rig in record time as Miss Emma regained her composure. Still, on the ride over, she had not been very forthcoming about the details. But Doc Odie was not born yesterday and had a pretty good idea of what had happened.

"Ouch!" Turley complained as the doctor probed his wound without much gentleness. "You're hurting me!"

The doctor gave him a wide-eyed look. "I thought big, tough cowboys didn't feel pain. Do you want a bullet to bite on?"

Turley didn't answer, but he sullenly seethed.

"How did this happen?" the doctor asked coolly.

"Didn't the bitch tell you?"

Doc Odie's hands stilled on the blood-matted

hair of his patient, but he resisted the desire to strike the fellow. "I haven't seen any bitches lately," he answered coldly as again he probed the wound. "It was Miss Emma who was concerned enough about your injuries to fetch me."

"Miss Emma?" Turley spoke her name with distinct insinuation and then spit on the floor. "That bitch could have killed me."

Not a great loss to the human race, Doc Odie thought as his eyes narrowed. "A young lady has the right to defend herself as best she can."

"Defend herself?" Turley chuckled without humor. "Hell, Doc, I didn't drag her up here. She wanted it. It was her idea."

Doc Odie seemed to ignore the words as he reached into his bag for a bottle of medicine. Liberally, he doused the open wound on Turley's temple with carbolic.

The young man screamed.

"Even if it was her idea," Doc Odie said to him quietly, "a young lady always has the option of changing her mind." The doctor poured more of the fiery carbolic on the back of Turley's head. The cowboy went rigid and momentarily fainted from the treatment.

The doctor sighed with satisfaction. "That should keep away any infection," he said aloud, as if the cowboy were not now beyond hearing.

Without Turley's foul-speaking tongue to anger him further, Doc Odie carefully dried and inspected the wounds before wrapping his entire head in soft, clean cotton bandages. He glanced around the dirty room, hating the sight of the place. He recalled the meticulous cleanliness of the Dix house. Miss Emma was much too beautiful to be seen in such squalor. But it wasn't simply her beauty that made her too fine for such a dwelling. She was a loving daughter and a splendid, strong woman. She should never have come to this disreputable flophouse.

But she had. Was she trying to get Turley to marry her? Doc Odie shook his head. Perhaps she had decided against Briggs, but surely there was better than Turley. Even *he* would be a better husband to her than Turley!

He looked down at his patient. Clearly the young man was not gravely ill and there had been little chance that he would have died. Still, Doc Odie couldn't help but be glad that Emma had come to him for help. She trusted him, and that was a very good thing. A lot of things could be built on trust.

Uncorking a bottle of smelling salts, Doc Odie passed it beneath the cowboy's nose and he revived immediately. He began moaning all over again.

"Well, you're all wrapped up nice and neat now," the doctor told him.

"Damn her, she could have killed me."

Doc Odie began loading his equipment in his bag. "Not likely, not with a head as hard as yours."

"You think I'm going to be all right then?" the cowboy asked.

"Yes, you'll be fine. That is, if you take a suggestion I would like to make for the sake of your health."

"What's that?"

"You ought to leave town."

Turley's brow furrowed. "What?"

"For the sake of your health," the doctor repeated quietly. "I don't think being ridden out of town on a rail would be very good for you with those head wounds. And that, of course, is what will happen when I tell the townspeople that you attacked Miss Emma."

"I didn't attack her!"

The doctor shrugged. "Yes, I do suppose it will be your word against mine."

Turley looked furious as he stared at Doc Odie. The man was at least fifteen years older than him, not even half his size, and looked like a good stiff wind could knock him down, not to mention a hard-living cowboy. Still, the doctor's expression was unyielding. His determination alone seemed to give him power that youth and muscles did not.

Turley raised his chin, determined to outstare the older man. The doctor, however, was not intimidated.

With calm finality, Doc Odie snapped the closure on his worn black leather case. "Change the bandage every three days and have a nice trip," he said evenly.

Unhurried, Odie made his way to leave. He turned back to give Turley a long look. "I would think that your health will greatly improve the minute you get out of this town."

There was anger in Turley's expression, but he didn't reply.

When Doc Odie opened the door he found Emma standing nervously on the landing.

"Will he live?" She tried to look past Odie's shoulder into the room.

"Certainly," the doctor answered. "I never kill my patients unless it's absolutely necessary."

Startled, Emma stared at him dumbstruck for a moment until she realized that he was making a joke. She sighed in relief and even managed a ghost of a giggle.

"I was so afraid," she said.

The doctor took her hand. It was as cold as if it were the dead of winter instead of a balmy evening.

"Yes, I know you were afraid," he said kindly. "But you needn't worry now. Mr. Turley's decided to leave town at the earliest opportunity, and you are quite safe with me."

Sighing, Emma stood limply on the stairway landing for a moment, shaking her head and simply counting her blessings. Doc Odie wrapped a comforting arm around her shoulders.

"He's really decided to leave town?" she asked in unfeigned relief.

The doctor glanced back into the dark, squalid room at the young man still lying on the bed. Then he leaned close to Emma's ear to answer her in a whisper. "I believe, Miss Emma, that you have plainly scared the daylights out of the man. I certainly wouldn't want to have you as an enemy of mine."

Emma's slack-jawed amazement brought a smile to the doctor's face.

"But then we've never been enemies, have we? We've always been the best of friends. May I have the pleasure of escorting you home, Miss Emma?"

She didn't have a chance to reply; Doc Odie took her arm as if stepping out at a grand cotillion.

As they descended the stairs, Turley looked after them, shaking his head in disbelief.

"Emma Dix and Doc Odie?" he speculated aloud with clear disbelief. "That gorgeous sugar-tail and the smelly old Doc?" Turley almost laughed at the idea. Then his thoughts cleared.

Again he heard the doctor's words and saw his unyielding expression. He remembered his own foolishness in picking a fight with Luther Briggs. A man would do a lot for a woman like Emma Dix.

Ignoring the pain in his head, Turley jumped from the bed and hurried to take action. In ten minutes flat his dirty laundry was stuffed in his saddlebags, his tilt-brimmed sombrero covered his bandages, his shattered shaving mirror was left in pieces on the floor, and he was noisily carrying his tack and saddle downstairs.

Chapter Eighteen

The lamplight glowed in Tulsa May's bedroom as she and her mother sat on the edge of the bed, having a mother-daughter talk. At least, that was allegedly why her mother was there. In fact, Constance Bruder had begun sobbing and sniveling the minute she walked into the room and she hadn't stopped yet, almost fifteen minutes later.

"Please, Mama," Tulsa May coaxed. "You really mustn't take on so."

"My baby!" Constance whined. "Married among strangers!"

Tulsa May had nothing really constructive to answer to that. She was sure her mother wouldn't feel any better to hear that she was actually not married at all.

"I just didn't want you to have to go to all that trouble."

That brought a near hysterical response. "You are my only child, my only baby. It wouldn't have been trouble. It would have been joy."

Tulsa May had no idea how to go on from there. Her mother had seemed at first stunned at the wedding news, then delighted. Now she had succumbed to disappointment at missing an opportunity for a gala celebration.

"Mama, what's done is done," Tulsa May insisted gently, stroking her mother's back reassuringly. "We just have to go on from here."

The admonition was as much for herself as for her mother. On the porch, when she'd made her declaration, it was almost a reflex action. Arthel was in trouble. Luther had to save him. She had to help.

Never had she imagined that Luther would claim holy wedlock. But then she had set the ball rolling. It no longer mattered. The milk was definitely spilt and she didn't know what she could do about it now.

"I know I should be happy," her mother sobbed.

"That's right, Mama," Tulsa May coaxed. "Luther and I want you to be happy for us."

Constance blew her nose loudly in a linen handkerchief and attempted to compose herself. "I know how Moses must have felt not being able to cross over Jordan."

"Moses?" Tulsa May looked at her mother with genuine puzzlement.

"You know the story," Constance said. "For forty years Moses led the children of Israel through the wilderness. Then when they finally got to the promised land, God didn't allow Moses to go in with them."

"What has that got to do with Luther and me?"

"For twenty years I've prayed and prayed," the woman answered. "And thank the Lord, now you've finally gotten married. But just like Moses, Heaven didn't see clear to let me be there." Mrs. Bruder wiped her tears on her handkerchief and looked at her daughter bravely. "I've simply got to stop feeling sad and be grateful that my prayers were answered."

Prayers were the order of the day downstairs as well. These were not the preacher's prayers, nor even the prayers of the deacons, city fathers, or the previously outraged upstanding citizens. The only silent entreaties emanating from the lower floor of the Bruder parsonage were coming from Luther Briggs.

"Please don't let anybody ask to see the marriage license," he begged fervently. "I'll change my ways, I'll sell my share of Ruggy's Place, but please don't allow anyone to ask to see the papers." Lack of a wedding ring could be explained away, but nobody marries without a license.

The crowd of men, who had been cheerfully toasting the bridegroom with lemonade, slapping him on the back repeatedly with congratulations, began to disperse. Luther found himself less and less eager to be alone with his fictional father-in-law. He had always tried to be open and truthful with the preacher. Lying to him now would be painful. But he had to protect Tulsa May. Even more than Arthel, Tulsa May deserved his protection.

Once they were alone, Reverend Bruder grasped Luther in a bear hug.

"Son," he said, "At last I can really call you that. Welcome to the family."

His stomach sank. It had been one thing to have the Rev as a temporary foster parent when he was sixteen. At twenty-six, the last thing in the world that he wanted was the good reverend to feel obliged to offer wedding night advice and counseling.

Luther smiled wanly. His only other option would be to hurry up to Tulsy's room. He was quite willing to do that — at least then they'd have a chance to get their stories straight — but Miz Constance was up there. Luther was sure that she would find it unseemly for him to be such an eager bridegroom. He seemed destined to listen to a "man-to-man" talk.

"Come and sit with me a moment," the reverend said, sighing expansively. "I've always thought we had a lot in common. Now, I guess little Tulsa May is one of those things."

"Yes, I suppose so, Rev," Luther answered.

"Please," the preacher said, clasping the younger man's hand in his own companionably. "Call me Pa."

"Pa?" Staring at the smiling man with the bright orange moustache, Luther found the word a little distasteful on his tongue. "Rev, I really prefer —"

"I know, I know," Reverend Bruder interrupted. "It will take time for you to get used to this new informality. But son, we are going to get along just fine."

"I hope so, sir." Luther swallowed nervously.

"I've known you for ten years," the preacher continued. "And I've watched you grow up. Your path has not always been down the straight and narrow, but I've always been proud of you."

"Thank you, Rev."

"Oh, you've got into some scrapes. But I've known from the beginning, from the way you took responsibility for your brother, as well as your own life, that you had integrity. You're a man that a man can trust," he said. "And that's a good thing. It's hard for me to entrust my little girl to anyone at all."

"I can understand that."

"Truth to tell," the preacher admitted, "I wasn't all that fond of Odie Foote. Oh, don't get me wrong, he's a good, honest man and all. But he never seemed to have any special feeling for my little Tulsa May."

"Apparently not," Luther replied woodenly.

"But you," the preacher went on with a smile. "Why, I've been seeing it in your eyes for weeks. You're in love with my little girl, and I know she's in love with you."

Luther tried to hide his astonishment. Were he and Tulsy that good at acting? Or was the good reverend unbelievably naïve?

"Well, Rev," he said, attempting an explanation. "Tulsy and I have known each other so long and we've been best friends practically from the day we met. And, well, we —"

The preacher seemed uninterested in his reasoning.

"There is one thing that I wanted to speak to you about, however."

Luther's blood chilled in his veins. *The papers,* he thought with near terror. *The reverend is going to ask to see the marriage papers.*

"What is that?" Luther asked bravely.

Reverend Bruder opened his mouth to speak, but then momentarily hesitated. He appeared to be as nervous and ill at ease as Luther was himself.

Clearing his throat, somewhat nervously, the preacher tried again. "I still find it difficult to believe that we had our little talk this afternoon and this evening you're my son-in-law."

Luther nodded. He could see how that might be a little hard for the reverend to comprehend. He found it pretty strange himself.

"It was . . ." He hesitated, unsure of what to say and wishing that he and Tulsa May had had time to cook up a story together. "It was a private thing, Rev," he said finally. "It was just between Tulsy and me."

Bruder's brow furrowed in concern. "Marriages are more than two people," he said, his tone the familiar one of the shepherd of the flock. "Marriages are the joining of families."

Luther raised his chin defensively. "Some families cannot be joined. Sometimes marriages can tear families apart." He spoke with conviction, knowing well of what he spoke. "But if you love someone, I mean really love, then what families, or friends, or even neighbors think is not important in the least."

The preacher looked at Luther for a long moment before nodding a tacit agreement. "What about what God thinks?" he asked.

Luther didn't even hesitate. "Seems to me, Rev, that if it's really love, God's already had a hand in it."

Reverend Bruder stared at the young man before him with a new admiration.

Confused at the meaning of his own words, Luther attempted a hasty retreat. "I suspect I should go upstairs to Tulsy now," he said, hoping the preacher's temporary astonishment would last until he was safely out of the room. He didn't quite make it.

"Wait!" the reverend called out.

Luther hesitated in the doorway.

"What I really wanted to say, son —" he began. "Well, what I was actually thinking was —" Again the older man struggled for words. "I realize that tonight, with you thinking your brother was at your home, and Mrs. Bruder and I here . . ." The reverend cleared his throat loudly. The bright orange moustache stood out vividly against the beet-red color in his cheeks. "Well, I just think that . . . that . . . well, on the ground in a deserted yard is just —"

Luther's face flamed; he was almost as discomfited as the preacher. "You are absolutely right," he said, nearly choking on the very idea of having . . . doing . . . well, his Tulsy on

337

the ground beneath a pecan tree. "I promise you that it will never happen again."

The knock at Tulsa May's bedroom door was not exactly welcome.

"Just a minute," Constance Bruder called.

"This is the sweetest, daintiest little nightgown that you own," she told her daughter earnestly as she held it out before her.

"Mama," Tulsa May answered quietly, but with conviction. "It's pink. I do *not* wear pink."

"Who can tell pink in the dark?"

"I can!"

"Now Tulsa May, I only want you to look as well as you can for your new husband. Every woman, even the loveliest natural beauty, must enhance herself."

"You are forgetting, Mama," she said bravely. "We got caught together in the Sparrow cottage yard. Luther has already seen me. I don't think a prissy gown will make him believe he got a better bargain."

"Oh!" Mrs. Bruder covered her mouth in shock. The reverend had told her the details, but she certainly didn't want to be reminded. "Tulsa May, don't you ever let me hear a word about that again. It's simply too unrefined to even be recalled."

Luther's knock sounded at the door once more, this time more insistently.

"I said just a minute!" Mrs. Bruder's voice was downright strident.

"I know we haven't talked about —" Constance

allowed her eyes to stray to the bed and then pursed her mouth with embarrassment.

"That's all right, Mama," Tulsa May assured her, blushing. "I'm sure that Luther knows . . . I mean, that we . . . I'm sure that we will manage fine."

Her mother sighed, apparently greatly relieved. "Just remember one thing," she whispered to her daughter. "This is what my mother told me." Constance raised her chin and clasped her hands as if reciting an important litany. "Man was only one of the animals until God created woman."

Tulsa May's expression was puzzled. "I'll keep that in mind, Mama."

The knocking sounded again.

"All right! All right!" Constance went over to the door. "For heaven's sake, young man," she scolded Luther. "Have some propriety!"

Luther gave a slight bow by way of apology. "Sorry, Miz Constance. Or do you want me to call you Mama now?" He hoped she didn't.

Dumbfounded, Constance Bruder stared at him as if he'd lost his reason. "Certainly not!"

"Then good night, Miz Constance," Luther said, shutting the door before she had a chance to make any further comment.

He leaned against the door, breathing heavily as if he had just been pulling the weights on the preacher's Whiteley Exerciser. He glanced over at Tulsa May. They sighed in unison and then smiled at each other as if they couldn't believe that they'd pulled it off.

It was then that Luther realized that Tulsa May was standing at the end of her bed wearing a button-front white muslin nightgown and a little lace cap. Obviously his imitation bride was dressed for bed.

It's simply Tulsy in her sleeping clothes, he reminded himself. He had lived in this house for almost a year. He'd seen her dressed for bed before. Somehow none of these facts could distract him from the sight of her before him.

Tulsa May felt his eyes upon her and dropped her gaze in embarrassment. Self-consciously she folded her arms across her chest. She didn't know what to do, what to say. What must Luther feel, being trapped like this?

She raised her chin bravely, her eyes wide; an idea that had come to her, a vain hope. "Perhaps you can send Arthel off to college early," she suggested. "If you can get him out of town on the morning train, then by tomorrow afternoon we can admit that we're not really married."

Luther forced his gaze from her thinly clad body up to the hopeful expression on her face. He shook his head slightly. "Tulsy, if I spend this night in this room, we *are* married. I'm sure that the Rev wouldn't have it any other way. And neither would I."

Tulsa May nodded solemnly, knowing what he said was absolutely true. "Luther, I'm so sorry I —"

"Sorry?" he asked, shaking his head with incredulity. "You shouldn't be sorry, you should

340

be proud. You were so brave. I couldn't believe that you were willing to give up your reputation for Arthel and Maybelle's sake."

Guilt flashed through Tulsa May. She wasn't sure her motives were pure. Had it been for them or for herself?

"Besides," Luther continued. "You didn't say we were married, I did." He sighed heavily and raised his eyes to her. "I'm the one who needs to be apologizing, Tulsy. I may have ruined your whole life."

She looked at him, but knew she was to blame. Tulsa May loved Luther Briggs. She had always loved him. Somehow, she was sure, this could not be just a lucky coincidence. She had maneuvered him into this marriage. Because she'd always wanted it to happen, it had. And she had ruined Luther's life, he hadn't ruined hers.

She felt selfish and ashamed. "I just should have thought of something else."

"Well, you didn't, and I didn't," Luther answered. "And it's done now."

"Yes, I guess it is," Tulsa May agreed quietly not knowing quite what done meant.

"Or rather," Luther corrected. "It's not *done* at all! First thing tomorrow we've got to get to Guthrie and get really, legally married."

"Do we have to?" Tulsa May's voice sounded uncharacteristically meek and distant.

"Absolutely! I swear my hair was going gray downstairs worrying that somebody would ask to see the marriage license."

341

"The marriage license!" Tulsa May was flabbergasted. "I hadn't even thought about it."

"Fortunately, neither did your father, but we have to come up with one and soon."

"Oh, I suppose you're right."

"Maybe if I cross the judge's palm with a little silver, we can even get it dated for yesterday."

"Is that necessary?"

"It is unless you want to celebrate two wedding anniversaries."

"I never even expected to celebrate one."

Luther was grinning at her then, and Tulsa May was feeling distinctly uncomfortable.

"It's just —"

"Tulsy, let's just make the best of this," he said easily. "I know I'm probably not the man you would have chosen, but I'll try to be a decent husband. I promise you'll never be cold or go hungry."

"Oh, I know that, Luther, but for you —"

"Me?" He shrugged with unconcern. "I hadn't thought of marrying so soon, Tulsy. But, truth to tell, I always thought to marry sometime, to have a family and all."

"But you wouldn't have married me," she said flatly.

Luther opened his mouth. He appeared momentarily surprised by her words. He hesitated only a moment. "I would have married someone like you, Tulsy," he said. "All the qualities I'd want in a wife are things that I've admired in you."

Tulsa May knew he was not talking about her gap-toothed smile or orange hair. What he meant, she was certain, was that he would have married a respectable young woman from a good family. But Tulsa May was just as sure that had he chosen his bride, she would have been a good deal prettier and much more desirable. Luther Briggs was just too honorable a man to say those things.

"You are very kind," she told him.

He chuckled as he pushed away from the door. "That's what you'd expect from a doting bridegroom on his honeymoon."

Tulsa May's cheeks flushed bright red and once more she nervously cast her gaze to the floor. He stepped toward her, gently raising her chin.

"Don't worry, Tulsy," he whispered. "You and I both know this is not our wedding night."

She flushed with embarrassment and tried to look away, fearing that he might see the longing in her eyes.

"Hush now," he whispered as he caressed her cheek. His hand caught on the tiny ribbon tie of her lace cap. He tugged on it until he had her attention. "Why do you wear this thing?"

"To keep my hair tidy," she answered too quickly.

Luther raised a skeptical eyebrow and grinned warmly. "I've known you for ten years, Tulsy Bruder, and keeping tidy was never one of your top priorities."

Her answering giggle was somewhat nervous. "That's one of the bad things about having a good friend," she said. "They know the truth about you and can always tell when you're lying."

Luther nodded. "That's right, Tulsy. I know the truth about you. Is this thing meant to cover and hide your hair?" he asked.

"Yes, of course. What else?"

"I thought maybe you were hoping to give up on youth, skip the dull life of the matron, and move directly into your dotage."

Her laughing reply was just the encouragement he needed. Like the young, mischievous boy he once had been, Luther jerked the cap from her head.

"Luther?"

He held it tauntingly out of reach. "I've got it and you can't have it," he declared in a singsong manner more familiar to the schoolyard than the wedding bower.

"Give me that back!" Tulsa May insisted, quickly following along with the game.

For reply, Luther laughed and waved the dainty piece of lace under her nose. Tulsa May made a grab for it, but she was not quick enough. She pulled at his arm, but he twirled out of her grasp and hurried across the room, still waving the lace cap like a flag.

"Come and get it, Tulsy," he teased. "Come and get your dotage cap, if you can."

With a growl of irritation, Tulsa May took up the challenge. Unexpectedly, she rushed toward him, nearly catching him unawares. Luther jumped out of the way; once, twice, three times he managed to feint, only to find himself blocked into the corner.

With the bed on one side and the window on the other, Luther clearly had no place to go.

"I've got you now," Tulsa May said in triumph.

Luther grinned. He hesitated only a minute before throwing himself across the bed in an escape attempt. Tulsa May threw herself on top of him.

In a wild, rolling tussle, like two young pups let out to play, Luther and Tulsa May struggled against each other on the bouncing bedsprings. The lace cap was still in Luther's hand, but Tulsa May held a firm grasp on his wrist. Laughing, they turned over and over from one end of the bed to the other, both teasing and threatening and determined to win the tiny lace headpiece that neither really wanted.

It was happenstance that Luther was on top when they reached the footboard. The iron bedstead stilled their movement; both took stock of where they lay. Luther felt the warmth of a soft, smooth body with delicate feminine curves beneath him. Tulsa May was surrounded by the hardened strength and masculine aroma of the handsome lover of her dreams. He stared down into her eyes with some emotion she couldn't fathom.

It was a long moment, punctuated only by the sound of two young bodies breathing quickly and uneasily.

Luther pulled away first. Rising to his feet,

he hurried to the window and cast the lace cap out to the wind.

"Luther!"

He shrugged and offered an uneasy grin. "It looks better on the catalpa tree than it does on you, Tulsy."

Tulsa May stared after it for only a moment, before her eyes returned to Luther. Nervously, she brought her hands to the neat little bun the cap had been so good at keeping tidy. To her dismay, the bun had almost completely unraveled and long curly strands of carrot-red hair waved around her shoulders.

"Oh, I must look a fright!" she said, hurriedly trying to repair the damage.

Luther reached for her hands. He held them for a minute in his own. "I like your hair down, Tulsy," he said. "I've told you that more than once now."

She shook her head. "Nobody likes orange hair."

He made a face. "I've been accused of being a lot of things," he answered. "But this is the first time I've been nobody."

"Oh, Luther," she protested with a laugh.

Gently he grasped a handful of the vivid curls in each of his hands. He held it there surveying it for a moment before he looked back into her eyes.

"I don't love *orange* hair, Tulsy," he said. "But I love this hair because it's yours. Because it's part of you. I guess I must love most everything about you."

Tulsa May dropped her gaze, fearful that he would see the tears that glistened in her eyes. "You are so sweet," she whispered.

Luther used a finger to raise her chin. "I certainly am sweet, ma'am," he said. "I'll undoubtedly make some lucky lady a wonderful husband."

She managed to smile and regain her composure.

Luther looked past her for a second. She could almost see the gleam come into his eye.

"Here, sit on the bed," he told her. Luther hurried to the far corner of the room. A free-standing oval beveled mirror of the new French style stood in the corner. Luther grabbed it from its swivelhooks and began to carry it across the room.

"Oh!" Tulsa May exclaimed. "Mama'll have a fit if you break that new mirror."

Luther only smiled. "I don't intend to break it," he said as he set it at an inward angle at the foot of the bed. "Besides, if your mama was going to have a fit at me, I suspect she would have had it tonight."

Luther stepped back, surveying the arrangement. "Perfect," he declared with some satisfaction. He walked over to Tulsa May's dressing table and retrieved the Russian bristle hairbrush.

"What are you doing?" she asked him.

"I'm going to brush your hair," Luther answered as he sat down beside her on the bed. He pointed to the glimmering image reflected in the sleek oval at the end of the bed. "You just watch in the mirror," he said. "I want you to see what I see."

As Tulsa May was not overly fond of mirrors, she had a difficult time keeping her attention on her own reflection.

"Eyes straight ahead," Luther insisted as he languidly drew the bristles through her hair. "Watch, Tulsy. Try to see what I see."

She raised her chin determinedly. She could do it, she assured herself. She would just imagine she was looking at someone else.

In the mirror a young couple sat on the edge of a girlishly beribboned pink quilt that covered a somewhat narrow iron-framed bed. The bed was so high that the young woman's feet did not quite reach the floor and her charming little pink toes peeked out from beneath her simple muslin nightgown. The young man sat behind her. He was somewhat taller than she. And one long, well-muscled leg jutted out from the bed at an angle while the other was bent at the knee and crossed casually to lay a booted ankle upon his thigh.

Calmly, carefully, as if he did it every day, he was brushing the young woman's hair. The hair was long and thick with curls of bright golden red.

Tulsa May's brow furrowed. "It's the lamplight," she said, almost to herself.

"What?"

"It's the lamplight that makes it look this color."

Luther's gaze caught hers in the mirror. "Yes, it's lamplight that makes it this color," he said.

"Sunshine makes it glimmer more gold and at dusk it looks like it's lit with fire."

Tulsa May tried to look away.

Luther dropped the hairbrush and grasped her chin. "Look, Tulsy," he said. "Look and see what you look like. You've been seeing yourself through your mother's eyes and the eyes of the people of this town. You've believed what they saw, what Miss Maimie saw." He turned her to face the mirror once again. "Tulsy, look at yourself, look at the truth. This is what I see."

Tulsa May still felt awkward.

"I remember you told me once that you like the countryside in winter, because the landscape isn't hidden by the leaves of trees or decorated with wildflowers and tall grasses. You always wanted to see the truth, to see what was really there and find beauty in that."

He grasped her hair into one long, thick, twisted coil and laid it along her shoulder until it hung nearly to her waist.

"This is the truth about you, Tulsy. Can't you look and see the beauty here? Can't you see the beauty that I see?"

Tulsa May stared at her reflection. She had not changed. The miracle she knew her mother had prayed for had not occurred. But Luther was right. She could see the truth. And the truth had flaws. But the truth was not the flaws, it was only enhanced by them.

The words formed on her lips, but she hesitated to speak them.

"Say it," Luther coaxed quietly next to her ear.

"I'm . . . I'm almost pretty in your eyes," she admitted.

Luther smiled. It was a warm and loving smile. A smile that she knew very well. "Not 'almost pretty'," he said. "Almost beautiful. Do you want to see yourself as beautiful?"

"What?"

"Do you want to see yourself beautiful as I see you beautiful?"

She tried to look away from the mirror again, but he wouldn't let her.

"Do you want to see my beautiful Tulsy?" he asked.

"Yes," she admitted finally, nervously.

She heard Luther take a deep gulp of air beside her and then felt the flurry of his breath exhaling against her neck. She watched in the mirror as slowly, so slowly, he brought his hand to the button of her nightgown.

It was Tulsa May who gasped then as he released the tiny pearl buttons from the delicate braid frogs.

"Luther," she whispered uneasily.

"Shhh, Tulsy," he answered. "I want to show you something beautiful, someone beautiful. I believe it is far too beautiful for me not to share it with you."

Slowly, inch by inch as each button was released, the pale flesh beneath her gown showed itself. She was trembling now, and there was gooseflesh on her arms and neck though the room was not cold. Through the thin muslin of her gown, Tulsa May saw the nipples that she had tried so hard to hide standing firm and dark and impudent against the thin cloth.

She wanted to stop him, to cover herself, to jump up and run away. But like a mesmerist's victim she sat stiffly staring at the reflection in the glass.

When the last button had been opened, Luther tenderly grasped each side of the button placket and slowly, almost reverently, parted the fabric of the gown.

Tulsa May watched, spellbound, as the generous cleavage of her bosom was displayed. Then the round, soft inner curves of her breasts were in view. She wanted to close her eyes. She wanted not to see. But as he pulled the cloth away from her thick, stiffened nipples they both became entranced.

"Tulsy," he sighed. "You are more beautiful than even I imagined."

She jerked her gaze away from her own exposed reflection to see the look in Luther's eyes. There was no hint of condolence in his expression, only . . . admiration.

"I . . . I . . . well . . . Mama says my . . . well that I have . . . that it means I can suckle a lot of babies."

Luther's gaze warmed into the gentlest of smiles. "Tulsy, I do hope so," he whispered. "But what about husbands?" He brought one long sun-browned finger up to caress a thick nipple. "Does Mama say that husbands get to suckle too?"

"What?" Tulsa May's jaw slacked in shock. But the meaning of his words zinged through her veins like lightning. She was breathing heavily as she watched the mirrored reflection of the labored rise and fall of her breasts.

Luther teased and tickled the nipple into hardness, then he smoothed it gently with the pad of his finger.

"I wish I could taste you now, Tulsy," he whispered. "You're so sweet and soft," he said as he palmed her breast. "And so hard." He tugged her nipple between his fingers. "I wish I could kiss you where you are soft. And also where you are hard."

Tulsa May closed her eyes against the wicked image she saw in the mirror. In her imagination she could feel his warm, damp lips where his fingers were now.

She opened her eyes to meet his own in the reflection. She saw hunger there, hunger, desire, need, all of it. And it was all directed toward her. An alarming, dissolute, wicked thrill surged through her, with frightful hunger to the little ball of fear in her stomach and then lower.

Her breath caught in her throat. "Luther, I don't think —" she began, jerking the sides of her nightgown back together modestly.

"Tulsy, I —" He reached out a hand to touch her. She was trembling. "Don't be afraid of me, Tulsy. I don't want to hurt you. I just want you."

She wanted him too. The frightening fear now quivered between her legs like an ache. She wanted him to soothe her. But as he reached out a hand to caress her cheek, fear overwhelmed desire.

"We're not really married," she said.

Luther's hand stopped in mid-motion. His eyes were glazed with want and he closed them to the sight of her. Taking a deep breath, he cleared his throat and nodded.

Abruptly, he got up from the bed and walked to the window. Pulling it open, he leaned outward, wishing it was a cold winter night instead of a mild spring one.

Tulsa May watched him as he allowed the cool evening breeze to ruffle his hair.

"Luther?" she asked quietly.

"I'm fine," he told her, glancing back with a wan smile. "You're right, Tulsy. We are not really married. Not tonight."

Chapter Nineteen

"We saved your neck last night. Don't you have anything to say about that!" Luther's tone of voice was close to furious as he stared down his younger brother.

Arthel appeared unmoved. He turned to Tulsa May, who sat somewhat uncomfortably on a hard wooden chair at the table. "Welcome to the family, Tulsa May. I always thought you'd make a terrific sister."

"Arthel!"

The younger brother turned back to the older, assessing the anger in his face, but not intimidated by it. "Luther," he said calmly. "I didn't ask for your help. I certainly didn't ask for you to marry Tulsa May." He glanced in her direction and grinned. "Although I'm real glad that you did."

Luther began pacing, his expression dangerous. "What in the blue blazes were you doing down there anyway?"

"That's none of your business," Arthel answered without even a hint of rancor.

"Was that Maybelle Penny you were with?"

Arthel shrugged. "My big brother taught me never to kiss and tell."

"Damn it!" Luther's glare was positively explosive. He held his fists clenched together at his side as if to keep himself from using them.

"I don't want you to curse in the presence of my sister-in-law." Arthel's wry words almost burst through the weary bonds that held Luther's temper in control.

"Please," Tulsa May pleaded quietly. "Arthel, stop baiting him. Luther, calm down a little. You're so angry now you won't be able to talk. And you two need to talk."

Luther turned to her and nodded. She was right. He was hopping mad right now, near ready to blow up, and that wouldn't do himself, Tulsa May, or Arthel any good.

Deliberately stopping his pacing, Luther rubbed his temples. He was tired and angry and sore. Last night he'd been thoroughly beaten up by a half-drunken cowboy. Except for one rather vivid black eye, most of his bruises didn't show. But that didn't keep them from hurting. If that weren't enough, he'd slept the night in Tulsa May's desk chair. All night he'd shifted and turned and attempted to find a comfortable position to sleep.

After the untoward intimacy of the mirror, he hadn't trusted himself to share Tulsa May's prissy pink bed. He had already frightened her. She hadn't asked to marry him. And she was right in pointing out that they weren't really married. Intimacy was something they would have to work at slowly. Just because he was eager didn't mean that she was too. Tulsa May was a lady as well as his best and closest friend. But as far as loving, he was a complete stranger.

He knew he had acted wisely. His back ached, his head pounded, and his unfulfilled desire still plagued him. It had been one of the longest nights he'd ever lived. And this morning hadn't gone much better.

By breakfast, Mrs. Bruder had already planned a reception for them at the parsonage that afternoon.

"We have other plans for today, Miz Constance," Luther had stated quite firmly. He sat at the Bruder table once again as he had when he was a boy. But he was not a boy now, and he was not about to be ordered around.

"Well, whatever plans you have will just have to be changed," the preacher's wife insisted with an unconcern that bordered on complete disregard. She passed Luther the plate of biscuits. As far as she was concerned, it was settled.

Glancing over at Tulsa May, Luther could see that she was also displeased. This morning she had dressed in a pretty blue-striped voile waist with panels of pin tucking and a smart navy skirt of cotton serge. It was not a typical wedding costume, but the style suited her well. And Luther found himself enjoying the sight of her. On the way downstairs he had teased her that she'd worn the dark blue to match his shiner. She'd giggled at his joke, but asked with concern about his other injuries. As usual her hair was done up in a fashionable little twist at the crown of her head, making it simpler to fit under the braided straw panama-style hat she carried. But today the hairstyle seemed a bit looser than customary, allowing a bit of her natural wave and curl to show. Luther remembered those sweet, silky curls from the moments before the mirror. Then, remembering the sight of her bosom, his eyes dropped to her decently covered bodice and he felt the heat of physical need stirring within him again. Determinedly, he turned his eyes to his plate and filled his mouth with hominy grits.

"Couldn't we have a reception next week sometime, Mama?" Tulsa May suggested. "Luther and I have so much to do today and I'm not sure that I'm really ready for a big to-do."

"It simply must be today," Mrs. Bruder said firmly. "Tomorrow is Sunday and your father will be announcing the wedding in church. We can't have everyone in the community knowing before we've had a chance to have all our friends and neighbors over for a little celebration first."

"But, darling." The reverend tried to intervene. "The way news spreads in this town, everybody will know the news by this morning anyway."

Constance Bruder couldn't be dissuaded. To Luther's dismay, he found himself agreeing to be back at the parsonage at two o'clock with Tulsa May and his best dress suit.

"I know you never thought to wear the concert dress again," Constance said. "But it will be perfect for the reception."

"Mama, I'm not wearing that pink dress," Tulsa May said flatly. "I'll burn it first."

"Well, let's not spoil the morning arguing," Mrs. Bruder said lightly. "I'll lay the gown out for you and we'll decide this afternoon."

Luther's eyes narrowed. Miz Constance could push him around all she wanted, but he would not allow her to bully Tulsa May again. "I hate that pink dress," he stated emphatically. "Instead of laying it out, why *don't* you spend the morning burning it?"

Mrs. Bruder was silenced into stunned shock.

But at least this morning Luther had had the satisfaction of having the last word. His discussion with his brother wasn't going nearly as well.

"All right, Arthel," Luther said, forcing calm into his voice. "Let's all take a seat at the table. There is no reason the three of us can't talk this thing out calmly and rationally."

Arthel nodded, but he kept his chin up defiantly. He grabbed one of the chairs and, straddling it, laid his arms casually along the top of the chair back. Although he'd done as he was bid, Luther saw the closed expression on his face and sighed.

"I don't want to argue with you," he told Arthel. "Even if I did, I honestly don't have the time. Tulsy and I have got to get to Guthrie, get married, and be back by two o'clock for a reception at the parsonage."

"Then I think you two had better get on the road," Arthel answered.

"Arthel, you've got to take this seriously," Luther said. "Titus Penny was ready to have your head on a platter last night."

"And maybe he should have," Arthel snapped.

"Probably so, but did you think I could just let that happen?"

"I wish you would have."

Luther stared at his brother, completely puzzled. "Do you want to be run out of town on a rail?"

"I want to live my own life," he answered quietly. "Succeed or fail, I want my life to be my own."

The silence between the two men was long and uncomfortable.

"Arthel, I promised Mammy and Dad —"

"Don't you think I know that," Arthel interrupted him. "You've loved me and cared for me for ten years and I'm grateful," he said. "You've been a good brother, a stern father, and even occasionally a comforting mother. But you can stop now, Luther. I'm all grown-up. I can take care of myself."

"You can take care of yourself?" Luther was obstinate. "What about Maybelle? Can she take care of herself too?"

"Maybelle is not your concern," Arthel answered.

"She will be if you get her with child!"

Tulsa May lowered her eyes.

Arthel glanced over at her and then gave his older brother a stern look of disapproval. "If Maybelle's with child, it's *my* child. And *my* child is only *my* concern."

"She's not? Is she?" Tulsa May whispered anxiously.

Arthel shook his head and patted her hand reassuringly.

Luther wasn't ready to give up the argument. "Arthel, what about your plans? What about college?"

"College was your plan, Luther."

His eyes wide with surprise, Luther shook his head. "You've always said you wanted to study engineering."

"And maybe I will," Arthel admitted. "College isn't a bad idea. I understand that you wanted to help me get a start in life and education would be a way to do that."

"It certainly is."

"But I'm not thinking about college these days," he confessed.

Luther's mouth formed into one long thin line of disapproval.

"What about your future?" Luther demanded.

As Arthel gazed at his brother, his expression became serious once more. "I am thinking about the future," he answered solemnly. "There is a war coming, Luther. We both know that. A war is coming and I'm just the right age to be a part of it."

"President Wilson says —" Luther interrupted.

"I know what Wilson says. And I know that we are going to be drawn into the war in Europe and it's going to be a war fought with machines as much as men." Arthel's solemn visage began to look hopeful. "I know about machines, Luther — Greasy. I know about machines because my brother taught me. There'll be a place in this war for a man like me. And that's where I'll want to be."

"My God, Arthel!" Luther exclaimed.

"I can't think about college until this is settled," Arthel explained. "When the future looks more hopeful, then I'll think of it again."

Luther covered his face with his hands for a moment and then squeezed them together. "Arthel, I don't want you fighting in a war. You could get killed."

His younger brother smiled at him. Leaning across the table, Arthel laid a hand on Luther's shoulder. His expression was earnest, anguished but determined. "I'm not the helpless papoose in the cradleboard anymore. I'm a grown man, Luther. Old enough to know what I can and what I must do. Older than you were when you became my protector. Older than you were when you took on the world. It's time now that I took it on myself."

The Guthrie and River Road was sloppy from an early morning rain. Luther had chosen to drive the Runabout as a more fitting wedding car than the A-2 Commercial. He had draped a tarp across his knees and Tulsa May's to keep the splatters of red mud from the roadway from soiling either her pretty blue outfit or his best dress suit.

"Try not to worry about Arthel," Tulsa May told him as she secured the pin on her braided straw hat. "In many ways, he is right. You have carried him on your shoulders much too long."

Luther nodded thoughtfully. "I know I have," he said. "In my head at least I know it. But in my heart I still feel so . . . so guilty."

"Guilty?" Tulsa May stared at him curiously.

"Yes," Luther repeated sadly. "I know it's foolish, but I feel guilty because I was the lucky one, the favored one."

"Lucky, favored?" Tulsa May shook her head. "What are you talking about?"

"I'm the one who looked like my father," he said. "I'm the one that Miss Maimie remembered in her will." Luther set his jaw tightly, as if to hold in the anguish in his heart. "Arthel was so little when our parents died," he said. "I promised to take care of him, but I couldn't give him all that he needed. He needed family. He needed his grandmother. I knew that, but I couldn't find a way to give that to him."

He shook his head in self-disgust. "I tried, Tulsy. I swear that I tried. Do you think I wanted to be Miss Maimie's chauffeur? To spend every day of my life listening to that old harpy complain about everyone and everything. I don't know how many times she told me that I was nothing, less than nothing, to her or anybody else."

His jaw tightened with the memory. "I thought if she came to know me, she'd come to accept me. I did that for Arthel. I knew she would never accept him unless I forced her to." He shrugged and shook his head. "But in the end, I couldn't even get her to do that. To Miss Maimie, Arthel was just another Indian."

"That's sad," Tulsa May admitted, her eyes misting.

"It's stupid!" Luther corrected forcefully.

"Well yes, that too. But it's sad for Arthel. And more so for Miss Maimie."

"For Miss Maimie?" Luther was incredulous.

"Yes," Tulsa May answered. "Much worse for her than for him. Arthel's had so many of us to love him, and he has so much love to give back. It was hard for anyone to love Miss Maimie, and I doubt many did. She could have used some of what Arthel had to give."

Luther looked at her in amazement and shook his head but didn't disagree with her.

"However," she continued, "Miss Maimie's foolishness is nothing that you should feel guilty about, Luther. Arthel said so himself. *You* were his family. You were anyone and everyone that he needed.

"Losing your parents, your home, everything that is known and familiar is a horrible thing for a child. But terrible things happen to all of us in our childhoods. None of us makes it through that time without our share of pain and horror and despair. You didn't know your own father until you were eight. I don't know why heaven lets things happen that way, but maybe hardship teaches us to face life. For as soon as we learn that we can live through adversity, we become an adult."

Tulsa May took Luther's hand and squeezed it tightly in her own. "Arthel has lived through and become a strong and gentle and caring young man. You haven't failed him, Luther. You've raised him. He's a man of whom you should be very proud."

Luther turned to stare at her. "I love you, Tulsy," he whispered.

He felt uncomfortable as soon as the words were out. This was no place for romantic declarations. They were sitting in an old-fashioned car, covered with a mud-splattered tarp, heading toward a forced wedding. And Tulsa May's expression of horrified surprise was so comical, Luther actually laughed. His laughter broke the tension and after a moment Tulsa May began giggling with him. Holding hands, they hurried along the muddy road to Guthrie and their wedding ceremony.

A loud blast beneath the seat startled them both.
"OH!"
"WHAT!"
They hollered in unison.

Before Luther could get the car stopped there was the slap, slap, slap of something broken.

"Good heavens, Luther, what is that?"

"Sounds like a belt," he answered as he pulled the Runabout to the side of the road. He'd just set the brake when the cap on the radiator shot off like a cannon and a spewing shower of boiling water shot three feet in the air.

"Lord have mercy!" Tulsa May cried. "What have you done to my car?"

"Your car?" Luther asked as soon as he'd assured himself that neither of them had been splashed by the scalding water. He jumped down to the ground and Tulsa May held out her hand for his help. He ignored the offered palm and grasped her around the waist. He carried her to a grassy area on the edge of the roadway that was out of the mud. "What have *I* done to *your* car?" He tweaked her nose in feigned fury. "Tulsy, you'd best be grateful that this car hasn't done something to us."

She shook her head and laughed. "You're right, I'm sorry. What in the world happened?"

Luther was putting the seat forward to look into the engine. "Well, it sounded like a belt broke," he said. "But the way that water boiled over, I think something must have been hung up somewhere."

Peering into the hot, smelly engine, Luther squinted. He reached in to touch something on the engine and cursed vividly.

"Luther!" Tulsa May scolded.

He stood shaking his hand furiously for a second before sticking his fingers in his mouth.

"What are you doing?" she asked.

"Burning myself," he answered tartly. "What else would a fellow want to do on his wedding day?"

"Let me see," Tulsa May said, coming forward.

"Stay out of the mud," he ordered. "You're in your good clothes."

"Well, so are you."

He looked at her, chin up and arms akimbo for a minute and then grinned by way of apology. "Are we about to have our first marital spat?" he asked.

Tulsa May raised an eyebrow. "We aren't married yet. I could still change my mind."

"Oh, really?" Luther asked with his eyebrows raised skeptically.

"Yes, I could. And you might as well know that if you and I were having a marital spat, I'd probably knock you flat in the mud."

"You think you could do that?" he asked.

"Well, it looked pretty easy last night when Turley did it."

"Why, you little —" Luther reached over and jerked Tulsa May toward him. She was bubbling with laughter.

"What's so funny?"

"Well," she answered, still giggling. "Nothing yet, but I bet the justice of the peace will find it humorous marrying a couple with equally muddy boots."

Luther looked down to see them both standing ankle-high in the muddy red clay. "You tricked me."

"I had to teach you not to order me around," she admitted.

"Even if it meant getting your feet muddy?"

"I don't care about my muddy feet, I just care about getting my car fixed."

With a long-suffering sigh and a shrug, Luther turned once again to look into the depths of the Model G Runabout engine.

"Can you see anything?" Tulsa May asked as she moved up beside him and gazed at the perplexing array of mechanical parts that made up the Buick two-cylinder engine.

Luther nodded. "Fan belt broke," he said. "It looks like it got gummed up in the generator before it snapped."

"Can you fix it?" Her voice sounded worried.

Luther raised his head and grinned at her as he removed his jacket and hung it over the steering wheel. "Tulsy, would I let you go riding in a car I couldn't fix?"

His smile reassured her.

"I'm going to have to clean out the bad rubber from the old belt," he said. He glanced down at the muddy ground. "Unfortunately, I'll need to be underneath the car to do it."

Tulsa May, too, looked at the mud-soaked roadway with dismay. "Luther, I don't mind marrying a man with muddy boots, but I might have to draw the line at a muddy shirt."

Luther shrugged. "I can buy a new shirt when we get to town. There is no way I can attach the belt from the top side."

Tulsa May nodded her understanding as she glanced around looking for another alternative. "Can we push the Runabout down that hill?"

she asked, indicating the far side of the road. "It's not nearly as muddy at the bottom of that maple grove."

Luther looked in the direction that she indicated and smiled. "That will be a whole lot better," he admitted. "It's a lucky man who gets himself a wife that's smarter than him."

She rolled her eyes. "For some men it's easier than others."

Luther turned to give her a thoughtful squint. "I think there was an insult somewhere in there."

She gave him a look of completely feigned innocence which brought a broader smile to his face.

"Hop in the car, Tulsy," he said. "You drive and I'll push. If we don't run the car into one of those maple trees, this will be one of the best ideas you've had today."

"It's still early yet," Tulsa May answered as she took her place in the driver's seat.

Getting across the muddy road was slow and, from the groans she heard, obviously painful. She glanced back once, only to notice that Luther would need more than a new shirt to keep the mud out of this wedding. As soon as the Runabout was on the down side of the far bank, however, Luther's manpower was no longer needed. The Buick went racing down the hill so quickly, Tulsa May cried out in delight at the exhilarating ride. She did, fortunately, remember to brake at the bottom of the hill and she actually brought the Runabout to a complete stop among, but not against, the maple trees. She set the brake.

"I'm all right!" she called back to Luther who was hurrying down the hill.

Tulsa May stepped down from the driver's seat and surveyed the area. The tall field grass kept the ground from being muddy, but the grass itself was quite wet. Tulsa May took the tarp that had covered her knees, and as neatly as a picnic cloth she laid the tarp beneath the frame of the Runabout. The bridegroom might be muddy, but he wasn't going to be damp. She was just straightening the last wrinkle in the tarp when a pair of muddy booted feet halted at her side.

"What are you doing?"

"Making a nice neat place for you to work," she answered.

Luther looked at the tarp spread beneath the car and smiled. "Thank you," he said. "I can't wait to put you to work in my shop."

She gave him a doubtful glance and he chuckled.

He dropped to the ground and slid himself beneath the Runabout. Grabbing the frame from the far side of the car, he pulled himself to the center of the vehicle, looking up into the bottom of the engine. The broken belt ran from the auto generator to the fan that cooled the radiator. The fan seemed in fine condition, but he used a screwdriver to scrape clean the spokes of the generator.

"How does it look?" Tulsa May asked above him.

"I've seen prettier sights," he answered.

"Under cars?" she asked.

There was a slight hesitation and a teasing in his voice. "No," he answered. "In a mirror."

Tulsa May felt a blush stain her cheek as she remembered the sight of herself glowing in the lamplight. She couldn't think of a thing to reply.

"It's fine, Tulsy," Luther answered as if sensing her discomfort. "Hand me that half-inch crescent."

She looked through the confusing array of tools in the box beneath the turtleback. Quietly, she picked up the wrench that she assumed he wanted and handed it under the car to him. "Is this the one you wanted?"

"Yes, ma'am," he said, clearly in a jovial mood. "And thank you. You're the best mechanic's assistant in a mile or more."

Tulsa May looked down through the top of the engine to see the teasing smirk on his face. Her expression was purposely unimpressed. "I'm the only *human* in a mile or more," she pointed out.

"You said that, Tulsy, not me."

Luther heard the sound of her laughter above him. They had laughed a lot today. It was surprising, with everything going like it had. But they had spent a lot of time laughing. He liked that sound. It made him feel warm and happy: a feeling he would certainly like to learn to live with. He wondered if living with Tulsa May would mean laughing every day. Somehow, he hoped that it would.

"That's got it," he said finally as he spun the

generator a couple of times to assure himself that there was no rubber left on it. "Clean as a whistle."

He reached down to the belt at his waist and found that it wasn't there. His smile faded.

"Damn," he whispered to himself.

Tulsa May heard him. "What's wrong?" she asked.

Luther crawled out from underneath the car, a perplexed expression on his face.

"Is it fixed already?" Tulsa May asked.

"Not yet." He opened the turtleback and rifled through it. There was nothing of any use.

"What's wrong?" she asked him again.

Luther touched the bright gray web of his suspenders. "My dress suit doesn't have stirrups for a belt," he said.

Her brow furrowed. "I don't mind," she said. "I think your dress suit is very attractive."

He saluted her with a courtly bow. "I wasn't fishing for compliments. I need my belt to fix the Runabout."

"What?"

"It takes a belt to make a belt."

Tulsa May stared at him for a moment and then looked back askance at the car. The situation became clear to her. With no belt, they had no car. With no car there was no way to drive to Guthrie and get married. And there was certainly no way to be back in Prattville in time for the reception. She glanced all around her looking for something, anything, that he could use.

"Can't you fashion a belt with your suspenders?"

"I don't think so."

"Have you tried?" Her tone of voice was clearly desperate.

"Well, no, I haven't but —"

"For heaven's sake, Luther. You have to try. We'll barely have time to make the reception as it is."

There was no arguing with the facts. Luther stripped himself of his suspenders and eased himself back under the Runabout.

Tulsa May paced nervously next to the car. Her optimism seemed to be failing her. Marrying Luther seemed to be the luckiest thing that had ever happened to her, yet this morning it was first one thing and then another. Perhaps it was a sign. Perhaps they shouldn't get married after all. Could she marry Luther with a clear conscience, knowing that he was only doing it because he thought it was his duty? Suddenly, she knew that she couldn't take advantage of his better nature because of her own selfish dreams.

"Luther," she called out through the top of the engine. "I need to talk to you."

Struggling to forge the suspenders into one long strong unit, Luther was less than responsive.

"I'm listening," he answered.

Tulsa May began pacing again. "Luther, there are things that you don't know about me. Things that you ought to know if we are going to marry."

She heard a chuckle coming from beneath the car.

"If you are going to confess that you snore, I already know it."

"No, it's not that, it's — I snore!"

"Not really loud," he answered. "Just kind of loud breathing, like a dog or something."

"I snore like a dog?"

"Well, not like a dog exactly."

"I most certainly do not snore!" she stated emphatically.

A howl of laughter exploded from beneath the car. "Oh, Tulsy, I wish I could see your face. I got you on that one."

"You were kidding?"

His answer was only more chuckling.

"Luther Briggs, I am trying to talk to you about a serious subject and you are making jokes. I feel that if you don't know the truth —" Tulsa May stared at the car. There was no way she could explain herself without coming face-to-face with the man in question.

With a sigh of disgust, she dropped to her knees on the tarp, grasped the Runabout's frame and slid under the car next to Luther.

"Tulsy! What are you —"

"I'm in love with you, Luther," she stated baldly. "I have been ever since I was a girl. I never let anyone know, especially not you." She swallowed nervously. "I've kept it as a secret all these years, but in my secret heart of hearts I dreamed that someday we would be together."

She stopped only long enough to catch her breath. He was looking at her closely. Those vivid blue eyes were unfathomable, and she hurried on to tell it all before she lost what little courage she had.

"Last night, when I blurted out that it was you and I at the Sparrow cottage, I didn't think in advance that it would be a way to trap you into marriage." She hesitated. "At least, I don't *think* that I thought it up in advance. But somehow . . . somehow, I feel like I maneuvered you into this whole thing. And even though I know that we will probably have to get married anyway, I wanted there to be truth between us from the start. So, this is the truth, Luther. I've loved you for years and I couldn't be happier about marrying you. If you are going to resent me for the rest of our lives for ruining your chance with Emma or some other woman you might have loved, well, I understand. Please, just go ahead and tell me now and let's get that over with."

Luther stared in disbelief at the woman who lay beside him beneath the old, rickety Runabout. The sunlight shone down through the top of the engine, lighting her cheeks and chin, but shadowing her eyes.

"Say it again."

"What?"

"Say it again."

"All of it?"

"Just the first part."

"The first part?"

"The part about loving me."

She tried to turn away. "Luther, I —"

He dropped the suspenders and turned to take her in his arms. He could feel her trembling.

"I said that I love you," she whispered. "I've always loved you."

"I'm so glad," he answered quietly. "I really didn't want to be the only person in love in this marriage."

Tulsa May turned in his arms so quickly, she hit her head on the exhaust pipe. "Ouch! What did you say?"

"I said that I love you too. I told you just a few minutes ago. Don't you remember?"

"Well yes, but you were joking. You laughed."

"I was embarrassed," he admitted. "I've never said that to anyone before, and I kind of caught myself unawares."

"But Luther, you can't —"

"Didn't I show you last night?" he asked. "What did you see when you looked in that mirror? Didn't you see a woman that was loved?"

"But you . . . I . . . do you really love me?" Her question was full of joyful astonishment.

"Yes, I do." He pulled her toward him, and they snuggled together in the cramped area beneath the car. "Kiss me, Tulsy. There's not a woman in the world who can kiss me like you kiss me."

"And there had better not be," she answered.

Chapter Twenty

Crawling out from under the car, Luther leaned down to help Tulsa May out behind him. He immediately pulled her into his arms.

"I just want to kiss you, Tulsy," he whispered, "I know we're not really married yet, and I know that this is not the best time or best place. But I love you and we're not going anywhere soon. I just can't wait another minute to really kiss you."

She wasn't much interested in waiting either. Tulsa May wrapped her arms around his neck and offered her lips. The taste of him was sweet and familiar, but the need that burned inside her was not.

"Oh, Luther," she whispered against his mouth.

He pulled her tighter against him. The strength of his arms held her securely as his body pressed close into her own. His hands moved all along her back from the nape of her neck to the indentation of her waist.

That encouraged her. Tulsa May let her own fingers slide upward into the thick mane of black hair that she had so long admired and had never dared to touch. She moaned deep inside her throat and the sound seemed to set him afire. His kiss deepened and she felt the warmly wicked intrusion of his tongue into her mouth. She opened wider to accommodate him. He teased her teeth and tongue, mimicking an action that was unknown to her experience, but was familiar within the primitive needs of her body.

Tulsa May gasped for breath and pulled away slightly. Luther, unperturbed, turned his attention to the gentle curve of her neck and the tempting taste of her ear.

"Oh, Luther, I feel so . . . so —" She didn't know how to continue.

"I know what you feel," he whispered against her flesh. His hand strayed down the curve of her buttocks. He caressed her flesh there. And even through her cotton serge skirt, her taffeta petticoat, and her muslin drawers, she could feel the heat of his hand. She tried to press closer against him.

With both hands now, he cupped her bottom and raised her up against him. The hard length of his erection was shocking, scary, and intensely thrilling. Amazingly, she found herself involuntarily straining to get closer.

"Oh, Tulsy!" he gasped as if in pain. "If you don't stop me soon, I don't know that I'll be able."

"Able to what?" she asked.

"Able to stop."

She squirmed against him eagerly. "Oh, Luther, please don't stop," she whispered.

Grinding his teeth together as if in pain, Luther

pulled back from her. "We can't do this, Tulsy," he said.

"Why not?" she asked, her voice languid with passion.

"Because we're not married?"

"We won't be the first," she answered. "And Luther, I don't care. I know you're going to marry me. I never intend to let you go."

"But out here?" he gestured around in dismay. "Out in the open, in the grass? Tulsy, you deserve a sweet-smelling marriage bed with clean sheets and fluffy pillows."

"And I'll have one tonight," she answered. "But Luther, I don't think that I can wait that long."

She threw herself in his arms and his better judgment began to wane. With one hand still wrapped around her waist, Luther leaned down to grasp the corner of the tarp. He pulled it out from beneath the Runabout and then dropped to his knees upon it and pulled Tulsa May down beside him.

He clasped her tightly against him and she squirmed and wiggled to get closer.

"I want you, Tulsy," he said. "I want you here and now. But I don't want you to regret our first time or our first place."

She pulled back from him only to lie down on the tarp, her eyes looking up at him. Taking his hand, she gently kissed it and then laid it upon her bosom. She saw the heat of desire light in his eyes and she smiled.

"According to some very reliable Prattville gossip," she told him, "our first time *was* out in the open and upon the ground. I understand it was under a pecan tree, and these are maples," she said, indicating the spring-green branches above their heads. "But in the middle of love-making, is a woman supposed to be a tree specialist?"

Luther swallowed, attempting to hang on to the last vestige of his control. "Making love to you is not something that I want to rush," he said.

Tulsa May smiled. "Then don't. The Runabout is broken down and you don't have a belt to fix it." She shrugged with unconcern. "I'm not going anywhere."

A smile teased the corners of his mouth as he leaned forward to taste another kiss. "I love you, Tulsy Bruder," he whispered.

"And I love you."

He lay down next to her and took her into his arms, kissing and caressing her slowly and tenderly. Luther's hand lay upon her voile-covered breast. As he trailed tiny kisses along her jaw and cheek, he eagerly began to fondle her. His brow furrowed. Her bosom felt strangely hard and unnatural and those wonderful nipples that he so admired had seemed to disappear completely. Curiously, he slipped the buttons on her bodice and probed inside.

"Tulsy, what are you wearing?" he asked.

"It's a brassiere," she answered in a whisper. "It's the latest thing in women's fashions."

"I know what it is," Luther answered, remembering the strange bits of elastic and lace he'd seen in Penny's store. "I just want to know how to take it off."

Tulsa May giggled almost wantonly.

Luther sat up and pulled her into a sitting position. Hurriedly, he undid the rest of the buttons on her blue-striped shirtwaist and slipped it off her shoulders. Tulsa May sat there in the afternoon sunlight, her breasts covered only by her fashionable new lingerie. She felt shy again.

"How does it come off?" he asked.

With businesslike promptness, she found the hooks for him. In another moment, he pulled the garment off her body and cast it away from them.

Tulsa May looked down to see herself unclothed from the waist up. Her courage failed her and she folded her arms across her nakedness.

Luther watched her lower lip tremble nervously and saw the first hint of fear in her eyes.

"It's all right, Tulsy," he said. "It's just me. It's just Luther. You've known me for a long time. And you've loved me for a long time."

She nodded mutely.

"I showed you how beautiful you were last night. I want you to let me touch that beauty. I want you to *let* me touch it, but I'll never demand that you allow me to."

"I know," she said quietly.

"It's just me, Tulsy," he repeated. "It's just Luther, the man who loves you."

Her eyes filled with tears. She threw herself into his arms and he held her close against him.

"I won't force you, Tulsy," he whispered against her hair.

"You won't have to," she answered. "I want you, Luther. I want to make love to you. It's so new and so . . . so intimate. I'm a little afraid."

"I'm afraid too," he told her.

She raised her eyes to look at him. "But you've . . . I mean you've . . . this is not a new thing for you."

"Touching a woman I love is totally new to me," he said softly, slipping an errant lock of bright orange hair out of her eyes. "And touching the woman that I am going to marry is like a dream come true. I'm afraid I'll hurt you, or embarrass you or maybe even disgust you."

"You don't need to be afraid. I can't even imagine doing anything with you that wouldn't be wonderful."

"Of course you can't even imagine it," he said. "But Tulsa May, everybody in Prattville knows what an optimist you are."

Her own fears seemed to melt at his words. A gentle smile came to her face that flourished until it was clearly a grin.

"I can even see my own headline now," she said. "BRIGGS MARRIAGE CONSUMMATED. WIFE SURVIVES."

Luther threw back his head and roared with laughter. "At least I can promise you that, Tulsy. You will survive."

But as she slowly allowed him access to her body, Tulsa May became less sure of that herself. The touch of his hands on her naked breasts made her nipples tight and achy. But when he replaced his hands with his lips, she gritted her teeth against a pleasure so powerful it gave her body a life of its own.

It was she who bent her knee to press her throbbing womanhood against the thick muscles of his thigh. Without her speaking a word, he understood the meaning of the uncontrollable rocking that beset her hips.

When he grabbed the hem of her skirts and casually pushed them up to her waist, it nearly took the breath out of her. He peeled her out of her corset with very little fuss, then he sat back slightly and just gazed down at her. Her stockings and drawers, which had formerly never seen the light of day except on the clothesline, were displayed before his eyes. And he didn't hesitate in the slightest to look his fill.

With a hand that trembled slightly, Luther caressed her long slim legs. Tulsa May found it hard to breathe, to think, she could only feel his hand gently caressing her thighs. Her bosom was cold and bereft without his caress. She brought her own hands to her breasts and kneaded them herself as Luther gently, oh so gently, grazed the glowing dampness of her drawers. When his hand lightly cupped her mound, Tulsy moaned aloud and raised her hips to press him more closely to her.

"Please, oh please," she whispered.

Luther kissed her again. This time his hand was firmer between her legs. And it was wonderful.

"We need to get these drawers off," he whispered into her ear. Clearly, he thought he would have to coax her.

Tulsa May jerked at the sturdy white muslin, so eager to be rid of the annoying barrier she nearly ripped them off.

It was Luther's turn then to pause. She lay near naked and trembling on the tarp before him. His hand shook as he brought it to rest on the springy curls at the apex of her thighs. He pressed his fingers into the silky fine hair and the curls twisted around his fingers. He swallowed.

"When I was trying to convince you that your orange hair is beautiful," he said, "this is the hair that I should have shown you."

Tulsa May's eyes widened, but before she could make a reply his touch had turned to caress and her thoughts into complete mush.

He found the secret, achy parts of her and stroked them until she begged for more. When his finger dipped into the hot, tight wetness inside her, she cried out.

"Did I hurt you?" he asked anxiously. His voice was low and ragged.

"Good," was the answer she whispered. "Feels good."

Luther resumed his exploration, his fondling, his caress. Tulsa May could not lie still or keep quiet. She moved in rhythm against the touch of his hand and murmured love words, moaned in appreciation, and pleaded for more.

Luther sat up on his knees. His breathing was quick and labored, like a man who'd just run an uphill race.

"Don't stop!" she begged him.

"I've got to get rid of my trousers," he told her. "I just can't wait any longer."

She watched as he released the buttons on his dress pants and her eyes widened in fear as she saw for the first time how differently men and women were made.

"It's so big!" she said, horrified.

"It's not," he assured her. "I'll try not to hurt you, but —"

The words he meant to speak flew out of his head as she reached a hesitant hand to that part of him that she had never seen and stroked it hesitantly.

"It's so smooth," she said. "And so hard."

Luther made a strangled noise in the back of his throat and then moved over her. His kiss was hot and eager and earthy. He allowed one of his hands to feel her breast. But the other he used to part her thighs.

"I've got to be inside you, Tulsy," he said. "I've got to feel you around me."

Tulsa May had no thought to argue as she raised her hips to try to accommodate him. He fitted his hand under her buttocks and slowly, carefully began pushing himself inside her.

Under his breath, Luther began a mumbling discussion with himself, designed to distract him from the pleasure that he felt and to keep him in control.

"What?" Tulsa May asked distractedly to words she heard that sounded vaguely like the Gettysburg Address.

"It feels *so* good," Luther answered.

It didn't feel good yet to Tulsa May. She was still aching, still needing, and although his entrance made her feel stretched and taut, it wasn't enough.

"More," she whispered. "More Luther, more."

He ground down his passion with a growl and gritted his teeth against the need that he felt. "Oh, Tulsy, my sweet, sweet Tulsy, I can't . . . no longer, can long . . . can long . . . oh, Tulsy."

He plunged deep within her.

She cried out.

His teeth bared like an enraged animal, Luther held himself in control as he cuddled Tulsa May and comforted her.

"Sweet Tulsy, my sweet Tulsy," he whispered. "It's so unfair that it should hurt you when to me it feels so good."

He cooed and rocked and held her as he regained control. Still deep inside her, he could feel the walls surrounding him relax gradually from the pain of the onslaught.

"Tulsy, oh Tulsy," he said as mentally he continued the speech that helped him to hold the last reins of his control. "I'm so sorry I've hurt you."

"No, it's all right."

"No it's not. I hate hurting you. I never want to hurt you again."

"I know, Luther," she said as the startling pain within her waned and the driving need that she felt before began to reemerge. "Remember, Luther, I am an optimist. And I am just certain that you are going to make this hurting feel a whole lot better in just a few minutes."

And he did.

It was nearly dusk when Luther awakened. Tulsa May lay snuggled up against his arm. They were both as naked as man and woman had been in the Garden of Eden, and Luther had only managed to cover them with Tulsy's blue serge skirt before they fell asleep. Tulsa May groaned slightly as she came awake.

"We've missed the reception at the parsonage," he said.

"At least I didn't have to wear that pink dress."

Luther nodded in agreement. "What you're wearing right now is much more suited to my taste."

She glanced down at her naked body. Her bright orange hair lay all about her in a tangled curtain. She gave him a cool expression, but he laughed at it because her eyes were filled with love. Eagerly she nestled closer and then winced.

"Are you okay?" he asked her.

Slowly she smiled with lazy satisfaction. "I've never felt better," she said. As she tried to sit up, she winced again. "Except for a little twinge or two."

"I think next time we should really try out a bed," Luther told her.

"If we have one," she answered. "If you can't fix the car, we may just have to live here forever."

"You want to live in a deserted wood, just you and me and the Runabout?"

"Sounds like heaven to me."

Luther smiled.

"Well, I don't think that we'll have to," he said. "I can surely find a farmhouse along this road someplace. Somebody will loan me something that I can use for a belt to move this contraption down the road."

"You're sure you don't want to live here forever?" Tulsa May asked as she gestured to nature's love bower all around them.

"I've told you already, Tulsy. You're a woman that deserves a sweet-smelling marriage bed with clean sheets and fluffy pillows."

She sighed grandly. "Well, all right. I guess I'd be willing to try that."

Luther shook his head, grinning. "Besides, I still have to marry you. Have you forgotten that little detail?"

"You don't have to marry me, Luther," she said. "I'd be perfectly willing just to be your love slave."

"Only if you promise to explain that to the Rev!" he said, coaxing her up from the tarp.

Luther found his trousers and her undermuslins

and they began to right themselves. The fact that there was a good deal of unnecessary nudging and occasional grasping and kissing notwithstanding, they did make progress toward getting dressed.

"Hand me my brassiere," Tulsa May asked.

Luther dutifully leaned down to retrieve the undergarment. Holding it in his hand, he stared at it for a long moment before turning to Tulsy.

"You know," he said. "If I didn't have to walk several miles to find a farmhouse, I could probably take you dancing in Guthrie tonight."

Tulsa May looked up at him curiously. His smile was hopeful, and he held her brassiere expectantly in his hand.

The Runabout chugged into Guthrie, Oklahoma, less than an hour later. Fortunately, no one on the street could see inside the engine or no doubt they would have been scandalized.

"First to the justice of the peace, then a telegram to your parents, and then dancing all night," Luther told her.

"We're a rather muddy, disheveled couple to be getting married," Tulsa May commented.

"Well," Luther said. "We can get a hotel room first to tidy up. I was just afraid that if we checked ourselves into the room, we wouldn't make it to the wedding." He gave her a knowing grin, and she smiled right back. "I don't know if I have enough money to bribe the judge to lie two days' worth."

She giggled. "All right, we'll have the wedding first, if you insist. But we can skip the dancing and go straight to the honeymoon."

"I thought you loved dancing with me?"

"I do, but we don't have to come to Guthrie for that," she said. "We can dance together anytime there is moonlight and a river."

Constance Bruder was flabbergasted, anxious, and generally horrified when neither the bride nor groom showed up for the wedding reception. Practically the whole town was in attendance. Important society matrons like Amelia Puser and Cora Sparrow were looking around curiously. Major sources of gossip like Fanny Penny whispered behind their fans. Even the bridegroom's brother, looking especially dashing, and sporting Maybelle Penny on his arm, showed up. The celebrated couple, however, were notably absent.

Clyde Avery was just suggesting contacting the county sheriff to make sure the young people were not the victims of foul play when Grady Ringwald arrived at the door with a telegram.

Reverend Bruder read it aloud.

UNABLE TO MAKE THE RECEPTION STOP WIFE AND I TO HONEYMOON IN GUTHRIE STOP HAVE DECIDED WHAT BUSINESS TO OPEN IN MY MAIN STREET BUILDING STOP LUTHER H. BRIGGS

BALLROOM OPENS ON MAIN STREET

Moonlight River Room Is Elegant Dancing

Mr. and Mrs. Luther Briggs shared a gala night of fine food and dancing at the opening of the new Moonlight River Room in the former Henniger building on Main Street in Prattville. The ballroom, which features a crystal chandelier with electric lights shipped all the way from Kansas City, will be open three nights a week throughout the year with a house band and guest appearances by musicians from all over the country. Mr. Elmer Tripten, manager of the ballroom, stated that "no expense was spared in creating an elegant and genteel atmosphere for the patrons of music and

Epilogue

The Prattville Spring Blossom Festival of 1919 was the biggest the town had seen in years. It could no longer be held on Cora's Knoll since the Martin Oil Company had drilled a well right on the peak of the hill. The huge metal derrick rose like a beacon over the river and gratefully assured that Cimarron Ornamental Flowers would be cushioned from bad times for years to come.

Since the festival had long ago become more of a community event than a company picnic, in 1919 it was held in downtown Prattville. The rides and games and booths were set up in the city park. A traveling carnival was there for the occasion, featuring a two-headed calf and a real live elephant. Fireworks were on tap for the evening, as well as a formal dance at the Moonlight River Ballroom.

A fancy new Stutz Bearcat was parked behind a barrier of waving red and white banners on Main Street. Philemon Bruder, the former church pastor and new executive director of the YMCA, had gotten the Briggs Motor Company to donate the vehicle. It was to be raffled off to raise money for the new gymnasium that was planned for Second Street.

Children swarmed and laughed and played as in years past, but the war had brought some changes. The booths where the townsfolk had once gobbled up wieners and sauerkraut on a roll now served only hot dogs and liberty cabbage. Where once boys held sticks they thought were swords and defended themselves against wild Indians, now the sticks they held were rifles and field cannon and they defended themselves against the Kaiser. Where the townsfolk once found political opinions and disagreement to be open to everyone, it was now considered suspect for anyone to express opposition to the war.

The peace treaty had been signed in January and slowly, so slowly, the young men of Prattville were returning to their homes. Rossie Crenshaw lost a foot to gangrene. Kirby Maitland's oldest boy, Eustace, had been gassed at the Marne River and his lungs still plagued him. Ferd Mitchum had taken a bullet to the head and no longer always knew where he had been or who he was.

And Fasel Auslander had been killed in the Meuse-Argonne Offensive and was buried somewhere on French soil. The day that the notice came from the War Department, John Auslander went to the courthouse and had his name changed.

"The name Auslander means a foreign person," he explained to the clerk. "My family are not foreigners in America." The old man was the first of his whole family to change his name to Landers.

But despite the war, many things in Prattville

had not changed at all. Clyde Avery was still mayor. Erwin Willers still ran the newspaper, although Tulsa May Briggs was now the editor. Fanny Penny still circulated through the crowd with the latest and juiciest gossip.

"Did you see how peaked and sickly Emma Foote is looking?" Fanny commented casually to a group of attractively attired young matrons. "I think she is *finally* on the nest." Fanny shook her head in dismay. "They have certainly taken their time about matters. Frankly, I had my doubts about that old doctor."

Elias Curley was running for Congress again. This time on a prowar stance. The congressman was roaring drunk even before the speeches began at noon, but everyone expected him to be easily reelected for the office anyway.

Mort Humley revved up his fiddle for dancing at the ballroom, although the house band was available to play.

There was homemade ice cream served to each and all and plenty of pretty girls to serve it.

When the evening train from Guthrie stopped at the station, half the travelers poured out, anxious and excited to join the festivities. One young man, however, still dressed in doughboy-brown, stepped off the train unaware that today was the festival. He glanced about the neat, clean little town, his eyes feasting on the sight.

With his kit bag over his shoulder, he made his way up Main Street, stopping by first one happy friend and then another. Handshakes and claps on the back were given by most. Occasionally, he was blessed with a warm hug by a teary-eyed matron. His jet-black hair was cut very short and his hat sat upon his head at a jaunty angle.

At the doorway to the Moonlight River Ballroom, he met up with Cora and Jedwin Sparrow. There was laughter and hugging all around as he stopped to ask about their children, mutual friends, and the town. As they talked, one after another of the townsfolk spotted them and came over to share a word and a welcome home.

It was a good half hour later before the young soldier made his way inside. Immediately, he began to scan the area until he found what he sought. Without hesitation, he made his way to the far corner of the ballroom where a pretty eighteen-year-old was dishing out bowls of peach ice cream. He stood before her, just watching her for a long moment. Until she felt the heat of his gaze and looked up. Their eyes met.

"Arthel!"

"Hello, Maybelle," he said quietly. "You want to dish me up some of that ice cream?"

Her mind was momentarily so muddled she attempted to dip with the bowl instead of the spoon. When she saw him smile at her confusion, the spine stiffened in her back, her chin came up, and a too bright smile came to her lips.

"Well, if it isn't Geronimo back from the wars," she said, a little too loudly. "I do hope you aren't carrying any smelly scalps on your belt."

Arthel actually chuckled. He took the bowl of peach ice cream she handed him and tasted it slowly, as if savoring its flavor. The minutes passed uncomfortably as he said not a word, merely ate his ice cream and watched the crowd.

Maybelle saw Patsy Panek across the room and motioned for her to come take over the booth. Hurriedly, she began fussing with her apron, hoping to quickly escape from Arthel Briggs's obnoxious presence.

"I see you waited for me, Maybelle," he said to her finally.

She saw red. "Waited for you?" Her tone was dangerously facetious. "Well, I haven't married yet, if that's what you consider 'waiting.' There are so many good-looking men in town these days, I just haven't been able to make up my mind."

Arthel smiled pleasantly. "Well, at least I can solve that problem for you, now that I'm back home."

He took one last bite of his ice cream and then handed the bowl back to her. She took it in her hand, but he didn't let go. He leaned forward and whispered to her. "I've got to go find Luther and Tulsa May, but why don't you meet me later under the pecan tree at the old Sparrow cottage?"

Maybelle's eyes flashed as she jerked the ice-cream bowl out of his hands. "I will not be meeting you," she snapped with fury. "Not under that pecan tree or anywhere else."

Arthel seemed to take her rejection with good grace. He nodded calmly and stuck his hands in his pockets. "I thought you might say that," he admitted. "So I suppose I'd better give you this here." He pulled a small box out of his pocket and offered it to her. "I hope you like it, 'cause it will be pretty hard for me to return it to that jeweler in Paris."

Maybelle jerked open the little box and screamed as loudly as if a whole band of raging redskins had just attacked with tomahawks. A minute later she was in Arthel's arms.

"I've rented the cottage, Maybelle," he whispered in her ear. "I remember you said that it was the most perfect place for a honeymoon."

Luther and Tulsa May Briggs were late leaving their new house on Fourth Street. Two-year-old Mavis would not leave until her daddy had told her, not one, but *three* good stories. Her daddy didn't really mind since the little girl was the apple of his eye. When she'd finally fallen asleep with her little chubby fist pressing against her mouth, Luther had stood for several moments just looking at the beautiful child that was his own.

Mavis had the best of both her parents. Her hair was red, not quite as orange as her mother's but a shiny dark auburn. And her eyes were the same deep vivid blue that her mother found so attractive in Luther.

"Are you ready to go?" he asked Tulsa May as he slipped out of the baby's room and encountered her on the landing.

"Whenever you are. Mrs. Crawford is in the kitchen fixing herself a cup of tea."

Luther nodded. "Then allow me to escort you, Mrs. Briggs," he said. "I know how fond you are of dancing and we are already late."

Arm in arm they made their way down the stairs. They called good-bye to Mrs. Crawford in the kitchen and headed out the side door. In the cool spring evening, Luther wrapped his arm loosely around Tulsy's waist and squeezed her to him lightly.

"Are you feeling all right?" he asked. "You're not queasy or anything?"

"I only feel that way in the mornings," she told him. "Right now I feel like I could dance all night."

He gently laid a hand on her still flat abdomen. "Well, I guess we'd better dance then. From what I remember when you were carrying Mavis, in a few months I won't be able to get close enough!"

She slugged him playfully in the ribs and he pretended great injury. They walked to the two-car garage at the far edge of their property. Luther pulled the cord that brought the electric light to life. The shiny, new 1919 Chevrolet touring car sat ready to go. Luther politely opened the door for his wife. She hesitated.

"Let's take the Runabout."

Luther's eyes widened in surprise. He turned his gaze to the rather sad-looking old-fashioned autocar whose snappy wine-colored body and shiny brass lamps were scarred and faded.

"I was hoping that you'd win the Bearcat and we could paint 'rest in pieces' on this thing and leave it out in the pasture."

Tulsa May tossed her head haughtily. "You are never getting rid of *my* car, Mr. Briggs. I intend to keep it always. We need it."

"We don't need it."

"Yes we do. We never know when we might get stranded and this is the only auto in the world that can wear a brassiere."

Luther shook his head and chuckled, but he set the spark on the tired old vehicle and cranked it until it sputtered.

"Your coach, ma'am," he said, handing her inside.

Laughing together, they backed out onto the street and set out for the festivities at the slow, sedate Runabout pace.

"Are you happy, Tulsy?" Luther asked as he leaned across to take her hand.

She looked at him and smiled. "I couldn't imagine a woman being any happier."

"Me too," he admitted with a sigh of gratitude.

"And Miss Maimie said it would never work," Tulsa May said with pleasant laughter.

"Miss Maimie?" Luther shook his head. "I bet that old biddy is rolling in her grave to see how happy we are."

"No, she's not in her grave, Luther," Tulsa May said softly. "She's in heaven with her husband."

Luther looked at his wife with surprise.

"She really loved him, I think," Tulsa May said quietly. "I imagine that she was a much kinder and happier woman before he left her a widow. Now that they are back together again I'm sure her disposition has improved."

Luther made no comment.

"Of course, by now I'm sure she's reconciled with your father and come to love your mother as well. I'm sure they all are delighted about Mavis and just as expectant as we are about the new baby." Tulsa May sighed pleasantly. "Yes, I suppose that all four of them are probably looking down on us right now full of joy that we've found such love together."

Luther raised an eyebrow skeptically. "None injured in overnight blaze," he mumbled.

"What did you say?"

"I said that I'm so glad I married a wife who is such an optimist."